The Hot Monkey Love Trial

Lawrence G. Townsend

Water street press

Published by Water Street Press
Healdsburg, California

Water Street Press trade paperback edition published 2016

Cover art by Mark Bartman
Interior design by Typeflow

Produced in the USA

ISBN: 978-1-62134-140-6

To my lovely wife, Lisa, for being my keeper,
the one with actual feet on the ground.

In the beginning
Was the SHOCK…

It pricked the smallest bit
And made the living hot,
Turning on the quick
From that which was not.

With time came a creature who,
Bound always to his lot,
Found a whiz-bang way
To mimic primal shock.

Now he holds the tool
For conjuring his stock,
For stunning combinations
That'll stop Darwin's clock.

TINA HALLIKSEN
Composed July 2019
on day two of The Hot Monkey Love Trial
Yolo County Courthouse
Woodland, California

"I'm your man. I was born for bioporn."

ERNIE PUTTERMAN
On being retained as patent lawyer for
Primal Urge,a company that combines biotech
and adult entertainment services

Prologue

FROM WASHINGTONPOST.COM

In a strange sequence of events today, the United States Patent and Trademark Office granted a new patent, but the successful new patent holder then promptly announced that it would appeal the award in its favor.

Leland Jones, an outspoken critic of the biotech industry, filed a patent application for the so-called Fowl-Man, a gene composed of both human and chicken genetic material. Jones's sole purpose in filing was to force the Patent Office to address whether it would allow someone to own a biological patent comprised of both human and animal constituents.

"This comes as a shock. We fully expected that the Patent Office would refuse our application and lay down the many legal and moral reasons why it should do so," Jones said. "Instead the system failed us. We will appeal."

Jones is head of Citizens Opposed to Unnaturally Twisted Helixes in Humans (COUTHH), a Washington-based think tank highly critical of recombinant DNA used in forming transgenic species, also known as chimera. The Fowl-Man gene was created by COUTHH using a combinatorial catalytic shock technology developed by the agri-biotech pharmaceutical and chemical giant, Pharm-Life. PharmLife's shock technology, called Undercurrent, is the subject of another, earlier patent application. In labs where scientists are developing a wide array of transgenic species, a rapidly evolving story in the world of biotech, Undercurrent is used throughout.

Professor Ellen Proskauer, a patent law expert at Georgetown University, believes the appeal by a successful applicant is a first. "They got what they asked for. It's done. Now they're trying to put that genetically modified horse—or in this case, that humanized chicken—back in the barn."

At a press conference at COUTHH headquarters, Senator Ray Hoffenworth of Tennessee, chair of the Senate Investigative Committee on Chimera, echoed Jones in denouncing the Patent Office decision: "Fowl-Man is against nature's laws. It's against divine law. Humans and chickens were never meant to interspeciate. It's a perversity of nature, a downright natural perversion. The rogues of biotech must be stopped. They're turning everything all upside down and which-a-way."

1

TEACHING FOURTEEN-YEAR-OLDS WASN'T easy. By their nature they were uncontrollably distracted by hormones roaring like the Colorado through the canyons of their unlived adulthoods. Bert Gropes knew this because, even at age twenty-six, as his own canyon started to fill up, most of the time he could barely hear his human voice above the din. So constant were the rivaling calls that he sometimes wondered which was his truer voice: Bert Gropes—Social Studies teacher, Mansfield Academy, Woodland, California—or the barely stifled creature who from deep within sounded like that deafening, downward-snaking, mud-mad river able to electrify the rawest of his desires at every turn.

Sure, he could have admitted to feeling just a little bit hornier than usual today, but that's not how he chose to see it. He was John Bertram Gropes, in search of a destiny just like the Giants of American History he lionized in his classroom. Maybe his wasn't as big, but it was his, whatever it was.

It was only five minutes into his second period—Advanced Social Studies, the only elective he taught—when Bert turned around to see Megan Burns giggling at something class cut-up Trevor Jamison whispered to her. Linda Nguyen in the front row turned around to look at Megan and Trevor, then back to Bert, searching his face. Relax, take a deep breath, Bert telegraphed to her. Linda's terrible stutter matched her darting eyes. In a far corner Alfonso Ruiz droned in a low dreamy voice to Alicia Benson.

"All right, let's settle down," Bert said. "Today is democracy-in-action day. We'll be watching another hearing on C-SPAN." He went over and tapped the top of the TV as if patting the head of a guest lecturer.

"What's it going to be about today?" someone asked.

"Hearings before a Senate Subcommittee chaired by Senator Hoffenworth of Tennessee. How or if government will regulate the creation of new species of plants and animals." Drawing blank stares, Bert added: "In agriculture."

That registered. Woodland, ten miles due northwest of Sacramento, where Cache Creek mixes into the Sacramento, was the Yolo County seat, aggie central. With its river-fed soil and dry-hot summers, the farmlands of Yolo County were legendarily adaptable: almond and prune orchards flourishing next door to wine vineyards, or fields of rice, tomatoes, wheat, and alfalfa adjoining acres of kumquats and kiwi vines. Any living thing could grow here.

"But first, on this promising first day of spring, we will begin our study of California history. We will continue with our year-long theme of bold adventurers—in their time, in their forays into uncharted spaces, and in their ability to be free thinkers—who embody the American spirit. Remember, the world is divided into two groups: the *ohs* and the *ahs*. Let me hear a very disappointed *oh* from all of you."

"Ohhh…" they expelled loudly and in unison.

"That's excellent, because remember, the *ohs* are the big zeroes in life. Nothing ventured, nothing gained. The naysayers.

The nameless. The nobodies that other nobodies never heard of. But thank goodness for the *ahs* of the world." He lifted his arms to the chorus. "Let's hear it for the *ahs*."

"Ahhh!" the class lilted on cue.

"Nice! That's what we're here for. You will never grow tired of hearing that the letters *A-H-S* in *ahs* stand for Adventurers of the Human Spirit. Right?"

There was a smattering of good-natured laughs at the indoctrination to which they'd been subjected since the school year began.

"We started out marveling at some of the explorers of the New World, even before our country existed, looking under their skins to see what moved them, what fired them up. Then we moved into Revolutionary times, and there was another feast of *ahs*. Let's hear it again!"

"Ahhh!" A group of boys in the corner, mimicking the soundtrack from *Scary Movie*, threatened to earn complaints from neighboring classroom teachers.

"That should do it. That should summon a few of our *ahs*. Whom have we brought up from Revolutionary times?"

Two entire rows of waving hands went up on the left: a giant insect struggling to right itself.

"Robert."

"Benjamin Franklin."

"I never tire of hearing that answer. The Wizard of *Ahs*, in my book. But why him, Robert?"

"He was a writer, a lawmaker, and a scientist. He experimented with electricity and invented things like the lightning rod, the Franklin stove, and bifocals. You said that he was one of the great *ahs* who kept remaking himself."

"Good answer, even if I did say so myself." Bert turned away from the class in order to compose his follow-on observations about Ben Franklin. From the window where he stood, he could see two AWOL ninth graders behind a tree pawing and probing each other with hands and tongues.

"I imagine Franklin had to struggle to find himself along

the way," Bert said as he swung around to face the class again. "When he was fifteen, he wrote for his brother's paper in Boston under the name Silence Dogood, a widow. Then he started *Poor Richard's Almanack* under the name Richard Saunders. It was only much later he knew who he was. When he died a beloved hero, they called him 'the harmonious human multitude.'"

"Are we going to study *ahs* of early California?" Megan asked.

"Of course, but be warned, there are no big names like Ben Franklin. Instead lots of smaller ones that make up the whole. That will make it more exciting for us to dig into it. Don't you think?"

"So who are the *ahs*?" someone asked, followed by a chorus of "yeahs."

"You'll decide that. We'll talk some more about Manifest Destiny—remember? That funny way of saying 'We'll keep eating land and eventually grow into that big pair of balloon pants we think we'd look good in.'" There were guffaws of laughter. "Or maybe it really is the normal growth of a young nation into its natural adult size. Which is it? Keep in mind that we're now entering a new time and place. You may decide that the greatest hero of the time was the common person—the people who left their old family farms in New England or Ohio, who came from Europe and China because there was this place of opportunity called California. Ordinary people. No big names, but they had the spirit we're talking about. Few of them found their fortunes. There were terrible failures, but they stayed and became pioneering farmers, engineers, and Social Studies teachers."

"But is that true, Mr. Gropes? Isn't there someone you can name like Ben Franklin who is one of the California *ahs*?"

"Perhaps you'll each come up with an answer by the time we're through." He turned his back on the class and faced the TV hoisted on its rolling mount.

"Yeah, but who is somebody *you* think is one? Come on, you're our teacher," Alicia Benson pleaded sweetly. It was easy to see why Alfonso was so engrossed with her.

Bert could see his own dim reflection on the darkened television screen. He glanced at his watch: 9:55. He had four to five minutes to play with before the 10:00 start. It was nowhere in the teacher's curriculum, but something inside him cried out to be expressed.

"All right," Bert said, turning around. "My own personal choice? To my mind, it would be Heinrich Schliemann."

"Who?" someone asked, followed quickly by four louder voices: "Who's that?"

Bert went to the left side of the chalkboard and drew a boomerang whose top was partially sawed off, underneath which he wrote "California." In the middle he drew a box and wrote "Europe" inside it. To the right he drew a large circle and wrote the word "Dream" inside it. "When Heinrich Schliemann was your age and living in Germany"—Bert tapped Europe with the chalk—"after studying the Trojan War celebrated in Homer's epic tale *The Iliad*, he came up with this farfetched idea that one day he would learn the Greek language, that he would find a way to travel to a remote and forgotten region in what is now Turkey, where he believed Troy once thrived, and that he would somehow dig up mountains of earth in hopes of finding the lost city. No one believed there was a place called Troy that existed thousands of years earlier. Everyone, including all the experts and scholars throughout Europe, thought that Troy was nothing but a make-believe place."

The classroom was quiet, without the usual pockets of conversation, laughter, and distractions. But Bert wasn't sure yet if they were interested in Schliemann or simply whether he could make the stunted boomerang way off to the left somehow come back and connect with the Dream far off to the right.

"In order to realize his dream, Schliemann knew he'd need a fortune. He also knew he'd have to remove himself from a mindset stuck in the past: the Old World thinkers and naysayers who lived inside the box here." He pecked at Europe again. "So in late 1850, at the height of the California Gold Rush, he packed up and left for America, ending up in Sacramento. That's right, just a few miles from where we are right here in the Valley." Bert put an *X* right at the bend in California on its eastern side. "Of course, family had a lot to do with it. His brother, a banker, arrived first in California, but he died. Schliemann came over to straighten out his brother's affairs and ended up staying here for two years. He was successful, not in digging up gold—the digging came later. He made a fortune as a gold broker."

Trevor's pal Jason was inspired to challenge Bert: "So he wasn't even from California. He was from Germany." He and a few other boys shook their heads skeptically.

"Who was? No U.S. citizens had been born in California back then either. That's not what puts the *ah* in Californi*a*. More than anywhere else, it's about living for and pursuing your dream," he said, tracing the Dream with three more circles of chalk.

"He stuck to his dream. It took him years and years for the government of Turkey to give him permission to start digging. By the way, he was a self-taught archaeologist at a time when all that most archaeologists did was sit around and debate in the universities…and scoff at dreamers like Heinrich Schliemann. But guess who had the last laugh? In the early 1870s, and with hundreds of men digging in that faraway place, Heinrich Schliemann stunned the world by unearthing the treasures of the ancient civilization of Troy. He proved it was a real place."

"Wow. What kinds of stuff did he find?"

"How did he know where to dig?"

"Did he just get lucky?"

"How did he know that's what he wanted to do with his life?"

"All good questions," Bert said, waving them off. "We can discuss them another time. Right now we're supposed to watch that Senate hearing."

Bert turned on the TV to the tape-delayed broadcast on C-SPAN just as the camera showed the witness table in a large Senate hearing room. The witness, scheduled to testify before the Senate subcommittee, was one of Mansfield Academy's own: an honorary trustee of its Board of Governors, a distinguished professor emeritus at nearby UC Davis. He also happened to be Professor Grover Seymour Gropes, Bert's adoptive uncle.

The image on the TV screen was a close-up of the old man. From between the brown eyes, his nose jutted out and then plunged precipitously to the ground like an Ansel Adams image of the south face of Yosemite's El Capitan. Wearing an old brown worsted coat and a blue shirt whose collar had been thoroughly scoured by his beard, his uncle sported a wingspan of white hair and, totally blind for the last fifteen years, dark glasses. To his University students he was known as Dr. Gro.

The C-SPAN camera moved to the person seated next to Uncle Gro. This had to be his assistant, Anna Brighton. Bert had never met her in person, although he knew she'd been working with his uncle for at least three to four months now. Of course, she'd spent more time with his uncle during those few months than he had over the same number of years. Uncle Gro visited his sister, Eugenia—Bert's mother—often enough, but Bert had been invisible to him for some twenty-six years now, more years than his uncle had been completely blind. That didn't bother Bert, who chose not to think about it. He had his own life to live. He shared a name with his uncle, the bigshot scientist, but that was about it.

Trevor let loose with a shrill, suggestive whistle when the screen filled with the pristine face of Anna Brighton. A few of Trevor's buddies laughed as if his outburst were not only inspired wit, but one of nature's surest mating cries. Trevor was offered fists from the others; he knocked each in turn.

"That's enough, Trevor," Bert said in a firm voice. "Or you'll be testifying silently to yourself in detention."

"That's your uncle, isn't it, Mr. Gropes?" the studious Dee Vasquez asked.

"That's right."

"What's he supposed to talk about?" she asked.

"As I mentioned, new breakthroughs in agriculture. Specifically, it has to do with applying molecular biology to animal husbandry."

All the faces, especially the boys', looked up to Bert, training blinkless eyes upon him. Animal husbandry was close enough to the real thing to compel their attention.

Molecular biology, on the other hand, Bert didn't in the least understand, nor did the class. And he was the last person to be able to instruct them on *the real thing*; that was a subject of which no one was less qualified to speak than Bert Gropes. At twenty-six, unmarried, and certifiably funny-looking—a heavy-footed six-two, with simian-brown eyes, a promontory-like nose of his own, and large, clumsy hands—he was not exactly the Casanova of the Sacramento Valley. Stuck in his daily routine—withdrawn into it, more like it—he hadn't had a date in six months, even if you could call escorting his cousin Fran to her company's banquet dinner a date. The kids could probably read that in his face right now.

"What does animal husbandry have to do with social studies?" someone asked.

"Will we be tested on this molecule biology?" another despairing voice asked.

"No. This is social studies. We're interested in observing a Senate hearing, democracy in action. Let's just watch, shall we? We'll discuss afterwards."

Dead air, C-SPAN's signature at the beginning and end of every program, was interrupted by a male studio voice so restrained and sober it was as if he were about to call the play-by-play action for a head-of-state funeral: *"We now join the Senate Investigative Committee on Chimera in the Everett Dirksen Building. Today, Professor Grover Seymour Gropes here, emeritus professor of molecular biology, will testify..."*

Bert was looking into the dark glasses of the man on TV but, as always, the face of his Uncle Gro was not looking back. The story of his life.

2

"THIS COMMITTEE WILL COME TO ORD*AH*," THE senior senator from Tennessee bellowed. When the noise subsided slightly inside the hearing room of the Everett Dirksen Building, Ray Hoffenworth struck the gavel. "There will be ord*ah*!"

Wearing a baseball cap and dark glasses, Ellis Peek drifted into the hearing room. Being skinnier than most, he could easily join a cluster of people and split off. Once inside, he peeled off to an empty seat in the back corner, still incognito. Not that he knew anyone in the room. That was exactly the point. *They* never tell you who they are, or that they're following you. Think about it. *They* were clever all right and would not be satisfied just to stop Ellis Peek from fulfilling his mission. No, they wanted to destroy the world, too. That's why Ellis Peek had to conduct his own investigation. That's why he had to secretly join forces with Senator Ray Hoffenworth. That's why he had to stop taking the medication *they* wanted him to take.

"Thank you," the senator drawled. "The Senate Investigative Committee on Chimera is now in session."

A self-taught cryptologist whose day job for the last eighteen years was a Decatur, Illinois fumigation technician, Peek was keenly attuned to hidden meanings in the sounds and words transmitted by others. Smells, too. It occurred to Ellis Peek that the senator purposely mutated the word *chimera*; "ki-MIR-a" became "kuh-MURR-ah." To the senior senator from Tennessee, a chimera was not just a bio-engineered animal containing genes from two species, like an eagle with chicken feathers. The word *chimera* was *America* upside down— twisted, perverted and plunged towards a godless world unreckoned since the fall of the Evil Empire. Ellis Peek agreed. More telling of the secret bond between the Tennessee senator and Ellis Peek was how strikingly close Ray Hoffenworth's pronunciation of *America* was to "uh-MURR-kah," a place inhabited by "uh-MURR-kins." The latter did not include *them* but rather was code for people like Ray and Ellis who'd undertaken a solemn mission. *They*—the *them* out there—had seized control of both the government and the universities, and right now they were creating monstrous chimeric soldiers under strict specifications of the biological warlords on the distant Planet Lusus Naturae. In Latin, of course, that meant freak of nature, but insiders like Ellis knew it as Planet Lusus.

Ellis Peek was privy to the Lusians' plan to destroy Earth. Under an unspoken pact, it was up to him, and him alone, to help Senator Ray Hoffenworth thwart the warlords' plans. He quietly checked under his coat to make sure he had everything in order for when the big moment came today.

"Before today's testimony, as is customary," the chairman said, "I'd like to have this Committee's charge read into the record." Ellis Peek racked his brain to glean what message the senator was beaming with that last word that he pronounced "wreck-ode"; it sounded like it might be an elegy following a naval disaster, but no, that couldn't be right.

"I call upon the clerk to the Committee, Mr. Trout."

A young clerk, seated below the lawmakers and in front of the witness, stood and read aloud: "The proliferation of chimera, or transgenic species, from the biotechnology industry has prompted the Senate Commerce Committee to form this investigative body to find answers to the challenging questions our society faces. Should their creation be legally permitted? Should the procreation of such animals be entirely controlled by their patent owners? What recommendations can be made to the Commerce Committee in the form of legislation or policies? We charge the Senate Investigative Committee on Chimera to evaluate these issues, to determine the role of informed Government, and to so advise the Senate." He closed an elegant black binder with an official seal on it and looked up to the senator.

"Thank you, Mr. Trout," the chairman said with a nod.

"Now Professor Gropes," Hoffenworth spoke into his microphone, "you've been sworn. Let us begin by learnin' somethin' about you. You're an emeritus professor of molecular biology. Is that right?"

"Yes, I *used* to teach molecular biology," the professor replied. "Now I am a molecular cosmologist."

"And what would that be?" the senator guffawed.

"Same thing except I ask much bigger questions." His face remained impassive.

"Like how all this foolin' with nature affects humans. I hope that's what you mean."

"I truly fear that most humans, including you, it sounds like, Senator, overrate their significance in the cosmos."

Ellis made a note on a Post-It that this witness was openly contemptuous of earthly inhabitants. He opened his notebook, pasted the note inside with the same attention to detail he would if he were crawling through sub-flooring to spray for cockroaches.

"We'll see who has some big questions, Professor," the senator said. "I got a big question about this government-funded genome project. How much has the federal treasury been sponged for so far?"

The professor's assistant, a Lusian disguised as a young, brown-haired woman with glasses, leaned over and whispered to the scientist. She was spitting data into his ear from a computer underneath latex skin masquerading as her face.

"I'm merely a special adviser, Senator, but I'm told the cost so far is somewhere to the tune of eighty-seven million dollars," the professor finally said.

Senator Hoffenworth shook his head, and traded like expressions of dismay from his fellow Republicans who must be grieving with him about all the starving arsenals of half-built bombs needed to thwart the Lusians. The Democrats on the Committee—fools, all of them—regarded the witness with an amiable glow, verging on misty-eyed, as if the project were all about kids, education, and developing medicines to save humanity.

"For the record, please tell the Committee what government-funded project did you apply this learnin' to that brings you here today?"

"I'm a special adviser to the Naked Chicken Genome Mapping Project," the professor said. "Naked chickens have been bio-engineered without feathers so that they are better able to survive in the hottest climates on earth."

"Now, Professor," the chairman said with a curled lip, unable to endure being civil much longer. "If I may interject, I'm lookin' at hundreds of pages of gobbledegook." An image flashed on the hearing room projection screen, a portion of the naked chicken genome with the letters representing the four building blocks of nucleotides the Lusians were after:

gaggataggctaaactgcggcccctcgtaaatttcggtaccggta
tttaacccggatcgtttaacgattgggcatttcgatatcccggtatat
gcccaatttgggcatggccctaatgcctacggaaattgcatcgta
cccggtacgaaattcgataaatcgatatccagccctttaattgcatcg
aaatccggtaatccggcctttattacccatatcgatgggcgggattt...

"Voodoo genomics, like all the other ones we've paid for. Four letters repeatin' over an' over. Then they are mishmashed in no order. Nothin' but chicken scratch, 'cept here the chicken been let loose with a computer. How are we better off knowin' any of this?"

The professor pulled his chin thoughtfully before speaking. "If by *we* you mean politicians, you're not going to get better. But there's value in knowing that large sequences of the chicken genome match up with humans, possibly explaining the reluctance to take a stand on sensitive issues."

The chairman gaveled once to squelch the laughter from the gallery. "This is no laughin' matter, sir."

Ellis knew what all those letters were about. His man Ray must have been acting stupid, maybe to draw out the witness who might let something slip. These so-called blueprints for various organisms, invented by Lusians like this Professor Gropes who—big coincidence!—were highly trained scientists speaking difficult-to-decipher languages. The text held military secrets of the warlords and described in detail when, where, and how the invasion would occur. Time was a dear commodity. Ellis opened the notebook, took out the old Post-It (a large one), crumpled it up and inserted it between his cheek and gum. As he secretively wrote out the words "American Leaders Under Attack!" on a fresh Post-It, the old one slowly dissolved, making it easier to chew and swallow. It tasted bitter yellow.

"Let's get down to business, shall we, Professor." The senator put his reading glasses on and leafed through a dossier. "You are here because you been workin' up some new kinda technology that might just be used for creatin' chimeric critters. Please tell this committee just exactly what you're up to?"

The professor removed an unlit pipe from his mouth and spoke. "Genes are the engines that express proteins. Some of these engines have been turned off in species for millions of years, while in related species they have continued to be turned on producing vital proteins. By studying the active genes in the related species, I have discovered a way to beneficially turn on dormant genes in the first species. I call it…"

"Flippin' switches on what the good Lord, in His wisdom, turned off?" Hoffenworth interjected. "Sounds like foolin' with nature in a way that can't be good."

"Fooling with nature or re-instilling nature, depending on how you use it, or your point of view," the professor said, curling his mouth thoughtfully into the shape of a crescent moon above Saturn. "In the case of naked chickens, they lost more than their feathers in the bio-engineering process. By studying and comparing their genome with that of their ancient cousin the jungle fowl, I can turn on the genes that had been switched off by the intervention of biotechnology and restore those natural functionalities."

Hoffenworth looked at him with an expression of both confusion and dreadful understanding. "Continue, sir."

The Lusian professor put his pipe down, leaned back in his chair and, folding his hands on his chest, peered up at the ceiling with his dark glasses. "Bear with me. Scientists, including molecular biologists, thought all along that the sequence was merely a set of instructions for assembling proteins. But I theorized that there was a more fundamental vital force at play here. I have deciphered from the thousands of pages larger patterns, clearer mathematical relationships, akin to music, actually. Using these relationships as a template, I've discovered a way to use modulated electrical shocks that simulate patterns from like functional genes in one species that activates non-functioning, non-protein-producing genes from another. At the molecular level, where these molecules are moving to these natural rhythms, the overwriting of the genetic code can be done without unnatural and invasive gene-splicing. It can be done by merely applying the electronic force at a level only the cells themselves can feel, if you will. It's a kind of subatomic gene therapy utilizing a mild electric shock and whose effects are an immediate re-sequencing of the amino acids to form different proteins. With repeated application, it rewrites the germ line, which is to say that the next generation of chickens is born with switched-on genes. The full name of this technology is Cell Shock-Transmitted Life Force, or Cell-STL Force." He rocked forward, staring blankly in the direction of the senator. "I call it Cell Shock."

There was silence for a few seconds. Several senators from both sides of the aisle stared at the witness in slack-jawed disbelief.

He held the pipe in his hands, its bowl acting as a satellite dish, probably serving as a receiver downloading digital transmissions from a faraway planet. Did he actually say that genes are rewritten, mutating the species back to its distant jungle cousin? Would there be Jurassic jungle chickens lumbering across the plains with thundering feet, crushing automobiles and bowling alleys, destroying the planet? Is that how the warlords would achieve their goal?

"Thank you," the senator finally said. "And I think we all feel better, Professor, knowin' that you were able ta write some pretty music for all the itty bits o' molecules inside a barnyard bird. Need I tell you, Professor, that I have concerns about eatin' chickens been switched on. And how do we know this bio-juju won't be used on humans?"

"Our goals are simple and purely nonhuman," he said. "We want to convert naked chickens to free range, to re-wild them. Returned to their natural state, but to do that we have to solve a problem they have."

"Go on, Professor. We're dyin' to know what this problem is you've solved. Lemme guess. You play some hoot-owl music to chicken molecules and make 'em birds a whole lot wiser." He chuckled. "Call 'em 'road' scholars if they make it across without gettin' run over!" He laughed, rejoined by others.

"The upshot of the bioengineering they've experienced is that they do not mate without human intervention in the form of artificial insemination. Although they are better suited to survive in the heat, our research shows that their neuro-hormonal sex drive is in large measure derived from a gene we've isolated. The so-named Rooster Booster gene."

Ellis Peek might have to make his move sooner, rather than later. As predicted by the ancient prophets—whose names escaped him right now, but their message surely had been repeated by his favorite hosts on all-angry-all-the-time radio over the last six months—the cataclysmic collapse of America would come from an abandonment of morals. His man Ray stared bravely back at the enemy, no doubt redoubling his resolve to launch the MPS—the far-flung, wildly expensive, yet desperately needed Moral Positioning System the Senator proposed and the centerpiece of his presidential designs.

"Through this technology we've isolated how chickens become sexually aroused," the professor said.

There was quiet in the hearing room except for some whispers from the gallery.

"In other words," the barefaced alien added, "we've figured out how to re-sex, re-invigorate these formerly feathered—"

"I heard you the first time, Professor," the senator interrupted him. "Eighty-seven million taxpayer dollars goin' to figure out how to give 'em birds a thrill…"

"OHHH!" THE CLASS CHORUSED IN DISAPPOINT-ment when Bert turned off the TV. Just when it was getting good. Not that Bert needed to understand the mating dance of chickens but, in a way, he was as curious as anyone about what made roosters captains of their domains. At the same time he'd found himself staring at Anna Brighton whenever there was a long view of the witness table.

"We've only got a few minutes for discussion," Bert said. "Any questions?"

No response.

"Is the professor really your uncle?" Jimmy Alvarez finally asked.

"He's not real—" Bert was about to explain that his mother was adopted, and therefore he was not related by blood to his uncle, but caught himself. Too much information.

"—close," Bert finished his thought. "He's always been very busy with his work, and we don't have a close relationship like many of you have with aunts and uncles. Now let's wrap it up. Does anyone see a connection between the testimony we just heard and our tireless search for ahs?"

Trevor's hand shot up. There was no wrong answer to Bert's question, but why give Mr. Smart Ass a chance to flourish in self-satisfaction when a more worthy creature needed some sunlight?

Bert made eye contact with the sylph-like Linda in the front row who never spoke. He knew she had things to say because her writing and testing proved it, but she didn't speak in class because of a speech impediment.

"Anyone?" He looked over in Linda's direction but her eyes remained cast down. Luckily a new hand went up.

"Yes, Patrick," Bert finally said.

"Your uncle sounds like an *ah*, a pioneer in science," the boy said. "He's made discoveries about genes no one else has."

"Good answer," Bert said. "What struck me was the explanation that genes *express* themselves. That's how molecular biologists describe it. In other words, when there's expression, genes produce the vital proteins that make us alive. I like that. Sound familiar? What in our Constitution keeps our democracy alive?"

Bert noticed that Linda's eyes were emboldened, lit up. "Linda, what do we call it?"

"Ffff....fffirst Ammm...mendment!" she managed. Ffffreedom of ssss...ssss...." Bert nodded vigorously at her with all the aching in his heart. She pressed on bravely. "Pee... eeech!

"Pee?" Trevor repeated, looking at her, as if he genuinely wanted to make sure he heard it right. Then he looked around to his band of rogues with a grin. Stifled guffaws from each followed.

It was only one syllable, but Bert felt it like an edge of sharp, cold steel, and it sounded like the abridged audio version of *The World History of Tyranny*—all twenty leather-bound volumes condensed into one vicious word. No one knew more about that subject than Bert, especially when it came to enduring cruel hazing from classmates at Linda's age.

The young girl didn't cry or flush with anger. Worse, she looked down, expressionless, withdrawn into a world she'd created just for these occasions.

"Thank you, Linda. That's exactly right," Bert said, taking care not to look at Trevor. "Free speech. The right to speak freely, the right to be left alone, even the right, with exceptions dictated by common sense..."—he scowled at Trevor—"to behave as we please."

The bell rang ending the class.

"Amen," Trevor said, standing up to leave.

"Trevor, you will remain," Bert said, letting the whole class know there would be consequences.

Five students remained after class to ask Bert more about Schliemann and the C-SPAN program. After a few quick answers or arrangements to meet later, they were gone. Bert then addressed Trevor, re-slouched in his seat. "Your outburst was inexcusably rude and cruel, and you know it." He took a deep breath. "I want to make sure we give you an assignment that will be instructive for both of us, that explains where that rudeness comes from."

"I'll do my homework," he said to Bert. "I'm fine. I don't need an assignment."

"We'd be cheating ourselves if we did that, Trevor," Bert said, the anger in his voice barely suppressed. "I couldn't help but think about what we saw on TV, the genome material. All those pages and pages of the same letters repeated over and over. That's what chickens copy and pass on from generation to generation. Unlike Linda Nguyen—a complex, thinking, and all-too-human creature—*Homo Trevoris* has almost nothing on his mind. Except the letters *p-e-e*." He pointed to the boy's head. "That's what's in there. Right?"

Trevor looked up, unease now taking hold of him.

"So for detention, you are to copy your genome—or is it *penome*?—which is composed of two letters, *p* and *e*, with the sequence *p-e-e*. You're to copy that sequence for one hour, single space, and no spaces between the letters."

"What?" he ranted.

"I want at least twenty pages of it by the time detention lets out. And no spaces," Bert told him. "Anywhere."

3

ANNA BRIGHTON FIDGETED IN HER SEAT. DR. Gro had raised the forbidden subject. There was only one thing that set off Senator Ray Hoffenworth more than the mention of human chimera, and that was deviant sex, or something he could interpret as deviant. They had been warned. Of course, it would have been hard not to touch his hot button since, unavoidably, at the heart of the Cell-STL Force technology was the libidinal priming of naked chickens.

"It's a simple way to stimulate sexual appetite among naked roosters to re-wild them," Dr. Gro explained.

"You figured out how to give 'em birds not just any thrill. It's a sexual one," the senator said, having his way with the word, pronouncing it *sek-shil.*

"That would be accurate," Dr. Gro said matter-of-factly. "Allow me to explain. For example, surely you've observed, Senator, that chickens don't fly." He spoke as if lecturing a room full of slow learners. "You see, chickens were domesticated thousands of years ago, and have become grounded; their flight genes, if you will, are turned off. Now, just like chickens over time lost their ability to fly, the same birds, subject to radical genetic alteration that nakedizes their morphology, are not mating the way nature intended. They need to be re-wilded, and that's what Cell Shock does in a natural, non-invasive way."

"And I suppose that the human race will be better for this," the senator sneered. "Is that about right, Professor?"

"The human race won't improve, but that doesn't mean I'm some kind of futilitarian. The planet will improve. If you want to hear something nice about humans, perhaps you should talk to my assistant, Anna Brighton, who's more likely to tell you something you want to hear."

Anna couldn't believe she'd been offered up as a sacrificial lamb. Suddenly her throat felt as tight, constricted, and at risk as one of the birds they'd been discussing. She was brought here to describe or retrieve papers for him, and to make sure he got around safely. She hated public speaking. She wasn't supposed to testify!

"Miss Brighton, consider yourself sworn." The senator leaned over with his readers lowered on his nose. "But first, introduce yourself. Tell us about you and your schoolin.'"

"Certainly, Mr. Chairman," she began, adjusting her own glasses. "My name is Anna Brighton. I received my undergraduate degree at Harvard where I majored in biology with a minor in statistical analysis. Last year I received my doctorate at MIT in computational molecular biology. I also grew up in the Boston area, but I came to California a few months ago to become Dr. Gropes's research assistant."

So far, so good. Of course, she should know her name and degrees pretty well.

"Now, for the benefit of the committee, kindly tell us what all it is to be a computational molecular biologist." Hoffenworth struggled—part real, part feigned—with the mouthful of words.

"Of course," she said. "It's the study of molecular biology by using computational, statistical and algorithmic methodologies as tools for accelerating and facilitating discoveries in the field of molecular biology."

Another easy one. Now a few words about the benefits for humans and she'd be done.

"Thank you. A whole lotta learnin' to be sure," the senator patronized. "Now, do tell us what's to learn from a buncha barnyard birds about makin' life better for human bein's?"

What's to learn? It wasn't about learning. It was about feeding people in the tropics who might otherwise starve.

Her mouth hung open, not sure what to say.

"Lemme guess. It's going to bring humans a whole lotta longevity. Tell us, Miss Brighton, how long does the average chicken live?"

"That's not—"

"How long?" he insisted.

"Broilers have a life expectancy of something in the neighborhood of seven weeks," she said. "That's when they're slaughtered."

Rude laughter erupted in the Senate hearing room.

"Seven weeks, ladies and gentlemen." The senator joined in the fun. "Think about the golden age of humanity bio-engineered broilers will bring. Now what about roasters?"

It was no use trying to put the senator back on track with the real human benefits.

"Roasters are allowed to live a little longer," she said, having been conscripted as the Senator's involuntary straight man. "Eight weeks, to be exact."

"Well, eight full weeks now!" Hoffenworth bellowed. "Scooch on over, Methuselah, and make room for Mr. Roaster. Why, with that whole extra week thrown in, I bet 'em roasters spend most of that last week sittin' in their Lazy Boys, pen an' paper in hand, writin' their memoirs."

More derisive laughter.

The senator shook his head and looked down as if shamed. With chin pointed at sternum, his fleshy wattle pushed out in all directions from his face like a compressed water balloon about to burst.

"This is nothin' more than some kinda welfare—*academic* welfare." He pronounced it *ackie*-demic. "Meal tickets for a whole lotta professors and their assistants. This was supposed to be about chicken, but..."—he shook his head in disgust— "it's lookin' to me a lot like that other white meat." He let out a sneering chuckle in the direction of a few senators whose large states were home to universities that received barrels full of pork.

Senator Hoffenworth leaned forward to engage Dr. Gro again, taking the heat off Anna, to her relief.

"Let me review, Professor, so the record is clear. You say this research of yours is only for sexin' up 'em chickens." He looked incredulously from side to side. "You got Miss Brighton here workin' a computer to conjure up a—what did she call it?— algorithm. The government's spent tens o' millions o' tax dollars allowin' you to invent some frisky Cell-STL music so's you can turn old jungle fowl genes on in these naked chickens, mixin' it up and makin' farm birds into some kinda newfangled hot wings. Hot'n'bothered, I should say!"

The senator leaned back and removed his readers.

"Do I have that about right? Why yes, I believe I do. Pretty far-fetched, Professor, if not downright preposterous, but so is just about all that goes on in biotech labs across this country day in, day out, hundreds of new plants and animals bein' created in laboratories. Scientists playin' God, that's what it is. So let me ask you the same thing I ask every scientist who comes before this committee. What assurance do we have this Cell Shock can't or won't be used to alter the sanctity of human life as we know it? How do we know you won't find rooster genes in people and switch them on? Or rats, dogs, or monkeys for that matter?"

"I think I've already answered this, but let me say it in a different way," Dr. Gro said, quietly disaffected. "Humans evolved to as high as they were going to get. I like to think there was an Atlantis once, if for no reason other than it had to be better than this. Thousands of years of wars, pillaging, raping and looting. Among the species, they account for nearly one hundred percent of the pollution of this planet, and their space junk is already turning the rest of the firmament into a roadside dump. If anyone thought humans could be made better by switching on genes from another species, I suppose they would, but it will never happen. You criticize the biotech industry. Fine. But in my view the human race, especially their appointed ones who've led the charge, are the ultimate experiment gone bad."

Hoffenworth was vibrating with rage, ready to pounce.

Just then Anna turned around to see a wild-eyed man in a business suit and baseball cap charge into the view of the television camera, planting himself in front of Dr. Gro. He tossed the cap and tore away his suit, revealing long skinny legs covered in yellow tights, topped with a matching yellow turtleneck. Now starkly visible were the black boots he'd been wearing under the suit. There were so many feathers stuffed into his underwear, it looked like he was wearing over-sized diapers beneath the tights. His face must have been covered by an invisible tacky substance because the handfuls of chicken feathers that he grabbed out of his crotch and slapped himself with stuck to his head and face quite effectively, with only half fluttering to the hearing room floor.

"Order!" Hoffenworth bellowed. "Cut him off!" he shouted at the C-SPAN cameraman with repeated cleaved-neck gestures.

"Is this what you want? Is this what you intend?" the crazed man shouted at the witness.

"Ah yes, I hear one of your precious human specimens," the blind Dr. Gro said calmly.

"Well, is it?" the man insisted, walking around stiff-legged between the witness and the panel of senators, an excess of feathers spilling out of the bottom of his turtleneck.

Two members of Senate security attacked the man and tugged at him, stretching his yellow top, then collided with each other and fell to the floor as the man broke free and lunged away. The turtleneck was now halfway off; only the point of his nose—or was that really his Adam's apple?—could be seen beneath the yellow o-ring upon which his head had formerly rested.

"Do you know what I am? Fowl-Man! That's right, a monstrous human! See? It's grotesque and horrible, isn't it?" He stalked over and stood before Senator Hoffenworth. "It must be stopped! We've got to do something!" Fowl-Man pleaded, a single feather now sticking straight out from that spot where his nose protruded from the fabric, flittering at the chairman.

"Calm down, sir!" the Sargeant-at Arms shouted. Four more security guards swooped in and dragged the protester away, his black boots flailing at the end of hapless yellow noodles.

"'Calm down?' What do you mean calm down? You're all losing your head!'" his voice shrieked, now from the back of the room. "That's a Lusian warlord! We're under attack! Don't you see? It's all part of a plan! The human race will be chickenized, rendered into nuggets, and served at fast food stores throughout their planet. Wake up, America!"

4

DAYS LATER, ARRIVING HOME FROM A DAY OF teaching, Bert sat in his old, beat-up Saab a few minutes, windows up, and listened to the silence and the *tick-tick* of his engine. Today he was not in a hurry to go inside. Parked in the driveway was his Uncle Gro's pickup truck that he'd converted into a hybrid vehicle. Newly painted, the old Ford was a loamy brown whose sheen gave the illusion of moisture; it inspired vivid scatological associations in Bert's mind, especially when he thought about the advice his uncle might feel compelled to impart if they actually had a conversation. Then there were those sporty lichen and moss-colored racing stripes that ran down the length of the electro-gas turd-mobile—a visual flare only a blind molecular cosmologist, only his Uncle Gro, could appreciate. Bert resolved to walk in, make a brief appearance—more like another nonappearance in the vacant eyes of his uncle—and escape to his room.

As soon as he opened the front door and stepped inside, his mother's voice called out, "Is that you, Bertie? Your uncle is here!"

WALKING INTO THE ROOM, BERT COULD SEE HIS mother and uncle seated on the couch. A young man, with his back to Bert, was poised in a chair in front of them.

"There you are," said his mother. She also must have just arrived home from the nearby university where she worked in Student Aid. But for the dyed red hair, and although she was his adopted sister, Eugenia Gropes looked a little like his uncle, only a softer version. Where his sharp-angled nose could probably open a can of soup, hers could tell across the room it was chicken alphabet.

"Come in and meet Joseph Cherp," she said. "Joseph is doing postgraduate work in… what was it? Computer modeling of—?"

"Molecular proteomics," Joseph said with a squeaky voice. "Sequencing of proteins." Cherp was skinny, with long legs and a giant head.

"Marvelous," his mother gushed.

Bert shook Joseph's hand. As if his uncle brought the boy genius along because of his mastery of molecules. Joseph had functioning eyeballs and could navigate a turdmobile.

Uncle Gro, seated with mouth open and head cocked, leaned forward in a mid-lecture pose, waiting for the interruption to pass so that he could continue. As was now hardwired into their relationship, neither Bert nor his uncle shook hands or greeted one another in any way.

His mother said, "Your uncle was just sharing with us highlights from his trip to Washington."

"Great balls, Eugenia! I'd hardly call them highlights!" Gro chided his sister. Bert had never bothered to ask him if "great balls," his favorite expression of alarm, used whenever roused from his lecture mode, were supposed to be "of fire," of dying stars hurtling through the dark recesses of space out in the middle of nowhere, or of something even more futile.

"Now, where was I? Oh yes. A democracy, the grand human experiment, is nevertheless in the earliest stages of evolution," his uncle continued when he sensed he had everyone's attention again. "Like the evolution of humankind, it had to start somewhere, but I believe other species were first. Ages ago, by chance, some amphibious water-worms and slime-slugs crawled out of the primordial ooze. Then one of them pulled all his friends up. It was all part of the progression but, in effect, they voted and installed themselves as governors of the bottomless muck."

This was his uncle's idea of funny. He neither smiled nor chuckled during his delivery, and he certainly never acknowledged Bert in the course of it.

"Soon the bottomless muck was too big for one governing body. So some of the slime-slugs evolved into reptiles and spun off to take charge of their own slime pools. Incidentally, reptiles are particularly adept at governing slime pools they call committees. The upshot is that slithery slime-slugs and reptiles have been governing themselves for a good deal longer than *Homo sapiens*, who came along much, much later. We need to be patient with the fledgling human efforts at a democratic political order that's both sustainable and intelligent." He placed an unlit pipe in his mouth and suckled thoughtfully.

It seemed Uncle Gro had not become an instant fan of the committee chair from Tennessee but, as long as he didn't have to watch, he was willing to give Senator Hoffenworth and his descendants a couple of million years to grow into the job.

"I confess we have a lot to learn about getting along with one another, but sitting up alone looking down is not going to change anything." Eugenia Gropes regarded her brother sternly. He remained silent and unapologetic. "You know how

I feel," she said, touching her heart and turning to her young guest. "I'm a believer in our own potential, Joseph. I believe it's what's inside that matters," she proclaimed as if defying her brother. "Even if we're only cosmic dust. I believe we humans, unlike all the other dust, have the power to change ourselves, to correct errors and misprints on our life maps, that kind of thing, and live our lives more fully." She cleared her throat and delivered from memory: "'You can strut out of your rut if you've got the gut to know what's what.' One of my group leaders said that, and I believe it. What do you think?"

Joseph nodded. "That's good! I think your leader is describing knowledge as a catalyst, one that's self-generated. In science we call that autocatalysis."

"Marvelous," she said, clasping her hands.

"Or, if it's generated by your own mind"—Egghead was going in for extra credit—"you could call it *psycho*-catalysis."

Eugenia heaved a sigh of rapture. Uncle Gro remained motionless and disengaged. Bert was slouched in a cushioned chair. His poor mother was truly excited about the prospects of being able to personally evolve and change, and now she had Joseph buying into it. Unfortunately, Bert was tainted by his long-held belief that she just wanted to crawl out of her skin and into someone, *anyone* else's. And if she couldn't do it, she wanted Bert to do it for her.

"I've been trying to get Bert to take a motivational seminar," she told Joseph. "Not that there's anything wrong with him. I just think if you can do more with what you're born with, you owe it to yourself to move off your cozy chair and, as they say, 'go for it.'"

"I promise not to get too cozy." Bert shrugged, a little embarrassed that she was bringing a stranger's attention, indirectly at least, to the fact that he still lived at home with his mother. "I don't need a motivational seminar to make the most of what I was born with. I have plans. I'm on the move. You'd be surprised."

"No, I wouldn't, Bertie," she said. "You're an exceptionally talented boy. You're future is large. I just want you take advantage of all the wonderful tools that I know are out there."

"Water-worms," Uncle Grover muttered to himself without looking up.

Joseph turned to Bert. "Where are you moving?"

"He means moving, like in spreading his wings," his mother said to Joseph, then turned back to her son. "Honestly, Bertie dear, I just want you to be happy. How about you, Joseph? Ever think about changing yourself, striving to make yourself even better than you already are?"

"Oh, definitely. I, for one, am interested in anything that will give me an edge," Joseph said. "Better tools for doing my work. That's what science is all about, isn't it?"

"Come with me, Joseph," his mother said as she stood up. "We'll go find some nibbles to bring back. And I want to show you something. I've got a special wall in my kitchen."

Joseph better not be thinking home improvement, Bert thought. Of course, he'd asked for it. Joseph was about to make a pilgrimage to the Altar of Self-Improvement, as Bert called it: a shrine constructed by its greatest devotee, Eugenia Gropes. Floor to ceiling, books, tapes, videos, and computer programs were crammed on shelves, the edges of which were plastered with Post-It notes of maxims, catch-phrases, pithy truisms, and positive affirmations.

"We'll leave the two of you to visit," she said. "Grover, dear, come down from your ivory tower. Maybe you could talk to Bertie about *his* future, if you can reflect for one minute on that and not the planet's. Get more involved with him. Encourage him to 'reach for the rung that's far above the dung,' that sort of thing."

Joseph followed her out of the living room.

Bert did not move from his chair, which was about fifteen feet from where his uncle sat. The two of them now alone, an awkward moment of silence hung in the air.

"I've started a search for my biological father," Bert said, hoping that he had the attention of this brilliant mind long enough that he might pick up one or two research tips.

"Yes, that can be useful," his uncle said, removing the pipe from his mouth. "Having ample genetic data and medical histories of bloodlines can be valuable for ascertaining disease susceptibility and prevention."

Bert squeezed his eyes shut and gave his brow a deep shiatsu massage, knowing his reaction was unseen. He took a breath. "I was thinking more along the lines of meeting him—learning about who he is and what he's about. Maybe grabbing a pizza or something."

"Why?" his uncle asked with sincere wonder.

"I don't know. I guess I'm curious." Now he felt foolish. He hadn't developed a good answer other than the one that couldn't be spoken: He wanted to upgrade to a product he imagined—Real Family 2.0, ads for which boasted a "father-son feature" not found in the original version, and a new search capability called Brighter Future.

"People let you down," his uncle said.

Really now? Bert thought to himself, as if there was some mystery as to how the old man felt about his fellow travelers in time and space.

"Unlike other adopteds," his uncle paused to confirm she was out of earshot, "your mother's never expressed an interest in finding her own biological parents. I suppose growing up in our house, watching your grandparents let each other down each day—with endless sabotage, plots, counter-plots, sandbagging, and shout-downs—was enough to leech any interest she may have had. That's why, when she wanted to have you, she made the decision to go the sperm-bank route."

"Any suggestions on how I might improve my chances of success?" Bert forged ahead. "I've filled out forms requesting records at the hospital, and the same at the sperm bank." He couldn't help smiling at the name American Gene Savings & Loan.

"I'm the one who referred your mother to that sperm bank. That was in nineteen-eighty-nine, a few years before you were conceived. Back then in-vitro was still relatively *primitive*." He pronounced the last word as if to suggest Bert were conceived with the help of a Yolo County equine service. Then he added: "The bank will say it's confidential, of course. Have you researched how to go about this? Do you have a strategic model?"

Bert was hoping for a few tips, not that his own questionably scientific approach be vetted.

"Heinrich Schliemann."

"Great balls! Who?"

"The adventurer who discovered Troy. He's my model."

Uncle Gro had a way of shaking his head in disappointment without actually moving his head or revealing the story his eyes told behind dark glasses. "I recall the figure. He did find Troy and the treasures of Mycenae. With no formal training as an archaeologist. He was also notorious for his self-aggrandizing lies and exaggeration."

Bert felt stung by this slap at one of his heroes. He rallied a defense. "I think he's an amazing example of digging into the truth about the past against all odds. He's an inspiration. I profiled him in my class at Mansfield. The students were quite interested—"

"Mansfield?" his uncle repeated. "Forgive my not remembering, Bret, but I thought your mother told me you were teaching at Warren Middle School."

Bret! There was no mistaking it. He called him Bret. Enough! It was time to make himself scarce. His uncle was a lost cause.

"Slime-slugs..." Bert muttered spontaneously.

"Huh?" his uncle grunted.

"Two kinds of chips," his mother announced, placing two bowls on the table in front of the couch and bailing Bert out, not for the first time in his life. "Potato and corn."

Joseph traipsed to his chair and tried to sit down delicately, but half a dozen books and videos fell out of his arms onto the floor.

"Did I hear talk about slime-slugs and muck again?" she scolded. "Remember, it starts with positive affirmations. Right, Joseph?"

Joseph nodded and grinned.

"I'm going to excuse myself. I have a stack of papers to grade," Bert fibbed.

A minute later he was upstairs, the door closed behind him, in the room of his childhood, a space he thought he'd outgrown long ago. When he taught at Warren Middle School for two years, he lived alone in an apartment in neighboring Davis. He left the Warren job for a good reason: He was fired on grounds of chronic failure to follow course curriculum, failure to turn in reports, and failure to attend mandatory faculty meetings. The least that should have earned him was a rep, even if a bad one. But instead, there were teachers at Warren who didn't even know who Bert Gropes was after two years on the job. Another reason to finally begin the search for his lost father: Bert might actually be somebody but just not know it yet.

When he lost his job at Warren, he had no choice but to move back into his room which hadn't changed in a dozen years: a twin bed now too small for him, a desk with a computer, a poster on one wall of Ben Franklin. The Dean of Social Studies struck a dynamic pose with lightning in the background that, on first glance, appeared to be leaping out of his head.

On another wall he'd hung a poster portrait of Heinrich Schliemann he'd had made from a photograph. When he was fourteen and making his way through a tough stretch in his life, his mother gave him Irving Stone's *The Greek Treasure*. It was also the first occasion his mother told him everything she could about how she'd chosen his donor-dad: "His profile told me that he was an engineer, a businessman, and of high intelligence. Just like Heinrich Schliemann. My intuition told me he was also handsome, and I was right. Just look at my Bertie!"

That did it. Bert read the book and identified wildly with the story of the famous adventurer and archaeologist. When Schliemann was Bert's age, he'd worked at a job he hated but vowed that some day he would learn Greek and discover Troy. Until he was thirteen, Bert had been popular at school, had many friends, and was elected vice-president of his sixth-grade class. Then a boy in his class learned from his mother, who learned it from another mother, that classmate Bert Gropes had been fabricated in a science lab by means of in vitro fertilization and a sperm bank. Kids began teasing him, calling him "The Experiment," or "Mr. X Periment," or simply "X"—as if it were a mere placeholder name for the otherwise nameless. Even in class when he was called upon, whispers of "X" echoed around the room.

Hurt by it, Bert withdrew (or he was constructively banished), and he quietly finished out the sixth grade. The next year he started at a private middle school where no one knew him, and he made sure it remained that way as much as possible. Being remote evolved from strategy to habit all through high school and later at UC Davis where he attended college while living at home.

Like his hero, Heinrich Schliemann, Bert vowed that some day he too would, against whatever odds, begin his quest when the time was right, when conditions were ripe, even if decades hence. For Bert the quest was to discover his biological father and find out who he really was, to supplant the "X" with a name he could be proud of. That time had come; he just knew it.

For now, however, he'd have to pursue his quest from this home base, at least until he could pay off his bills. His finances were in the process of turning from red to black, rendering them brownish right now—decidedly darker than red, verging on a fiscally desirable black. He'd already transformed his childhood room into a staging area for the big plans he had. His next move, the escape he dreamed about, would send him far beyond Woodland and its environs.

He couldn't wait.

5

ONE THOUSAND MILES SOUTHEAST OF WASH-
ington, D.C., three hundred twenty-two miles due east of the
last Virgin Island, and more than ten thousand miles due west
of ancient Sodom, the tiny paradise of Isle Libido beckons. A
six-by-nine mile dollop of dirt splashed into the Lesser Antilles
by a rummy volcano about nine hundred years ago, Isle Libido
has emerged as a sovereign nation—but rogue to be sure.

The island was discovered in 1623 by René Louis Pardon, a
swashbuckling French sea captain whose badly off-course ship
had somehow been pulled into the swirling currents surrounding it. "Libido, Fraternité, Egalité," the captain is said to have
exclaimed upon stepping down from his ship to greet the warm
and friendly natives. Scholars of the region say that the natives,
unfamiliar with the parlance of French pirates, may have not
heard Pardon correctly. On the other hand, the captain may
have actually said that, what with all the free time he'd had to
daydream over the prior eight months while he'd been adrift at

sea. This much is known for sure: Captain Pardon's utterance was spontaneous, if not prescient, and it occurred a century and a half before the French Revolution.

The unofficial motto of Isle Libido was "Laissez Faire" which reputedly was the *bon mot* freely repeated by Captain René Louis Pardon during that first lost weekend in 1623. Although it was clear to the native Libidoans that economic policy was not the primary thrust the ghost-colored stranger intended to impart by his words, the people of the island had, in fact, since their beginning, promulgated, or perhaps acquiesced to, the most transparently toothless standards of government regulation on the surface of the Earth. A draft constitution had been circulating for longer than anyone could remember and was said to be on the verge of ratification by the Provisional Government of Isle Libido.

For all but the last twenty years the inhabitants of the island managed to eke out a modest trade by growing sugar cane, producing rum, and catering to the small number of visitors passing through who would discover Libido's irresistible island charm. Then, twenty-five years ago, the island endured another sea change, bigger than any since its seminal eruption—the volcanic one eight hundred years earlier, long before Captain René Louis Pardon first explored the island's treasures. Another rogue, of the American entrepreneurial variety, arrived on the island to set up world headquarters for the business known as Primal Urge Entertainment.

By all appearances Primal Urge took the island's traditional sugar cane and evolved it into highly-processed eye candy. From its main operations on a former two-thousand-acre sugar cane plantation, the company commanded a network of pornographic websites that dominated the Internet's digital skin trade. Primal Urge Entertainment was the brainchild of the one who put Libido on the map: founder, chairman, and expatriate American, Dick Slayde. Ernie Putterman clutched his briefcase and gawked out the window of the helicopter about to land on the roof of a building perched atop Isle Libido on the grounds of the Estate: the personal residence of Dick Slayde and world headquarters of Primal Urge Entertainment. A few years ago, when Putterman had flown into Hawaii's Hilo airport for a conference of patent lawyers, a woman had put a lei around his neck as he stepped off the plane. This time he fantasized that a Slayve—one of Primal Urge's exotic dancers who performed at The Urge—would be waiting for him as he stepped off the plane.

Ernie Putterman was practically drooling at the prospect of this new client. Primal Urge Entertainment brought together everything that made for a perfect client: exotic location, sex, and mountains of money. The pirate theme on Libido—dolls, pendants and merchandise everywhere of Captain Pardon— was a favorite of Ernie's. He especially loved it in the old movies when the pirates ran their dirty fingers through the treasure chests brimming with gold coins, doubloons, and precious jewels. *Filthy lucre*, that's what they called it. Putterman's hands began to itch just thinking about it finally being *his turn*.

Of course, he was hoping to do more than run his fingers through it. He wanted to put it into the bank account of his Miami-based firm, Pynne, Pencilgirth & Needlemeister. He'd heard about the kind of money that Primal Urge made from its operations. He'd also read about what it paid its First Amendment lawyers who defended the company against obscenity charges back in the States. They were always outfoxing prosecutors by getting jurors to become cushy-comfy with the idea that their own community standards of decency were much lower than they'd first imagined.

The call had come into the office and was directed to Hanford Bland, the managing partner and the biggest rainmaker in the firm. Putterman had been in the front lobby when the receptionist was fielding the call. He'd heard her say: "I'm sorry, but Mr. Bland is out of town on business… Yes, he's taking new clients… I'll put you through to his secretary. Who shall I say is calling? Simon Debree of Primal Urge? Please hold—"

That's when Ernie Putterman made his move. "Hanny told me he expected that call," he said to the receptionist. "I'll take it in my office."

Putterman did not see it as stealing a client; he saw it as taking a load off his partner, Hanford Bland: married twenty-six years, four children, a deacon in his church. Then there was Ernie Putterman: married twice, divorced twice, no kids, too much free time on his hands...

Upon disembarking from the helicopter, Ernie was met by a tall, gorgeous-looking Slayve named Tina, who escorted him to an elevator that took the two of them down to her golf cart. She chauffeured him from there to the plantation mansion at the top of the hill a quarter of a mile away, surrounded by more buildings, lawn areas and acres of sugar cane. Another Slayve opened the front door for him. Yet another welcomed him and handed him a large drink—a SplUrge, the five-kinds-of-rum signature drink served at The Urge Casino Hotel—and ushered him into a room full of white wicker furniture. He was accustomed to meeting with clients in drab offices and sterile laboratories, a far cry from this room where he found himself ogling framed photographs of various Slayves—fully unclothed, alluringly baking themselves under the steaming Libidoan sun.

"You must be Ernest," a young, barely-covered woman greeted him. Her familiar address, along with her wry smile, imparted that she was both friendly and amused—amused perhaps by his startled demeanor and business suit.

"Hi, I'm Ernie," he said, peeling off his glasses with an awkward stab at a devil-may-care swagger. He was really feeling the heat now.

"I'm Tinkie... *Ernie*." She giggled.

Putterman loosened his tie a smidgeon, just enough to make sure she got the message that he would rip it all off and have her right here and now, but for the fact that he had to conduct some legal business first.

"So, Tinkie, you look familiar. Could we have met?"

Without moving her head, she rolled her eyes up at one of the large photographs that had been thrust in front of Putterman's eyes upon his arrival. On her back. wearing only spiked heels, the woman was parting the way with both hands—what he had once heard referred to as a "bubblegum shot"—with a look that urgently demanded attention from any passerby in the waiting room. It was captioned "Ms. Tinkie Periwinkle: January Slayve of the Month" for an issue of *Slayve Quarterly* two years earlier. He was a little embarrassed that he didn't realize that the large framed image was the reason she seemed familiar, having focused on details in the photo other than her face.

"Follow me," she said, now with a teasingly flirtatious smile.

Breathless, the patent lawyer was led down a hall and into a great room with red and black pillows and exotic flowering tropical plants everywhere.

"Ernie Putterman, the patent lawyer," Tinkie announced him to a man and a woman seated in oversized, generously cushioned swivel chairs. Tinkie departed, closing the doors behind her.

"Slayde," the man said without rising from his seat. "Dick Slayde." They shook hands. Ernie Putterman, at five-nine, was at least four or five inches taller than his new client. Dick Slayde wore a silk, collarless black shirt with pink pearl buttons, white cotton pants, and flip-flops.

"This is my vice-president of public relations, Tatiana Lurenski." Slayde gestured toward the woman.

"I please to meet you," she said in a thick Russian accent. She was also in black, except her pants were of some shiny, moisture-impervious material. At six feet, plus her heels, she towered over Slayde. She was tanned, with shoulder-length black hair. It was so dark in and around her green eyes, Putterman suspected that she applied eyeliner with a latex roller.

She gave Ernie Putterman a smile that chilled him. Suddenly her shiny pants looked like black ice. The rum drink in his right hand felt like it had dropped to fifteen-below. Instinctively, he switched the glass to his left hand and pressed his freezing fingers against his throat—the only exposed flesh—to warm them up. Then, realizing that he looked like he was choking himself, he felt himself turning red. He impulsively thrust his right hand into his pocket and withdrew it when he considered what message, in context, he was sending. Another long second passed, and he nervously touched his throat again. He could feel Tatiana Lurenksi's eyes fixed on him. Glancing sideways, he saw her licking her lips ever so slightly. Her right hand—which had been resting on her hip—gently took hold of her gleaming black leather belt. Her fingers thrust back up inside the belt and shiny black pants until the chrome painted fingernails emerged and squeezed whatever life, real or imaginary, was between them and her thumb.

"Sit here," Slayde said to Putterman, waving his left hand at a couch.

"No, lawyer *eez* here." Tatiana Lurenksi pointed a long finger at a straight-backed chair.

Ernie Putterman sat down in the chair. She smiled as if he'd been outfitted in a darling choke collar.

The walls in the drawing room were covered in large framed images of monkeys—Libidoan monkeys—natives to the island. Appreciably larger than their eastern counterparts, African chimpanzees, Libidoan monkeys had faces of animated black rubber, puckish white teeth when bared, and long hair the color of bittersweet chocolate. Most prized were male Libidoans' sex organs, twice the size of average humans'. That Libidoan monkeys were so prodigiously endowed made them stand-outs among apes generally, and the envy of naked apes specifically. Each subject was captured in oil and acrylic (photorealistic and abstract), mixed media, in museum-quality photographs, or Cibachrome prints.

To Ernie's way of thinking, the exhibition was more powerful than the exhibit. Staring open-mouthed at the images, he caught himself crossing his legs tightly and leaning forward as if hiding something from those leering at him from the walls—as if, in a bad dream, he'd been hurtled back in time to another epoch, millennia before his miserable high school years, to Hell's Primordial Locker Room.

"Let me just say, I'm very comfortable writing patents in your... line of work," Putterman offered. "I wrote a patent once for a 'dual action mattress with coiled undulation.'" He suggestively bounced his eyebrow on his end of the imaginary box springs. But there was no counter-bounce forthcoming from their end. "It was a state-of-the-art 'magic fingers' bed developed by a major motel chain," he added.

Dick Slayde stared at a far wall, his body language making clear that he didn't care.

"We are a biological technology company," Slayde finally said.

"You mean biotech, of course." The lawyer chuckled as if there was a joke in the offing.

Nothing back again. This time no counter-chuckle.

"Everything we do is about biology," Slayde said, nodding to Lurenski, who nodded back.

"It *eez* who we are," she agreed. "The company *eez*, how you say, on all fours at the front."

"You're no doubt familiar with what's depicted on our websites," Slayde said.

"Biology," Putterman agreed and then added: "Depicted, definitely."

"And technology. Three hundred yards from here, we run all of our Internet operations. Next door, in an air-conditioned building the size of an airplane hangar, where you landed with the helicopter, we maintain one of the largest server farms in the world. That's how we manage a billion hits a day." Slayde picked up a remote and scrolled through a dozen Primal Urge websites on a giant flat panel mounted above a three-foot-high rock waterfall. "Nobody streams media like we do." A dozen pictures flashed on the screen: attractive cybermodels engaged in an endless variety of unnatural poses, couplings, conjoined contortions, and multi-corporeal pretzelizations.

"I was in Northern California in the eighties, a grad student at UCSF, when it was all happening," he said. "*Biological technology* scientists in the seventies created *biotech*, a combination word. Genentech ,too, is a blend word. As the pictures tell us, it's all about combinations. Two*sies*, three*sies*, group*sies*. But unlike old-fashioned biology, biotech is about accelerated combinations—nature accelerated."

"Exactly," Putterman said. "And you should know I've filed lots of gene patents that combine animal and plant genes."

"What I have is not a combination gene. Better, it's combinatorial in its biological sequela." He paused. "Did you hear that someone claims to have invented a shock technology that turns on genes in naked chicks?"

"No, but if you give me the background material, I'd be happy, no charge, to bone up on it," Putterman offered. "I mean, you know, study the technology."

"It's mine. It was stolen," Slayde hissed. "The technology was stolen from me a long time ago. I'm going to get it back, and you're going to help me. If you're willing."

A Slayve drifted into the room and replaced Putterman's rum drink that, with the jet lag and the excitement of this new client, already had him irrevocably caught up in those swirling Libidoan currents.

"I'm eager to help."

"I'll have you meet with my chief operating officer, Simon Debree, and we can make whatever financial arrangements you require. You're going to be part of finally bringing biotech to mainstream consumers. You'll be part of history. I've coined a word for it that combines the multiple scientific disciplines involved—two*sie* at least. How do you feel about writing patents in the emerging field of *biopornology*?"

Putterman smiled and lifted his rum drink. "I'm your man. I was born for bioporn."

6

HAVING REMOVED HIMSELF FROM THE SCENE downstairs with his mother, his uncle and Joseph, the human Hoover suck-up machine, Bert kicked off his shoes and sat down at the computer in his room. He booted up and checked his mail: ten spam messages, one pathetically unfunny joke forwarded by Jack Burnside who taught English at Mansfield, and a confirmation of an online order for another book about adopted children searching for parents.

Nothing. More time to devote to his dream.

He selected "Favorites," then *SactoValleyRanches.com*. He quickly scanned for new listings. There was a ranchito twenty miles north of Woodland. Nice amenities, but way too expensive—$625,000, and not much of a ranch property. A few acres suitable for ag development, but not the bucolic escape his body and soul craved.

He clicked through a few properties he hadn't seen. All too expensive or too geographically remote. When he got to the bottom of the new listings, there it was: exactly what he was looking for, the home of his dreams, the metes and bounds that would define his destiny, and all inside his target price range:

Ranchito Joaquin Murietta: two-bedroom two-bath rustic ranch-style home in the Sierra foothills. Far from everything. 2.5 acres, access by long dirt road; well water; stream runs through with fishing pool. Ideal for chicken hatchery, horses, etc. $480,000. Owner is motivated. Ten percent down.

One picture showed an enticing pool of stream water; another depicted an old ranch house. It had a roof on it; it looked great to Bert. He lapsed into a reverie, seeing himself fishing in the morning before driving an hour to Woodland to teach at the Academy.

If he could only get his hands on forty-eight grand.... That was a big if. He didn't have any of it right now. He hit the virtual PLAY button in his mind to continue his reverie. Now he was standing on the ground of his own ranch up in the hills, looking out at the Valley, breathing out a most gratifying *ahhh....*

Just then a bell rang, and a pop-up graphic announced that an e-mail had arrived. He clicked and saw it was from American Gene Savings & Loan. The sperm bank! The computer clock showed 5:37 P.M. Obviously they didn't keep traditional bankers' hours at sperm banks. He quickly opened the e-mail.

Dear Mr. Gropes:

We have received your written information release forms and are replying by e-mail at your request. Your records have been located, and your biological father has also been contacted. We are pleased to tell you that he is alive and carefully considering your invitation. He writes: "To make a responsible decision as to whether at this point in our lives we share enough in the way of interests, values, and experiences that will make this rewarding for both of us, I ask that he write a letter telling me all about himself, including his accomplishments and aspirations for the future. Because of my travel schedule over the next three months, I request that he wait until the beginning of July to send his letter (through the bank, of course) as I will then be able to devote the necessary time and attention to this communication that it requires."

If your biological father consents, we will send you each other's contact information. If he does not consent, his identity will not be disclosed and, barring a court order, it shall remain confidential.

Unless you tell us that you do not wish to correspond with your biological father, we will expect that you will be sending us the invited letter by no later than July 1, 2019.

Sincerely, Barbara Helms

Manager, Customer Relations

Bert jumped up from his chair. He had a father, a real connection to the past! His father was alive and wanted to hear from him! All he had to do was write a reasonably intelligent letter describing the highlights of his life.

Then he caught himself in the full-length mirror across the room: He was in the middle of an endzone celebration, all but spiking the mouse. Yet the truth was that he was flailing, not dancing, and he wasn't even close to the goal line. He remembered what he'd been told in one of a number of articles on the subject. Biological fathers were naturally suspicious that children seeking contact wanted money, compatible blood, a kidney or vital organ—but mostly financial assistance. No surprise that donor-dads were reticent, especially when most of them deposited at the bank in the first place just to earn a few dollars. There it was at the bottom of her e-mail message, the bank's tagline:

What Are You Saving It For?

American Gene Savings & Loan

Sure enough, next to the link beneath the tagline that targeted would-be mothers, another pitched donor-dads to make a "savings deposit" and "get paid." How could Bert write an honest letter when the only thing he wanted more than to meet his father was $48,000?

But for his money needs, he would write the most compelling letter to his father. He could tantalize him with details about…what? That—with no girlfriend and few real friends—he lived at home with his mother? That his adoptive uncle was a blind molecular cosmologist who invented Viagra for naked chickens? That it was only because of the same uncle that he was able to land a job teaching Social Studies at the charter school where he'd be lucky if he were asked back next year?

His CV was DOA, all right. He had three months to do something about it.

7

THE HEARING ROOM INSIDE THE DIRKSEN
Building was bustling, the largest crowd ever to attend the
Senate Investigative Committee on Chimera. Ellis Peek
savored his success. His patriotic demonstration as Fowl-
Man the last time out brought major primetime coverage
and propelled Ray Hoffenworth's committee into the national
spotlight. Guerilla warfare by way of guerilla theater was a
venerated American tradition. Members of the defiant Boston
Tea Party had dressed as Native Americans when they pulled
their stunt. The direct connection between the American
Revolution and the Planet Lusus Resistance surely did not
escape the authorities who arrested Ellis, or at least someone
with juice who put the fix in. All charges were dropped. The
next thing he knew he began receiving encrypted messages
from Ray Hoffenworth himself, begging Ellis Peek, American
hero, to accept a secret assignment—secret to both the public
and the rest of the Senate Committee—as the Committee's

new press secretary. In planning today's events, Senator Hoffenworth had asked Ellis to sit quietly and anonymously in the middle of the audience until further notice. Carrying out those orders, Ellis had taken it upon himself to assume the identity of a woman. Outfitted in a velour leopard-print tunic and black leggings, bracelets, blonde wig, and sturdy shoes, Ellis had whisked through security, no doubt because the senator discreetly had whispered instructions to security in advance of his arrival.

"You've been sworn in, Mr. Carnotta," the senator began, leaning forward. "You are the President of Novelty Farms, with headquarters in New York City. Accordin' to the CV you've provided the Committee, prior to that you worked for the World Wrestlin' Federation in 'new markets development and image management.' Is that accurate?"

"You got it," Carnotta said brashly, as if about to drop a silk robe, jump into the ring and go a few rounds with the senator.

The burly Louis Carnotta, despite his expensive gray suit, looked like the operator of the Tilt-A-Whirl at the annual Carnival of the Fourth Galaxy held in Xanaxia, the Lusian capital city, known for its vomit-inducing amusement rides. Even when not talking, his mouth was always open, in constant motion. Right now it was difficult to tell whether he was chewing a phantom stick of gum or his own tongue. His longish black bristly hair resembled a well worn brush used to clean toilets at the quark-stop rest area en route from his planet.

"Mr. Carnotta, this Committee recognizes that you are represented today by Ms. Dare," the senator said to the attorney, who nodded back.

It was hardly a surprise that Louis Carnotta hired an attorney from his own planet. Ellis was sure that beneath the neat shiny-black hair and handsome features of her face, a real monster lurked—as if at the dramatic moment she was going to reach under her chin and rip the latex mask off, revealing her extraterrestrial identity.

Ellis had done some research and found out that, in addition to being a past president of the Xanaxian Bar Association, Clarene Eliza Dare had been famous for years now on this planet for chipping away at the human race by successfully defending those lowest on the food chain, convincing juries that mayhem, savagery, and murder—along with all preparatory acts, including double-parking during commute hours—were justified under the circumstances. The intelligence that informed Ellis also revealed that her plan was to convince the world that the same mayhem and savagery were acceptable human behavior. She cleverly disguised her plans under the mantle of the First Amendment. Ironically, she professed to be a champion of "human" rights. Lately, the truth about that had begun to percolate to the surface. It was well known she spoke out on behalf of universities and the biotechnology industry as an advocate of unrestricted research and development with one notable exception: elimination of cruelty to animals. Yes, she'd stepped to the forefront as an advocate of *animal* rights, claiming that certain animals—not just apes and dolphins but possibly weasels and snakes able to hire big-bucks trial lawyers—were entitled to special rights, rights apparently not for sharing with last-surviving human beings like Ellis Peek.

Before today's hearing a grim Senator Ray Hoffenworth had telepathically transmitted these words to Ellis: "It's all about the proper sequence. Everything has its time. That's how you're goin' to help me tell the world about the threats we face. That's the battle of public relations that I'm countin' on you to win for me. Just like human DNA, it's all about preservin', creatin' and recreatin' the proper sequence, and wardin' off the alien ones," he said. "Timin'. In public relations that's the whole ball game."

As the Committee's new but double-secret press secretary, Ellis took these words to heart.

TRANSCRIPT OF HEARING BEFORE THE SENATE INVESTIGATIVE COMMITTEE ON CHIMERA
CHAIRMAN: SENATOR RAY HOFFENWORTH, TENNESSEE
WITNESS: LOUIS CARNOTTA

SEN. HOFFENWORTH: Let's begin, Mr. Carnotta, by having you describe the nature, if any there is, of your business enterprise.

MR. CARNOTTA: We are innovators in the meats and vegetables food sector. Using freely available biotechnology, Novelty Farms ever so slightly alters the genotypes in living things—less than one thousandth of one percent of their genomes—but enough to give them pizzaz. It's quite easy for scientists to scrape a little DNA into the embryo of a sheep or slap a gene gun upside the head of some cabbage. But before you get your knickers all in a twist, you can relax; we only use what they call junk DNA. That doesn't mean it's junk food. Our meats and vegetables are as high in nutrients as any. They call it junk DNA simply because it doesn't perform any known genetic function in the host animal, which has nothing to do with nutrition. It's like genetic white noise, completely harmless.

Novelty Farms was founded five years ago by me and my brother, but last year we came to market with our first product: Chicken L'Orange. We spliced genetic material from an orange into a chicken, bred the birds, and brought them to market. With junk DNA this product doesn't taste orange or have any attributes of an orange. It was a bust. Who cares about inert DNA from an orange that's sound asleep inside a chicken? What were we thinking? We realized that consumers in America want sizzle—sex appeal or, better yet, something sensational. Even if it's just entertainment.

SEN. HOFFENWORTH: Just entertainment to you, Mr. Carnotta. Outside this country there are places that allow human cloning. There are places that use viable human genetic material in breeding animals to raise and harvest organs for human transplant. And we are receiving daily reports of more disturbing efforts to transform the world we live in into somebody's idea of entertainment, whether the rest of us like it or not. By the way, sir, it's my understanding that scientists call it junk DNA because they just haven't figured out exactly what those genes do.

Now, describe to this Committee the devil-may-care nature of your latest offering, food that takes and uses the same technology they used to develop the Fowl-Man gene.

MR. CARNOTTA: We heard about the Fowl-Man and read the patent that described the Undercurrent shock technology they used to combine genes from two species—chickens and humans—and decided to do some research into whether there might be a market. Indeed there was. So we used the Undercurrent technology to create a line of celebrity products that will be coming to market shortly. For example, The Human Octopus—one of the biggest stars in the WWF right now—has licensed his genes and name rights to mix into a sports drink. It's going to be a huge hit with the kids. Using Undercurrent tech, we've combined real octopus genes with the Human Octopus and put it in the drink. It tastes like any other sports drink; the genes have no nutritional significance, but kids will believe it's easier to body-slam their friends. Just for laughs, we've got a nationally known comedian signed on—I can't say who—and we're going to squirt some of his genetic material into corn. Get it? Corny, huh? The big seller though is going to be our chicken. Wait'll you see whose DNA is going into our signature chicken breasts. Not Dolly Parton, and better than a pro wrestler, the very gifted and genetically endowed adult entertainment diva, Sayla V, will be throwing her weight around. In bright twin-packs, these babies will be bulging in their frozen shrinkwrap.

SEN. HOFFENWORTH: Disgusting. You are an animal, Mr. Carnotta. A low loathsome animal. No more than a snake wriggling across the dirt. Now, let me understand, this chicken you sell as a 'novelty' item has part of a human being in it. Is that right?

MR. CARNOTTA: It's marketing, Senator. Like your campaign ads, except mine aren't misleading. In reality, the amount of human DNA in these products is infinitesimal, inconsequential.

SEN. MILLARD: Excuse me, Mr. Chairman, but Mr. Carnotta seems to be inviting another line of question here—

SEN. HOFFENWORTH: I yield to the gentleman from Iowa.

SEN. MILLARD: What about false advertising laws? Aren't you falsely implying, sir, that these sports drinks will improve performance?

MR. CARNOTTA: The sports drinks will accurately state that they contain the athlete's genes. Nothing else is promised. Purchasers can decide for themselves if it's pure entertainment or a magic potion. As for the chicken breasts, there's nothing false about them. Underneath that package, what you see is all real, genuine U.S.D.A. quality.

SEN. HOFFENWORTH: Tell me, sir, why do you think there's a demand for such a putrid piece of perverted poultry?

MS. DARE: No matter how unsavory you may find it, Senator, it is a lawful and protected expression.

SEN. HOFFENWORTH: Taxpayer dollars paid to learn how to be an animal, human scum? I think not. America can plainly see for itself that this must stop. There will be legislation—I will sponsor it—that will make sure your kind of titillatin' business is shut down, Mr. Carnotta. This is contamination of our species, the vilest form of pollution.

MR. CARNOTTA: What I'm doing is perfectly legal, and let me say I resent your threat to put us out of business, causing us and our shareholders to lose millions in investment. Besides, whether you want to know it or not, this is what America wants. Call it amusement or titillation, I don't care; this is what they want.

SEN. HOFFENWORTH: You are wrong, sir. I know what decent Americans who love this country want. They want to preserve human dignity.

MR. CARNOTTA: You need to fire your polling company, Senator. If you're going to put me out of business, I might as well let you in on one quick secret. Our research shows there's an interest in imitating some of the quirkier aspects of popular culture. Right now there are a number of movies and video games that have depicted characters who relish the eating of human flesh. Our research shows that with the right marketing and packaging, a significant number of Americans are eager to buy into a vicarious experience along those lines. We've found a way to grab a little of that harmless bloodlust and put it on America's dinner plate. Like it or not, in a democracy people vote every day with their pocketbooks.

SEN. HOFFENWORTH: You are a disgrace, sir. And you will not provoke me. I promise you I will introduce legislation to put a stop to any further intrusion of this kind into our way of life. Where I come from in Tennessee, your business is already outlawed.

MR. CARNOTTA: Because of the law you wrote there, we aren't selling into Tennessee.

SEN. HOFFENWORTH: I'm moved to call the federal version the Louis Carnotta Blight Abatement Law.

MR. CARNOTTA: Who's provoking who? We will succeed, regardless of what you say. If I can convince you my company has a product that a refined man of your special tastes really wants, I may get you to change your mind. I brought with me—right here in my pocket—a forthcoming product that's our most innovative. Take a look at this. This juicy kiwi has a famous celebrity inside. His genes anyway. I can't say who at this point but, unlike the other products I described, these genes are active. This kiwi's been genetically altered so that the skin is hairless and the meat is extra sweet. Like a bite?

SEN. HOFFENWORTH: You…you will not make a mockery of these proceedings. This will not stand in my…in the House of Congress. I want and this great country wants no part of you or anything connected with you or your entire immoral enterprise. If we allow you to grow those things, fruits that are homosexual either by diabolic genetic engineering or Hollywood lifestyle choice, just as surely—

MR. CARNOTTA: Who said anything about Hollywood or gay? It's a star basketball player who's—

SEN. HOFFENWORTH: An evil wind will rise up and blow your seeds into our communities, into the bedrock of America, causing—

BEWIGGED MAN IN LEOPARD-PRINT TUNIC: Excuse me, Senator. Would this be a good time to introduce myself as your new press secretary?

SEN. HOFFENWORTH: What? How did that lunatic get in here again?

BEWIGGED MAN: Please, Senator! Not another word about our close working relationship. Message received and decoded. We can't keep it a secret any longer. Now, before I take questions from the press corps, let me just say—

SEN. HOFFENWORTH: Remove him. Please. Quickly.

BEWIGGED MAN: The Committee knows that alien forces are infiltrating. They've crept in! They're in security uniforms! Everywhere!

(Bewigged Man removed from hearing room.)

8

AT 2:00 PM THURSDAY AFTERNOON BERT
received a message marked URGENT from Principal Margaret
Tillman. It said: "See me before leaving today." An URGENT
message from Margaret Tillman was never good, certainly not
for Bert Gropes—on probation for the last three months. Now
what? He'd only started this teaching assignment in August,
five months ago, yet this was the fourth time he'd been tagged
with one of her URGENT missives.

When he arrived at her open door, she was standing rig-
idly in the corner of the office squinting at a report and leafing
through it with short, jerky motions, as if shooing one pesky fly
after another. In her mid-forties, she wore her bleached blonde
hair pulled back and perennially pinned into a brutish fist
that crouched upon the back of her head and ruled her every
move. Bert believed the Fist actually housed her brains, rendering the small skull beneath—the severe facial expressions

in particular—a mere projection screen for the Fist's nonstop PowerPoint presentation, featuring an endless stream of reactive images: impatience, bitterness, disgust, horror and contempt, to name a few. Always fastidiously attired, today she wore a black pantsuit and black shoes. As usual the pants were a little too tight around her somewhat hefty thighs, just hefty enough for her to pretend they weren't. More strikingly tight, however, was the white blouse displaying her large, pointed, weapons-grade breasts.

"You were looking for me?" he announced himself.

She turned and took aim.

"Be seated, Bert." She waved at a straight-backed chair as she walked quickly to her desk. After he sat down, she dropped swiftly into her chair and placed two fingers of each hand on the desk. That assured her breasts would continue training on him, possibly acting as precision sights—the details of which were no doubt all meticulously calculated by the Fist.

"Need I remind you"—a phrase she relished using so as to position herself somehow forced against her will to bludgeon others with their failings—"that you are on probation at Mansfield."

They stared at each other for an intense moment. He knew it would win him no favor but found himself slouching ever so slightly in his seat. He thought he detected a slight tightening of the Fist; that would explain the expression of growing impatience.

"I'm a good Social Studies teacher." He couldn't let her get away with reducing him to nothing, although that seemed to be her primary gift in her chosen field of education.

"Good? This is your idea of good?" She reached into her desk, grabbed a stack of papers and tossed them across the desk, two falling to the floor. They were in the handwriting of Trevor Jamison, who'd attended detention yesterday afternoon—twenty pages of single-spaced scrawl that redefined *run-on sentence*:

peepeepeepeepeepeepeepeepeepeepeepeepeepeepee-
peepeepeepeepeepeepeepeepeepeepeepeepeepeepee-
peepeepeepeepeepeepeepeepeepeepeepeepeepeepee-
peepeepeepeepeepeepeepeepeepeepeepeepeepeepee-
peepeepeepeepeepeepeepeepeepeepeepeepeepeepee-
peepeepeepeepeepeepeepeepeepeepeepeepeepeepee-
peepeepeepeepeepeepeepeepeepeepeepeepeepeepee-
peepeepeepeepeepeepeepeepeepeepeepeepeepeepee-
peepeepeepeepeepeepeepeepeepeepeepeepeepeepee-
peepeepeepeepeepeepeepeepeepeepeepeepeepeepee-
peepeepeepeepeepeepeepeepeepeepeepeepeepeepee-
peepeepeepeepeepeepeepeepeepeepeepeepeepeepee-
peepeepeepeepeepeepeepeepeepeepeepeepeepeepee-
peepeepeepeepeepeepeepeepeepeepeepeepeepeepee-
peepeepeepee

"I was walking past Trevor Jamison in the hallway late yes-terday," she said, "when he happened to drop these pages. I asked him to explain himself. He said *you* told him to write that down in detention." She now appeared more rigid than when he'd arrived but a few minutes ago. "What low regard do you have for this school and the students we are trying to cultivate? This is your idea of being a good Social Studies teacher?"

Bert examined each of the pages. "Yes."

She treated him to an expression of controlled severity. "Charter schools have enough challenges. Can you imagine if it leaked…got out to the press that this is what we have students do? Writing over and over an infantile word for the male sex organ?" She shook her head slowly. "Pee-pee…"

"Wait. It's just pee," he said. "And the reason I—"

"Pee-pee!" she insisted, cutting him off. "I know it when I see it!" She grabbed a handful of pages and shook them.

"Pee." He remained calm. "Trust me. I assigned it."

She rose from her chair. Her eyes grew large. The Fist,

quivering, was more clenched, giving her bleached blonde hair more of a white-knuckles look.

Bert pressed on. "He was vicious to Linda Nguyen, who doesn't need it. It was for his own good. That's because, unless he gets the message, his already wayward life is going down the toilet. I think I exercised good judgment in crafting a just punishment for his blurting the word out in class."

"Judgment?" she repeated. "That's the last thing I'm seeing." She walked over behind Bert and straightened a prized photograph of her late father smiling weakly while getting his phalanges crushed in the mortar of Governor Schwarzenegger's right hand. "I learned a few other things from Trevor about what goes on in your class. You're studying California history, and who is introduced as the celebrated historical figure? Father Junipero Serra? Fremont? Vallejo? No. Heinrich Schliemann. Heinrich What-The-Hell Schliemann! For God's sake, what's wrong with you?"

"You obviously didn't hear my tie-in." Bert twisted around in his chair. "I was bolstering their interest in the subject. Minutes later I was going to have to turn on C-SPAN and answer the question burning in all their young minds: Why are we studying the sex lives of naked chickens in Advanced Social Studies?"

"Try 'Democracy In Action.' Of course, that's in bold print in the teachers' guide. I wouldn't expect you to look there." Standing in front of her desk, arms akimbo, her breasts threatened and demanded his respect.

"Let's cut to the chase, shall we?" She sat down again. "Need I say, barring the miracle of proving your merit as a first-rate Social Studies teacher, you are not on track to be rehired after this school year. However, there is a window of opportunity for you should you wish to succeed." She clasped her hands on the desk and looked up toward the ceiling. "Running a charter school, everything's my responsibility. That means overseeing expenditures and identifying all revenue opportunities." She reached one hand back and lightly massaged the knuckles atop the Fist. Then she leaned forward, looking him in the eye. "It would behoove you"—she emphasized *behoove* as if commanding a dumb ox to be fitted with more sensible footwear— "to exert whatever influence you have to land a major gift from your uncle when he sees income from his new technology. If you can do that, well, then, I give you my word that there will be a slot for you next year."

Bert avoided her gaze. "Is that it?"

"I believe I've made myself clear." She sat stiffly and glared.

He stood up and walked over to the door.

"I want to take you up on your offer," he said.

She smiled and relaxed her posture slightly.

"Your first offer," he added. "That is, if I prove to be a first-rate Social Studies teacher. I am, and you'll see. As far as my uncle is concerned, I'm not aware that he has any big deals out there for his technology. If he does, I hope you land a major gift. It would be good for the Academy. We'd all like that, but it's not going to be me. I simply don't have that kind of relationship with him. So, I wish you luck. We all want you to succeed."

As he opened the door to let himself out, he glanced back to see the Fist once more shaking at him silently, furiously, and menacingly atop a glowering Margaret Tillman.

9

ERNIE PUTTERMAN HAD SPENT LESS THAN AN hour yesterday afternoon with Dick Slayde and Tatiana Lurenski, the company's vice-president of public relations. When an emergency call for Slayde interrupted their meeting, Putterman was taken to his guest cabin by the same hot-looking Slayve named Tina who'd picked him up after the helicopter ride. When she dropped him off and carried his bags into his guest quarters—a *stabbin' cabin* if ever there was!—he suggested she stay for a while. She must not have heard him because she turned and left in a hurry. He hadn't sold her on Ernie Putterman, Stud Package—yet. But give him time.

The next morning Slayde met him in the drawing room. "We're having breakfast outside this morning," his host said.

They walked out on the southeast side of the mansion to a spacious veranda shaded with banyan trees. A large lawn lay beyond which, in turn, was flanked by buildings in the distance. Elsewhere untamed jungle abounded.

"All of my Internet operations are here on the plantation. Down there"—Slayde gestured in the direction of the harbor—"is the heart of my latest initiative that brings you here."

"The Urge?" Ernie asked. "I was in the casino last night."

"My biotech startup, Mother DNAture."

"De-nature?"

"That's how I pronounce it, as in the sense of derived from nature. But it's D-N-A-ture. Remember, everything I do is in the life sciences."

Slayde was resting one hand on a sculptured head—a mermaid riding side saddle on a supine Neptune; their facial expressions revealed the throes of Primal Urge freestyle aquatics.

"I bring people what they want, their most fundamental yearning: to interface…biologically."

"So tell me, as your patent lawyer, what I can protect?" Putterman said with a vocal rubbing-of-hands.

"We'll need patent applications to be filed all over the world," Slayde said. "I've got something old with a new face on it—still a ways from going online—and something completely new. The old that's new is what we're calling the BioBUD technology."

"Bud, like in plant? Bio-engineered sugar cane? I happen to be an expert in plant patents," Putterman boasted.

"Any experience with blow-up dolls?" Slayde asked in his most matter-of-fact tone.

"Excuse me?" Putterman hesitated. He had to indicate some familiarity with the art or he might not land the job as Slayde's patent lawyer. He just wasn't used to being treated this way by his clients, much less being asked these kinds of questions. "Well, once…I wasn't dating at the time. A friend introduced me. We didn't actually go out. We, as you say, interfaced once or twice."

This was sounding too candid. He'd already said too much. "Nothing serious, you understand. We were *so* different." He hoped that would earn a wink and a chuckle from his host, but instead Slayde stared at him without expression.

"Then you can appreciate the next generation product," Slayde said. "BioBUD—a Biological Blow-Up Doll. Within a year or so we expect to develop a full-sized novelty that will be so realistic—specifications call for live, humanized skin that will operate on a platform of goat blood."

Putterman was losing his appetite for the food that servers had just placed on the table a few feet away. "There could be some legal problems with that," he said. Before he could explain what the problems were, a Libidoan monkey jumped down two feet away and screeched. It had apparently been perched in the banyan tree whose limb hung over the veranda.

"Bruno!" Slayde exclaimed. "Meet Ernie Putterman, patent attorney to the Libidoan monkeys. Say: 'Hello, Counselor.'"

With the fingers of his left hand still touching the ground, Bruno extended a large right hairy one at the attorney. When Putterman reciprocated, the animal grabbed it, stood up as high as he could, and thrust Putterman's hand—soft and somehow attractive to Bruno—onto his semi-erect penis. Bruno began grinding his hips and screeching with pleasure.

Horrified, Putterman tried to withdraw his hand, but to no avail. The monkey was strong and determined. His penis—now engorged with blood and hot to the touch—enlarged with each passing second. The attorney bent over under the animal's force that twisted his arm. Suddenly he fell to his knees; the monkey, behind him now, kept a firm grip on his hand. Before he could imagine a worse-case scenario, it happened: A hot steel rod, or what felt like it, plunged between the cheeks of his buttocks. Although his humility was complete, the only thing separating him from the beast's total penetration was the thin, stay-pressed fabric of the khakis he bought for this trip. Speechless and in shock, Putterman looked desperately up to his host for help. To his dismay, Slayde was standing four feet away speaking calmly into a recorder: "Libidoan achieves rapid erectile deployment. Eyes dilated, vigorous adrenalin production in evidence—"

Putterman struggled with all his will, but without success. The monkey's pelvic thrusts matched that of a pile driver: steady, mechanical, and violent.

"Bruno, that's enough. Let go of your lawyer," Slayde finally said, without the slightest hint of scolding. He took the pitcher of ice water from the breakfast table and doused the hot spot, hitting his target and soaking the seat of Putterman's pants in the process. The monkey ceased, protesting, and lumbered away.

"Thanks for volunteering. Every bit of research helps," Slayde said. He was serious.

Wincing and still speechless, Putterman wiped his hand on his new khakis and reached back to feel in and around the seam to check for a breach in the fabric. His boxer shorts were drubbed so deeply into the crack of his butt that it felt like he was wearing thong panties, best left for a later excavation project.

"Bruno can't help himself," Slayde said. "It's his nature, you know. I've been saying for years: If I could bottle that. Now we know the means is available, making it feasible to bring it to millions of eager consumers. I want to call it what it is: Hot Monkey Love. It's the advent of biopornology we talked about."

Putterman was still reeling from the assault, but he was starting to get his bearings back. Slayde signaled to a female server who instantly appeared with a hot, rolled washcloth so that he might remove the residue and fetid odor of amorous monkey moisture from his hands. She was polite and discreet, but he thought he detected in her the slightest smirk. His male mystique was still intact, but only by the barest of threads from The Gap. Still hoping to get lucky here, the last thing he needed was a rumor to spread around Libido that he'd nearly been ravished on the veranda—that he was Bruno's bitch.

Slayde gestured for Putterman to have a seat at the breakfast table. "I'll need your professional assistance."

Suddenly the indignities suffered seemed manageable after all. Putterman scooped up an extra napkin and laid it on his seat.

"So, what can I do? File a patent? Protect the name?" he asked as he sat down.

"First thing is we have to get the source code for the software algorithm."

"You need me to negotiate a license for it?"

"It's going to be more complicated than that. It's the shock technology I told you that was stolen from me thirty years ago."

"Stolen? Why, that's a brazen case of trade secrets theft, unfair competition, and conversion," Putterman said with a new tone of aggression. As if pity were a stranger to him, he discarded a lemon wedge to the tabletop, leaving it for dead, lying on its back, all the juice squeezed out of it. "Just say it. I'll file suit." He plunged a spoon into the flesh of his melon.

"No, I have in mind more direct ways of ensuring the cooperation of my old academic colleague, Professor Grover Gropes. More personal ways, to be sure." He chuckled quietly to himself. "I've already exacted a small but satisfying measure of revenge." Slayde savored his coffee.

Putterman squinted at him.

"Attorney-client privilege?" Slayde seemed eager to kiss and tell.

"Absolutely."

"You will be the only other person in the world to know this. Two years after the theft, I was working in a lab in Baltimore when—wouldn't you know it?—if it wasn't the egg of Dr. Gropes's sister... there for an in-vitro procedure. I had recently reconstructed enough of my stolen research to perform a gene-splice. Unfortunately, I was never able to do the same with the gene-reactivation tech."

Putterman felt a chill, and it wasn't from the ice water still soaking his seat.

"But, using a primitive shock technology, I was able to insert

a single Libidoan monkey gene into the embryo, and it took."
Self-satisfied, Slayde stuck a spoon into his own melon.

"A human embryo?"

"It's a boy," he said, mocking natural fathers.

"You did it for revenge?"

"Yes and no. I did it because I *could* do it, long before anyone
else. I was curious. It was a random gene I selected. This was
decades before we completed the Libidoan genome. We still
don't know the function of that gene."

"Is he…normal?" Putterman was dying to know.

"That's a relative term." Slayde laughed. "John Bertram
Gropes is the name. The young man may figure into our plans
to get the shock technology back, depending on the cooperation we get from Professor Gropes. Young Gropes lives in
California with his mother. A schoolteacher. More than a loner.
Loser is more like it. Not sexually active, from the little we
know about him. Let's just say that Young Gropes will never be
my pitchman for Hot Monkey Love."

10

BERT PULLED INTO THE FIRST AVAILABLE space in the Beth Shalom Temple parking lot. The front tires of his old Saab abruptly pushed up against the cement wheel stop he couldn't see, lurching him to a standstill. He cut off the motor—wondering again what he was doing here—and replayed the conversation he'd had last night with his mother.

"Bertie, you know it's time for you to start getting out more," she said. "Sarah told me over lunch today just the thing: speed dating at her temple." Sarah Goldman worked with his mother in the Student Aid office at the university.

"At a temple? With a rabbi? Why would I do that? I'm not even Jewish."

"It would be good for you. The young people at her temple have loved it so much that they talked Rabbi Zach into running a session for their goyim friends. I told her to hold a spot for you."

"It sounds Jewish. I don't think so. Besides, I've got papers and stuff to look at."

"Bertie, I'm telling you, it's time to get out," she pressed him.

"And why not at a temple? What makes you so sure your biological father isn't Jewish?"

As much as he really didn't want to do this, she made a point. Based on the letter to the sperm bank, his bio-dad sounded like a man on the move. For all he knew, his father could be a modern-day Heinrich Schliemann: an adventurer, a world traveler, and Jewish.

Bert climbed out of his car and entered the community center building next door to the temple. He checked in and pasted a large name tag on his shirt: "Bert." There were about twenty others standing around shuffling their feet, staring at nondescript artifacts on the wall—a building donor plaque with a long list of unrecognizable names, a map of some obscure place in Israel—and a few participants talking to one another with brief comments designed to make a conversation last for no more than ten seconds. "Is this your first time at one of these?" one fellow asked a young woman. A look of guilt flashed across his face, suggesting the rules had been broken by hustling up a conversation before the formalities were underway.

The gathering appeared to be half women, half men, with the exception of one prospect who appeared to be half woman, half man. With an angelic smile but a bit broad-shouldered to be a woman, he or she had thick short brown hair and wore a purple shirt and a large shapeless jacket that concealed vital clues, along with khaki pants and loafers. A glance at the sticky tag revealed a name but nothing more: "Lee."

Again swearing to himself that he didn't care if he met someone tonight, Bert nevertheless sized up the competition and his odds with computer-like quickness. There were a few reasonably attractive women in the room, but most of the other men in the room were better-looking and no doubt more charming than he was. He was self-conscious about his big feet and large nose. Even he had seen that his large brown eyes spoke of a distant sadness.

With these calculations in mind, Bert was already in a state of despair. It was this simple: If Lee proved to be a man, Bert felt he could beat him out to win the attention of the least attractive woman left over after the others had picked through the choices. But if Lee turned out to be a woman, she would no doubt fall for Bert, adopt him, marry him, abuse him, and eventually abandon him. So much for natural selection. Why go through the motions?

One of the men who appeared to be well outside the thirty-five-year age limit for tonight's get-together turned out to be the rabbi, casually dressed. "Hi everyone, and welcome. I'm Rabbi Zach." Rabbi Zach was athletically built, olive-skinned, and had a mouth full of large, whitening-kit-whitened teeth.

"Let's get started, shall we? First, let's see who we have here tonight." Smiling, the rabbi panned over the room, his mouth silently moving, counting out the numbers of each sex. Discreetly, halfway through the process, the rabbi must have registered the problem of classifying Lee. At that same moment Bert detected a faintly pained expression on Lee's face, and in that instant felt a strange kinship with him or her. Bert was compelled to recalculate his own geek quotient. His pants were hiked up a little higher than necessary, highlighting the contrast of yellow socks against dark pants and loafers—loafers so remarkably similar to Lee's.

"Why don't we do this?" the rabbi finally said. "Let's have the women stay here and the men over there, so I can get a quicker count." A large showing of teeth went a long way in convincing everyone that this was the usual routine. Lee walked over to the men's side with renewed lilt in his shoes.

"OK, we've got seven women and nine men," he said, assigning a number to each person. Bert was man number nine. "Let's have you men facing the women with your corresponding number. Marla," he called over to the receptionist, "you and I will be women eight and nine to keep the rotation going smoothly."

Great! Bert thought to himself. He'd managed to do worse than his death-plunge imagination could conjure up. On cue he was supposed to make the moves on Rabbi Choppers.

There were two rows of nine chairs facing each other. "OK," the rabbi announced. "Remember, speed dating follows the same natural course you already know—meeting, dating, and mating—only accelerated. The rules are simple. Start with your first date and get acquainted for seven minutes. Remember, no talking about your work. When I say 'switch,' you switch. The men will rotate. Then switch again. Seven minutes with your next date. And so on. Any questions?"

Can I go home now and log onto the real estate site, Bert asked himself. Instead, Lee asked how exactly the men were supposed to switch. Just then, when everyone was listening to the rabbi explain how the women were to stay put and the men were to move down the row, Bert noticed the door open at the far end of the room. A quiet beauty peered in, then entered. It was Anna Brighton! He had never seen her in person. He was instantly mesmerized. The way her small and delicate frame hurried to a halt in front of the reception table seemed to him like a perfect snowdrift, deep within a white forest a million miles from civilization, its pristine form never to be observed by human eyes but for the grace of God... *So far from anything, you would never have reason to come upon it unless you were lost, possibly for weeks and starving to death, sustaining yourself on bark torn from trees and snow you'd eaten for hydration. But you'd sooner die than eat the perfect snowdrift clinging so exquisitely to a rock. That's because it has become your altar of hope, your reason for living, your willingness to die lost and forgotten...*

Marla, the greeter, saw Anna and hurried over to check her in. As the all took their seats for the first of nine dates, Bert had to pause and wipe away a tear in each eye, moved as he was by the visualization of his own sublime death. He lifted his face—his eyes still a little watery—and his eyes met hers coming toward him. Marla escorted the new arrival to her seat, replacing herself as woman number eight.

"Ready? Begin everyone!" Rabbi Zach held up his watch to mark the time.

The new arrival was now seated across from him and only one to the left. Her name—a perfect palindrome, gorgeously scripted with a Magic Marker—stood out from all the others: "Anna." He could see up close her eyes, bright yellow brown, modestly shying back behind a pair of dark-framed glasses, and her short, reddish-brown hair, outlining the most unspoiled, snow-driven white skin he'd ever seen. The thought of her skin transported him again into the delicious rapture of a martyr's death face down in the ice, prostrate before a mantle of snow enshrouding a rock.

Rabbi Zach spoke first: "Tell me about yourself, Bert. What kind of interests do you have?"

"I…I…" Bert began, avoiding eye contact with the rabbi, continuing his gaze on Anna, whose eyes were focused on her partner.

"Speaking our mind can be hard sometimes. Even talking about the things we love. But I hope you'll speak freely, Bert. I'd like to get to know you better," the rabbi spoke gently.

Caught up in his freshly conjured emotions, Bert felt strangely liberated, free to speak his mind. "What is beautiful—"

"On that we share. Beauty is the image of God," the rabbi added. "Where do *you* find it, Bert?"

Suddenly shaken from his trance, Bert regarded Rabbi Zach. The face of his first date was fifteen inches in front of him, leaning towards him, with a beard dark and skin as gritty as sandpaper. Two black hairs poked out of each nostril, the pairs curling like pincers towards each other.

"Kahlua and Dr Pepper? That's my favorite drink, too!" Bert

heard Lee exclaim. Everyone was connecting with the opposite sex, even Lee. Everyone except Bert. For Bert, it was only in his dreams.

Bert lamely answered the question by describing his favorite Ben Franklin poster. Then he made the mistake of reciprocating, asking the rabbi where he found beauty. The answer went on at length about when the rabbi met his wife, whose eyes twinkled in a way that resembled a particular configuration of Hanukkah candles. The conversation was so devoid of the sexual electricity Bert felt when he peeked over at Anna, he was determined not to do that again. If the rabbi asked for his phone number, he was resolved not to ask for his in return.

"Switch!" Rabbi Zach, jumping up, called out.

Bert moved down one seat.

"OK, seven minutes," Rabbi Zach reminded. "Begin!"

"I'm Anna," she said with a bright, unhesitating smile.

"I'm Bert."

"Nice to meet you, Bert. So," she shifted to a low conspiratorial voice, "how was your date with the rabbi?"

"Are there no secrets about my torrid love life?" he said. "We got along great but—to be truthful—there was no future there. The religious thing."

She giggled. His eyes plunged into hers, all within a second—a very long one that launched his stomach on a thrill ride.

"Bert, you look so familiar. I've been racking my brain since I walked in the door. Have we met before?"

"No, we haven't, but I know who you are. I saw you on C-SPAN last week. You appeared before the Senate Investigative Committee on Chimera."

Her eyes widened, mildly astonished that anyone would admit to using a TV to watch a SICC hearing.

"You work for my uncle." Bert glanced around to make sure he wasn't breaking a rule talking about work. "You're his new assistant."

"You're kidding? He's never mentioned—" She stopped herself. "What's your last name?"

"Gropes."

"Amazing. I knew he had a sister."

"My mother."

The roar in the room picked up again.

"Your uncle is brilliant and wonderful." She was effusive. "I know we're not supposed to talk about work here," she said glancing furtively at Rabbi Zach ten feet away, "but since you already know what I do, can I ask: Are you in life sciences, too? I bet we have lots of common friends."

"I figured one molecular cosmologist in the family is enough," Bert said. "I'm in the field of social studies. I teach ninth graders at Mansfield Academy."

"You work with kids." She seemed genuinely enthusiastic. "Teaching, no less. My work is so removed. I'd love to do something with kids."

Bert's heart leapt. She was as pure as the snow he'd imagined when she swept into the room.

"One minute!" Rabbi Zach announced.

Bert had to make it count now.

"How romantic!" Lee cooed at a woman's description of a date who invited her to a late candlelight dinner and then served eggs and champagne, blurring the line between dinner and brunch.

There was a moment of awkward silence between Bert and Anna.

"Why don't you try it? See if you like it," Bert said.

"What do you mean?" She looked at him as if a dark, yet intriguing stranger asked her to spend a week sailing to a tropical island.

"I'm saying you should come to my class and tell them all about your work. It'd be a big hit."

"Really?" She was doubtful that this was a good idea. "Talk

about computational molecular biology to your social studies class?"

"Absolutely. They've already got the basics since they saw you on C-SPAN, and they've expressed a keen interest in anything to do with animal husbandry."

"OK," she said thoughtfully, then let a smile spread across her face.

"Time!" the rabbi shouted. "Switch!"

11

"NOW!" DR. GRO SHOUTED ABOVE THE NOISE. "Let me go!"

Joseph Cherp nodded and pulled the three ropes that, in turn, released slipknots tied to stakes in the ground surrounding the hovering balloon Dr. Gro had boarded.

The bright blue and gold globe, once untethered, took off like a giant bubble at the bottom of an aquarium. Dr. Gro released the ropes hitched to the rim of the basket and let them drop to the ground. Joseph gathered them up into coils and dumped them in the back of Dr. Gro's hybrid pickup truck.

When he looked up again, the balloon—two hundred feet high and almost a quarter mile away—was heading north as planned. Joseph could still easily make out the large white letters on the one side of Dr. Gro's balloon: *WHAT*. The first time he volunteered to be the pre-dawn flight crew he'd asked where the name came from.

"It's an acronym," Dr. Gro told him.

"For what?"

"I don't know yet," the old man explained without the slightest hint of irony. "I just know those are all the letters and that the sequence is correct."

Dr. Gro was an excellent teacher. Quite frequently, however, his response to a question was more conundrum than answer. The professor explained to him in graphic terms the type of infinite regress problem the two of them shared: "As scientists we are the personal groomers of the universe. The questions we must ask, that no one else will, are analogs of unsightly, unwanted facial hairs. For every one we pluck, two more appear in its place."

Dr. Gro had also pointed out to Joseph the perfect design of a hot-air balloon. In flight it looked like two question marks, facing each other—the first one backwards—while the basket stood in as the two dots, merged into one. He'd told Joseph: "A balloon, like a perfectly framed scientific question, soars high and true to its conclusion."

That spoke of his love of science and solo flight. As far as humans were concerned, the story was that years ago, before he'd lost his eyesight, he'd said that, from way above, human activity never looked better. Nor had the onset of blindness cooled his ardor for hot-air ballooning. In fact, he was all the more determined to fly in spite of it. His balloon was fully computerized with a voice-commanded burner, and both an altimeter and GPS capable of giving audio readings. On the other end, Joseph could track the flight with the GPS readings from Dr. Gro's pickup truck and, during a typical two-hour flight, he could easily keep up or stay ahead of the balloon's course. In contact with Dr. Gro by radio, Joseph could guide him down into an open space, help load up the truck, and head back to Davis.

The balloon continued to rise quickly and steadily.

"Earth to Dr. Gro. Level your altitude. Do you copy? Over."

An answer came back, but it was too garbled by too much electronic interference to be intelligible.

"Ground Control to Dr. Gro. Do you copy?"

Nothing came back this time. The burner kept burning, blasting more and more heat, causing the balloon to rise higher and higher. Soon it reached nearly a thousand feet and picked up a strong easterly current, hurtling toward the lightly reddish sunrise. If he continued in that direction, there would be no way for Joseph to chase him with the truck. Dr. Gro was headed into the foothills and an area where there were no roads, or if there were any, it would take Joseph hours to get there by some roundabout way.

"Dr. Gro! Do you copy?" he shouted into the radio.

The aircraft continued its ascent upwards and eastward. Joseph watched helplessly as the balloon became a bigger dot on his land-based computer screen than in the sky, heading into uncharted territory. He didn't know what to think. It was as if the professor's curiosity about the heavens had gotten the better of him and he couldn't resist their allure, or the computerized balloon had somehow developed a mind of its own.

"Ground Control to WHAT! Do you copy? Over!"

12

April 18, 2019

Dear Dad:

I am starting this letter now, even though you will not see it until the beginning of July. My name is Bert—John Bertram Gropes. I want to tell you about me, my work as a teacher, and some of the dreams I have.

I must tell you that right now there's been some disturbing news that you should know about, that affects everyone around me. My adoptive uncle is a rather eccentric fellow. He's a scientist who flies a hot-air balloon, and he's totally blind. Unfortunately, he's missing, following a flight that got away a few days ago. My mother is devastated and I'm trying to do the best I can to keep her spirits up. Coincidentally, I met my uncle's assistant at a speed-dating event recently. She's a beautiful woman (I'll send you a photo in a future letter) and a brilliant computational molecular biologist here at Davis. Naturally, the fact that my uncle is missing has been a terrible blow to her, too. I've invited her to come in and give a guest lecture for one of my classes at Mansfield Academy. I'm hoping that will be a positive experience for her. I know it will be for me. That's coming up next week.

Beyond that…

"THESE PHOTOGRAPHS SHOW THE BALLOON where we located it in the foothills," Special Agent Nina Carera said, laying photographs out on the table. Bert and his mother looked at them, at Uncle Gro's basket in a clearing next to a grove of connifers, the nylon fabric spread lifelessly over the ground; the letter *A*, albeit upside down, was all of *WHAT* that could be made out.

"In a wooded area about eight miles northeast of Auburn. Elevation approximately twenty-five hundred feet," the agent explained.

Eugenia Gropes burst into tears. The photos starkly depicted what she already knew: Her brother Grover was nowhere near the grounded balloon. Bert put his arm around her in an effort to comfort her. She studied the photographs carefully.

Bert continued with his examination of the compelling image before him: Special Agent Nina Carera only inches away across the conference table in the FBI field office in Sacramento. Wide-shouldered and snugly fit into a dark blue blouse and skirt, she had the most incandescent skin he'd been near since... well, meeting Anna. Her long hair fell around her shoulders and face as she leaned over the table, propping herself with her arms. He was imagining the training she endured to become an FBI agent, visualizing the various drills she went through, picturing her efforts to escape a full nelson on a wrestling mat, possibly of the horizontal variety, expertly applied by Special Agent and master instructor Bert Gropes....

Lately it also seemed to take less for him to be lit up in the presence of an attractive woman. He had to get hold of himself. He may not be able to feel the loss his mother did right now, but he had to maintain his composure, at least for her sake.

"The search continues, Mrs. Gropes," Agent Carera said. "We're leaving it primarily to local law enforcement unless and until there is sufficient evidence of a kidnapping or other crime—"

"That crosses state borders," Bert Gropes, scholar and teacher of American government, explained to his mother. He glanced back at Agent Carera where he was treated to a surprisingly sweet, roger-ten-four nod.

Just then an older G-man walked into the conference room. She introduced him.

"I'd like you to meet the supervising agent for this investigation, Dennis Clamp."

Balding, fiftyish, blue eyes constantly darting around like wildly crisscrossing search lights, Dennis Clamp delivered a firm handshake while quickly scanning Bert's airspace. His jaw pushed out from his neck and jowl, possibly acting as a crime detection sensor; his mouth hung slightly open, exposing teeth that were ever parted a quarter inch in a display of readiness.

"Let me explain how we see it thus far," Clamp said. "Although it's possible he fell out of the balloon before it landed, we think that's unlikely. He was too experienced an aeronaut. He may have landed and tried to hike out on his own, although with his condition, total blindness, that would seem unlikely."

"He was kidnapped," Bert's mother said, choking back the tears.

"It's because of that scenario the Bureau is involved," Clamp assured her. "We're looking into why the radio, computer system and manual override didn't work. It looks like tampering. But we come back to—"

"Why would someone want to kidnap the professor, Mrs. Gropes?" Agent Carera chimed in.

Bert and his mother looked at each other. They'd had this conversation earlier and were yet to come up with a plausible answer.

"We're examining that onboard computer system thoroughly," Agent Carera added. "We have reason to believe a remote-controlled electronic robot commandeered the aircraft and guided it to this location." She tapped a spot on one of the photos with her pen. "You can see an old dirt road in the background here. We're scrutinizing the all-terrain tracks. Unfortunately, it looks like a number of ATVs have traversed that road recently, but that's where he'd be taken by kidnappers or—"

"There is the scenario," Clamp spoke carefully, glancing at his colleague, "that he staged his own kidnapping or...withdrawal, we'll call it."

"That's ridiculous," Eugenia Gropes said. "For heaven's sake, why would he do that?"

Bert nodded agreeably at his mother, but he knew full well what the agent was going to say.

"Mrs. Gropes, it is no secret that your brother was not fond of... You would never describe him, for example, as a social animal? Right?"

Eugenia Gropes squinted at them in disbelief.

"You know what I'm talking about." Clamp turned to Nina Carera. "He was not active in the Davis Rotary Club. Were you able to confirm that?"

Agent Carera nodded and patted some files as though the forensic reports had only just come in.

"In fact, correct me if I'm wrong," Clamp pressed his point, "but it appears he never joined much of any group, club, or organization."

Eugenia Gropes pursed her lips in defiance. "He preferred spending his free time alone. He wouldn't kidnap himself."

"But don't you see, Mrs. Gropes?" Clamp said with a self-satisfied smile. "You're more upset at the thought that he would do that than if there were an actual kidnap. That's exactly why he'd do it. He didn't want you to think he'd abandoned you."

"There's something else that's curious we found inside the basket," Carera said, now seated. "A well-worn copy of *Stargazing In Tibet.*"

"Why would he have that?" Bert jumped in. "He's blind. Wouldn't that be the kind of thing a sloppy kidnapper would leave behind to make it look like that's where to look for him?"

"Right," Clamp said. "Or it's a ruse to make us think that

sloppy kidnappers were involved. And maybe not that sloppy. It was a *Braille* copy."

The agents winked at one another.

It still didn't make any sense to Bert.

"He was kidnapped," Eugenia Gropes repeated. She turned to Bert. "People that would do that are a pathetic lot who do not feel whole or complete as human beings." She composed herself and straightened her posture. "Rather than dig deep within themselves to see what they might reap"—she tapped her chest to convey she'd been there—"they reach to the outside for others in an unnatural, entirely *un*wholesome way. Unscrupulous lawyers, leeches and career politicians are famous for taking others, but kidnappers are the worst." She shook her head as if her observation were beyond challenge, and there was no point asking what others thought.

The two agents quietly scratched the tops of their heads and stared down and away during her lecture to Bert.

"It's just a scenario, ma'am," Clamp finally said, dropping his scratching hand to his side. "If we get a ransom demand or find a suspect and a motive, you can call me the fool for mentioning it. But if it's not a kidnapping, I must say, a blind man working with unknowns using remote-controlled robots in computers onboard his hot-air balloon and leaving behind mixed-message clues like Braille Tibetan stargazing books to make it all look like a kidnapping is, well, pretty ingenious. I gotta hand it to him."

13

"HI," ANNA GREETED BERT, BREATHLESSLY HUR-rying towards him in the hallway outside his classroom. It was 9:45 and, as the ninth graders streamed into class to find their seats, they stopped and scrutinized her in the mode reserved for new teachers, friends of parents, and those most deserving the rigors of age profiling.

"I'm a little nervous," Anna said.

"No, you're not. You'll be great," Bert said.

She was a wreck all right, but indeed looked great wearing a tan skirt and royal blue blouse. Impulsively, she touched one of the buttons and pinched it just above the navel and pulled it down in a phantom gesture of tucking it in.

"Just be yourself. You know, what it was like when you were in school. They'll like that," Bert said. "Ready?"

She smiled and, confining her head to a vertical-plane motion, vibrated a yes.

"Any new word on your uncle?" she asked as Bert put his hand on the door.

"Not yet," he said sympathetically.

She let out a pained sigh. Then she nodded at the door. Ready.

Bert walked into the classroom, Anna behind him. Usually the first words out of his mouth were "settle down." Not today. They were as quiet as Roman cats watching doomed mice at sport.

"Today we were supposed to... we were going to continue with our California history," Bert said. "But we're going to do something a little different instead. You saw our guest on TV last week, appearing in the Senate on C-SPAN.

"She holds a Ph.D. and is a full-time computational molecular biologist. I thought we could expand on last week's lesson by letting her talk a little about her work. So, why don't we get started. Let me introduce, and please extend a Mansfield Academy welcome to Ms. Anna Brighton."

"Hi," she said, lifting her right hand in a humble gesture of peace and friendship. "Thanks for having me." The class gave her an Easter Island reception: stone faces—*ancient* stone faces—faces that showed no signs of changing their *stone*-itude anytime in the near geological term.

Except Trevor Jamison who rolled his eyes just when Anna looked right at him.

Bert sat down in a chair in the front corner of the room and signaled to Anna with an open palm. "Please be kind enough to tell us a little about you and what you do. Then we'll open it up for questions."

"Let's see now...what I do," Anna began, pausing. She appeared as if she suddenly decided to abandon plans to open up, at the risk of sacrificing herself, by letting loose with her life story. Instead she waxed serious and looked at Trevor and the others as though they were a dissertation committee. "As a CMB, it's my job to conduct, study, and log sequence analysis, genomics, and protein folding. That's actually a really *interesting* area." She paused to let them catch up just in case they needed a little extra time to digest that. "I get to explore things like computational approaches to sequence homology and alignment... you know, physical and genetic mapping, gene recognition, protein structure prediction, distance geometry, virus shell assembly, and phylogeny. That kind of thing. Fun stuff." She turned and nodded at Bert in search of a life line. "There's so much to learn, right?"

"Right. Absolutely," Bert said, acting as if he personally didn't know where to begin sharing his own fascination with virus shell assembly.

Class eyeballs were as heavily glazed over as cheap sweet rolls. The room was so silent Bert was certain it was causing him permanent ear damage.

"So, questions?" In presenting her personal story, she'd run out of ideas to launch without ever launching a first one. Not a flicker of interest from the class. Forty-seven minutes to go. Eternity in real-time.

"What kind of educational background should one have if he or she wants to become a *CMB*?" Bert tossed one out. He and Anna weren't going to reach out and grab their adolescent attention like *Spring Break* on MTV. Instead, Bert was stirring the kind of excitement reserved for *The Cloudies*, the Weather Channel's annual awards show recognizing achievements in five-day forecasts.

"If you think you might want to be a CMB," she said, then paused to add a real *intime* aside: "It's a great field. You'll meet fun and interesting people. Let's see, you'll want a solid background in probability and statistics. And loads of math for the algorithms and data structures. And computer programming. You like computers, don't you?"

Even the computer nerds in Bert's class were stone-faced— or more than was their usual petrologic demeanor—no doubt contemplating a future gone awry. Rather than writing killer apps or video games, wearing chick-bait-black leather coats and roaring in Porsches to their beach condos, all by no later than age twenty-two, they were instead seeing themselves in hospital-white lab coats in Gary, Indiana, staring for days on end at a computer screen display of a single molecule, one of billions inside a rat's lower intestine.

"Especially for writing programs for data analysis," Anna continued, stating the obvious. "Of course, you'll want to take as many courses as you can in molecular biology, biochemistry and genetics."

Still no questions. Some students now wore pouting faces, perhaps finding that they yearned to watch re-runs on C-SPAN of committee hearings flyspecking regulatory compliance, anything but this.

"So tell us, what exactly is the study of genomics?" Bert asked.

There were never going to be questions from the class. It had quickly reduced to a boring interview format. Forty-six minutes to go, and it was the *Bert Gropes Show*. He was excoriating himself with network teasers he imagined: *Tonight, Bert's guest is unknown computational molecular biologist, Anna Brighton, talking about her big opening on C-SPAN. Be sure and tune in.*

"Genomics is the study of genomes," Anna said. "A genome is a complete set of genes, the biological units that are inherited by an organism. A genome is set forth in a genetic map or sequence made up of segments of DNA—nucleotides, the building block components that make up genes, with the letter *A, C, T* and *G*." After this rote, Anna looked at Bert with an expression that said: *This was a mistake. I'm dying up here. How could you have talked me into this?*

"What exactly is a gene?" Bert instinctively filled the dead air.

"A gene is a biological unit that repeats itself," Anna said, flashing another look of frustration at Bert, "from generation to generation, that occupies a specific location on a chromosome in an organism, like a human being, and determines a particular characteristic. In a human being," she continued, stretching her hands out to the class as if the stat applied to them and not her, "it's estimated there are approximately twenty-five thousand genes."

The class had been stirred from its collective coma. A restlessness rippled from left to right across the room.

"Yes, a question." Bert said hopefully, nodding to Sue Milligan whose hand had ventured up.

"Mr. Gropes, I'm not understanding what this has to do with social studies," she said. "Are we going to be tested on this?"

A number of other faces in the room expressed concurrence, albeit not as politely. He could see that Anna was visibly distressed but maintaining her poise.

"Really? I'm surprised you're not getting it," Bert said. "This is democracy in action. Remember how we talked about the relationship of the words *elect*, *electoral*, and *electrical*. We said that full participation makes for a charged electorate. Charged, as in alive. Hello? Is anyone alive here? Doesn't anyone see how this connects to democracy in action?"

Guffaws of incredulity.

"All right, speaking of action," Bert pressed on, "tell us, Ms. Brighton, what do the genes actually do?"

"Genes express themselves by defining the recipes for proteins which are transcribed from the DNA and delivered to the parts of a cell where those proteins carry out a function." Hers was the stone face now, a talking one.

"Do all genes send protein recipes to cells?" Bert pressed on, as if the future of democracy depended on it.

"No," Anna said with some resignation, hinting in her tone that she joined the rest of the class in skepticism. "Genes that are switched on express proteins. The rest are turned off and perform no apparent function."

"So," Bert jumped up from his chair, "a human chromosome has a body, if you will, of voters made up of about twenty-five thousand citizen-genes."

The class laughed in appreciation. Instantly, Anna smiled and relaxed her demeanor.

"The genes elect the proteins," Robert volunteered.

"Good," Bert said.

Anna turned and drew a double helix on the board and an arrow from "voting genes" to a box with the words "elected proteins."

"And the elected proteins carry out policy. Right?" Miguel observed.

"That's right," Bert said.

Anna eagerly drew a line from the "elected proteins" box to another marked "policy."

"Right," Bert continued. "But who is making policy, and is it democratic policy? In our 'governing body' we see that not all voters vote. Some are registered to vote but don't vote; some aren't even registered. What happens in a democracy when only a few vote?"

More than a dozen hands sprang into the air and waved like a field of wildflowers shaken by a warm breeze.

"It's not a true democracy," Whitney observed when called on.

"It's not government of the people, by the people and for the people," Tom said.

"Individuals have no power, no freedom," the studious Robert said. "It's an oligarchy, not a democracy."

Bert was in heaven. They had been listening to him for the last few months after all. They were feeding his words back, but better, they were discovering what it all meant. And they were doing it with Anna as his witness.

"Now what's with these unregistered genes?" Bert said, nodding to Anna. "I mean, in a chromosome is that good or bad?"

"Scientists just don't know," Anna said. "It may be that particular genes are switched off due to an evolutionary adaptation that serves a good purpose, or it could be that if the same genes were switched back on, they might cure a hereditary disease or lead to a better life."

"What does this class think?" Bert said. "I'm taking a poll. What shall we do with all these unregistered slacker genes?"

Linda's hand ventured up. Bert's heart leapt.

"What do you say, Linda?"

"I ssss…say: Turn 'em on!" She smiled triumphantly.

The CMB dissolved from Anna's face, and a carefree smile lit up her face. The class saw it and fell in love with her. He knew because he caught a glimpse of her drinking it in.

Bert whisked through the room and switched on the TV, the VCR, a window fan and a boom box that lay dormant at Ramon's feet. "Turn 'em on!" he echoed. At the back of the room he pointed with both hands at the light panel on the wall near the front door. Anna responded and flipped on five of the eight overhead light switches that, under edict from Margaret Tillman, were to remain off to conserve electricity. Bert scurried to the front of the class and stood next to Anna, now beaming with delight.

Ramon's thumping rap music mixed in with the voice of Senator Hoffenworth on tape gaveling to open a subcommittee hearing: "There will be ord*ah*!" Above the din, Bert proclaimed: "I say turn 'em all on! Let the will of the people rise up and be heard!"

Bert grabbed Anna's hand and raised it with his as if they'd just received the party's nomination by acclamation. The class went wild.

14

TINA HALLIKSEN ARRIVED AT THE PLANTATION guest cottage in a covered golf cart to pick up the newest guest. When the twenty-two-year old knocked on the door and it opened, she was surprised to find an old man—a blind one at that—awaiting her. That was different, way different for Isle Libido, bordering on the exotic. All she'd been told was to pick up Professor Gropes.

For the last month she'd been taxiing that creepy patent law-yer around, doing his bidding—strictly chauffeuring, that is. Turns out he's here consulting Mr. Slayde about a biotech busi-ness called Mother DNAture that she didn't even know existed before working on the Plantation Estate. That Primal Urge's flesh peddling was combined with a casino seemed almost predictable, a good bet. But a biotech biz on top of that? That made her curious, and a little uneasy.

"I'm taking you to your meeting with Mr. Slayde," she told the old guy.

He nodded soberly. She was wearing a watermelon-colored halter top and lime green short shorts that, on her long legs, made heads turn. But not this guest. He seemed more interested in finishing his breakfast of mangoes, tea, and guava juice.

"Here on business?" she asked after she'd walked the elderly professor to the cart and seated him.

He nodded faintly, distantly, as if preoccupied, not saying a word.

As they descended from the damp gardens of the estate toward the buildings and beachfront of downtown Libido below, Tina negotiated the cart around a bend and swerved wildly to avoid a Libidoan monkey relieving himself on the paved path. The curious old man didn't explain himself further during the ride. He didn't seem to possess the usual social compulsion to make small talk, but she was sure something was on his mind. His white wings of hair suggested he was in flight to a theoretical place.

"I started out as an exotic dancer in the casino," she said. "Then I got transferred two months ago to this job on the Plantation, driving people around, things like that. It worked out great. I'd just broken up with my boyfriend who also works in the casino." She paused, then added: "Couldn't get him to talk. About him, about us. Drove me crazy. Know what I mean?"

For some reason she had a strong compulsion to tell this old man about her life, brief as it was compared to his—spare as her short shorts compared to his long faded khakis. Although an exhibitionist by nature, she didn't usually open up about her aspirations with total strangers. There was just something about this old man that she trusted.

"I graduated from the University of Iowa. I thought it would be fun to spend a year or two on a tropical island doing something completely different before going back to get my masters in Victorian literature. I thought that's what I wanted to do. Honestly, now I'm not sure *what* I want to do."

No response. She wondered if he was listening at all. "I was going to leave here six months ago, and then guess what? I started writing a novel." She waited for the usual question: "Really? What's it about?" But nothing. That didn't stop her from forging ahead. "It takes place in nineteenth-century England. Genre-wise, it's kind of a Victorian sci-fi, gothic romance, suspense novel. It's about a young woman born to royal family, the daughter of the Duke and Duchess of Sandwich. Through a series of revelations she becomes convinced that she is not a royal Sandwich and that she was actually born of a lowly working-class family. Her royal family has kept it secret from her for reasons she realizes will put her in danger. Meanwhile, in her heart she knows she will never find a true love until she connects with her real family and humble past. As the story unfolds, we see the protagonist attending teas and ladies' functions by day while at night, under an alias, she's an exotic dancer in one of the seedier parts of London. In the course of stripping, she meets a series of characters, including Victor Frankenstein, a young doctor, before the events in the Mary Shelley novel. He's in a position to use his knowledge of science to match her to her parents. She falls in love with him, but there's a problem. She sees the horror he's going to create some day—the destruction, the stiff lurching about, the clunky shoes, the human debasement—if he doesn't relax, open up and talk a little bit about himself and their relationship, you know, about *them*. Oh, I should have mentioned on the genre? There are definite comic overtones."

No reaction.

"I still have quite a bit more fleshing out to do, but..." She didn't finish the thought.

They passed near the back nine of a virtually empty municipal golf course. Four Libidoan monkeys played on the seventeenth green, re-enacting a ritual they'd seen. One monkey was pulling his chin in deep thought trying to figure out how, with a twenty-two-foot lie, he could roll and sink a fallen coconut that was larger than the hole. Just as he stepped up to roll it with two hands from between his legs, his concentration was unraveled by the rude squawking and jumping up and down of the other three, including a female who'd insisted on tending the pin.

"Of course, the stripping is sort of a metaphor…"

The dark glasses and facial features remained placid. *Why did I say that?* she thought. As if this old man, a no-doubt brilliant university professor, hadn't figured that out.

"I was best known at the casino for my mirror dance. Four mirrors."

A moment passed and she let out a sigh. "Try to imagine what it's like. The alternating joy and trepidation you feel. What it's like to look at yourself face-to-face while doing it, seeing yourself for exactly what you are: groveling, wincing in pain and pleasure, revealing the quirky rhythms inside you that are bursting to be expressed, opening yourself up and, totally without shame, inviting a crowd of strangers to go ahead, grope with their eyes and thoughts, and have their way with your utter nakedness. Can you relate to that?"

She glanced over. This time his lips were actually parted. He spoke.

"I'm sorry. I am unable to relate." A moment was lost as they coasted a downgrade; the only sound was the muffled squeal of where the rubber met the road. Then the old man spoke again: "I'm not a dancer, but I believe the planets, the stars and, deep down, perfect molecules are dancers."

That was worth the wait. "What a cool way to see the world," she said, ruminating on it another moment. "By the way, I was talking about what it's like writing for an audience, real or imagined."

He looked like he was going to give in to a smile, but then his thoughts seemed to drift off.

Five minutes later, they approached the casino, a ten-story building with neon-lit letters: THE URGE. Tina rolled the cart up to a small entryway in the back of the building with a dis-creetly-stenciled sign on the glass door: "Mother DNAture Bioinformatics."

Entering a service elevator, Tina pushed "Mezzanine." When the doors opened, a hotel carpet of dried-blood bur-gundy and random colored spots rolled down the hall and splashed against gray doors, one lettered "Mother DNAture" and the other "Bioinformatics." Underneath was the slogan "Betting on a Better Tomorrow." Tina led Dr. Gro inside. Floor-to-ceiling one-way windows overlooked the casino below. A sliding window was open, a cacophony of bells and voices, croupiers and clinking cocktail glasses called up, punctuated by the occasional yelp of agony from a disappointed gamer. Men and women of all shapes, colors, and sizes wandered through mazes of slot machines carrying buckets of the gold tokens called Urges.

Pulsing music from a nearby floor show—a weird fusion of Reggae and rap—trumpeted a Rastafarian Promised Land where murder and anarchy were rampant. A tipsy young man at a blackjack table wore a Plantation souvenir straw hat with a Libidoan monkey holding onto the brim with a "Let's Party" expression. Its head bobbled up and down to the tropical rhythm.

A side door opened and Dick Slayde appeared, wearing a silky black shirt, gold monkey pendant, red pants and black slippers. He was accompanied by Putterman, the dweeb lawyer.

"Well, Professor Gropes, if the courses of our lives don't recombine." Slayde smiled in appreciation of his own wit. "We meet again. Sheer *co-accidence*. An amazing *conflu-currence* of events, to put it recombinantly. Wouldn't you say?"

Dr. Gro said nothing.

"This is our patent attorney, Ernie Putterman." Slayde ges-tured to Tina to stay put in the room.

To her surprise the professor reached out to shake the law-yer's hand, held onto it, and leaned closer to him, as if sensing something. Then he turned to Tina and said: "Be so kind to describe the configuration of Mr. Putterman's hair."

She got that the old man wanted to use the lawyer as Dick Slayde's whipping boy, perhaps a warm-up act for things to come.

"Let's just say that if he were a stripper from the neck up, he'd already be topless," she observed, letting her eyes pan over his scalp.

"Forgive my asking," the professor said to the lawyer, "but I've rarely encountered an aura so small. Truly. Not just the usual receding auric corona so common an industrial hazard in your profession. I mean no disrespect. Being a molecular cosmologist, I'm interested in the larger mysteries behind small things. What do you suppose would account for your condition? Surely something extraordinary and grossly devitalizing."

Tina wanted to pump her fist and say "Yes!"

Putterman, speechless, touched his oily white scalp and rubbed slightly where, to protect against the tropical sun, he'd slathered on too much sunscreen. Evidently at a loss for a retort, he widened his stance and planted his hands on his hips. "I'm a partner with the firm of Pynne, Pencilgirth & Needlemeister. We're the first American patent firm to establish a presence in the Libido market."

"How big an outpost is it?" the professor asked.

"Well, right now—and if you count me—one lawyer. But with the Primal Urge account we're projecting solid growth."

"No, I can't help with your de-vitality problem," the professor said, answering an asked-for but unasked question. "There are no quick fixes like aura plugs or coronic comb-overs. I personally don't give a rat's ass about any of this New Age crap, but some people swear by karma therapy."

Slayde chuckled, no doubt relieved that the barbs struck his decoy. He walked over to the window where the noise came from. "So, you probably ask, what's with both gambling and bioinformatics under one roof? The problem with mainstream bioinformatics is that these companies think they can load all the genetic data in the computer, slap an algorithm at billions upon billions of combinations in search of patterns, hoping they will reveal gene locations associated with cures, triggers of vital proteins, etcetera." He slammed the window shut. It was quiet again. "A sterile, detached approach, indeed. As if that's all there was to it."

Slayde picked up a bucket of Urges and waved his free hand out at the casino below. "My research is tied directly to what goes on down there. With each bet—whether electronic poker or a slot machine—an algorithm derived from gut chance determines what genetic combination to investigate. That way my research is limited to what counts and excludes worthless queries. It searches only combinations that have the intangibles that count in the real world. My algorithm automatically factors in greed, compulsion, thirst for power, raw economic survival and—last but not least—lust. There are billions of promiscuous proteins roiling their hips at one another inside a human being. I only want the sexually dominant ones."

"And when you find some really fetching proteins, we can't wait to see them published in *Slayve Quarterly*," the professor said. "Get to the point, Dick. What do you want?"

"All of this would have been unnecessary but for the fact that I'd come up with the algorithm thirty years ago, and it disappeared."

"You say you had it back then," the lawyer said, as if about to ask for the first time. "What happened?" He was a lousy actor.

Slayde ignored the new arrivals and spoke directly to Putterman. "Back then, I was one of the Professor here's graduate students when he was teaching at UCSF. We were working on the cutting edge of molecular biology, at the epicenter of the emerging biotech era, when I was suddenly shaken by a series of earth-moving discoveries. A once-in-a-lifetime experience. I walked around in a trance for a week." Slayde paced around the room to demonstrate precisely what inspired walking looked like. "I didn't sleep. As if possessed by another intelligence, my hand moved and moved and I filled an entire notebook with formulas, notes, mathematical equations, and—most critically—the algorithm for a new catalytic shock technology that could prick dormant genes into action. On the sixth day, delirious, I told Dr. Gropes about my discoveries, and he marveled at it. He even suggested I call the notebook *The Shocking Details* which, then and there, I wrote on the cover. I left the notebook in a drawer at the lab, went home and collapsed. I slept for two days. When I returned to the lab, the notebook was gone. I'd suffered a mild form of amnesia and was never able to reconstruct but a fraction of its content."

The professor shook his head in denial, almost pity, and directed his response to Tina, ignoring the other two. "Overnight, the quiet and studious Richard Sleigh became what you see. Dick Slayde, the *enfant terrible* of biotech." The blind-man gestured in the direction of the man in the silk shirt and loose-fitting vermillion pants as if he could have guessed what Slayde was wearing. "By all accounts, including his own unwitting one, he'd suffered a severe mental breakdown. He dropped out of graduate school. He's been living in his alternate world ever since. A shame."

"Let's talk about shame, shall we?" Slayde's tone was sharp. "I learned that a year later, after I'd left San Francisco for Johns Hopkins, you used my insights in a trial balloon presentation to the department faculty. Triggering gene expression to help heal genetic defects in humans. You saw a brave new world. In your enthusiasm you proposed that relationship of genes was both mathematical and musical. That got you laughed out of the hall. They called you both a quack and a hack. You were angry and upset at the ridicule. That's right about when you withdrew from your save-humanity idealism, isn't it?"

The professor was silent, even sullen.

"But that didn't stop the always-ambitious Dr. Gropes,"

Slayde said, now speaking directly to the lawyer. "He moved away from UCSF to Davis and reinvented himself from the biologist to the molecular cosmologist. It's interesting that right about the time he lost his grand vision for an improved human race, he lost his eyesight. He didn't think much of helping humans, but he got the nickname Dr. Gro when he proved, after a series of papers on the galaxies, that he could do wonders for chickens."

"Your twisted interpretation of events." The professor's shrug was a study in controlled fury. "That's all it is. What do you want from me?"

"I will be brief." Slayde placed a token in the slot and pulled the handle. Spinning and whirring, it came up a mango, a papaya, and bananas. No payoff. "You stole my notebook thirty years ago. You waited, thinking I wouldn't be watching, and you used it to create your Celestial Force of Shocked Chickens."

"Cell Shock-Transmitted Life Force," Dr. Gro corrected.

"Oh, that's even better than the picture I had of randy roosters with angel wings doing the nasty," Slayde said, pulling his chin. "'Shock-transmitted life force?' Sounds like a living, throbbing offense to one's sense of propriety. I definitely own that."

"Mine is not that kind of shock," Dr. Gro said. "Consistent with all the work I've done over the years, it's more like a healing, invigorating splash of cold water to the face of a dormant gene."

"No! It's mine!" Slayde shot back. "You were never working on shock technology. Thirty years ago you were spinning your wheels studying human sperm. Even I found it shamefully self-indulgent."

"My start toward becoming a molecular cosmologist," the professor said defensively. "Important findings came out of that—"

"Seminal research," Slayde said sarcastically. "You found yourself all right."

"I had to study my own…lab specimens," the professor stammered.

Tina detected some embarrassment.

"I couldn't ask my male graduate students to…contribute," he added. "Not with female students on the team."

Slayde frowned superciliously and inserted another one of the Urges. He grasped the handle and—once, slowly—stroked the shaft top to bottom. "Such a noble inquiry," Slayde said, his voice thick with venom. Then he grabbed the top of the shaft and jerked it down swiftly. Mango. Monkey. Bananas. "But sorry. Zilch. No payoff."

Slayde was quiet for a moment. Then he inserted another Urge. The handle dropped. Spinning. . .Monkey. . .Bananas. . .Monkey. Two monkeys. A spasm of coins spilled into the slot tray. He scraped it into a bucket which he set on the table in front of Putterman. The patent lawyer ran his little fingers through the bucket and picked out one of the coins. Lost in his thoughts, he held the gold monkey token with the tips of both thumbs and forefingers in an act of twisted consecration.

Slayde turned to Tina. "You are excused. I need to speak with Professor Gropes about some private business. Wait in reception until he's ready to be taken back to his room."

No one spoke while Tina stood up and walked out of the room. Back in the reception area she plopped herself down on a chair and picked up a magazine, but she couldn't focus on it. She was thinking about how easy it would be to eavesdrop. Two months ago a company executive named Tatiana Lurenski had shown her how to video the same conference room from a remote location in the building. It had been a meeting where Primal Urge sought to merge with and take over a conglomerate of successful but competitive adult websites. The target company was quickly devoured by the masterful Lurenski, who struck Tina as some kind of corporate species of black widow.

She tossed the magazine on the table and hurried down

the hall. The door to the tech room was open. Once inside, she flipped a switch that silently turned the camera on in the conference room. Tina leaned toward the monitor, earnestly drinking in what was probably as close as she'd ever get to a godhead experience on Isle Libido: video omniscience.

DICK SLAYDE'S OLD PROFESSOR WAS A STUDY OF controlled fury; he didn't want to give his host the satisfaction of knowing that he, Dick Slayde, was calling the shots now.

"Give me my notebook back," Slayde demanded. "And we want the source code for your new software re-interpretation of the shock technology. If you were able to figure out how to shoehorn the gene action of free-range chickens back into genetically-altered naked chickens, well then, surely the magnificence of the Libidoan monkey can be shock-driven into the naked ape."

"Triggering dormant ape genes in humans?" Gropes asked with sarcasm.

"That's what people want."

"Reversing evolution? Taking us back to monkeys?" Gropes asked himself out loud, then turned to Slayde. "No doubt you were the first successful lab experiment. You think that's a worthy goal? Among the billions of delusional humans, a good number I have known personally, you stand out."

"I know there's demand and a commercial future." Slayde spoke with confidence. "That's one of the biggest differences between you and me. I understand people. You don't. You never did."

Gropes laughed with contempt. "I know enough about the species. You think that would-be *Homo sapiens* parents will pay to use shock technology so that their children will carry monkey genes? This is your scientific legacy?" He shook his head.

"I only regret that, but for your theft, I would have done it sooner."

"You've been on this island too long," Gropes said. "So have I! How long are you going to hold me here?" He was seething. "What is it you want, Dick?"

"Here's my business proposition for you, Professor," Slayde said. "What I need you to do. You will issue a press release from Libido. In it you will announce that you're still very much alive. You've been in top secret meetings with Dick Slayde, entrepreneur and biotech visionary—"

"You're wasting your time."

"—That you are retiring to this island but that you will serve on the scientific advisory board of Mother DNAture Bioinformatics. But first, before the press release, you must turn over what is rightfully mine. See that my notebook is returned, and sign over to me everything you have that's based on my shock technology including the new Cell-STL Force software."

Gropes angrily shook his head.

Slayde picked up the bucket of tokens he'd set down and rattled it once, rousing Ernie Putterman from his semi-hypnotic state. The lawyer placed the golden Urge he was examining into Slayde's outstretched palm. Slayde dropped it into the bucket.

"Thank you, counselor. Now, please explain to our guest what it is he needs to sign."

The lawyer pulled a sheaf of papers from a large envelope. "To secure patent protection worldwide, we'll need you to sign this technology transfer agreement. Basically, it's an assignment to Mother DNAture of all existing patents, to-be-filed patents, and related intellectual property."

"I've never patented any of my inventions," Gropes snorted, the same self-righteous professor Slayde remembered from thirty year ago. "I know what patent lawyers do. You take inspired discoveries and unraveled mysteries and describe them in a dead language so you can squirrel them into a legal strongbox where, for the rest of the world, they must lie fallow.

Tell the truth. Isn't that all you do?" He spoke with the same tone reserved for questioning a veterinarian who, when asked about what happened to a child's pet, is slow to admit he's only licensed in taxidermy.

The lawyer separated a set of papers from a larger stack and rustled it around in front of the old man. "I even had a Braille version prepared for you." He dropped the papers in the professor's lap.

"So far, counselor," Gropes said with undisguised contempt, letting the papers fall to the floor, "looks like you're an accomplice to kidnapping, extortion, racketeering, to name a few of your little escapades. How's your state bar going to size this up?"

"You took what's mine," Slayde interjected. "The most despicable kind of plagiarism. Worse, you stole from a student of yours."

"I did no such thing," Gropes insisted. "And you're neurologically imbalanced enough to compare academic plagiarism with kidnapping?"

"Plagiarism. From *plagiarius*," said the lawyer. "In Latin it means *kidnapper*. They share the same gravamen."

"You see?" Slayde said. "An eye for an eye."

Putterman smiled back at Slayde. "And rest assured, I've done nothing illegal under the sovereign laws of this country. I've researched it. Nothing is forbidden in Libido if done pursuant to the unofficial policies of the Provisional Government."

"'Unofficial?'" Gropes repeated. "Who decides that?"

"Officially, here on Isle Libido, that would be the Primal Minister," the lawyer explained.

"Enough of the legal gobbledegook," the professor griped. "Just take me to the Primal Minister. I'd like him or her to know exactly what's going on here."

"Naturally I'm flattered that you'd like me to be more involved with your future," Slayde said. "The people of Isle

Libido still haven't been able to agree on a Constitution or a governing body, but twelve years ago we were able to scratch out a new draft of the provisional charter late one night at one of the casino lounges on the back of a cocktail napkin. The document creates governance and puts our priorities in order. Wouldn't you know? As the Primal Minister, at least for the temporarily indefinite term, I am the highest ranking official on the Island."

Gropes heaved a breath of resignation. "And if I don't sign your papers?"

"Have you been given a tour of nearby Shady Pines? Go on the informational presentation, and you get two hundred Urges." He rattled the bucket.

"Pines trees?" Gropes repeated in disbelief. "What kind could thrive in this equatorial climate?"

"The really shady kind." Slayde stretched his arms out like branches in a visual demonstration to himself. "Genetically altered, of course, to maximize their shadiness. It's the island's new retirement community. We're just putting our final touches on the Phase One build-out, fifty luxury units. Saturday night, bingo. Sunday, all-you-can-eat buffet. For you, no more fussing over how molecular structures mimic those of the galaxies. Trust me, you'll love it."

"Let's cut the crap, shall we, Dick?" Gropes said, the dark glasses staring grimly away from Slayde. "If I don't sign it over, I'm stuck here forever. My life work over. But even if I do sign it over, you still won't let me leave or communicate with the outside. Right? Because, once back on the mainland, I could sue to nullify your naked act of coercion."

"That's why I want you on my advisory board," Slayde said in mock flattery. "You're smart. But I assure you I'll get back what is rightfully mine. In fact, the longer you are here, the easier we will be able to gain control of it back on the mainland. Do it now or I'll do it soon."

Slayde stabbed the slot with one more of the monkey tokens.

"What sequence will it be? Sign it and you can continue with at least some of your life work here, or don't sign it and become the bingo champ at Shady Pines?" He pulled the lever.

Monkey. Monkey. Monkey. *Jackpot.*

A crush of coins roared from the bowels of the machine and into the tray. A bell rang and rang in a synchronized hoopla of spinning lights and whirligig sounds. The more noise it made, the more it seemed the golden Urges kept pouring from inside the machine until they were spilling onto the floor.

"Remember," Dick Slayde smiled, "the house always wins."

TINA WAS BACK IN THE RECEPTION AREA BY THE time Professor Gropes, Dick Slayde and Ernie Putterman met her there. Once outside the offices of Mother DNAture and before reaching her golf cart, she was determined to toss him a lifeline, if he wanted one.

"Is there anything I can do for you, Professor Gropes? Anything?"

"Thank you, but I'm finding my way around quite well, actually."

"You don't have a phone. After I drop you off up at the Plantation, I have to come back down to the casino. Anyone you'd like me to call? Or send an e-mail message?"

No response. Why didn't he take her up? Was he protecting her from knowing too much? Too late for that. Or did he not trust her the way she'd found she naturally trusted him? He was a funny old guy.

Even with her earlier suspicions, Tina was truly shocked at the scene she saw unfold in the conference room, but she wasn't sure what to do about it. The sordidness she witnessed stretched well beyond the playful themes of The Urge. Underneath the silk shirt and red pants, Dick Slayde was a genuine scumbag. Unfortunately, it was true that there were no

law enforcement officials on the island that didn't share with
her the same boss.

"I *really* want to help you." She gave his upper arm an urgent
squeeze as she guided him along.

"If you can find me some good pipe tobacco, I'd be grateful,"
was all he said. "I hear you can buy Cuban."

15

AFTER DROPPING PROFESSOR GROPES OFF AT his guest quarters, Tina had to attend a brunch—to mingle in her semi-celebrity status as a Slayve—inside the mansion, where technology and telecommunications vendors from New York were being entertained. After what started as a bad day at the office—witnessing that her employer was a thug actively engaged in kidnapping and extortion—it was bizarre to find herself then thrust into a group of guests and co-workers who were so charming and pleasant.

After the brunch, she headed back down toward the casino for a group photo shoot with about twenty other Slayves for the cover of a travel magazine doing a spread on vacations on Isle Libido. Halfway to the edge of the Estate, a monkey emerged from the bushes. He scurried to the cart and, jumping onto the back, hitched a ride.

"Hi, Scooter doll." Tina turned her head and greeted him. A

fixture on the Estate, the fourteen-year-old Libidoan loved to ride around with her when she was on taxi duty.

She pulled her cart up to the security post at the edge of the Estate. As was customary, the guard, dressed in khaki—shorts, shirt and the Primal Urge trademark red belt—put his hand up for her to check through.

As she drew closer, another man—in his late forties, round face, glasses and black hair too well coiffed for a tropical island—emerged from the security hut and stood in front of the young man. On him, especially with his paunch, the khaki shorts looked like a costume. Tina recognized the second man as Simon Debree, the company's vice-president of operations.

Prior to this job, Debree had worked in personnel for Disney and two or three other hotels at the Epcot Center. At each he'd been let go. A few years back, early in his tenure with Primal Urge, the company had been the subject of public criticism in a number of articles in the U.S. for calling women Slayves. Because public relations determined that it would look foolish to have Slayde defend "Slayves," the task fell to Simon Debree, VP of human resources, to demonstrate that nothing serious was meant by the moniker and that women were treated with the same respectful accord as men. Debree announced that all the young male employees—waiters, croupiers, maintenance workers, security guards, etc.—were also Slayves. Primal Urge had to be sensitive to the fact that eighty-nine percent of the tourist traffic came to the island from the U.S. Although male tourists were generally eager to board a plane (or a guided missile for that matter) in order to touch down in Libido, the company needed to make sure the wives and girlfriends were willing to go along for the ride. Following Debree's public announcement, the male employees were officially Slayves, too. After that, although visitors and employees continued to refer to only the women as Slayves, Debree had managed to subdue the outcry.

"Hi," Tina said, rolling to a stop.

"Hello there, Tina." Debree smiled unctuously.

"I'm on my way down to the casino for the reception in the Rum Barrel Room. Need a ride? Hop in."

"I'll take you up on a ride, but we'll need to head back to the mansion." He plopped himself into the seat next to her and she lurched into a U-turn.

"We have a small problem," he began, as if about to tell her he needed help because they were short one dancer this evening for the midnight show. "I'm told you, shall we say, *took it upon yourself* to make sure Mr. Slayde's business meeting earlier today was recorded."

The warm tropical air did nothing to stave off the chill that swept over her. Although she hit DELETE for that recording session, there must have been a computer back-up. And who would have found it?

"At Primal Urge we value employees who are self-starters, make no mistake," he said.

Tina stared straight ahead. Whatever he was trying to gloss over this time, the real substance was already transparent.

"Unfortunately, I think you know sensitive information was discussed that should have only been shared by those in attendance. You can see the dilemma we're in. At Primal Urge we try to balance the needs, values, goals, and aspirations of our employees against the greater good of the company. Mr. Slayde has said that if that information leaks to anyone outside the Plantation Estate, there would be serious repercussions for everyone involved. We need to talk about your future here."

"Wait," she said. "I came here to work, to be a dancer for what I thought was purely an entertainment company. I don't have an employee manual for this biotech company. Nobody's ever told me their rules. I was shown how to record meetings. I thought I was being helpful."

He let out a sigh and, reflexively, his shoulders gave way. He looked out at the uncontrolled growth they were passing on the right. Debree's body language, particularly the now unconcealed absence of a vertebra, said: *Look, I'm just following my orders.*

"I get my paycheck from Primal Urge, too, you know," he explained to her. "But, off the books, I also work for Mother DNAture. As it was explained to me, 'It's all about biology, the same as it ever was.' And 'All companies today are biotech concerns. They just don't know it yet.'"

There was no need for attribution—Dick Slayde: The Signature Collection.

"The more I've thought about it, the more I see that he's right. As vice-president of operations, it's ultimately my charge to be steward of human capital. Think about that. Where are the boundaries for that? There aren't any," he assured himself.

He wasn't getting around to firing her. Maybe there was some wiggle room on that decision. For some perverse reason, she didn't want to leave this job right now. Her new hours and duties really agreed with the writing she had taken up.

"So, you tell me, I work for...?"

"Both," Debree said as they bounced along, "whether you knew it or not. You're a hybrid employee. But now, because of what's happened, you're a possible safety and security risk. On your own, you've managed to solidify your status as an employee for the biotech company. Mr. Slayde says you know things about it that you shouldn't. It's hard-wired into your brain tissue, biologically speaking. If prematurely set free into the environment, who knows what could happen?" He held his hands out, open-palmed, conveying his genuine confoundedness.

"I know we're in a foreign country, but can you give me that again, this time in English?"

"Keep driving past the mansion, out to the cottages to the west," he pointed, referring to guest quarters that were at a remote corner of the Estate, a half mile from the mansion. "Better yet, let's switch. I should drive."

She hit the brake. While he got out and walked around, she slid over to the passenger side.

"We'll call this a reassignment." He relaunched the cart. "You won't be working with others. No dancing or driver duties. For the time being, you'll no longer be living back in town at the Slayve Quarters. You'll be staying in one of the guest cottages."

"Are you kidding?" She startled him, causing his foot to come off the accelerator. "You can't do this. No way, I quit." She spoke with defiance, but she knew the gears of something much bigger and more frightening than losing her job had been set in motion, closing in all around her.

"Sorry, we can't let you quit," he said in the most flattering tone. "The proof of how much you're valued is in the new package I've prepared for you. You'll be getting a paycheck now from both companies. See, we're doing this very professionally, I assure you. You've still got health and disability, of course. Longevity incentives. Although you won't be able to take any vacation time until this blows over, there will be accrual. I promise. Finally, as long as you're on this assignment, we'll even waive your annual review."

Scooter screeched in what sounded like a scornful laugh. Tina sat in stunned silence for a moment. They pulled up to a guest cottage next door to another.

"You're at liberty to do as you please while living here on the Plantation," Debree said as she stepped from the cart. "Provided you always stay within a hundred feet of your quarters." If it was possible, his last words stung her anew. This tiny island, the one she'd circled on a map a little over two years ago, just got tinier—more like molecular.

"As is company policy, and especially where you're drawing two paychecks, we will likely ask you to perform a few assignments while you're here," Debree continued, idly stroking the steering wheel with his right hand. "Since we know you write, we may bring you articles from *Slayve Quarterly*, for example, so that we can take advantage of your editorial skills."

"Oh, would you? That would be such a thrill," she said sarcastically, then changed her tone. "Do me a favor. Tell Dick Slayde I hope that the world's smallest, genetically engineered gnat gets into his shorts and severs his namesake with one itsy-bitsy bite. I'd say the same for you, but I'd be insulting the gnat."

She sucked in a cleansing breath. She didn't know where the verbal machine-gun fire came from in her terrified state, but it sure made her feel better.

"I'll take that as a refusal to perform assigned tasks," he said, all but stuttering. "You're fired. All compensation and benefits are terminated, but you'll have to wait here. You can't leave until there's been an exit interview. In the meantime, we'll tell everyone in the Quarters that you're on a special project that's under wraps at the Plantation. That's because there may be some delay in conducting your exit interview."

Simon Debree took off, traveled about twenty feet, and stopped.

"Get off. Shoo! You're not wanted!" Debree reached back and shoved the monkey off the cart. Scooter yelped in protest but landed defiantly on his feet, near where Tatiana Lurenski had walked her Rottweiler this morning. He reached down and, picking up a large chunk with his left hand, hurled it at the back of Debree's head. Perfect strike!

"Good shot, Scooter!" Tina yelled with glee. "Brain transplant! Big improvement! Huge!"

"Fucking monkey!" Debree shouted, wiping the back of his head, then scraping his hand on the empty seat next to him. The cart took off again.

The monkey waddled his way back towards Tina.

"Scooter doll," she said affectionately, "Way to nail old shit-for-brains. Really, you didn't want to go where he's going."

Scooter came up and put his right arm around her; she put her hand on his shoulder. Then he dropped his hand down to her left buttock and copped a squeeze.

"Shame on you, you big rascal," she said, disengaging him

without any resistance. He squawked in delight. She laughed. "Let's see what's inside. I may have to send you on a banana mission. Stick around, you."

Out of nowhere she heard a familiar voice.

"I've always lived alone."

She looked across the way and saw that the blind old man had been sitting quietly in a chair in front of his cottage the whole time. He spoke slowly and deliberately as if summarizing a day of sitting and thinking. "Although not really... I was always content to live with my work."

"We need to talk," she said.

"Do me a favor," he said. "Bring that Scooter fellow with you. He might be the most evolved creature on this island."

16

ONLY A FEW WEEKS AGO WHEN THE WIND AND
rain pressed against all sides of his mother's house, he'd had a
nightmare about principal Margaret Tillman—actually hundreds of Margaret Tillman *zombies*—drumming fingers against
and clawing at the windows of his home, bent on reaching all
the way inside and ripping his soul, along with any chance he
had at social studies immortality, clean out of his chest cavity.

Tonight, however, the pounding rain of the late spring storm
only compounded the thrilled beating of Bert's heart. Tuesday,
the first day of May, and Anna would be arriving any moment
now. She would be stepping inside his world. She would share
a meal with him. His mother would not be arriving home until
late. Who knew what was in store for him?

Last night—a week after she'd come to his class, and a day
after he'd driven her to Vacaville to examine one of the chickens that was part of the study she and Uncle Gro were conducting—she'd called him and said: "There's something very

important I need to speak to you about. I apologize, but it's important. I can't put it off for another day." Bert thrilled to hear it since he'd been thinking the same thing. Now it was his turn to send a warm smoke signal back her way. When he suggested that she come over for dinner at his house, she hesitated at first. Perhaps she was thinking what he was thinking.

"That would work," she finally said.

Music, Bert thought. Tonight there should be music to fit the mood he wanted. In their drive to Vacaville, they'd come to discover that they both loved and missed everything about summer: the hot sun, the bounty of fruits and vegetables, the carefreeness of it all. He picked out a CD compilation he'd recorded and which he'd given the name "Perfect Summer." First up: the Drifters singing "Under the Boardwalk"—classic, sweet and bouncy. Should he wait for her to arrive before he hit PLAY? He hit PLAY and REPEAT; then, like a ballet-dancing walrus from a Disney animation, he plunged back into the kitchen with a few sweeping ballet steps. Any moment now Anna would be coming in out of the winter rain and into the warmth of his meticulously staged summer Shangri-la.

The doorbell rang. Suddenly all oxygen on deck bailed ship. He turned the music down and hurried over to open the front door. It was the taker of breath, Anna, holding an umbrella, the rain pouring down behind her.

"My car!" she shouted above the roar. "Can you come out and help me?"

As he followed her out to her car, he screamed into the downpour and to her: "I've got summer! Hamburgers! Waldorf salad! Wait'll you see!"

Anna flashed him a smile and then pointed to the problem. A large fallen branch, twisted and gnarled, had ensnared itself into the right rear wheel well. "About two blocks away," she said. "I can't get it out…" The last word trailed off in despair.

She'd managed to park in the middle of a large puddle about two inches deep. She waded in and renewed her tugging in a display of helplessness. Bert sloshed in and grabbed the heftiest handle he could find. He used all of his strength and, with a tremendous force, the stubborn tendrils gave way. The two of them staggered back, nearly falling into the puddle.

"Oh!" they both grunted in shock. She started to laugh. And continued laughing as they splashed and trotted to the front door and back into the house.

"So, this is where you grew up," she said, stepping back to take it in, while removing her glasses to wipe away the rainwater. "Would you at all mind if I put something different on?"

Bert couldn't believe how forward she'd become. For sure that was a testosterone-churning rescue he'd just performed. He was huffing, his blood still racing. She already wanted to slip into something more comfortable than the jeans she was wearing.

"No," he said, keeping cool.

"I ran into a marine biologist grad student just back from an outing in Alaska. He gave me this to listen to." She pulled a CD out of her bag. "The sounds of Beluga whales in the wild." She went over to the CD player and crouched down.

He wasn't that disappointed. She wanted to share *something* with him, although, it was true, her in a negligee could've beat the pants off those Beluga whales. The night was still young.

"Your feet are soaking," Bert said. "You better put those on the heater." He pointed at the lime-green canvas shoes she wore with purple socks. "I'll get you something dry."

He ducked into the bedroom and opened a drawer. He found a pair of clean gray thermal socks, too large for her small feet, but they'd have to do. He took off his own wet shoes and socks. He was about to put on an identical pair of socks when he saw a few pairs of his slippers on the floor of his closet—plush Ultra-Woolies slippers he'd embellished with animal designs. It was part of a grander plan, and as close as he could come to rising above the excruciating limits of a charter schoolteacher to fulfill his home-in-the-hills dream. Bert had designs of coming up with a whole line of Ultra-Woolies retrofitted with animal themes, selling them, and making some real money. What would Anna think about that? He walked over and slipped into a pair, and walked back towards the living room.

Anna was sitting on a chair in the corner, taking her second sock off and laying it on the nearby furnace vent.

The Drifters were gone, washed out from under the boardwalk by a sudden high tide for marine mammals to cavort in. The living room was filled with the strange and beautiful voices of Beluga whales.

Bert shuffled towards her.

"Look at those slippers!"

"You like 'em?" he asked tentatively. "I made them. They're plain Ultra-Woolies that I've modified into designs for children. A year ago I was a substitute teacher in a high school craft and design class. That's how I learned. The monkeys are my favorites. I call them Jungle Heat." The slippers, adorned with smiling monkey faces, were big enough to let his toes wriggle freely; a tail protruded from the heel and shot up and out in an unwavering vector with a curl at the top in the shape of a walking cane.

"When I give you a tour of the house, I'll show you the other ones I have—the leopards are Quiet Spots and, of course, the lions are Comfort Kings."

"What fun," she said. "I wish I was creative like that. I bet kids will love them. What are you going to do with them?"

"I've got plans," Bert said with renewed confidence. "Big plans. I'm thinking of not teaching this summer so that I can devote full time to finishing the development and trying to sell the whole line to a manufacturer."

"How would that work? Would you just sell them, or do you get a piece of the action?"

"A license is the way to go. I'd be looking to get royalties for the commercial life of the product." He conjured up an image of him shuffling out to his mailbox for a big check. Easy money.

"That's what they do in my industry," she said. "I guess you could say it's just a different technology." She pointed to his feet and laughed.

Bert released an undetected sigh of relief, feeling vindicated for letting her in on his top-secret project. Anna put on the pair of thermal socks, and Bert gave her a tour of the house. As they moved from room to room, he was charmed by her three inches of toe-flap that slapped the hardwood floors.

They ended up in the kitchen.

"I just have a few things to finish up and we'll eat," Bert said.

"Can I help?"

"Sure. You can finish this." He pointed to piles of cubed apples and chopped walnuts on a cutting board next to a cup of grapes and a yogurt-mayo dressing.

She reached for the knife on the counter. "No celery?"

"Cucumber. It's better than celery." He pulled one out of the refrigerator. "Armenian cucumber, actually. It's tastier, has fewer seeds than other cukes, and doesn't need to be peeled."

"I'm impressed," she said, taking the cucumber from him and bopping him lightly on the head with it.

Anna took a sip of the zinfandel he'd poured and started to chop. Bert drank in the domestic tranquility as he readied to boil the corn and prepare a topping for the vanilla ice cream dessert. Whales crooned gently in the background. It was all so sweet; he couldn't help but imagine this could be a typical evening home on the ranch.

"Bert, I need to talk to you about something. The reason I wanted to see you."

She seemed a little ill at ease. He knew exactly how she felt. These things weren't easy to talk about. But he was going to let her do it. Besides, women were so much better at that sort of thing.

"Please."

"Where shall I start?" she asked herself. She continued chopping. "You're familiar with your uncle's WHAT Trust?"

"What?"

"Right," she said, not looking up. "That's the acronym. It's a non-profit he set up to fund research into his *big questions.* Although he believes people are messing things up, he was actually doing lots of good to help the planet as a whole, you know. He used to joke that it was his way of coming to terms with his own fears of dysteleology, the assumed absence of meaning or purpose in nature."

"Of course," Bert nodded. He had no idea what this had to do with getting on with their burgeoning relationship or their future together. He was aware his uncle had coined the word "teleologistics": a far-off notion that one could provide large and impersonal groups of people in distant places with not only the bare essentials for existence but what he said was "knowledge that will help them discover what they're doing here." If Anna were not present, Bert would gag himself with the spoon he was using to stir frozen blueberries in a sauce pan.

"I work for WHAT as a paid researcher for your uncle. That's where the paychecks come from. I've been in the final beta testing stages, running the computations that will define the shock technology algorithm, just the way he'd envisioned it be done. At the same time, an agency of the United Nations— well meaning, I guess—is airlifting a hundred thousand baby chicks to aborigines in the Amazon. But, of course, these are the naked chickens." She nodded at Bert with a certainty that he knew what the difficulty was with those birds.

He recalled hearing about the intimacy problems of featherless fryers and roasters aired on a government-sponsored afternoon talk show, courtesy of C-SPAN. "Those birds can't… are unable to—"

"Right…breed without bio-technical intervention," she said, stepping in, sparing him more tongue tripping.

"The Trust project I'm working on is called WHAT Relief. If we don't deliver the algorithm to our Relief partners in the Amazon, the biotech giant PharmLife will move in and seize the opportunity to make a big PR splash with the biotech drug they're touting. They call it VigoRoost. It's an insidious compound, but it works. Chickens will breed without need of artificial insemination. Problem is the compound doesn't break down in chicken manure, it gets into the water table and is absorbed by indigenous trees. The trees can't break it down either, and worse, our studies show many tropical varieties will die. It's a disaster. Rain forests in Brazil, Venezuela and Ecuador are at stake. That, in turn, could bring even more global warming."

Bert was beginning to wonder whether she was building up to a discussion about the two of them, or whether, in fact, she was as far removed from him as his uncle. Global warming wasn't exactly the hot talk he'd hoped for.

"So what can I do?" he asked.

"This is awkward asking, with your uncle still missing. You know I'm worried sick about him, but I just believe he'll turn up somewhere, hopefully soon."

"Me, too."

"Meanwhile, WHAT's at a complete standstill right now with your uncle gone. No one is managing the Trust. No one is there to license the technology even if I were finished, and—" She broke off, a little embarrassed. "No one is there to sign my paycheck. I'd do it for no charge if I could," she hastily added, "but I just can't. I've got rent, student loans—"

"You need to be paid. Tell me what we need to do," he said.

"Ordinarily a court would handle this by naming your mother executor of his affairs. She's next of kin. But the law says that until enough time has passed or"—she gave it a respectful breath—"his body is recovered, they won't pronounce him dead. So, while we're in this limbo, the court will have to appoint a trustee, an interim trustee, someone to stand in his legal shoes."

She paused. "This is a big favor I'm asking of you. Do you think you could talk to your mother and ask if she would be willing to go to court to become the trustee? We've got to cut off PharmLife before they get in and pull a big publicity stunt with VigoRoost."

Bert thought for a moment. "You need to understand that she's very different from her brother. She likes people but guards her privacy."

Anna nodded her head to indicate she would never impose, prepared as she was to accept no for an answer.

"And when it comes to legal proceedings," Bert went on, "let's just say she would rather not. My thinking is, it makes more sense to have me do it. She would prefer it and, after all, I'm next of kin after her. Would that work?"

"Really?" Anna lit up. "You'd do it?"

"Sure, why not? Remember, I teach Social Studies. That includes a whole week on the judicial branch of American government. So, I'm really quite comfortable in the milieu of law."

"You would do it!" she repeated, facing Bert. "That's fantastic." She stepped forward and hugged him tightly. Her sweet-smelling shampoo, reactivated by the raindrops, played havoc in his nostrils. She released him, turned back to her salad; she poured the dressing into the salad bowl and began stirring.

"You'd be running a small biotech business," she said. "Not exactly social studies, but you'll get the hang of it. Oh, Bert, I knew I could count on you!"

"No big deal."

She turned and faced him again. "There!" Standing with perfect posture, holding the beautiful Waldorf salad just below her breasts, she glowed. Bert glowed too. Inside that moment he felt absurdly wonderful and newly created—part human, part archangel, and, inexplicably, a little Armenian cucumber thrown into the mix. Instinctively he leaned forward and kissed her full on the lips. Startled, she took a step back—

Or at least she tried to. Her left leg moved but her foot didn't; his right slipper—the monkey he'd fashioned on the toe-tip wild and hellbent and beyond Bert's control—pinned the toe-flap of her left thermal sock solidly to the kitchen floor. Mayday, mayday! She lost her balance. When she dropped the salad, it was as if a crystal chandelier of no less than its namesake, the Waldorf Astoria, had disengaged from the high ceiling and shattered onto the lobby floor. Bert and Anna came crashing down after it. He managed to avoid landing directly on top of her, breaking his fall with his arms on either side of Anna, fully reclined. As she lay there in shock, he found himself in a position both beastly and preposterous. It was as though a lizard—*his* inner lizard—had emerged and taken over. Perched on all fours atop a hot rock, it scouted for more prey. In that instant Bert was afraid to open his mouth to gush his apology, lest his tongue dart out to pluck an imaginary fly off her forehead.

He shifted to one side and dumped himself on the kitchen floor, rolling over onto a smear of yogurt and mayonnaise dressing. Anna sat up in a daze. He jumped to his feet and offered her a hand. "I am so sorry. Are you all right?"

"I'm fine. It was just… I was startled… obviously." She looked down, wiping her jeans with her hands. Luckily only a grape, now smashed, had stuck to her seat, but it was doubtful that it had helped much to break her fall.

"I don't know what I was thinking," Bert said, still shaken.

"Don't… it's not a big deal." She looked at him. "I can't recall much of anything I've done or said tonight, but I may have inadvertently sent the wrong message—"

"You didn't do anything wrong. I—"

"Bert, I really like you. You're like… I feel like you could be the brother I never had. But we're so different, too. I'm sorry if I misled you. I mean, I'd understand it if now you don't want to help me with—"

"Really, I'm fine with it."

"—WHAT Relief."

"Never mind my… blunder," he assured her. "I want to help."

Bert realized that she didn't have her glasses on. They'd

fallen to the floor but she hadn't retrieved them yet. In the past whenever she paused to clean them, she was always looking down. He'd never gazed straight into her eyes before as he was now. They were deep and ripe and yellow brown.

"You're sure?" she asked.

"I'm sure." He bent over to pick up her glasses.

"Let's eat then. I'm starved. Where are those cheeseburgers? They've got to be a whole lot better than that Top Ramen I was going to have tonight for the fourth night in a row."

All during dinner, conversation remained light and cordial. But Bert's faux pas, together with his raw desire, hung like a cloud over the table.

On her way out, Anna asked Bert once more whether he was sure he wanted to help. He was grateful for the oblique reference to the pain he suffered but could not show.

"I'm in," he said. "I'll call my uncle's lawyer. I'll take care of it."

She smiled and started to move towards him as if to give him a hug, but she caught herself. Instead she rubbed his left upper arm a few times with her right hand in a solicitous gesture. "Thanks, Bert."

When the door closed, and after he'd been standing there like an ice sculpture for a minute, he realized that she'd forgotten her Beluga whales. With all the distractions, he had ceased to notice the CD playing low in the background the whole time. Now that the sounds of those deep-sea dwellers registered again, it was impossible not to hear them for what they were: big, sad-sack Quasimodo creatures drowning in watery wind tunnels, piping their final farewells in the hope some listener would hear them from a place where no one is heard.

17

"HELLO, EVERYONE... BENTON COFFEY," THE TV host blurted on cue. "Tonight on *Think Fast* we have Senator Ray Hoffenworth of Tennessee, chair of the Senate Investigative Committee on Chimera. Welcome, Senator."

The senator nodded.

"And from Sacramento, California, Clarene Eliza Dare, prominent criminal defense First Amendment animal-rights lawyer."

Benton Coffey spoke in such breathless rapid fire that a growing number of cardiologists were forbidding at-risk patients from watching his program.

"Welcome, counselor."

She bowed her head with a thin smile.

"Let's start with you, Senator, you're sponsoring a bill to regulate the biotech industry, the Abatement of Chimera and Beastly Degradation of Humanity Act. Catchy. That your title?"

"Skinned down a bit from the one I introduced." Then he

added with a smile: "Always prepared to compromise 'cept, of course, where my principles are concerned. It's the same law I wrote when I was a state senator back in Tennessee. It's already the law in Tennessee. I'm lookin' for the Congress to make it the law of the land."

"So tell us what the law will do."

Senator Ray Hoffenworth looked straight into the camera. "It would be a felony for anyone—whether doctor, scientist or any individual—to create human chimera with gene therapy, splicin', transplantin', engraftment, or by any means whatsoever. Now, let me explain, therapies that don't fool with nature, they're OK. By that I mean therapies that don't fool with the germline—the very earliest cells that become human eggs and sperm that we know were created by God to carry out His will. Same thing goes for any therapies that cause animal behavior in humans. We won't stand for it. But we have no problem with an organ transplant from an animal to save lives or reduce human sufferin'. We leave that up to the judgment o' doctors. What we aim to forbid is makin' any kinda animal DNA that's genetically heritable, that is to say where the germline is affected, permittin' animal tissues or traits or genes of any kind to be passed on from generation to generation, pollutin' our human gene pool with animals. As I said into the *Congressional Record,* some scientists don't seem to be satisfied with creatin' Frankenstein. They wanna take the human Frank an' make Frank an' Fido, or Frank an' Mister Ed, or whatever beast from the field they can an' see what kinda animal stew they can cook up in one o' them biotech labs. They wanna let Frank the Chimera out with other humans, bein' let loose for frolickin' an' interspeciatin.'"

The *s* in "interspeciatin'" hissed with disgust and conjured up droves of new human-beast creatures "out in the field" with traditional, unsuspecting "normal" humans, all doing what they would naturally do out there if given a chance to socialize, fraternize, and canoodle-ize among themselves. "Man was made in the image o' God, an' it should stay that way. To me it's inconceivable that another member of the human family would oppose this common sense law."

"Thank you, Senator. Now, Clarene Eliza Dare, you represent a group of university scientists who say the proposed law would go too far. Tell us about that."

The television screen bloomed three picture boxes: one on the far right with Senator Ray Hoffenworth and another on the far left with the defense attorney. A smaller one, below and center, was the talking head of Benton Coffey. Clarene Eliza Dare was a regular on *Think Fast*. Originally from New York, with a law degree from Columbia, she had come to the Sacramento area, where she based her law practice while teaching animal rights at the UC Davis Law School.

"Benton, we were extremely disappointed when this became law in Tennessee, and we intend to prevent that happening at the federal level. It represents a blow to the advancement of science and our basic First Amendment right to inquire. Recall how Galileo was persecuted for advocating that the sun was the center of the universe—by the big Church which, just like Senator Hoffenworth's Big Brother government, imposed its worldview that only unspeakable evil could come from pursuing such a line of thinking. This law sets the clock back and will prevent important research leading to potential treatments of disease and animal suffering, both human and nonhuman."

"But what do you say to the suggestion that without these laws we may someday have part-human part-animal chimera walking around, maybe on all fours?" Coffey rat-a-tat-tatted.

"There's no threat of that. It's pure science fiction. What is more realistic is that a handful of the twenty-five thousand genes in the human genome get rearranged—move this *c* here and this *t* over there—so that some malfunctioning human genes can be switched on and produce life-saving proteins for a human being. Technically, that trivial adjustment to the gene might be derived from an animal, making that scenario illegal under Senator Hoffenworth's ill-advised proposed law."

The head in the right box squirmed and shook incredulously. "Horse pucky," it muttered. "She's got it wrong—"

The screen collapsed into two large boxes, pushing *Think Fast*'s host out of the picture.

Clarene Eliza Dare rolled her eyes. "I suppose those with slightly more extreme views than the senator from Tennessee would say that all inter-species procedures should be outlawed. We all know that Senator Hoffenworth had a heart attack three years ago. What's not widely known is that doctors repaired his malfunctioning heart with tissues from a pig."

"Tissues, not DNA!" he protested, pronouncing it "tish-*ooze*."

"Those same extremists," she continued, ignoring him, "might point to the fact that animal tissues were introduced into and mingled with his blood which coursed into and through his brain, causing symptomatic pigheadedness. Now wouldn't that be unfair?" She smiled at her backhanded defense of the senator. "I think the senator and I should agree there is no room for extremism when it comes to alleviating human suffering."

Hoffenworth was practically coming out of his box to get at her. "I didn't give you all o' that nice statement I made into the *Congressional Record* about Frank an' Mister Ed, concludin' that a horse is a horse unless o' course the horse's got Frank's head stuck on it. But I s'pose that's fine with Miss Dare. She got all the book learnin' in the world but not a lick o' horse sense."

Her eyeballs bulged in fury. "A horse is a horse of course unless it's only the south end of a horse from Tennessee charging north hellbent towards its dream stables at sixteen-hundred Pennsylvania Avenue." She all but whinnied, then gained a semblance of control. "Because, for humans at least, ignorance is a known mutogen, capable of causing the most frightful mutations. It's a shame—"

"OK, that's all that we have time for," Coffey shouted over the continued sparring. "I think you two ought to rent a hall and have a public debate."

"Any ol' time," the senator said with a smile and feigned calm.

"Say when," she said.

18

THE GALLERY OF DEPARTMENT 3 IN THE OLD
Yolo County Courthouse, abuzz with a visiting social studies
class, was indeed filled with ninth graders. Bert positioned
himself in the front row next to the aisle just in case the judge
asked him to step forward. His lawyer, Ollie Tweed, sat quietly at the table with a sign that said "Plaintiff/Petitioner." The
lawyer table on the other side of the lectern said "Defendant/
Respondent." With Bert's petition to be named trustee of
WHAT unopposed, no one was seated there.

Ordinarily, it would be impossible for Bert to obtain
approval from Margaret Tillman for such a field trip, but this
was the exception. When Bert told her that he was going to
be named trustee—read: control funds coming into the trust—
she beamed and winked at Bert. So he decided to sell her on a
field trip rather than hire a substitute. She even started actively
fantasizing about what might come of Bert's appointment.

"Lots of money will come in from his new technology. You'll

need to make decisions about grants. I certainly hope your uncle is found soon, but if he's not, well, you may have to start the first educational arm of WHAT. Maybe call it WHAT Learning, or WHAT's To Learn, or whatever. Bear in mind there's a naming opportunity for a building. The new library wing could be the Gropes Learning Center."

Today the class had already toured the historic beaux arts-style courthouse—a combination Roman-Greek-Tuscan creation located in the center of downtown Woodland. When Bert was a boy riding his bike past the front of the building, he used to stare up at the giant letters engraved on its front above the pillars: COVRT HOVSE. He found it hard to believe that a *V* was inserted in place of a *U* not once, but copied again in the second word, making the ordinary "COURT HOUSE" something freakish, incomprehensible, and unpronounceable. It wasn't until he was in junior high that someone explained that the Romans didn't have a *U* and that the architect, for some inexplicable reason, was trying to bring back what had been gone for centuries.

The plan today was to watch a courtroom procedure beginning to end, namely, the hearing appointing Bert as trustee. Bert's hearing wasn't exactly a classic petition of human rights grievances torn from the pages of their textbook, especially since it was uncontested, but it would do.

Ollie Tweed sat quietly at the counsel table. His long white hair hung over his ears in a demi-Prince Valiant cut; everywhere from an inch or so above the top of his ear was bald. It was hard to believe Ollie and Uncle Grover were best friends. Bert was convinced Uncle Gro didn't even like Ollie.

In his practice Ollie did a little bit of everything: wills and trusts, contracts, and landlord-tenant disputes for mostly students at the University. But what he loved to do most was sit around with Uncle Gro and theorize about order in the universe. Sometimes these discussions droned on in tBert's mother's living room. It was Bert's custom to excuse himself—announcing his desperate need to prepare for a class or to organize his sock drawer, it didn't matter.

"Good morning," Judge David Winton McGrath said, after everyone had stood and been seated again. "Let me acknowledge and welcome our guests in the courtroom today. We have with us from Mansfield Academy Mr. Gropes's ninth-grade Advanced Social Studies class. Mr. Gropes is also the Petitioner today in the matter about to be heard. I'm glad he's Petitioner and not Defendant," the judge added in a good-natured way.

Ollie Tweed let out a mirthful giggle. A few students around Bert laughed, but the rest had only stopped momentarily from whatever occupied them to stare dumbly at the judge. Trevor and his boys were off to the left goofing off and not paying attention. A few boys and girls to his right were fidgety and casting about, disengaged. Girls in the front row were secretively texting each other.

Judge David Winton McGrath's appearance featured a full head of shiny black hair, parted to one side, perfect teeth, and skin tanned from outdoor activity—according to Ollie: hunting, fishing, and trap shooting.

"Now, ordinarily, with an uncontested hearing I would simply review the papers, ask a question or two, and then take the necessary legal action," the judge explained to the class. "Today, however, for the benefit of the class, I'm going to ask you, Mr. Tweed, to briefly summarize the petition—that, for example, due to circumstances the trustee is unable to act and that a temporary trustee must be put in his place. There," the judge chuckled, "I suppose I've already done it, but let's hear it from you." The judge turned to the clerk. "Let's have the matter called."

As the clerk stood to read the case name, the court reporter swiveled around in her chair and raised her hands above the keys of her transcriber as if poising to begin a concert recital.

"*In the matter of WHAT Trust*, Number 07-289781. Counsel, state your appearance for the record."

"Oliver Tweed, your honor." He rose and buttoned his brown worsted sport coat. "Appearing for John Bertram Gropes, who petitions this honorable court to act on behalf of my longtime friend and object of admiration, Professor Grover Seymour Gropes."

He paused reflectively, staring at the floor, then back to the judge. "Dear Dr. Gro. Let me just say how much we do miss him." He was choking up.

The judge, perhaps surprised by the spontaneous emotion, nodded sympathetically.

Ollie Tweed read the cue and continued. "How I do miss him and our cozy chats. Oh, if he'd only listened to me and not gone up in that balloon, albeit filled with life-warming breath of air, his spirit to soar. But it was not to be. Alas! Did he, when he reached the sky, make a connection to an airship providing nonstop service to the twinkling shores of the empyrean? We don't know. Oh, if we only knew."

There were a few snickers from the fringes around Bert. The judge looked at his watch but said nothing. Eight weeks out and Uncle Gro had not been declared dead, but the implications of his disappearance were clear. The judge recognized that Ollie Tweed's digression was no less than a eulogy that had been pent up for too long. It would be indelicate, to say the least, to interrupt the lawyer and insist on adhering to the strict request he'd made.

"Let me say, in summarizing this petition, how much it means to me, as a practicing holistic lawyer that this is an *uncontested* hearing. This is the harmony in judicial process to which we aspire. I believe, and I know Dr. Gro believes, that all disputes, but for human folly, are destined for harmonious accord; we need only reduce the realization time to a fraction of what it normally is. Now, as a *holistic* lawyer, I am also duty bound to treat the entire subject of a pending legal matter. Thus, to understand this petition you must not merely understand that a trustee needs to fill in;

you must understand the life and work of Professor Grover Seymour Gropes."

He shook his head as if at a loss where to begin such an explication. Students, not following or no longer interested, resumed their distractions. A bike messenger in spandex shorts, waiting for the clerk to stamp some papers, watched Ollie Tweed and scratched his head.

"To even think one could summarize and understand such a life causes me to stagger back in awe at the sheer sight of the towering edifice that is the life of Grover Seymour Gropes. Professor Gropes would love this hearing if he were here. He would say it is infinitely small and insignificant in the great order of things, but therein one finds the secrets of the larger. He devoted his life to the study of mathematical harmonics, the examination of disparate elements in conflict with no apparent relation and how they aligned and organized themselves into cooperative systems. As a molecular cosmologist, he asked: How is it that four billion years ago a bunch of amino acids and seemingly unrelated molecules managed to organize themselves into the first *living* cell? How did more unrelated cells organize themselves into more complex organisms? The odds of it happening are preposterous, as those that believe in a Guiding Hand are quick to point out. Dr. Gro was never interested in ruling out that the answer was wrapped in a divine ribbon, but as a molecular cosmologist he was more interested in the scientific knowledge underneath the ribbon. The truth and reckoning *behind* a simple uncontested hearing to substitute the trustee. You see? He would dare to ask—"

"Mr. Tweed, I'm ready to rule. I'm granting—"

"—how something so simple could become so complicated."

"That will be enough. Thank you." The judge paused and rubbed his chin thoughtfully. "Amazing. You've just given me an idea how I might settle a complex case I'm overseeing in a jury room right now. I'm granting the petition. Mr. Gropes, you are now the acting trustee of the trust." The class turned and stared at Bert. "As trustee you are now a fiduciary. That means that you must treat matters of the trust with the highest degree of care. Knowing, as I do now, something about the life work of Dr. Gro, you have an awesome responsibility. I'm sure you will act accordingly. If you need direction in how to proceed, be aware that you can always come back and request guidance from the court. Mr. Tweed, I am now signing an order to that effect.

"And to the guests today of this courtroom, I apologize that I can't spend more time, but I must get back to that settlement conference. But I'd like to make it up. I'll be taking over the criminal calendar in mid-June. I know that's during your summer break. Would any of you be interested in coming back to see how we handle criminal matters?"

When all hands went up, Bert felt a cool breeze on his face, as if on a mountaintop—a moment of triumph. He was now the interim trustee of a trust with great responsibilities. The judge was inviting him and his class back as if they were local dignitaries and, best of all, the class had embraced it all, wanting to come back during their summer vacation. A moment to be savored.

"Excellent," the judge said. "I'll ask my clerk to give us a date in early July. I suggest a Wednesday."

The female clerk stared at a computer screen. "July eleventh."

"Your honor, let me be the first to say that I'd be pleased to act as one of the chaperones that day," Ollie volunteered.

"How about you, Mr. Gropes?" the judge asked him directly. "I don't know if you're teaching this summer. Will you be free that day?"

"No," he said. "I'll be here." He hadn't quite emerged from his reverie. Realizing what the judge asked, he added: "I mean, yes. Count me in."

19

FROM THAT BRIEF EXALTED MOMENT IN
court, Bert quickly bottomed out again. He was on the floor in
Uncle Gro's office on campus, surrounded by twelve stacks of
bank statements, each about eight inches high. It struck Bert
that he was seated at the center of a miniaturized Stonehenge,
only more inscrutable. Not even the Druids could divine his
uncle's finances.

The office itself actually appeared to be in some semblance
of order but through no doing of his uncle. Beginning a few
weeks after Uncle Gro's disappearance, Bert's mother had come
in and sorted through the mail and neatly stacked and organized the papers and garbage on his desk. Although blind for
the last twenty years, Uncle Gro could envision obscure patterns of molecular order across diverse species—from amoe-
bas to humans, microbes to muskrats—but apparently he
couldn't see how to put order in his office.

Bert found twelve years' worth of bank statements dumped

into two file cabinet drawers in no particular order. Now having sorted and stacked them by year, he thumbed through several file folders, each marked TRUST, followed by a more specific file name. The term "file" was a euphemism; the tan-colored folders more closely resembled large pockets of pita bread stuffed with everything *but* garbanzo beans: a hodge-podge of letters, bills, business cards and random notes, thoughts—"questions and conundra," Bert had heard them described—written in dozens of handwriting styles, preserved at the request of the blind man. Hasps, clips, staples, and fasteners did not exist in the Pita Universe. Nothing in TRUST was fixed.

At some point in time he'd heard his uncle tell Ollie he didn't believe in corporations. "Great balls, Ollie! What a misnomer. There's nothing corporeal about them. They're legal life support for the DOA." But when Ollie told him about "living trusts," he knew that was how he wanted his projects to spawn and thrive. Trusts, unlike corporations, were also easy to create, Bert was discovering, file by file. With the help of Ollie Tweed, a series of trusts were created, and trusts inside of trusts, that made Enron's labyrinth of partnerships look like an off-the-shelf puzzle "recommended for ages 6 and under."

At the bottom of each file was a document entitled "Trust Agreement." Each followed the same format: A trustor (Uncle Gro) placed some kind of property or future right to proceeds (highly speculative) in the trust care of a trustee (Uncle Gro again), with instructions to the trustee that any income or benefits from the trust be provided to the trust's beneficiaries (other trusts he'd created). Notably among those sub-trusts was WHAT Relief that Anna was working on to aid naked chickens in the Amazon. His uncle even had a contingency trust set up in case PharmLife moved in and created a mess with its chicken droppings. Uncle Gro had more of a sense of humor than Bert had given him credit for. His contingency trust project was named WHAT Manure.

The upshot of all of it, the good news, was that there was only one checkbook and one bank account that regularly received income. The bad news: There was no money. Trust revenue came from various consulting projects, no longer producing income in his absence, and the occasional generous donation, typically (and ironically) from trust brats who seemed to delight in giving their parents heart failure. Bert found a photocopy of a check for $25,000 paid to the order of WHAT and signed by one B. Roger Throckmorton III with a handwritten memo in the lower left: "WHAT the Hell!" Bottom line, right now there was less than two hundred dollars in the account. His uncle had paid Anna on time, along with other expenses, then disappeared. Her next paycheck was perhaps to be funded by a loan from a personal account, but that didn't do Bert any good since he was responsible only for the trust records; his uncle's personal accounts were off limits. All he wanted to do was write paychecks to Anna as they became due. As luck—or was it destiny?—would have it, he found himself shortchanged.

He began to think about Anna again. He replayed in his head her words that night—that he was like the brother she never had and that, besides, she couldn't "make a commitment right now." Can you spell BRUSH-OFF? She wasn't interested in him, plain and simple.

He wished July would get here faster. He'd meet his biological father, a wiser and older man able to guide his wayward son—lovelorn, lost, and clueless in the jungle he couldn't hack through that was his life. In the month since Anna had politely, perhaps unintentionally, banished him into exile from the human race, Bert wished he were dead. He also wondered how at the same time he could feel both his morbid, consuming self-pity and a growing, awakening sadness that had him feeling more painfully alive than ever before. He hardly needed more evidence that he was strange.

His eyes wandered around the room, settling finally on the glass bookcase directly in front of where he sat cross-legged.

Along with Braille volumes of Plato, Shakespeare, William Blake, Walt Whitman, and Aristotle, there were endless science books, including one he'd heard his uncle discuss with Ollie in the living room: Horace Freedland Judson's *The Eighth Day of Creation*, chronicling the history of molecular biology.

It occurred to Bert that when all was said and done, his uncle must have had a lonely life. Never married, it seemed he managed to form liaisons through the years. In his uncle's earlier years, the purely *molecular* years when he was teaching biology and was more of a traditional scientist, the evidence was legion from the inscribed photos and gifts around his office (and his mother had told him) that he was involved with a number of women. They couldn't resist him. He and his uncle truly were unrelated, and not just because his mother was adopted; Uncle Gro had real fun in his younger days while Bert, trying to figure out how to make a buck, was sitting at home these days gluing slippers together. In later years, the last twenty when he'd pronounced himself not just a biologist but a molecular *cosmologist*, Uncle Gro seemed to have lost interest in the casual liaisons, in search as he was for something that he described as "more enduring yet ephemeral, whatever it is."

Adjusting his view, Bert no longer saw the books in the case but rather the image reflected by the glass. A large, oafish-looking man was seated, hulking awkwardly over meaningless files on the floor. As he stared at himself, space and time were transformed, and he could easily make out his mutant destiny:

It's ten years from now, and he's arriving home from work. He walks in the back door wearing a McDonald's hat and hangs it on, so that it covers, a bathrobe hook he'd transformed into a whimsical monkey's tail—the last thing he could honestly say he created ten years earlier. He greets his mother. Although she hugs him closely, he can sense her profound disappointment in his failed future. Margaret Tillman had fired him, and he'd quit looking for a new job as a teacher. Having long abandoned a search for a woman, and gained a few pounds in the interim, he now embodies the amorphous shape and sex appeal of a colossal McNugget. He's forgotten about moving out of his mother's house and into his dream home up in the hills above Sacramento. He sees, to his chagrin, that somehow he's been promoted from temporary trustee of WHAT to a lifetime appointment. Apparently the judge, in his wisdom, decided that Bert needed to do something with his life and since WHAT had no income, no outflow (Anna gone for ten years, there were no expenses), and no assets to manage, what harm could there be in vesting Bert Gropes with the honorary, permanent yet indefinite title: Trustee of WHAT?

He took some comfort in the scene. Seeing himself ten years out, Bert had to admit his mother was right about how a relationship, a prolonged visit to and with the foreign sex, was a singular opportunity to learn more about himself. He'd gotten to know himself all too well just by approaching the landing strip, without actually touching down.

He was Bert Gropes, in love and in life, nobody.

20

TINA REREAD HER DESCRIPTION OF THE
island's endless surf:

> *A warm Libidoan wave breaks and rushes the shore with
> a foam tongue that licks and slurps and probes her bight
> until spent. Eight seconds later, with a sure resurrection of
> force—fully recharged more than ten thousand times this
> day and every day for the last nine hundred years—again
> he nudges her, flat upon a sand-encrusted back, and
> mutters: "Hey, you still awake?"*

She closed her notebook and from her cottage window
looked out at the blue sea two miles away and eight hundred feet below. At least there were signs she was maintaining her sense of humor, but enough for today. Her writing had
devolved to doodling, wandering far from her Victorian sci-fi
novel in progress. In the last week, while an involuntary guest

of her employer, Primal Urge—or was it Mother DNAture?—
she needed whatever escape she could find.

For the first time in her two years here, she felt gravely
homesick. She missed her mom and dad, her two younger sisters and her brother. She missed the small town where she
grew up twenty miles west of Des Moines. Her fantasy right
now was for her whole family to have good seats to watch the
town's annual Fourth of July parade, coming up in a few weeks.
She'd marched in it herself, first as a Girl Scout and later as one
of the high school's pom-pom girls.

She turned out the overhead reading light and began nav-
igating her way across the air mattress to the far edge, ending up on her back, wildly swinging her legs around like some
kind of helpless insect. It reminded her of an old college boyfriend who had one of these, part of a whole line of air mattresses from Primal Urge branded UnderAir, including Silk,
Black Leather, Thong (twins pushed together with the narrow
pad forever disappearing down the middle), and Nothing-On
(no pad). The product line was a bust. Now Tina knew where
some of the leftover inventory was land-filled: her guest cottage, the repository of a Silk.

At last Tina's feet found the wooden floor. She stood up and
stepped into the bathroom. The cottage was appointed with
amenities, glaringly useless, especially the generous supply of
condoms next to the soaps and shampoos with The Urge logo.
The condoms were Primal Urge's Great Ape brand, fresh from
the nearby factory, each package emblazoned with the tag-line
"Because You *Can* Go Back". The only accessory she wanted to
find in the bathroom was a dashing pilot with a chopper outside ready to go. No such luck.

It was nearly eleven o'clock and time to check in next door.
When she stepped out of her cottage, a man in a golf cart lifted
his binoculars from his watch position two hundred feet away.
Three goons a day, three shifts each of eight hours. Even if she
could outrun them, there was nowhere to go. Heading south

toward the town meant the security check-through. East and
west there was nothing but impassable jungle. The path to the
north, should she make it that far, would bring her to another
dead end, the River Libido.

Since her unceremonious "reassignment," she had fallen
into a practice of walking with the old professor every day
about this time. Fifty feet directly to the south of their two cottages was a dirt path on the edge of a precipice that dropped
off about a hundred feet to volcanic rocks below—a relatively
level promenade of a hundred feet back and forth, suitable
for stretching a little but no place for a blindman to go hik-
ing alone.

This morning they had done one lap along the cliff-side trail,
walking arm in arm, when a screech was heard.

"Scooter!" the old man, newly re-animated, cried out.

When the ape reached them, the professor dropped her
arm and took the hand of the new arrival to guide him. Male
visitors to the island (including deaf, dumb and blind ones),
Tina observed, if forced to choose between walking arm in
arm with an attractive, long-legged Slayve or a hairy but well-
endowed monkey, varied none in their choice. She took no
umbrage though. In his funny way, the old man was consistent too: eccentric. She was used to forming fast friendships,
getting on with others and getting them to do the same, but
her fellow captive was a slow-go. Scooter, who had succeeded
where she had failed, understood his marching orders and led
the blind man down the narrow dirt path while Tina walked
behind the two of them.

"This morning I was thinking about my family back home
in Iowa." She spoke loudly enough to be heard in front. "My
brother and two sisters—Jimmy, Lea and Megan. We're very
close. I miss them terribly. Do you ever have those feelings?"
She knew the answer, but she wanted to hear what he'd say.

He thought about it before speaking. "The longing to be
near and part of what you love? Yes, especially being here on

a volcanic island. When I was six, I abruptly abandoned my study of molecular formation and, for the first time, found myself gravitating toward the study I love the most, to which I feel the greatest kinship: volcanoes, supernovae, and like natural phenomena. A theme that's continued throughout my life until twenty years ago when I bit the bullet to pursue molecular cosmology exclusively. Supernovae—stars in the final stages of death—are like volcanoes about to blow," he explained, as if going out of his way to answer her question. "When a supernova explodes, it increases its brightness a staggering thousand-fold and lights up the nebulae, the cosmic dust and gas that flows like lava from atomized galaxies. The nuclear reaction from the explosion is so far-reaching—"

As he swept his free hand heavenward for emphasis, his right foot struck a bulging, dirt-covered root, causing him to tumble headlong to the ground. Immediately, Scooter began wailing and jumping up and down. Tina rushed over. The professor was face down in the dirt, and she could see he'd cut his forehead.

"Oh my gosh! You all right?"

He didn't say anything. Instead he stretched his hand out to the edge of the cliff and, confirming that his head was within a foot, he withdrew it and rolled over. He lay on his back with an oddball, dumbstruck look on his face until slowly a mischievous smile took hold, ripening into a laugh. Scooter began pounding the earth nearby with his fist, and the old man laughed harder. Scooter must have been in on the joke as he now joined the laugh fest.

"Here, let me help you up," she said, grounding one foot behind the other.

He reached out for her, both hands. Her sturdy dancer's legs made him an easy lift.

He insisted he was fine to continue and that there was no need to go back to his cottage. She had a clean piece of tissue in the pocket of her shorts which he used to cover the small cut on his forehead. They set out again. He took her arm and Scooter followed.

"Where was I?"

"The nebulae."

"Right." His tone was self-effacing. "Great balls! I couldn't just have my head in the clouds like an ordinary fool."

"Why do you say that?"

"While I was going on a minute ago, I was having a rather distracting parallel conversation, with myself, asking why I resisted answering your question. I've spent a lifetime lecturing on molecular structure and galaxies, asking all the big questions, but not much about the in-between phenomena, the kind that walk around on the earth with two feet. So what do I know about close relations? To be honest, very little. I never married. No children. The words *friends* and *colleagues* are frightfully interchangeable. I have no one except my sister who also never married, and with whom my relationship is more out of habit than intimacy."

She felt emboldened to ask more. "Is it true what Dick Slayde said—that twenty-five years ago you were more involved with the human side of biology?"

"That was a long time ago. I believed in a lot of things back then. But when I saw the proof, I had to conclude that we call it the human race because our headlong and purposeful rush to extinction puts lemmings to shame."

"You don't really believe that."

"Believe me, I do. Except for the problem of the stunning new data I cannot reconcile with my conclusion."

"What?"

"You," he said, stopping his walk and leveling his dark glasses at her. "I'm a complete stranger, and you put yourself in harm's way on my account, only to end up a prisoner like me. Why would you do that?"

"You were in trouble, and I wanted to help," she said. "It's not complicated. And let's not forget, I'm incorrigibly nosey."

"I know I said 'thank you' that first day you were brought here, but I'm afraid saying it is not always the same as actually giving it." He paused, evidently not satisfied with that statement. "I suspect the two are separate but by no means entirely congruent." He laughed at himself. "There I go trying to explain nonlinear human behavior in mathematical terms. I can't believe I'm talking like this out here in the middle of nowhere, baring my soul—"

"To a stripper," Tina said with a laugh.

"I'm not cut out for it. I told you, I don't dance."

"But you're a natural," she said with a smile in her voice. "You're the only person I know who actually grasps the relationship between space and time. But only in your head, like all the science-niks I've known. You need to bring it out onto the floor." She glanced over and detected the barest trace of mirth around his mouth. "Tell you what. It'll start with you and me. Please, keep talking. But about something more than the galaxies. I'm really lonely out here."

He picked up the pace, reaching a little further with each step on the dirt path, as if getting a better feel for that floor.

"All right, let's talk." He started to walk again. "You first. How did you end up on this infernal island working for Dick Slayde? What were you thinking?"

"Oh, no, not the revealing mirror dance," she fake-fretted. "And out here? OK, here goes. Believe it or not, there was thinking involved, just not of much quality. Remember, I told you I'm searching. I was looking to graduate in a year with a degree in literature, then go on for my master's. I saw my best path to a writer's life by starting out as a teacher, maybe at a junior college somewhere. All told, looks like a lot of years of nothing but the ivory tower world. Then along comes my friend Karen who says she's got a job on an exotic island, and she persuades me to try out. I figured what did I have to lose? I love to dance. I love adventure. I thought I might even collect a few experiences along the way to write about. So, the next thing I knew,

I dropped my academic robe, stood up on that tower top and took the plunge. Except one small problem. What I thought was the fountain of life turned out to be Dick Slayde's cesspool."

"With the gravitational pull of dark matter, the kind that warps and bends space." He stopped again in his path and turned to her. "I just want to know. Is there some way out of here?"

Tina squeezed his arm. "Now we're talking!"

21

"EXCUSE ME, IS IT THAT YOU ARE JOHN Bertram Gropes?"

A woman's voice spoke to him in an exotic accent, rolling the *g* and *r* into the gently guttural sound of a tigress purr—*gurr-rOPES*. Although Bert had never been to Europe (had never been east of the Grand Canyon), he felt confident enough to place the source of her inflection, ball-parking it somewhere between Russia and Bulgaria.

He was seated at the bar restaurant in the terminal of the Sacramento International Airport. Especially for someone who just walked off a plane, she was striking. Having taken pains to spare no detail with makeup, her voracious red lips were set off by assiduously whitened teeth. Along with shoulder-length black hair, a sheen reminiscent of a panther, her meticulously groomed dark eyebrows complemented her eyes with like power. Statuesque, she wore a chrome-colored skirt and black silk blouse revealing more than two inches below the tan line—not that all of these features were noticed in that particular order. Could all this effort have been put in solely for the purpose of meeting Bert Gropes, trustee of WHAT?

"That's me."

"Tatiana Lurenski. Public Relations, Mother D-NAture Bioinformat*iques*. I please to meet you."

"Nice to meet you, Ms. Lurenski."

"Please to call me Tati."

He stood up to shake her hand. She squeezed his fingers gently and held them.

"Tati? OK. Call me—"

"John Bertram, you are a JB, no? I love a name JB. It *eez* so, how you say, complete with force."

"Forceful?"

"Listen to you…" She smiled. "JB is a sure man. I like that."

Bert invited her to join him. He hastily folded the new slipper design he'd been sketching—a monkey with absurdly anthropomorphic features—and tucked it into his book. Tati Lurenski glided into the seat next to him.

A waitress came and took orders: for her a double espresso with a side shot of "extra ice-chilling" vodka. It was some obscure and foreign brand he'd never heard of, but the waitress didn't flinch; they had it in the freezer. Bert ordered a diet Dr Pepper with a squeeze of lime.

Three days ago he'd received a call from an Ernest Putterman who identified himself as a patent attorney based in Miami, telling Bert that he represented a company called Mother DNAture Bioinformatics. Bert had never heard of bioinformatics until Anna explained it to him, but the name Mother DNAture sounded like a real biotech company. When he agreed to fly to Sacremento, the attorney mentioned that he might be joined by someone from the company.

It wasn't the first such inquiry from the few out there interested in licensing the so-called Cell-STL Force technology. Five inquiries had trickled in, resulting in two in-person meetings.

All were from New Agers whom his uncle loathed, lost souls, or the altogether strange. They wanted to license the technology in order to advance their own research on the fringes of animal husbandry: raising animals (family pets, mostly dogs) from the dead by "flipping on that whiz-bang gene thingy," or isolating and switching on the "laid-back gene" as a strategy for world peace. One woman thought Cell-STL Force could be used to turn on the "gospel-singing gene" in her parakeet, which could lead to entire choirs of parakeets in need of "Hollywood record producers." Another, a sad case indeed, called to see if he could use the technology to turn something *off*, namely, the tissue-embedded radio in his skull playing coded hits from the seventies, controlled by operatives from the CIA and Interpol.

The two live meetings Bert had were with a woman who lived in nearby Dixon and the other with a man who drove in from the coast in Humboldt County. With each one, Bert patiently listened to their business plan and scientific methodology—such as they were—and then brought up the question of money, knowing full well, after hearing the hare-brained schemes, that none there was. Each said he or she was willing to share with a generous ten percent royalty payment but could offer nothing as an advance. (The parakeet lady was quite serious in her conviction that the profits to be derived from her bird choirs would be "like getting money to copy itself.")

"Where is Mr. Putterman?" Bert asked.

"He flies from Miami. He *eez* late." She seemed annoyed that the lawyer was not there. "But that is *gooed*." The word *good* rhymed with *mood* except it was stretched beyond the limits: *gooed*. "You and I talk business. Professor Gropes *eez* your uncle, no?"

"No. I mean, yes. He's my uncle."

"I am so sorry to hear he *eez* disappearing. And so you are the boss now, yes?"

"I'm the trustee of WHAT," Bert said. "It's a trust."

"I know your WHAT, but I don't understand all the

legal-legal," she said, shooing with her long fingernails. She narrowed her eyes slightly and looked deeply into his. "I can see that you are a *gooed* man of business. You are boss for more companies, yes?"

"Oh no, I'm just standing in for my uncle. My regular job—I teach Social Studies."

She thought for a moment. "Ah, that eez *gooed* to study. All business *eez* social, no? It *eez* sales and making for people to do what you want. I see nobody can say no at you." She smirked. "You are the same to a woman, yes?"

"I don't know about that," he said, letting a nervous laugh gush forth.

Bert knew that he was being treated to a good stroking, by no less than a world-class *artiste,* but she was so convincing in her portrayal of sincerity he couldn't resist. Of course, he wasn't going to be giving any licenses away today without cash on the barrelhead, and Ollie Tweed looking over the contract. She wouldn't be treated any differently than the other comers. Besides, spending half an hour listening to a European beauty whisper in his ear that he was a captain of industry and a lady killer was needed medicine for his lonely soul.

"I am so happy you to meet. If we not to talk soon, it would be no *gooed.* Today *eez* thirty of May, no? Thirty-one, you see, it *eez* last day for Mother DNAture to write check, seed money for new company. Books and taxes," she said, shooing her nails again. "That *eez* why I must fly to you now. See?"

Bert nodded. The waitress came and set drinks on the table.

"You must to be a busy man, JB. Please to let me be fast with you. Is OK?"

"OK."

"Mother D-NAture, the company *eez* fantast*ique.* I work one year now. Believe to me, the most excited farming and biological company in this world. Animal husbanding, it *eez* always on top, ahead for the time. Mother D-NAture *eez,* how you say, on all foure at the front."

"At the forefront." Bert nodded, eager to show he understood.

"Yes, that *eez* it. Now it makes a new company, a startup so that you and me, WHAT and Mother D-NAture, we can be partners, yes? You must to give me your, how you call, Cell-ACS Force—"

"Cell-STL Force."

"Yes, all of it. Here, you see." She handed him a business card.

WHAT/Mother
A Biotech Joint Venture
100 René Louis Pardon Blvd.
Libido, Isle Libido

Tatiana Lurenski
Vice-President, Public Relations

"You see the future, you and me, no? We are combined. We must to make something new, not known. It will be with JB's Force. It *eez* excited, yes?"

No wonder Bert couldn't find anything on the Internet about Mother DNAture. He'd vaguely heard of the tiny Caribbean Island, but he was mostly unfamiliar with that region of the world, as it was close to the southeastern coast of the States. Although it was a haven for offshore banking, it was best known—and Bert had seen the ads in the Sunday travel section—for tourism at a number of island resorts that featured a week of eating, drinking, gambling, and running around naked. It was an unlikely place to run an agricultural technology company.

While he held the card in his hand and looked down at it, she took a delicate, almost meditative sip of her coffee with one hand. Then, using the other hand, she leaned her head back, seized the vodka tumbler and threw down its content, all with the seamless zoom of a pneumatic drill replacing a lug nut to the wheel of her open mouth. As she rocked her head forward, her supple black hair falling in front of her face, Bert could not help but stare as her tongue slowly explored the cavity of the tumbler for a last drop, her eyes half closed and dreamy; then she licked her red, glistening, vodka-ripened lips. When she opened her eyes and saw that Bert was watching her, it was as if she'd regained her consciousness. She didn't blush, but she giggled out loud at the excess of her own pleasure.

Those European women—Bert concluded—they know how to mix business and pleasure without it getting complicated. He wished Anna could meet her. It wouldn't hurt if a little Tati rubbed off on his friend, the computational molecular biologist, maybe loosen her up a bit, have her not take her life so seriously. With Tatiana Lurenski there was nothing to hide. What you see is what you get. He liked that about her.

Just then Bert looked to his other side. A man stood there.

"Let me to introduce you to the patent attorney, Mr. Putterman," Tati said, then turned to the lawyer. "Please to meet Mr. Gropes. JB."

The two men shook hands.

"Ernie Putterman," he said.

"You are late," she said. "You must not to keep Mr. Gropes waiting."

"My plane was late. There was nothing—"

"Please, I do not want to hear it." She was annoyed with him. Bert was embarrassed by her zealousness on his behalf.

The lawyer stood there blankly until she made a brusque gesture for him to sit. Obediently, he did so. The two were an unlikely pair.

The patent lawyer looked to be about fifty. The shape and geographic scope of his bald spot closely resembled the Bay of Fundy. The purely functional nature of his cheap, black-framed eyeglasses was simply unassailable. His unsmiling face also struck Bert as remarkably featureless.

"I tell Mr. Gropes about the new company we make," Tati said. "But we must to make it all legal and *gooed*, no?" She turned to the lawyer. "You have papers?"

On command the lawyer opened his briefcase and pulled out two documents, clipped together, each five pages. He handed Bert one copy.

Ernie Putterman cleared his throat and began: "Why don't we start on page one at the top? First up, the 'whereas' recitals. They stipulate that you own and control the Cell Shock-Transmitted Life Force aka the Cell-STL Force, software, know-how, formulas, and algorithms, all referred to in the agreement as the Technology. It is further recited—"

"Stop," she interrupted him. "He knows what he has and what he *eez* here for. Tell him what we agree. Mr. Gropes *eez* boring himself to hear you. Do not torture him."

Bert's mouth hung open in disbelief. "Honest, I'm fine."

"I need to set up the framework first," the lawyer protested. "And for once I'd appreciate a modicum of professional respect. I don't have to take this."

"Oh, stop. You make me laugh." She turned to Bert. "We have an expression in my country: 'Your speech *eez* a baking potato that *eez* put on the table cold and with no delicious dressing.'" She shook her head. "I am so sorry."

"There's nothing wrong. I understand him, and it's OK."

The lawyer, harshly chastened, pressed on: "Paragraph one says you license the Technology to Mother DNAture exclusively. Which means—"

"That it can't be licensed to anyone else," Bert chimed in. "That's fine." A dream was more like it. If given enough money for an exclusive, Bert would never have to sit through another one of these meetings. "Except commitments have been made to farmers, in the Amazon, who raise—"

"*Poulet au naturel*," Tati said. "We know."

Bert was impressed by their level of research.

"And that's covered in paragraph two," the lawyer said. "Once

you give us the source code, we'll deliver to your Amazon partners, royalty-free—that is, no charge to them."

"It also says that you own everything," Putterman continued.
"If Mother DNAture develops any improvements, the patents
will be filed in your name, as Trustee for WHAT, but they'll be
exclusively licensed to us."

"Papers are *gooed*," Tati conceded. "Not so bad for a baking
potato. But where *eez* his money?" She leafed through it impa-
tiently. "He must to be paid."

"That's on Schedule A in the back. A ten percent royalty will
be paid with an advance of—" He flipped Bert's copy to the last
page for him and pointed to Schedule A. Tati cozied nearer to
Bert for a closer look. "—this amount," the lawyer said. Under
"Advance" appeared the amount "$1750."

Money! Actual payment. At least on paper. Enough to be
of some immediate help to Anna, but it wouldn't go very far.
Unless royalties started to roll in, but realistically that was a
long time off, and a long shot. Naturally, he would have to run
it by Ollie Tweed, especially the advance amount.

"This *eez* mistake," she said. "This *eez* not advance. It *eez*
insult. I did not today fly at him for deal so little."

The lawyer leafed through his legal pad. "It is correct. That's
the precise amount Mr. Debree authorized in a discussion I
had with him about this license proposal." He tapped the
handwritten "$1750" on his notes.

"I talk with him and chairman," she said. "No need I discuss
exacting amount for Mr. Gropes. It *eez* understood. But I know
this *eez* ridiculous. My friend here will not to sign such thing."
She turned to Bert. "Tell him, JB!"

"I don't know. Probably not. But I need to talk to my own
lawyer before I sign anything."

"We can't wait," Putterman said. "I need to deliver a signed
copy of the agreement to the Board tomorrow to be approved
and countersigned, or declined." He turned to her. "We can't
wait for Mr. Gropes's signature."

Tati let out a sigh of frustration. She picked up the contract and spent a minute reading through it. "The deal *eez gooed*, except the money. If it *eez* enough, you will sign, yes?"

"Depends on what you mean by enough. Sure, but—"

"Thanks to God JB *eez* here. He make decisions. But it must absolutely not be insulting amount." She was hissing at the lawyer. "What if we not fool around and just change to this?" She grabbed Putterman's pen and scribbled in two zeroes, obliterating the decimal point, making it $175,000. "It *eez gooed*, no?"

The lawyer was coming out of his chair. "You can't do that! This is a startup. That amount of money is obscene. Who do you think we are? It will never be approved."

"I have no care," she said dismissively. "And what about JB's time? He has to run around so as to make sure the technology *eez* finished and delivered to new company. And that *eez* not all. He must to be our adviser and be paid." She reached in her bag and pulled out a white box of business cards. A specimen was taped to the lid:

WHAT/Mother
A Biotech Joint Venture
100 René Louis Pardon Blvd.
Libido, Isle Libido

John Bertram Gropes
Technology Adviser

Bert was stunned. He could never have imagined this. While he was searching for words, she snapped her fingers at him. "Write down that JB Gropes, personal to him, not trustee, must to be paid $75,000 flat fee for to be adviser to new company."

All Bert could do was shake his head. Another part of him

wanted to believe this could be happening. His head was swimming down below the surface of some warm tropical water in
some remote equatorial place, and he was staring at the strange,
soundless, and mesmerizing sea life on the ocean's floor. He
wasn't the least interested in looking up right now. He was seeing a big cushion for payroll expense, and the adviser's fee was
more than enough for the down payment to his dream. So viv-
idly he could see it all: the ranch, the life on his own, the cachet.
If this could be real, he'd get another set of cards made up with
the ranch address and his private telephone number:

> John Bertram "JB" Gropes
> Rancher, Tech Adviser, Babe Magnet

"Please! Do it now," Tati urged him.

Bert wrote it in.

"Now, so that there *eez* no funny business, write down that
the agreement *eez* no *gooed*, how you say—"

"Void?" the lawyer said, pained. All his legal work, and the
very reason for his existence, all of it, about to be rejected by a
giant rubber stamp: VOID.

"Yes, that *eez* it." She spoke to Bert. "If they not to send you
the checks in one week."

Bert wrote that down.

"I see now, JB, why you are a *gooed* man of business. Now
put your initials close to it." She was leaning against his shoulder. Her perfume was an intoxicating mix of guava, passion
fruit, roses, and high performance vodka. Bert glanced over
and fully down her blouse at her sun-licked breasts. "And next
to the money I make for you. *Gooed.*"

"Now to sign here," she said, pointing to the line on the last
page.

"Are you sure?" Bert asked. Wrong person to ask if he were

willing to hear no, and her smile told him so. He already knew what he wanted; he just wasn't sure he could believe any of it would come to pass. The temptation was there to give his resumé an instant makeover so that he could write the letter to his father he'd be proud of. Entrusted with his uncle's futuristic hotrod, he found himself at the intersection of biology and technology without a road map. Instead, he had to rely on one more gut check to ensure that his desire to help Anna, and not his raging desires for her, were guiding him, not getting him into any trouble. He read and reread the words he'd written that the contract was void if he did not receive $250,000 within one week of today, May 30.

His pen—primed, self-lubricated with ink—slid across the page: "John Bertram Gropes." His signature was no less than graphological DNA, except for one change. On an impulse, after his eyeballs dipped into Tati's blouse, triggering a charge that roared through Bert's—no, JB's—conductive parts that, in turn, somehow, inexplicably, physically connected him to Anna, the *s* in *Gropes* swaggered into a curlicue, screeched to a halt, and exploded into a blotch of ink.

"This is highly irregular," the lawyer said, sweeping up the signed contract. "If for any reason this offer is accepted—and it would certainly be against my advice—we would express mail you a copy signed by the chairman."

"And the checks," she reminded him.

As if to show off his emotional range, the lawyer waxed from flat serious to a sobering grave. "We ask that you not say anything at this time to anyone about our business discussions, even if they fall through. Competitors could try to take advantage of the situation and cause harm for both of us."

"Sure," Bert said, not sure what that could be.

"We must to be going now to fly back at Libido," Tati said. "Ever been down to there, JB?"

"No. I hear it's wild."

"*Gooed*. You will be going down. You must to be my guest."

Putterman tossed a bill on the table for the drinks. When the two visitors turned to walk away, Bert dropped to his seat and stared at the business cards and the unsigned, unchanged copy he'd been left. If this new company was funded enough to write checks for $250,000, keeping the contract in play, how risky could this be?

Bert looked up and saw his new friend Tati and the patent attorney, Ernie Putterman, walking down the airport corridor together. From a distance it looked like she was berating him over something. He also noticed for the first time that Putterman walked gingerly on his right foot, favoring the left, perhaps suffering a recent injury. The man was in obvious pain.

22

TURNING INTO THE DRIVEWAY AT ABOUT 3:30 in the afternoon, Bert noticed a FedEx truck parked on the street in front of his mother's home. It was not an unfamiliar sight, especially since several home-based businesses were in the neighborhood.

The driver leapt out of the truck just as Bert was heading to the front door.

"John Bertram Gropes?"

"Yes."

"For you," he said, handing Bert a letter-sized package, a clipboard, and pen.

As he signed for it and the driver departed, Bert's heart began to race. He'd been thinking about his encounter a week ago with Tatiana Lurenski and the lawyer. Actually, obsessing was more like it, punctuated by moments of stark anxiety. He didn't even have a copy of the agreement he'd signed.

Anna never knew the trust account was empty. Instead, all he'd told her was that there was a delay at the bank in clearing Bert to sign checks. He didn't want to worry her; he would find a way to get her paid.

Sure enough, he could see that the FedEx package originated in Isle Libido, with the name and address of WHAT/Mother on it. He sat down on the front stoop and pulled the tear-strip to open the nine-by-thirteen package. He found and opened a sealed white envelope inside. A letter, a copy of the agreement, and two checks—both red—spilled out: one made out to WHAT for $175,000 and another made out to John Bertram Gropes for the promised $75,000. The tearaway memo on the first referenced "Advance on Royalties for Cell-STL Force Technology License"; the other said simply "Adviser Fee."

Bert began blinking rapidly as if trying to pinch himself with his own eyelids. Picking up the cover letter that accompanied the delivery, he skimmed over it. It was from "Tatiana Lurenski, Vice-President of Public Relations," written on new WHAT/Mother letterhead. The stationery matched the fonts on the business cards shown at the meeting, except that the paper was pink with a red border:

My dear JB:

I was so charming to meet you. In here is your copy to show the license we take from you. You see I must to send you checks straightly from our investor because we still making new company. Next time we send you from new account.

You must to send your source code now. Please, JB, I want you to be fast. I wait for you.

With warmest affectations,

Tati

Tatiana Lurenski

Vice-President, Public Relations

He put the letter aside and stared at the checks. Except for the payee and amount, they were identical, drawn from the First United Bank of Libido. Bert's eyes darted around the checks. Then he noticed something that he had completely missed on the first pass. Nowhere did it say Mother DNAture or the new company, WHAT/Mother. Instead the red checks were drawn from the account of "Primal Urge Entertainment, Inc." whose address appeared to be identical to Mother DNAture.

Primal Urge? The one and only Primal Urge? The most notorious flesh-peddling company in the Western Hemisphere? Bert leafed to the back of his copy of the license. Above the typewritten words "Chief Executive Officer" appeared the signature on behalf of WHAT/Mother in black ink: "Dick Slayde." The *i* in *Dick*—or at least the dot on the *i*—was smudged into an obscene bell-shaped blob melded onto the graphological column beneath. Bert had heard the name Dick Slayde, a smutmeister who, along with the likes of Larry Flynt of *Hustler*, seemed to relish his lurid celebrity status. The more Bert stared at the signature, the larger it seemed to get. If it got any bigger the neighbors would be able to see it from across the street.

He stuffed the checks back in the FedEx envelope and stared at the letter again. What had he done? Given a license to Primal Urge instead of an obscure but harmless biotech company called Mother DNAture? Exactly what was the connection between Primal Urge and Mother DNAture? What were their intentions for the technology he'd licensed them? What would Anna say if she found out? What would…?

His mother opened the front door just then and walked out with a plate of blueberry muffins. "I thought I heard you out here, Bertie. Look what I've made. Your favorite."

He quickly turned the letter face down and looked up at his mother from where he was seated.

"What is it, dear?"

"Nothing."

"You can talk with me, dear. Is it something about your search for your biological father? You know I support you, but I've told you: If you dig too deep, it might get too steep. I don't want you to get hurt, Bertie."

"Really, nothing, Mom. It's just some routine trust business."

She put the plate down next to him. There were flowers painted on it. Steam was rising from the muffins. They smelled great. He took one, tore its head off and stuffed half in his mouth. "Delicious," he garbled. "What's for dinner?" He picked up the FedEx envelope and the letter underneath. He quietly put the letter back in where the checks were already tucked away.

"Bertie, dear, I can see the candy pink paper," she said, strongly implying he had fibbed about trust business. "A woman doesn't send notes in that color unless she's interested in the same business you are. And I wouldn't call it routine, either. Tell me, you're in love with the scientist girl, aren't you?"

Bert had managed to swerve this conversation with his mother away from his exclusive relationship with the porn industry, only to set it on a collision course with his relationship with Anna. For an instant he considered not hitting the brakes. He wanted to die.

"Anna? Anna Brighton, the one who's finishing the software project for the trust? Is that who you're talking about? No, no, no. She's a friend, that's all."

His mother stood in front of him, reached out and lightly rubbed his neck. His muscles, tense as crack addict's checking into court-ordered rehab, squealed on him. "Bertie, dear, I know the signs. You're in love. I empathize with what you're going through. You're experiencing intense physical yearning. You're jumpy, and you probably feel like a press is exerting a thousand pounds of pressure on your heart in order to squeeze out one cup of juice. A single cup of juice that's your life. That's the way someone described it in a seminar last year.

I love that. But it's OK. It's a joyous, life-affirming experience. There's nothing to be ashamed of."

"Who's ashamed? What's there to be ashamed of?"

"Well, I don't know what the note says, because you won't share. She may be saying 'not now,' and that hurts, but I'm telling you as a woman who knows something, that neon pink paper with a red border—"

"I'm telling you it's trust business."

"Be honest."

"I am."

"OK, then let me see what's going on." She made a move towards the FedEx envelope. "After all, it's my own dear brother's life work—"

Bert placed his palm firmly on the envelope to kabosh that idea. "I can't show these to you, as much as I'd like to. The judge said I'm the trustee. I have to be confidential… I've been entrusted."

She wrinkled her mouth in a combination of pity and doubt. "I just want you to be happy, Bertie. I want you to know yourself, not fool yourself. I'd really like you to think about a workshop coming up in a few weekends that's for men only. It's about getting in touch with the things we're talking about. It's called *Three's Company: You, Beauty, and the Beast Within.* It'll make you more knowledgeable, more comfortable with the intense physical yearning you feel."

"Shouldn't that be private?" he protested.

"There will be other men like you to share with. That's not going public."

"I don't want to take any workshop." Bert put his foot down. "And I don't have anything to share. I'm twenty-six. I know myself. Besides, who wants to spend a weekend in a windowless, air-conditioned room with plastic chairs, talking about intimate details with a bunch of strangers? Thanks, but I'd rather spend that time outdoors in the fresh air."

Bert snatched up the papers, covering his chest with them.

"The muffins are great," he said. "Thanks for the treat." With his free hand he picked up the rest of the decapitated muffin and an extra to see him through the rest of the day.

BERT SPENT THE REMAINDER OF THE AFTERNOON in his room with the door closed. He pored over the papers he'd received and tried to resolve in his own mind what had happened. He logged onto the Primal Urge website and found, just as he expected, graphic depictions of men with women, several men with one woman, multiple men with multiple women, women with women, women with foreign objects, and foreign objects mingling in with men and women. The website's content came as no surprise to Bert; nevertheless, he checked all the images again just to make sure he hadn't missed any important investigative detail. One woman faintly reminded him of Anna, although, it's true, he'd never seen her narrow her eyes in fervor or curl her lip up above the gum-line on one side quite like that. He even imagined for a moment that he was the cause of her rapture, logically extending his own observations of her—Anna excited by one of her computational discoveries or, better, Anna laughing at one of his witty remarks—and engrafting them onto the computer JPEG image.

Attempting to log onto *www.whatmother.com*, he was somewhat comforted to find that it was "Under Construction," that is, a separate website. Even if the money for the new company came from Primal Urge or Dick Slayde personally, that didn't necessarily mean there was something wrong. People made money all kinds of ways—some good, some bad. The money then gets reinvested in what they think will make more money. Bert had read an article about how cable companies, some of them Fortune 500 American icons, piped everything from porno to Pinocchio into the bedrooms of America. So, what's the big deal that Dick Slayde is involved in WHAT/ Mother? Bert had done good landing a solid, paying biotech licensee, at least twice removed from the porn industry; there was Primal Urge, then Mother DNAture, and finally WHAT/ Mother.

Most importantly, he could provide for Anna, who needed him, and pursue his own dreams. It all looked smart on paper. He should be proud of what he'd accomplished.

So why didn't that gnawing feeling, aroused inside him, go away?

23

FUNNY THING, TINA WAS FIRED TWO WEEKS ago, yet Simon Debree hadn't been back for that promised exit interview. Instead, only a faceless peeping Tom in a golf cart watched from two hundred feet away, occasionally lifting binoculars up to his eyes to get a closer look.

Sometimes Tina imagined the man with the binoculars watching them was really an anthropologist observing their routine and daily life for a book that would shock the scientific community. They made for a strange family all right: an elderly, blind molecular cosmologist and a twenty-two-year-old exotic dancer sitting like Ma and Pa Kettle on their front porch. On this day "Junior," played by Scooter, was plopped on the ground in the front yard wearing a pair of Raybans he'd found, lost by someone on the Estate grounds. To complete his aping shtick, he'd found a two-foot stick fallen from a banyan tree. He walked around with it, poking it at the ground before him with such ferocious determination that Tina laughed out loud. That's when Scooter dropped to the ground and, scratching his head, began to examine the stick in search of clues as to how it could be so funny.

Tina looked up and noticed a shiny new golf cart rumbling down the path toward the guest cottages. Since she could see that Ernie Putterman was at the wheel, she concluded that it was the new electric cart he'd special ordered so that he didn't need to be driven around by a Slayve. "I've ordered it from a golf *car* dealership," he'd impressed upon her. "Gun-metal gray, just like my Beamer back in Florida."

The cart stopped briefly for an exchange of words with the phantom anthropologist. When the cart came to a halt in front of the cottage, Scooter waddled towards it.

"Get that crazy monkey away from me!" the lawyer screamed, glued to his seat and gripping the steering wheel.

"Relax. There's no problem," Tina told him. "Everybody knows that you were—Let's just say Scooter can hear and smell that you belong to another alpha male."

"That's not a problem?" Putterman whined.

Having an uncanny sense of where the hot buttons were, Scooter immediately began poking his stick, repeatedly and with increasing determination, at a rear panel behind the tires. By the way the lawyer grimaced and continued to clutch the steering wheel, it seemed to Tina that he was not only being outsmarted by the monkey (able to work adeptly and simultaneously with both tools and symbols); Ernie Putterman was also having to take, with chin up, what was plain to everyone who watched: golf-cart sodomy.

"Scooter doll, come with me," Tina called. She and Scooter walked away from the others and sat down on the grass nearby.

The lawyer extended his right leg to engage the parking brake, stood and advanced to within five feet of the seated professor. "Dr. Gropes, I'm in the process of preparing a patent application I've entitled *Method for Activating Targeted DNA in Primates as Means for Achieving Penile Erectility.*"

"That's marvelous," the professor said in a blasé tone, "but are you sure that describes the patent and not one of your lifetime dreams?"

The lawyer bristled. "Your nephew John, or JB, or whatever he goes by, is our business partner in an entity called WHAT/Mother."

"Who? JB? I don't have any relatives by that name."

"John Bertram Gropes. Your nephew," the lawyer said. "Since you've made yourself scarce back home, someone had to step in and act for your trust. Your nephew volunteered and was named interim trustee. We met with him and negotiated for a license on your DNA shock technology." The lawyer spoke in a slow, even pace, relishing that he was evoking the stunned expression now on the professor's face. "He gave us an exclusive license."

"I don't believe a word you're saying. And I don't know why you've invented this story that you have a license."

"Believe me we do," he pressed on. "I'm leaving a copy of the signed agreement along with a copy of our initial check of one-hundred-seventy-five dollars, cashed at your bank, Davis Community Green Bank, signed by John Bertram Gropes, trustee of WHAT, should you care to have someone verify this to you," he said, casting a glance over his shoulder at Tina. He tossed a full letter-sized envelope on the porch stoop.

"My nephew? *My* nephew." The professor stood up, in shock. "He knows nothing about this field. He teaches Social Studies, for God's sake, at a middle school."

"We're also paying him a fee for his personal time as a technical consultant for overseeing the details," Putterman said, rubbing it in. "And we're working with your research assistant, Anna Brighton, in completing the software development and delivering to us the source code. We paid your nephew so well, in fact, that he's bought himself a small ranch and a brand new pick-up truck."

"That would be how he'd handle something this delicate."

The old man shook his head in frustration. "Not that we're close, but I think I know him well enough to say he's a boy trapped inside the body of a giant infant. I don't fault him, but what you describe, entrusting him with the crown jewel of my life's work, is wildly irresponsible—"

"Believe me, he knew what he was doing when he signed this contract." Putterman wished the old guy could see his smile.

"Are you kidding?" retorted the professor. "In biotech? He doesn't know an allele from a schlemiel."

"Under the license, we decide what improvements to make and what patents to file. In your trust name but, of course, only we can exploit the technology or any patents obtained," the lawyer said. "Now, a serious problem has arisen with the erectility patent—"

"On top of everything else," the professor cut him off, raising his voice. "I've been kidnapped and held captive." He aspirated, exasperated. "Why are you here? There can't be more. Tell me, Slayde wants what from me now?"

"The notebook. *The Shocking Details*," the lawyer said.

"How many times do I have to tell you? I didn't take his notebook loaded with gibberish."

"It's essential," the lawyer explained. "Even if we get the erectility patent, potentially there's a huge roadblock ahead."

"What now?"

"We'll control the Cell Shock software and algorithm, but the shock technology, which is crucial for us to use, may be off limits if PharmLife's patent for Undercurrent gets issued. We have to show that Dick Slayde used shock technology before—decades before—PharmLife. That would invalidate their patent, free up the technology, and let anyone, including us, use it."

"I don't know what you're talking about, but I'm sure it's not my problem," Dr. Grofumed.

"Put it this way, Professor. It would be like us owning a parcel of land but with no way to use it or get to it because there are no public roads to it, and PharmLife owns all the land around it. We'll need to prove that when PharmLife filed for protection, Undercurrent was not inventive enough to merit a patent because Dick Slayde developed it long ago. Without the notebook as proof on that point, our erectility-method patent will infringe the Undercurrent patent."

"Thank you, counselor, for your persuasive presentation. Let me see if I can come to a decision." The old man allowed a deliberative nanosecond to pass. "Kindly tell Dick Slayde that Hell, and not coincidentally this infernal island, will freeze over before he ever gets any cooperation from me."

The lawyer, who'd leaned his head forward hopefully, slouched his shoulders in disappointment. "Mr. Slayde is running out of patience. He said it would be extremely damaging to your scientific reputation to not cooperate. All I'm trying to achieve—"

"We know. It's your lifetime dream," Tina said, approaching and standing by her fellow prisoner's side.

The lawyer scowled at her, started to open his mouth in retort, but abandoned the idea.

"I think Professor Gropes has made himself clear. Leave him alone." Tina scowled back at him.

Putterman made a dismissive gesture with his hand, climbed awkwardly back into his new cart, released the brake, and lurched off.

"He's awful," Tina muttered. "They're all awful."

Scooter, seated by himself on the grass, banged the stick on the ground five times, then stopped and watched his friends.

There was quiet. Tina inhaled the perfume of tropical flowers and paused to notice the explosion of green all around them, stretching up and out toward the bright blue sky. She pitied the old man for what he couldn't see and envied him for what he understood. They both stood for a moment until he finally spoke, staring at Tina as if he could actually make her out: "You have a remarkably generous spirit. That means something. It's large. Far larger than any field I've consumed myself with in the past. And I've looked at some large fields."

"Believe me, there are no regrets." She put a gentle hand on his shoulder. "I wouldn't have met you."

They both were quiet again for another moment. She took a deep breath and, picking up and opening the envelope left for him, began leafing through the papers.

"Shock," he said. "That's Slayde's modus. He didn't invent it, but nobody's ever exploited it like him. And the biggest shock is that my nephew, whom, I am not proud to say, I barely know, volunteered to work with a computational molecular biologist—Anna Brighton, a very promising young scientist—and that he took over the trust, no doubt having to wade through my papers, which I must also confess represent years of disarray. The sheer drudgery of it. Why would he—"

"You should see the contract he signed." Tina flipped to the last page to look at it again. "The sheer exuberance of his signature, 'John Bertram Gropes.'"

"He did it for the money. Is that it?"

"No," she said. "Trust me. This is a man in love."

24

BERT BREATHED IN THE HEAVENLY AIR.

Wearing his new jean jacket, Stetson hat, and cowboy boots, he placed his right foot on a rock and—hands on hips—tilted into the horizon, stretching the left hamstring and calf muscles, surveying his domain, drinking in the intoxicating stillness. He didn't just look out at the valley from the ridge top near his ranchito in the foothills east of Sacramento. Instead he practiced his impassive gaze, holding the bottom half of his face perfectly still—mouth shut—while the eyes above squinted stoically ahead. In this mode, Mansfield Academy was no more than a speck somewhere out there on the flatland before him. Behind Bert, a gleaming cobalt blue Ford Ranger—dealer stickers branding the windows and plates— grazed on the dirt road behind him. He snapped a mental photo of himself, one that captains of industry probably would envy to have of themselves commanding the cover of *Fortune* or *Entrepreneur*. Under the guidelines his donor-dad had laid down, would it be all right to include photographs? How could he be stopped?

The sale hadn't yet been finalized due to a delay in obtaining approval of financing from the bank, but the owner of the ranchito, who was eager to sell, had taken Bert's nonrefundable down payment and let him move in. With a teacher's salary, financing was not a shoe-in. He'd submitted his tech advisory agreement with WHAT/Mother as part of his loan application. Because the bank needed to verify income from Isle Libido, a foreign country, loan approval was going to take longer than usual.

Bert began blinking his eyes and rubbing his forehead, which ached from all the squinting exercises. He leapt back in his truck and drove back down the hill. Pulling up to his ranch house—a muddy red with off-white trim—and stepping down from his truck, he made sure his boot heels hit the ground first. It had been impossible in the two-minute drive back down to his ranch house to keep both hands on his hips but, back on dirt—*his* dirt—he assumed the stance and continued his vigilant survey.

The ranch. The truck. Money in the bank. More on the way. Not a problem. Not for the new Bert Gropes—JB, self-styled rugged individualist.

Could it get any better? As if merely willed and it was so, Anna was driving toward him. From the bottom of the driveway, a cloud of dust announced her arrival. She had called him at home in Woodland yesterday to tell him the Cell Shock software was ready for Bert who, in turn, could deliver it to his license partners. He told her he'd bought a ranch and was moving a first load of boxes up there on Saturday; would she like to check out his new place? "A ranch? Are you kidding? I'd love to see it."

Bert couldn't see her car yet, but he could faintly hear it getting closer. He imagined that the billowing trail of dust it left behind was actually smoke. He wanted to believe the smoke found its source in body heat, smouldering and volatile, that now propelled her up the hill toward him. Bert pictured that when she saw him on his ranch in his jean jacket, his Stetson angled just so, she would burst into flames of passion. He wouldn't take her in his arms right away. Sorry, but she'd have to suffer a little first. There were things he'd need to do before he swept her up in his arms. For example, he'd have to hitch up his pants. After all, he'd gone to a lot of trouble last week to purchase the right belt buckle. Not so fast, his look would tell her as she started towards him, parched for his cool waters. He would look sideways, calmly plucking the toothpick from between his teeth and flicking it twenty feet, sailing it end over end through the window of his cobalt blue Ford Ranger, landing it perfectly on the console tray...

Just then he heard a car door open. It was Anna in the flesh. The first thing he saw was her scrumptious lime-green tennis shoe emerging from the car pointing toe first at the ground.

"Hi," she said. When she emerged and stood, her form-fitting jeans trumped the big-galoot ones he wore. Suddenly the hat felt silly on his head.

"Look at this place," she said, smiling. Today he detected a smile of approval he'd never seen before. "And look at this setting. Pristine. This is the way it's supposed to be." She did a slow one-hundred-eighty degrees that came back to Bert. She gave him a full head-to-toe and then back up again.

"And look at you. New pick-up, new get-up. I never pictured you in Western. It's immutable fashion but always the fittest, biologically speaking. Out here anyway. I like it."

He felt a delicious hot flash: Anna's mark of approval searing his flesh, branding the new Bert—rancher, tech adviser, babe magnet.

"Don't just stand there with your hands on your hips giving me that funny look. Give me a tour."

"I've got two and a half acres." He was feeling his oats now. "It's a real working ranch." Pinching the brim of his hat, he made an imperceptible adjustment, then waved a finger out to where she had just surveyed. "Those are almond trees. Over there figs. A creek runs through it. I'll show you. But first, right this way, ma'am."

They started in the front hall and moved into a hallway towards the master bedroom, entirely vacant but for three boxes against a wall. She walked into the space between two windows where the bed belonged.

"No bed? Where are you sleeping?"

She seemed surprised, almost disappointed. That's when Bert's imagination barged into the room like a stallion, causing a riotous clackety-clacking on the empty hardwood floors. Out of the pandemonium his desires, riding atop his imagination, managed to organize themselves into a loop, a lasso wildly whirling at her.

He kept his cool. "The bed arrives next weekend." When she came for dinner that night, she'd seen the forlorn twin of his in his mother's house. "A California king," he felt compelled to add. Curious eyes darted up at his and swiftly away.

"Bert, this place is fantastic. How did you do it? I'd love to wake up in a place like this. My apartment bedroom looks out at a stucco wall next door." Now she was standing with hands on her hips. Bert felt a stronger stirring of desire.

They moved into the living room. Anna bounced on light feet around the room, taking it all in. "I love this," she said, stroking the stone on the fireplace, flanked by French windows in natural wood that looked out at a cluster of oak trees.

"What about a couch? You can't have a fireplace without a couch for sitting in front…" She spread her hands where it should go.

"Arriving next Friday after class. It's blue."

"Perfect. Let me help you practice sitting in front of a roaring fire in your *house* on your *ranch* up in the mountains."

Bert couldn't help but think that she really did regard him more favorably now that he was a rancher, and a landed one at that. For a moment he considered how unfair it was—that someone in his position only a few weeks earlier didn't stand a chance against those with means, especially substantial real estate holdings—but after seeing Anna drifting through his new house in a trance, the born-again rugged individualist concluded: Tough, that's the way the fortune cookie crumbles.

Anna slid two sturdy boxes marked "Books" in front of the fireplace. She perched herself on one and pulled him down by the right hand onto the other. "Sit down. I'm going to read your palm."

"Palm reading? Where did you learn that?"

"My aunt Delia taught me. She lived with my family when I was in high school." Anna paused and bit her lip reflectively. "I was already deep into science courses back then. What Aunt Delia taught me was considered anti-science. But I didn't see it that way. In retrospect, I think she was a strong influence in my deciding much later to take a year off and work with your uncle."

As she spoke, and in some kind of ritual to begin the reading, she drew light circles in the center of his palm as if to cause the significance of the lines to become more visible. She then grew quiet, slowly tracing the lines, examining them under an invisible microscope. He felt an exquisite glowing sensation run through his hand and up into a hidden recess of his brain, until then asleep. He recalled experiments with lab monkeys he'd read about. When shown how to activate the pleasure center in their brains with a push of a button, the monkeys would choose pleasure, forsake eating, and starve themselves to death. Bert's understanding of the choices monkeys made was deep and abiding.

"This line just below the pinky is your heart line. See how yours extends all the way to your index finger. That means you're an incorrigible romantic." She didn't look up.

Romantic was not the most accurate description of how he was feeling right now. Did palm readers have a rote word they used that meant *savagely hungry for the touch of a woman*?

"Really?" he asked.

"Why, I see that you will grow old here," she read on. "I see three children and a fourth on the way. I guess you were right. This *is* a real working ranch." She laughed at her own joke. He couldn't tell if she was really seeing that or just teasing him, but he forced a breathless laugh anyway.

"See here? This is what's really interesting." She tapped a spot where his wrist and hand intersected. "This line here that circumnavigates the thumb—that's your life line. Where it begins down here at the wrist is about your origins, where you come from. Yours is very curious." He could tell she was serious now, the way she squinted through her glasses. "This little one that feeds into the life line—this short one on the right that seems to come straight from the base of the thumb—I've never seen this on anyone else. Look how thick it is. I'm not sure what it is but I know it's powerful. We know it shapes your destiny because look here. See where your lifeline suddenly thickens the same way? I see a big event in your life. Look how the life line, head line, and heart line all parallel one another right there. A big event, Bert—that's exciting—involving life, love, intellect."

Bert fully bought into it all, but there was only one future event that mattered to him. He wanted to take her and kiss her, this time in a way that she would connect with him and all that was inside him. But he couldn't take her in his arms. It had been a complete disaster the last time out. Nothing had changed since that fateful dinner, except they'd become better friends, just as she'd wanted.

"Is it good or bad?"

She hesitated for what seemed an eternity. "Well," she said slowly and with only a dim smile. While she thought it out, she kneaded the sides of his hand with both of her own. "It's what we'd call a life event. That's definitely major." She squeezed his hand and stood up.

"Right," he echoed on cue, but he couldn't stand up with her.

A big problem had come up, bigger than his heart line and thicker than his aberrant lifeline. Until now he had successfully contained the wild horse in his head, but now his desire—having jumped out of the saddle, bent on recognition—was rattling in its cage, poking its head into his jeans, right below the shiny belt buckle.

"My hope is," he sent up a smoke signal, "that this is my year to win the Harold Bonner Civics Award. Presented to the outstanding Civics, History or American Government teacher in Yolo County 'who demonstrates exceptional innovation and effectiveness in imparting the values of our Founding Fathers.' That would be a big breakthrough in my career as a teacher. That's my dream anyway."

"That would be great," she encouraged with a lovely smile. "Now, I have to get going pretty quick. But before we finish the tour, let's take care of business." She reached into the bag strapped over her shoulder and, pulling out an envelope, held it out toward him. "Here's the software."

"Great!" He reached for the envelope, leaning towards it awkwardly from his low seat atop the box.

She withdrew it to her side. "Not so fast. We need to talk."

"What is it?"

"I've done a little checking around." She shook her head. "No one at the University or anyone in the industry I've talked to has ever heard of this company Mother DNAture."

"I told you they're new, one of those emerging growth companies." He couldn't believe he'd said "emerging growth."

"I went on the Internet. Not much information there. The new WHAT/Mother site is under construction. Mother DNAture's site, however, says they're headquartered on the tiny Caribbean island of Libido, not exactly a hotbed for biotech. More like tourism and gambling. It looks like they're doing legitimate bioinformatics, looking to expand into agri-tech, but the site didn't list any of their principals. Usually, there's something about a lead scientist. Strange. Are you comfortable with that?"

"Me? I'm comfortable." He crossed his legs, nearly falling off the box in the process. Technology was, to his way of thinking, synonymous with control. Right now he was all biology and no technology.

"I know, but I just want to make sure they do a good job. That they do honor to your uncle. Especially if he's…you know, not found." She paused once again to quietly air her grief. "I'm sure you and I both want that legacy to be in as dignified a way as possible. Cell-STL Force represents the breakthrough, the crowning achievement of his life's work."

"I was just thinking about that."

She stood silently a respectful moment. That, together with the image forced upon him of his grizzled Uncle Gro, acted as a bucket of cold water—splash!—right on the mark, minimizing his problem.

"I knew you'd agree," she said. "OK, here it is in object and source code." She handed him a disk inside a sleeve. "Do not let this get into the wrong hands."

Bert took a sobered breath. "Relax. Trust me, I've got the situation under control."

"Good." She grabbed him by the hand. "Now, get up and take me to see this 'creek that runs through it.'"

25

SAYLA V, THE VIDEO-PORN DIVA, WAS SLINK-
ing down the hallway toward Ernie Putterman, who was standing outside a reception room in the casino hotel. She was
wearing tight pink pants, a tighter white halter top, and white
pumps. Putterman prided himself in having worked with top
scientists, high-tech and biotech startups, university research-
ers and inventors, but this gathering set a new benchmark for
his career. Luminaries from the online adult-entertainment
industry had flown in earlier today, Saturday, from around
the world, mostly the U.S., for two full days and a series of
sales presentations. Their stay at The Urge, of course, was fully
comped by Dick Slayde.

Arriving at the door for the evening's first event—a cocktail party, welcome and overview presentation, Sayla V herself
stood face-to-face with the lawyer. She was holding a paper
cup of coffee in one hand and a jelly sweet roll on a napkin in
the other.

"Hi, Sayla. I'm Ernie Putterman, Primal Urge's patent attorney. Loved you in *Vampish Vixen*. Rented it twice."

"Ernie-Ernie, the patent attorney," she said in her familiar, slightly hoarse voice, her mouth half full. "How sweet." The jelly smudge on her upper lip seemed to iterate the candy red lipstick and makeup she wore, at the ready for bright lights and cameras, up close and personal.

"Paid late charges both times," he added.

Vampish Vixen, the first in the now-celebrated *V Is For* series, launched her career. Putterman was tempted to show off and recite the whole *V* series from memory, including *Venal Desires, Vacuum-atic Villainess* (winner of an X-cellence Award last year at the ceremony in Los Angeles), and *Valley Girl Interrupted and Corrupted*. He read in *Triple X News and Reviews* that "Sayla continues to have her V namesake explored thematically," having recently performed in *Piece to All Men* and *Five Is Company*—soon to be released, shot in two weeks back to back—and that she was currently studying the script for *Widespread Hunger*. She was such a celebrity now that she was producing her own films. Her *www.saylav.com* website, what brought her here today, got more hits in an hour than all the sluggers of Major League Baseball did in a decade.

"How 'bout you lettin' me give it to you?" Putterman asked, his wink implicit, as he held up a three-ring binder of materials. He stood next to a table where two seated Slayves were helping hand out a stack of them.

"Sure," she laughed throatily. "Stick it right here." While still holding her coffee on one side, on the other she parted her jelly sweet roll arm just enough to give him an opening. He inserted it, taking care to place the binding directly under her armpit so it could be held securely. He could tell she appreciated that.

"How am I doing?" he said.

"Oh, yeah, that's good."

When she clamped her arm down on it, his right hand became caught between the binder and what felt like a fully inflated soccer ball. It was one of Sayla V's cosmetically re-engineered and equally world-famous breasts. She giggled when she realized his hand was caught and squeezed tighter. Ernie Putterman was in heaven.

"Thanks, Ernie, you're a love." Ernie extracted his hand and Sayla V disappeared into the room.

Putterman was aflutter, beside himself. Right out in the middle of the hallway at the Primal Urge Casino, he'd slid into second base with no less than the Vampish Vixen herself. Hearing the distant ring of a jackpot, he couldn't help but think he was overdue to get lucky beyond second base. He'd made several extended trips here over the last six weeks, but unfortunately the airport was the only destination he'd been in and out of. He hadn't seen any of the action he'd dreamed about. But it was not too late… if he played his cards right.

He and the two Slayves continued to hand out copies of the binder until the last arrived. Some stood there in the hallway to scan the content. The bright cover, large red letters on pink, announced:

WHO SAYS YOU CAN NEVER GO BACK?

DELIVERING WHAT HUMANS WANT DEEP DOWN

PRIMAL URGE PROUDLY ANNOUNCES

HOT MONKEY LOVE

A legend was printed at the bottom: "CONFIDENTIAL: FOR VIEWING BY PRIMAL URGE VIPs ONLY." Inside, opposite the title page, today's visitors were further enticed:

Our HOT MONKEY LOVE technology is the missing link to maximum profits. When you see and, better yet, *feel* what it does, especially to your revenue projections swinging higher and higher, we're sure you'll go ape. To become one of our Monkey Love partners, you'll need to sign the included "Website Linking Agreement" with the newest member of the Primal Urge family of companies, WHAT/Mother. As a VIP (Very Important Pornographer) you'll be taking advantage of our obscenely high referral rates.

Dick Slayde, wearing a pair of smooth, flesh-colored leather pants and a red silk shirt, emerged from the theater and spoke to Putterman: "I'll let them know they can ask questions about the agreement tomorrow in your presentation. We'll keep it to a minimum today and start collecting sign-ups."

The two of them walked into the theater. Tatiana Lurenski was on stage at the mic. "Thanks to each and all ones of you for coming," she said. "We cannot be waiting to tell you what is new and so excited. So, I please myself to introduce the founder of Primal Urge Entertainment. Please to welcome our chairman, Dick Slayde."

The VIPs of the online entertainment world, almost two hundred of them in the audience, clapped as Dick Slayde walked down the aisle in front of Putterman and took the stage. An overhead screen dropped down and showed two Libidoan monkeys *in flagrante*.

"Today we are not here simply to supercharge revenue for your websites. That would be an understatement. By unleashing Hot Monkey Love on the world, as you will come to see, we are rewriting the evolution of our species. We're also creating a new science, a new industry. Combining both pornography and biotechnology, I've named it *biopornology*."

The screen split; the image on the left was a human couple in the throes, and on the right was a scientist in a lab coat, examining a test tube.

"Hot Monkey Love brings together the very best of shameless, unbridled sexual abandon and cutting-edge biotech. We're not talking about Viagra, herbal medicines, or club drugs—mere fluff on dandelions that will never withstand the gale winds." He paused for effect. "Are you ready? The biopornological solution I'm introducing to you is *three-hundred-fifty-seven* times more effective."

The crowd of pornographers gasped, screamed, and groaned. Instantly they were on the edge of their seats.

"And unlike the others, the effects are not transitory. With repeated use, they're permanent."

More gasps of amazement.

"Let your imagination recall, if you can, the golden age of sexual fervor. Forget about high school. Let's go all the way back to a million years ago. Back when doing it was not a mere amusement to bide your time on a rainy afternoon in your apartment, your cushy suburban bedroom. Rather, when the shrieks of pleasure announced to the surrounding jungle that yours would be the species to survive."

The screen displayed a graph with a vertical line for "Male Hominid Sustainability" and, left to right, a horizontal timeline. The graphic line peaked impressively with "ape/early primate," dropped but maintained with "Paleolithic" and "Mesolithic," and then, starting with "Neolithic" ten thousand years ago to "modern man," it lost its vector altogether, going from drop to droop to a hands-down free fall.

"Yet the genes of modern *Homo sapiens* are virtually identical to the early primates. What happened? The genes are still there, but they've been decommissioned, one by one switched off over the course of a million years. The biopornological technology, Hot Monkey Love, switches them back on, all at once."

Someone behind Putterman tapped him on the shoulder and handed him a stack of about thirty agreements. Signed! The presentation was already a huge success.

"Now let me tell you briefly how it works. To understand how anything works or behaves you have to strip it down first. Am I right?" He got laughs and murmurs of shared agreement. "For this I need to tell you about naked chickens, naked mice, and how your customers, naked apes, will access and use the technology. Hot Monkey Love is based on pioneering shock technology I developed thirty years ago."

A black and white photograph of a rooster filled the screen.

"While I used principles of shock technology to found and run my publishing business, our business partner applied my shock technology to chickens. Seems that genetically engineered naked, or featherless, chickens have a plight far worse than modern man. By taking key sequences in the genome of the jungle chicken—who's akin to the ape/early primate on our graph—and deriving from the genome a series of electrical charges that can be applied to the naked chicken, the dormant genes in the latter switched back on. Think of a computer screen freezing up. If the computer is turned off and then turned back on, what didn't work at all—was frozen up—fires up again. No new software is loaded in; you've just switched the old stuff back on. Think of it this way: We're just rebooting the Hot Monkey Love that's already inside all of us."

An illustration was displayed of a naked rooster with wires to his head.

"The software that makes this happen is called Cell Shock-Transmitted Life Force. We've simply taken the algorithm that delivers jungle chicken genome to the naked ones and substituted in sequences of the Libidoan monkey which, incidentally, was mapped right here in Libido by our own Mother DNAture Bioinformatics."

Approving mutters ensued as an illustration of a man seated in front of a personal computer flashed onto the screen. More signed agreements were landing on Putterman's lap.

"So how do visitors to your site actually use the monkey tech? Of course, we provide free digital advertising on your site. The user then links to our WHAT/Mother site where the user must then choose between two doors to click open: a pink "Her Hot Button" which turns on a different set of genes in the human genome—viva la difference!—or, as in our example, a blue "His Hot Button." He enters a credit card number and clicks once to show agreement to the terms of use. Now he's set to download the software." A series of images showed the familiar sequence of an online transaction.

"The app is downloaded into the notebook computer, tablet or mobile device. The vibrational tone from the proprietary audio file modulates a pulse that mimics key sequences in the monkey genome. The ears are the portal to the target molecules where there are billions of strands of DNA. So the user need only plug in and put on his earbuds or his headset, tightly fitted and with the volume turned up. Now he's ready. By clicking on START, the modulated current rhythmically pulses into the targeted control center in the brain, activating dormant genes the same way they are active in the Libidoan monkey."

An image flashed on the screen of a smiling Libidoan monkey in the wild holding a tablet computer and wearing a wireless headset, evidently Bluetooth enabled.

"Within a minute those genes are warming up, cooking in their own stew and, before you know it, only one thing will douse the fires in his flesh."

The final image showed the man transplanted from his four-walled room into a lush jungle scene. With a synthesized drumbeat added, he was standing tall under a roaring waterfall, a Sayla V look-alike fully attending to him.

"...And that would be Hot Monkey Love!"

The audience broke into spontaneous applause.

26

BERT'S BOOTS STOOD SENTRY AT THE FRONT door while he spent the last hour dusting around the house. What else was there to do until his furniture arrived next week? It wasn't just that his animal slippers were more comfortable; with each insufferably loud step he took in his cowboy boots in each hollow room of the big empty house, he was reminded just how all alone he was.

While taking a break from dusting detail in the bedroom, he walked out into the living room and stood, hands on hips again. He had so much to think about. Where to do it? He could put his boots on and walk out to the creek to stare at the water crossing his land or, for the second time today, he could drive up to the top of the hill in his pickup, put his left boot on the rock, and then lean into his expanded universe.

While leaning earlier in the day, he thought about what he liked now about his life. The ranch and the truck definitely. He liked his teaching job; it would be even better if he could lose

Margaret Tillman. He liked the deal he struck with Tatiana Lurenski—although holding only a few wild cards, it might have been the best move of his life. The first of July was a few weeks away and he was ready to finish that letter to his father. The key to surviving today was to channel his aching desire the only way he knew how—compulsive, obsessive dusting.

Bert heard a rap on the window in the living room coming from behind him. Turning to see what it was, he had to blink twice. It was Anna! She was waving her hand and smiling. Was this another one of his hopelessly wishful dream sequences? When she saw his face registering both surprise and recognition, she stepped back from the window and opened the palms of her hands as if to say—

He had no idea what she was saying, or what was going on. Had she forgotten something yesterday? It couldn't be the Beluga whale CD. He'd told her weeks ago she'd left it, but for some reason she'd wanted him to hold onto it.

He opened the front door.

"Hi…" Her voice seemed strained, slightly distant.

"Hey, Anna, come in."

She drifted past him, going straight for the fireplace. "I have to go to Vacaville today." Her right hand traced the stones and she gazed at them, not Bert. "When I got to the freeway, instead of going west, I watched myself go to the next ramp and head east. That was forty minutes ago. Can you believe that?"

"I've been dusting," he said as if all she had just said was: "What kind of house-cleaning have you been doing today?" He stared at his feet covered in large-sized Ultra-Woolies retrofitted with leopard motif—twin Quiet Spots. "But not with these. I have a dust mop, dust cloths, Handi-Wipes. The works." He waved a hand in the direction of the other rooms.

"Bert." She looked up at him. "There's something we need to talk about."

"OK."

He had a foreboding feeling that this was a continuation of

the brief conversation they'd had yesterday about business. He dreaded to learn from her what more she'd found out concerning the biotech firm, Mother DNAture, or the possible connection of Primal Urge to the license he'd given.

"I'd like to sit down, if you don't mind. I'd be more comfortable."

"Sure." He glanced around, as if furniture might have materialized in the last two minutes. "Will this be OK?" He pointed to the two boxes, still together, they'd sat upon yesterday.

"No. I'm sorry. Isn't there a normal place to sit?" She, too, cast about, seemed irritated.

"How about my truck?"

"OK."

Bert opened the door and she walked out first. He saw his boots and paused. No time to put them back on. Was there something in the Ford Ranger owner's manual that said you had to wear boots at all times in the truck? Probably not, but there might be something that warns against using "anything that poses a risk of impeding the driver's accelerator-to-brake foot motion, e.g., excessively fluffy slippers." At this moment his problem was figuring out where she was going to steer this serious discussion. What if she'd been contacted directly by Tatiana Lurenski? He doubted Anna would be favorably impressed. What if she were to find out, from someone other than him, that he'd received a big check from Primal Urge and bought the house with it? She might never speak to him again.

They walked across the yard, opened the doors, and crawled into the truck—he in the driver's seat, she in the passenger's.

"Bert," she said, wasting no time. "I think I'm falling in love. I've fallen in love."

He must have flashed her an especially quizzical look. "With you," she added.

She was beautiful. She was brilliant. She was filled with the kind of goodness he adored, and she said she loved him. For the second time today—on cue, now an encoded response—he leaned forward into his new and boundless universe. He put his right hand gently around her neck and pulled her near to him. Her lips reached for his. They kissed. Sweeter than even he'd imagined, she tasted of a warm and wildly tropical fruit compote, zestily fresh yet fermented to the point he could become drunk.

Anna took a breath and hugged him closely, ear to ear. "Oh, Bert, when I said no... that time at your house... at the other house, I was saying no because, well, I didn't know you. I was afraid. But you are such a dear friend. You're a great teacher. Your students love you. You're smart, like your uncle. You have a good heart. You've been so good." She laughed breathlessly. "I'm getting swept away."

Her wave of gushing washed over him. His heart was racing. "I'm overwhelmed," he finally said. "I've always loved you. It's never been a secret. You know how I feel."

"I do. Perhaps more than you're aware." An impish curl adorned the corner of her mouth. "Yesterday, as always, you were a perfect gentleman. I could see what agony you were in when, you know, we were sitting on the boxes. Before I got into computer biology, I'd seen that look in lab animals sacrificed for life-saving research. Back then it would always break my heart. You were so selfless about it."

Bert blushed. He was so sure the shares in his emerging growth company had been privately held. "So you know how I feel. All too well."

"I feel the same way." She paused and assumed the voice of a breathless seductress. "Such a tiger..." Glancing down at his leopard slippers, she appeared to suppress laughing out loud, staying in character. "You're one sexy guy, Bert Gropes." His toes wiggled involuntarily. That caused the two leopard heads to bob affirmatively.

They laughed and kissed again, this time with more hunger.

Bert took a breath. "Then if I feel a particular—a special particular—way about you, and you know exactly how I feel...

Then if it's true you feel the same way I do, and if I got this right…" His syllogism needed a lot more premise-building, but he made up for it with inflection.

"I *do* feel the same way you do. Believe me I do." She laughed. "But we gotta cool our jets for now. For starters, there's not a stick of furniture in your house. If we were to…you know, there's no place here…"

"You're right," he said. "We should wait."

Their conversation had evolved, or devolved, into good old-fashioned hot talk. Fine with him. The man with nothing better to do a short while ago was a thing of the past. Now Bert was a man with a mission. He turned his head all the way around and appraised the bed of his pickup. There were two old canvas drop cloths strewn about, together with the ropes he'd used to cover and secure the boxes he'd moved from Woodland this morning. Now that he thought about it, the payload of his pickup put to shame that California king he'd scheduled for delivery later this week.

"No," she said, reading the large-print open book that was his mind. "Don't even think about it."

"Just trying to be a problem solver."

"I love the gentleman. It's the animal in him that I don't know and who frightens me a little." She laughed again and, after running her fingers through his hair, gave the back of his neck a rub. "When you have your new furniture next weekend, I'd love to come for a slumber party on Saturday. If you're throwing one, that is."

"Huge sleep-over party," he hastened to assure her. "And you're definitely on the guest list. Along with the usual party animals: leopards, cheetahs, lions, monkeys—"

"I got dibs on Jungle Heat."

"Yours." His heart leapt that she remembered the name of the infamous monkey slippers that sexually assaulted her that night, and that now she wanted to wear them, and hopefully nothing else, around his house next weekend.

"Great," she said. "I've got to go. Off to Vacaville. What are you doing now?"

"I'm leaving shortly. Shopping for kitchen items and cookware."

"Mr. Domestic." She smiled with approval. "Maybe not such a wild and wooly cat after all." She reached over and pinched his calf above the right slipper. "Promise you'll call later."

"I will."

She gave him a quick kiss, jumped out of the truck and headed for her car.

Bert sat in his Ranger for another fifteen minutes. There was so much he liked about his life, but all of it could be reduced to two words: Saturday night.

27

ERNIE PUTTERMAN WAITED OUTSIDE THE RENÉ
Louis Pardon conference room in hopes that he could have
another one-on-one encounter with Sayla V. His desire to see if
he could get her attention was irrational but irresistible. Didn't
the Vampish Vixen and the star of over one hundred fifty porn
films flirt with all the men she encountered? But he swore yesterday that she was flirting with him—with him and him alone.
Could she really have just wanted him? No getting around it.
Ernie Putterman was special. His animal magnetism didn't
need activating.

The nine o'clock Sunday morning breakfast and briefing,
according to the program, after more remarks from Dick Slayde,
featured *The Linking Agreement: Questions and Answers* presented by Ernest Putterman, Esq., patent counsel to Primal
Urge; partner, Pynne, Pencilgirth & Needlemeister, with offices
in Miami and Libido. Within a few minutes Putterman would
be introduced, and his opportunity of turning the tables—of

letting her see *him* in action—would be missed if she didn't show up soon.

He could hear Dick Slayde's muffled voice through the closed door of the banquet room. His client had not been happy when he returned from visiting Professor Gropes without any prospects of acquiring his notebook that proved his pioneering work. He'd never had a client with such unrealistic expectations. He'd tried to explain to him several times—the legal reason, not just the ego vindication—why they needed it. Armed with *The Shocking Details*, under the legal doctrine of *anticipation*, Putterman could have the Undercurrent patent declared invalid, paving the way for its use by anyone. Without it, PharmLife's Undercurrent patent would issue and prevent Primal Urge from using a vital feature of Hot Monkey Love everywhere in the world outside of Libido, where there were no such laws.

"I didn't hire you to hear about problems," Slayde growled. "Just tell me how I get control."

Just then, back in the hallway of the casino and undulating toward him—a human wave machine in white short shorts, pink halter top, disheveled blonde hair, all hoisted on a pair of Manolos—came the object of Putterman's rash desire. This time Sayla V was carrying a SplUrge the size of a Big Gulp, garnished on top with slices of orange, papaya and lime. In the center, under a neon-colored umbrella, two plastic monkeys embraced, each with his and her ludicrously large tongue unfurled. Another hung upside down on the rim of the bucket-shaped container without need of arms or legs.

"Good morning, Sayla," Ernie said eagerly. "I'm the first act this morning. Hope you like it." He was in the world of entertainers now; *act* sounded so right.

"Ernie-Ernie, *the* patent attorney!" She licked the inside of the container still three-quarters full. "Are you kidding, Ernie? I'm not going to miss it. The all-Ernie scene."

"Great," he said. "You won't be disappointed."

As she wiggled away from him, she glanced once over her shoulder, her tongue pitched deeply into her SplUrge. Putterman was beaming as he entered the banquet room and stood in the back. He started to think about what kind of stroke her last remark actually was. The "all-Ernie scene?" Did she mean like a Sayla soliloquy—one of those dramatically erotic scenes with just her and a plaything of such heft that, when plugged in and switched on, dimmed all the lights on the set?

"What's going to be the launch strategy?" a woman was asking. "When you go live this Thursday, are you going to carpet bomb the net with pop-ups?"

"No," Dick Slayde answered. He was taking questions, following a few introductory remarks. "We're soft-launching at first. Since, under the Linking Agreement, we are taking a percentage of your entire business, we want to drive as much traffic through your site before they get to ours. To do that, we need some good data to be able to target customers and customize our ads. Once we have all that, we'll go big. But, to talk about the Linking Agreement and legal, let's go to what's next on our program, our patent attorney, Ernie Putterman."

Putterman had hoped for a splashier introduction to get the crowd pumped up for his presentation. Instead, as he walked toward the podium, the clapping—subdued, perfunctory, and sporadic—sounded more like the spanking of soft and helpless flesh. Was that good or bad? In context it seemed like a good sign.

"Remember," Slayde whispered to him sternly before he reached the mic, "we own everything. What we don't own, we control. That's what they want to hear."

From behind the podium, Putterman looked out at the hundred ninety-eight webmasters and webmistresses gathered before him. There were the ex-porn stars, along with twenty-something entrepreneurs, Boy Scout look-alikes, housewives, hairy-chested loudmouths draped with gold chains, and everything in between. Once he was through—a half hour max—the partition would open to a buffet breakfast served on the other side.

"The agreement we've prepared is similar to many others you've seen in the course of your business," Putterman began his presentation. "With ours, however, you have a thirty-day period to cancel and your sign-on fee will be returned. Plus, you'll all have a chance to test drive the technology later today to see for yourself."

"OK," a husky, fortyish-looking fellow wearing large, thick-framed reading glasses, blurted out in a gruff voice. "Let's say I'm more than thirty days out and committed to this thing. I've paid my sign-up fee and I'm paying a percentage of my business to you, and then suddenly it gets Napstered. I'm not going to want to be paying you a percentage of my business when everyone else is using it for free. How do I know that's not going to happen?"

It was Arturo "Jack" Hammer, an adult film star now in retirement, or recovery as the case may be. He'd starred in nearly three hundred and fifty films, a number with Sayla V. The Hammer-V pair-ups probably represented his best work. Putterman had read in *Triple X News and Reviews* that now there was an ongoing quarrel between Jack and Sayla involving their warring websites, something about his using still shots on his website from a film set featuring Sayla, two other men, and a bathtub full of lime-green Jell-O. The film was released but the stills from that scene were never approved by her and, she claimed, were so unflattering that they damaged her professional reputation. Putterman had noticed that Sayla and Jack didn't speak to each other at the cocktail party last night, if that meant anything. Over the course of ten films together, excluding grunts and single word yelps, they'd *never* actually spoken to each other.

"The software, which is protected by copyright, is delivered encrypted and it's programmed for a single use," Putterman said. "The user has to come back each time, maximizing your revenue."

"What are you doing about locking up ownership?" Hammer's tone was now outright surly. "Do you have a patent?"

Putterman, who felt like he was being personally sized up, shifted his stance nervously. "We've applied for a patent under the name *Method for Activating Targeted DNA in Primates as Means for Achieving Penile Erectility*. I've got it completely covered. We own and control this technology."

He glanced at Slayde, who'd taken a seat at a table near the front. His client was smiling approvingly.

"We've filed in the U.S. and just about everywhere in the world except where you're sitting," Putterman added to garner more confidence. "There are no intellectual property laws in Libido, no patents or copyrights granted to anyone that would prevent anyone from doing anything. You could say there's nothing but license to do whatever you want here."

There were a smattering of chuckles and cheers. "Unless there are other questions—"

"If you're switching on monkey genes, aren't you in effect creating a human chimera?"

Putterman knew where this question from the middle of the room was going but never dreamed it would come up this soon. It came from a slope-shouldered young man with dark hair who looked like his skin drew whatever color it had from the cathode rays of a computer screen.

"I don't see how merely turning genes on is a human chimera," Putterman said, pursing his lips with doubt. "Besides, we're not trying to obtain a patent on a human chimera like the Fowl-Man gene, if that's your point."

"I'm talking about the law in Tennessee where I'm from," the young man said. "Since everyone here's website is accessible in Tennessee, any of us could be prosecuted. I'm talking about the Abatement of Human Chimera—"

"And Beastly Degradation of Humanity Act," Putterman spoke over him, showing he was up on it.

"I love it!" piped Sayla V from the back row. "I want a scene of that in my next film!"

"She should!" shouted Jack Hammer, stubbornly refusing to say it directly to her. "It would only improve her reputation."

"A bill has been introduced by Senator Ray Hoffenworth to make it a federal offense," Putterman said. He was amazed to find the adult entertainment crowd the most legally sophisticated he'd ever encountered, more so than venture capitalists, or university scientists. They knew more about the First Amendment and what is legally obscene than all but the lawyers who specialized in that area.

"Oh, that kind of *act*," a disappointed Sayla V said. The tables around her all laughed.

"I'm aware the law makes it a felony to create a human chimera by any means whatsoever, but I don't think that anything like this was intended—"

"I don't know," someone else said. "I've been following that, too. Turning human genes into monkey genes sounds like just the kind of thing that zealous prosecutors would love."

"That's right," said another.

"I don't need that."

"Count me out, too."

"I've been hassled before. Not worth it."

"You've got my signed agreement, but I hereby cancel."

They were caving left and right. Dick Slayde was turned around in his chair and talking rapidly to a table of five. Others were standing up to leave.

"Wait!" Putterman pleaded. "They can't stop us from delivering the software from this Island. This is another country." He was clutching the podium, not concealing his distress.

"Yeah, so all the more reason they'll be looking for American citizens to prosecute who they'll say are doin' some good old fashioned aidin' and abettin'," said a middle-aged woman with a Southern accent. "You all do what you want, but I'm stickin' to a less risky game plan. Who's ready for some beach volley-ball?"

The conference room emptied out in less than a minute. Sayla V was leaving with another woman Putterman recognized from non-lead roles in adult films. "Are you going to come out and play?" she asked him. Her voice this time was more tentative than flirtatious.

"Sure. Be out in a little bit."

"Good, because we've got a court just waiting, all for you." She shared a malicious smile with the other woman.

"So he can play with himself?" her companion said, looking back at Sayla, not at Putterman. They both burst into laughter and walked out.

Slayde stared at the last two out the door then turned around with a grim face. "We are soft-launching this Thursday with or without our linking affiliate program in place."

"That's a good idea," Putterman said. "Libido is a sovereign state. You can do what you want."

"Are you sure?"

"Absolutely."

"Good," Slayde snapped. "Because you're fired. Absolutely. And don't ever even think about sending me a bill."

28

WHEN BERT ARRIVED HOME IN WOODLAND that Sunday evening, he was floating off the ground. Stepping out of his pickup truck, it was as if he'd been outfitted with a special pair of hovercraft cowboy boots. He and Anna had magically connected earlier that day. She'd said he was *one sexy guy*. Bert swooned to think what Anna plainly implied was in store this coming Saturday night. She said she wanted it as much as he did. He knew what *it* was. Within moments of her leaving the ranch, he was counting the days, the hours, to Saturday.

Although not the least bit hungry, he automatically drifted into the kitchen and, without turning the light on, went straight for the refrigerator. He grabbed a Dr. Pepper and shut the refrigerator door. *Pcccht!* He popped open the can and took a gulp.

Remain calm, focus on your job the next few days, and get the new place ready. All should go well, a nameless but trusted voice inside told him. *Just be yourself.*

Bert sighed, relieved. It made sense. As an extra measure of confidence he tried to form a picture in his mind of what that actually looked like, so he could lock it in and not have to think about it anymore. Unfortunately, all he could see was a single shot of himself standing in the living room of his ranch house with his hands on his hips in his new cowboy boots, looking purposeful—a purpose that escaped him right now. He looked like he was wearing a costume; the colors and details in the picture appeared cartoonish. Meanwhile, heaped on top of that image were two dozen more still shots of Anna and him—full-on graphic, with more posing hands on hips: his on his, his on hers.

Bert plopped himself on the upholstered bench in the breakfast nook, clinked the can on the table, and stared blankly at the wall. He recalled one of the things she'd said to him this afternoon when he called her: "You seem to know who you are and what you want. You love being a teacher. You wanted a certain kind of home and you figured out a way to have it. I really respect that." He wasn't sure if that was all true. He didn't know himself as well as she thought he did.

He had to do better. If he expected to hold onto a girl of Anna's caliber, he had to be certain of his own strengths, his core, who he was as a man. This was no occasion to be winging it, as he often did to fill dead air in a listless class. Right now he was in love, by all definitions not in his right mind, and hurtling towards the uncharted and unknown Planet Saturday Night. Now, better late than never, would be a good time to establish contact with air traffic control.

Take A You-Turn: Time to Get Back to You, a paperback spine invited him from the bookshelf four feet away. Up until now he'd rolled his eyeballs at, or glossed over, his mother's Altar of Self-Improvement. He pulled out the *You-Turn* volume and scanned the jacket copy that, in the most accessible terms, promised to help him prepare a "road map to his true self" for peaceful and lasting happiness. It talked about digging down to the "bedrock of your you-ness" for "building your f*you*ture." There were journal exercises to facilitate digging down. Visions of Heinrich Schliemann, master excavator, danced in his head.

He went through more books, pulling the ones that promised to lead him to the "essential you inside" that was the real Bert Gropes. It made sense the more he read about it. Imagine if he tried to teach an American Government class with only a minimal understanding of American history. He'd told his students that they were fooling themselves if they thought they'd be ready to vote in a few years without knowing American history or what the essential American experience was. The more Bert thought about it, the more he realized how he'd stubbornly resisted his mother's invitations to explore who he was and how he got here.

He glommed onto *Being A Human Sponge: The Virtues of Self-Absorption* and another entitled *Knock Knock! Who's There?* subtitled *Who You Are Doesn't Have To Be A Joke.* The latter came with workbook pages of questions about significant events and choices in the reader's life, details concerning perceptions about the reader's parents, their best and most ill-conceived choices, and on and on. When he was done, he looked at five books stacked in front of him on the breakfast table. He put them under his arm and headed off to his room. He was struck by the inescapable similarities between the ordeal of his hero, Heinrich Schliemann, and his own. Having finally received permits from the Turkish government and loaded for bear with more than a hundred men, shovels, and equipment to abrade the earth of a distant land, Schliemann set out to expose the blurred line between truth and fiction; after thousands of years he would bring to daylight the Troy of legend.

Heinrich Schliemann. Ben Franklin. Bert Gropes. Men who dared.

29

IT WAS ANOTHER BEAUTIFUL DAY IN SAN Diego: warm, but not too warm, with a gentle breeze stirring up scents of eucalyptus trees, ocean essence, and a nature's bounty of droppings from animals the way they're supposed to be—real, unengineered, and in captivity. A small stage with podium was set up near the entryway to the world-reknowned zoo. Of the fewer than one hundred people in attendance, most were media or, more discouraging to the promoters of the event, television tech people. It was early yet—9:00 AM—so that clips would be timely for news reports on the East Coast. Tourists seemed to dodge or beeline their way to the front gate, not the least interested in stopping to listen. Finally, with a nod from the TV crews, the speaker took the podium.

"Today I announce my candidacy for the presidency of the United States of America." Amidst the cackles, screeches, and baying emanating from the adjacent community, it was music to Ellis Peek's ears to hear Senator Ray Hoffenworth utter his mantra, *"uh-MURR-kah."*

"I've chosen this setting to speak to my fellow Americans today for two reasons. One, I know I need to carry California if I want to win in November." He paused to offer a self-effacing smile to accompany the implicit laugh track.

A recent poll showed that Vice President Sam Boswell, the presumed nominee to succeed the termed-out President Moon, was ahead in California. Among registered Republicans likely to vote, Boswell led with 42%, followed by a smattering of other candidates, last of whom was Senator Ray Hoffenworth with a paltry 6%. Ellis Peek was not the least concerned, aware as he was that the polls were controlled by Lusians.

"And two, I stand here today to declare a foreign policy that is entirely, irresponsibly, missin' from the current administration. I pledge to all the animals gathered at this zoo that, if elected, we will not invade your species with human genes to create godless chimera. By the same token, let me be clear about what I will do to defend the sacro-sanctity of the human bein'. I will use all the resources at my disposal as President—the Food and Drug Administration, the Office of Homeland Security, the Patent and Trademark Office, or the Armed Forces, exercisin' my powers as Commander-in-Chief—to ensure that this great land, or anywhere in the world that ultimately may pose a threat of a border crossin' of a contaminatin' nature into America, is not invaded by foreign species with foreign genes used as pawns by unscrupulous scientists, evil-doers, or ambitious politicians who may think they can preserve their edge in the polls—"

Just then a burst of banshee cries rose up, together with a wild cacophony of caterwauling, chittering, baying and cackling from the interior of the zoological gardens, the sounds roaring through the trees. Ellis Peek interpreted this ovation, entirely produced by nature, as a sign of the emerging populist appeal of the candidate and what he stood for: Ray Hoffenworth for President of the United States in 2020.

30

WHEN BERT PULLED HIS PICKUP TRUCK INTO the school parking lot, he was bleary-eyed from reading until four in the morning. He'd fallen asleep with *You-Turn* open and face down on his chest. He crooked the rearview mirror down to look at himself. Although tired, his eyes still held a gleam, even a swagger, if that was possible, not there the week before. On this Monday he was eager to start his week.

It was early June and the last week of class, with the temperatures in the mid-eighties—a gorgeous spring day that hinted of nearing summer and much hotter weather to come. On his way into the faculty lounge for a quick cup of coffee before his 9:45 class, Bert gulped air and tried to emerge from his subterranean fantasy world where sexually alluring images of Anna lined the cave walls of his mind.

Margaret Tillman, unfortunately, was leaving just as Bert came in. She looked startled, if not slightly frightened, to behold him. As they met at the door, he found himself beaming a foolish, devil-may-care grin and looking steadily at her in a way that demanded her own eyes look at him. When they finally obliged, his lost interest, and she saw him automatically glance down at her chest. She hurried past, the Fist driving her down the hall to its office command center. But then, "Oh, Bert." Tillman had stopped and was speaking in a pleasant tone. He turned around and faced her.

"Did I hear correctly that you signed some kind of lucrative technology deal for your uncle's trust?" Her breasts ogled him.

Bert smiled. "I don't know how lucrative, but yes, I found a taker."

"I heard you bought a home in the hills and a new truck. That sounds lucrative."

Bert displayed open palms in a gesture of modesty.

"Congratulations," she effused. "You and I are going to sit down and talk next week about what's in store for the fall. I'd like to help you ensure your uncle's legacy."

"I'm just trustee, and doing a little tech advisory on the side. I—"

"Can see you're willing to give some thought to the Gropes Theater, a choice naming opportunity I'm going to hold until we get a chance to sit down. I look forward to it, Bert."

When she turned and was gone, he took a deep breath. He'd managed not to put his foot in his mouth talking to Margaret Tillman this time but, with only two hours sleep, he needed to be on the alert for missteps.

After the bell rang for class to begin, Bert stood silently facing his class for a full count of five before speaking: "This is our last week. I'd like to do an overview of our American and California history, and reflect on some unifying themes. Earlier this year we talked about the laws and conditions that brought about the American Revolution. The Stamp Act. Taxation without representation. English rule was out of touch with life in the colonies. Think about it: Wasn't America like an unhappy, unfulfilled person, like we all feel sometimes?

Someone who leads a miserable life for years and then one day wakes up and says: 'I can't go on this way anymore. I'm going to change.'"

The class—fourteen-year-olds who must have felt they'd been there and plumbed those depths—locked into the image Bert painted as if they'd caught their own reflection in a passing storefront window.

"Last night I happened to read stories of people who went through major turmoil in their lives. In each case, their lives were marked by years of agony and worry, which then brought on upheaval and glorious change. Isn't that personal transformation just like the American Revolution?"

With the mention of "personal transformation," a number of students reacted with expressions of "Huh?" Trevor already started taking notes—unusual for him—as if for later study. For his part, Bert was enthusiastic about today's subject and the approach he'd chosen but, inevitably, thoughts of Anna were competing for his attention.

"You'll see," he continued. "Let's take a closer look and then open it up for discussion, shall we? Before the Revolution colonial America was a rough copy of England, or at least it was supposed to be. The difference was England was the parent, making all the rules, and America was the child, and was supposed to follow them. Now, after the Revolution, the Founding Fathers could have simply copied England with its monarchy and Parliamentarian democracy. And guess what? America's governance would have been just like its parent's."

There were groans at that nightmare.

"Yuck," a few said.

"Gross," said one.

"Boring."

"But they didn't do that," Bert forged on. "The Founding Fathers created something entirely new: a democracy never seen before. Later, and from the United States, California was born. With recalls and referenda, perhaps more wildly democratic than its parent. One democracy inside another over the ages. Believe it or not, this is something right out of some books I was reading last night." His voice rose to pitch his excitement. "Fantastic patterns emerge. And by the way, discovering all this at once was amazingly synchronous, wonderful things all of a sudden happening in my own life. Synchronicity: That's something Carl Jung, a founding father from another realm, came up with and which I can't go into right now—have to stay focused on our social studies panorama—but it reminds me of Manifest Destiny and James Marshall, one happy-go-lucky guy who, you'll remember, found gold in his bed—in his *creek*bed—I mean, in a *California* creekbed at Sutter's Mill in eighteen-forty-eight."

"Mr. Gropes, are you in love or something?" asked Leticia Mariposa, a sweet girl with dark eyes. She looked up at him in bewilderment wearing large, clunky glasses.

It was a much needed sober-up slap. "I can safely say you won't need to know all that for the test," he said with a wry smile. That was all he could think to utter, but it didn't stop the chorus of hoots and catcalls.

"All right, all right, let's settle down—"

"Well," another voice pressed, "are you?"

"None of your bee's wax," he said with a polite but firm tone. "Just as it's none of mine to parade around in front of the class what's going on in your private lives. Remember how we've talked about the right of privacy, the right to be left alone? It's not just for your protection. Your teacher's, too. Now that we've come this far," he continued before there could be a retort to that, "I think you'll enjoy how this all connects with the American Revolution and California history."

Bert held up a book with a woman, a celebrated psychologist, smiling on the jacket cover. "This is a famous book written about twenty-three years ago called *Your Inner Creature* by Dr. Dawn Marie Fletcher. In it she says that we each have in us a perfect creature suited for our lives. This book is practically the bible for the personal growth movement. Dr. Fletcher describes our Inner Creature as something that doesn't have to be in the mold of our parents, society, or what she calls 'self-limiting notions of what nature has in store for us'; blueprints for your Inner Creature have no bounds and come from what is true and fulfilling of your personal destiny and right for the time. She calls it a *creature* because it's something that *you* create—not your parents, not anyone or anything else. But, important to Dr. Fletcher's thesis, finding your Inner Creature is a gradual, long-term process—years, a decade, maybe a lifetime." Bert paused to let that sink in and put the book down.

"What's this got to do with our social studies?" Megan asked, elbow on desk, hand smooshed into her cheek.

"Everything." Bert was clear about the vision he wanted to share with the class. "Then along comes Dr. Albert Berzarian about two years ago and he writes a book, *SLICE of Life: Re-engineering Your Inner Creature For Today's World*—thirty-nine weeks on the *New York Times* bestseller list—that evolves, expands and contemporizes what Fletcher had to say." Bert held up a dog-eared paperback copy that his mother had obviously read and reread. "In it he confirms the quest to bring forth our Inner Creature, but he says it doesn't have to be a lifetime process. Dr. Al, as he goes by, says that, sure enough, we've all got an Inner Creature but it's waiting there—near ready-made, all but fully developed—and it's right below the surface. We are capable of bringing it forth instantly, or relatively instantly compared to the process Dr. Fletcher described. Dr. Al calls the accelerated process the Spring-Loaded Inner Creature Experience, or SLICE." He put the book down.

"It's pretty obvious to me," he spoke with confidence, "that England's Inner Creature was America, and America's Inner Creature was California, and California, even more than the country as a whole, has been in search of its own Inner Creature, probably a spring-loaded one. Maybe it's Yolo County. A place people can speak their feelings freely and do whatever they please in terms of life, liberty, and the pursuit of happiness."

Bert took a breath and pressed his lips together in an expression that conveyed he was satisfied he'd laid the foundation for the discussion to fill the remainder of the hour. It wasn't the model of clarity he strove for but, on short notice and two hours sleep, it wasn't bad either. "Any questions about the gradually emerging Inner Creature, the SLICE of Life, or anything we've covered so far?"

There was silence. Trevor was still scribbling notes. Several in the class looked like they'd been gassed and beaten silly with Nerf pillows. Finally, studious Robert spoke up: "I sort of understand how the Inner Creature is connected to the American Revolution. But I don't get what SLICE is or what Dr. Al has to do with the discovery of gold at Sutter's Mill. The 'spring something experience.' I didn't get it. What is that?"

"Ah, good question," Bert said. "And yes, I certainly can answer it. The Spring-Loaded Inner Creature Experience. That's *spring-loaded*, like a jack-in-the-box—you know, one of those clown-like puppets, stuffed down inside a box, ready to spring out instantly when the top is opened. That's what it means when you combine the two seemingly unrelated words *spring* and *loaded*, but I should also mention that Dr. Al has a nice discussion about both of the stand-alone words in there, *spring* and *loaded*. *Spring*, because that's also the season of new life and, of course, the season of romantic love, for which there are huge chapters in both books. Big agent of change: Think revolution. Following me?" Bert's mouth was moving but he could feel his brain was no longer keeping up. He was exhausted. "And *loaded*, which I recall he said meant having it all, like when they say a new pickup truck comes off the dealer lot fully loaded. Not loaded like when you're intoxicated, as when you don't know what you're doing or saying because of an impairment of your mental faculties, letting your feelings take over and—"

"It's the computer biology lady, isn't it?" Leticia again.

"Anna Brighton," someone piped, followed by a smattering of "yeahs" and whistles of approval.

"Anna Brighton!" another echoed. The sheer sound of her name caused a giant wave of emotion to flood into his face and fill all eyes in the room with a picture—as clear as water from a high mountain hot spring gurgling, bubbling over—of a madman in rapture. He didn't know where it came from. He was grinning uncontrollably, on the verge of laughing for joy.

"All right now," he said, "why don't we open it up?"

31

"AREN'T YOU CURIOUS," TINA ASKED, "WHAT your life would have been like if you'd had a family?" She'd gotten bolder in her questions, only because he'd become, in his funny way, more accessible.

"Naturally," Dr. Gro answered from his wicker chair while Tina sat on the three steps leading up to his porch. "The way I see it is that I've lived my life as a free electron. From an atomic standpoint, that's an electron that's free to move under the influence of an electric field. It's not attached to an atom, an ion, or molecule. I suppose it sounds rather romantic, and perhaps it is, but free electrons are subject to Heisenberg's uncertainty principle, which recognizes that the subatomic world is a roiling chaotic realm in a constant state of quantum fluctuations. Despite my own lifelong inquiry, what it all is remains unknown."

"That doesn't sound fun," Tina said. "Have you been happy?"

"I've been content, but we're talking *Malus pumila* and *Citrus sinensis* here—"

"What?"

"Apples and oranges. If I'd had a family, that would have made me a nucleus…or nuclear, part of a nucleus. Very different from a free electron. From a biological standpoint, a nucleus is programmed to carry genetic material, and control reproduction, metabolism, and growth. That's a lot of responsibility. By the same token, there's more to be known, more certainty in that world. I suppose if I'd reconstituted myself, I could have been happy in that role." He paused and let his lips clasp his empty pipe for a moment. "If I had it to live all over again, I'd choose the best of both worlds. I'd get a dog."

"Dogs are good," she agreed.

"I wouldn't own him though," he added. "I don't believe in that. But if he were of like mind, I see now I could have had the benefit of his friendship." He leaned forward on his cane, his dark glasses motionless.

He'd come a long way since mid-April, almost two months now. He was saying he appreciated having a friend—namely, Tina. She felt his warmth radiating from a strange and distant star. Just then Scooter tumbled twice across the grassy flat in front of the cottage and laughed in the direction of Tina before disappearing into the jungle.

"That's a ten, Scooter!" she shouted after him as she stood up. "I don't care what the other judges say." She stretched her hips from side to side and responded to the old man's last words. "It's not too late. We're going to get out of this hellhole." She went up onto her tiptoes and reached her clasped hands toward the sky. "And when we do, we'll find you that new friend."

Tina let her gaze take in the whole landscape. "Uh oh," she let out. "Looks like we have company." A golf cart, the gunmetal gray one special-ordered by the attorney, was arriving, this time without him. Instead, Dick Slayde was alone in the driver's seat. After he spoke to the security henchman assigned to watch them, the two carts came down the hill to the guest cottages and stopped in front of Tina and Dr. Gro.

Both drivers stepped out. Dick Slayde, apparently fresh off the tennis court, was top to bottom in white, with a vermilion towel around his neck. His sidekick was a burly no-necker, thirtyish, wearing an Urge Casino red t-shirt, sleeves rolled up to expose a mishmash of tattoos covering both arms.

"I'm afraid, Professor, my patience has expired," Slayde said smugly, having fused *expired* with *terminated*.

"If anything's expired, Dick, it's the sell-by date of you and your bad ideas," Tina shouted at Slayde from where she stood on the porch. "Eggs cracked open, rotten, and totally worthless. Pew! You really stink to high heaven!"

Dr. Gro held his free hand up to her as if to say: "Allow me to deal with him." Stepping in front of her, he approached and tapped the new cart with his cane. "I recognize the sound of this one. A whir that's more of a whine. Your lawyer's. Is he—?" Dr. Gro moved his head around with pursed lips as if trying to pick up the whiff of an identifying stench.

"No, he's also been expired."

"Too bad. I found him an interesting study. We talked about that. Remember?" Dr. Gro turned to Tina with a smile that winked.

"Yeah," she said. "He got off just *telling* me he'd ordered the damn machine, before he actually possessed it."

Dr. Gro took a few steps, ran his hands around the outside of the cart and onto the seat, climbed into the cart and put his hands on the wheel. "Imagine, his mere thoughts about it were more thrilling and stimulating than actually operating it. How farfetched is that technology?"

"Primal Urge Biology one-oh-one," Slayde said. "You were the first to teach me that the large organ between the ears— large compared to other primates, anyway—is the most easily excitable of all." He nodded to his thug who scratched his head to let him know he'd never thought about that before.

But I'm not here to ruminate on school days," he said, standing in front of the cart. "Time's up. If you don't see to it that *The*

Shocking Details is delivered to me immediately and agree to join my board, then—"

"You don't seem to comprehend, do you?" Dr. Gro, incredulous and irate, shook his head. "Some things were never intended to be joined together. You and I are two such things." He released the parking brake and let the golf cart slowly roll back a few feet.

"You're wrong and making a big—"

"Fine, Dick. We'll test your theory. Let's smash particles of matter and anti-matter together with our own homemade collider and see what we get. Shall we?" Dr. Gro shoved his foot down on the accelerator and lunged forward at Slayde who easily dodged out of the way. His goon moved at the errant cart, but Slayde waved him off. Dr. Gro negotiated a one-eighty and stopped. Tina watched in amazement as the blind man confidently navigated space he'd only walked upon.

"Be careful!" she shouted from the porch.

"There are some things you should know," Slayde said. "It has to do with your adopted sister. Eugenia."

"I'm beyond your reach," he said, stopping the cart once again.

Tina could see that something was building inside the old man, an anger that pushed at his jaw.

"I'm sure you recall that Eugenia brought her donor sperm to Baltimore where this in-vitro was done," Slayde said. "That was in nineteen-ninety-two. You'll never guess what young geneticist/cellular biologist did the honors."

"I have no doubt." Dr. Gro maintained an even but edgy voice. "You were at Johns Hopkins back then. That's what you do. You pop up in my life. Why should I be the least surprised?"

"I think you should know I took some liberties before implantation."

Dr. Gro began to roll the cart slowly forward again, bird-dogging Slayde's voice. Slayde retreated as he spoke, nimbly weaving a snake-like path, flapping out in front of him the red towel he'd pulled from around his neck. "At the time I'd recon-structed a small part of what you stole from me. Even without having it, I was able to splice in a tiny amount of nonhuman DNA into the embryo. Quite elementary these days but prob-ably a first back then. I'd already begun my study of Libidoan monkeys, and I was able to insert a small amount of Scooter's dad—a marvelous Libidoan named Primo—into the embryo."

"You're sick!" Tina hissed at him. If anyone else had made such a claim, she simply wouldn't have believed it. Now she knew better. This was Dick Slayde—half-genius, one hundred percent slime mold.

"Sordid," Dr. Gro said, slightly increasing the speed of his cart. "Cruel and gravely unethical, to be sure. But shocking? I don't think so. Not from you. Fortunately, the boy is normal. I think I would know if my nephew had some health problem, or exceptional gift for that matter. Before I lost my eyesight, I would have noticed if he were brachiating from room to room by means of fixtures hanging form the ceiling. But no such thing. Your sick experiment was genetically inert."

"Maybe. Maybe not." Slayde was breathing hard from exer-tion. He seemed to relish the sport as he backpedaled, weaving and cutting figure-eights in the grassy area. "But it's another example of my scientific primacy."

Dr. Gro lurched forward, nearly hitting him, but Slayde managed to recover from a staggered step and sweep his cape at the passing bull with a flourish. Slayde's muscleman, having remounted his cart, was now the picador for the improvised contest, edging forward, implicitly offering to subdue the ani-mal with violence. Again Slayde waved him off.

"If—*when* I get off this island, I'll…" Dr. Gro left to Slayde's imagination what he'd do.

"On the contrary, the information will get out, but not you," Slayde shouted at Dr. Gro's backside. "There's a file cabinet in a storage locker in Baltimore that I will lead the police to. Everything is there. They'll confirm by conducting DNA tests and find sequences in his DNA that unmistakably point to what I've told you. Of course, they'll think you're awful. The paper trail I've left will make it appear that you had a hand in it. That will be the scientific legacy they'll remember. Are you sure you don't want to change your mind before that happens?"

The cart turned around again on a small downhill slope and slowly crept back toward Slayde. Tina could tell by the way Dr. Gro's head moved that he responded to even the slightest breath or footstep, but she couldn't believe the game being played out before her eyes, or the stakes for that matter. It was well beyond the world of high rollers regularly flown into Libido, given the VIP treatment, and set loose to gamble away fortunes.

"My driving ambition right now is extermination." Dr. Gro gritted his teeth. "I have to ensure it doesn't breed, spread, and destroy the planet."

"Oh, and speaking of propagation, don't you want to know who your sister's sperm donor was?" Slayde's smile was malicious enough to be heard.

Dr. Gro stopped the cart, his jaw open. "It's true, a monster would not have used the donor she selected. You are a blight on this planet beyond imagining. Is that what you did?" His voice was rising. "Is it you?"

"No. It's you." There was silence. Slayde advanced a full step to within five feet of the cart and paused, letting each of his last three words pummel Dr. Gro over the head. "'G.S. Gropes sperm specimen' the container was labeled, dated nineteen-eighty-nine, and stored in that lab freezer at UCSF. I helped myself to a little of it back then when you were doing your ridiculous human sperm studies. I stole it because you'd stolen my research. Tit for tat. I thought I might need it some day. You've delayed the launch of my career as a biotech pioneer until now. It must have been my good karma, because I couldn't have been luckier when your sister showed up."

"Barbaric! Obscene and twisted," Tina gasped, stunned at the revelation.

Dr. Gro floored it. As the cart instantly gained speed from the down slope, he was plainly bent on nothing less than a bloody goring.

Slayde was ready for him. With cape presented, he light-footed to one side just in time. "Congratulations, Dad," he shouted. He swept the red towel over the top of the oncoming cart as it rushed past. "It's a *humonkey*. Have a banana!"

Dr. Gro didn't let up. He kept going full bore past Tina and the cottage, rumbling out onto rougher terrain, heading toward the cliff that overlooked the ocean.

Tina jumped down from the porch and chased after him. "No! Stop!"

With a little more than fifteen feet separating him from the cliff, Dr. Gro's cart plunged at full speed into a dip, which, upon impact with the other side, sent him airborne. When he hit the path—the same one they walked every day—he went into a roll, coming to within an inch of the edge where he'd ended up in his fall only three weeks earlier. The cart dove off the cliff and was heard crunching into what was now a pile of scrap metal below.

"Dr. Gro!" She was breathless when she reached him.

He was flat on his back, his eyes eerily blank. His dark glasses had landed ten feet away.

"You're inches from the cliff! Thank God you fell out."

"Jumped," he corrected her. His voice was weak. "From the electron path."

She turned around quickly and saw Slayde seventy-five feet away, glowering at the cart-less landscape. He climbed into the one that remained, and the two men departed.

Bruised, but up on one elbow, the old man started to wipe the dirt from his pants.

"Are you sure you're all right?" Tina asked. "Can you stand up?"

"Not yet." He seemed disoriented. "I'm composing myself." He turned his head toward her. "I'm nuclear now." His free hand was shaking, and he must have known she'd seen it. "I'll be all right. It's just shock."

32

June 14, 2019
  Dear Dad:
  I must tell you I've started this letter over and over, never sure what is the most important thing to tell you about me. Whenever I pick up the pen, I ask: Where to begin? My life as a teacher? My new home in the mountains? My startup venture in the children's market? My work as a fiduciary appointed by the court? Or that I moonlight as tech adviser?
  Those are all good, but the best thing that ever happened to me is my girlfriend. Her name is Anna Brighton.

SATURDAY NIGHT ARRIVED AT LAST. SINCE LAST Sunday—when Anna promised to stay over with him once his place was furnished with a real bed—cities had been founded, had thrived, and succumbed to rubble through which tourists now trudged, led by cheery docents; endless wars were waged, and obscure civilizations, known only to a handful of grizzled savants, had come and gone.

At least it seemed that long to Bert.

His house looked like a real home. He'd taken pictures of the living room to Macy's in Roseville where a saleswoman in home furnishings was eager to help him select a burgundy rug "with indigo tones," matching couch and love seat (both dark blue), lamps, and a coffee table. He lit the two scented candles he'd bought while he was in Auburn at a small store featuring an eclectic mix of gifts, household items, and bric-a-brac. When the woman saw him looking at a display with dozens of candles to choose from, she'd asked in a friendly way, "Hot date tonight?"

His rafter-to-rafter smile gave him away. He put one of the candles she recommended on the coffee table and another on the two-seater table where Anna and he would dine. His home was filled with the aroma of pasta primavera with vegetables handpicked by him at the farmer's market in nearby Auburn— easy on the garlic, so as to avoid collateral damage to the evening's Main Event.

When the doorbell rang, Bert wasn't just ready. Everything had come together so flawlessly in the last two days it was as if the universe itself had agreed to step up into the role of Jeeves for him. With no artifice from him, at that precise moment the sound system (winking at him from across the room) launched the Beatles *Greatest Hits*, given to him by his mother on his birthday. They began singing *Penny Lane*—indefatigably lilting, the perfect mood.

With only two days until the official start of summer, the air outside was warm and balmy. Anna stood at his front door— looking fully ripened in his eyes—smiling, bouncing on her heels, and holding a small overnight bag.

"I love it," she said after walking in, putting her bag down on the floors. "Look at how great—" She gazed into the living room.

"I had some help," he said.

She turned around and looked down at his feet. "I'll bet you didn't need any help running that wild animal motif through the house." She laughed at his leonine Comfort Kings.

He turned and stared at the wall facing the front door.

"Brighton? Let's see...Anna?" After scouring the imaginary shelves, his gaze dropped down to the small table in front of him. He plucked the only item on it, a pair of monkey-themed Jungle Heat slippers, and held them out to her. "Ah yes, here, I believe you asked us to hold these."

"I can't wait to slip into them," she purred. She took one in each hand and wrapped her arms around him. He returned her embrace, and when they kissed, it was with such naked ardor Bert had the sensation that wild screeches of brightly colored birds were deafening them, insulating them from the noise of the outside world.

"I'm going to freshen up and put away a few things." She picked up her overnight in the entryway. "Give me about ten minutes. Don't go away."

"Don't worry," Bert said.

He watched longingly at her backside as she moved away from him and disappeared into the far end of the house. He wasn't hungry anymore for pasta primavera. His appetite had become more specialized, more focused and targeted than even he imagined it would. As the currents from her touch coursed through him, his manhood tingled and felt like some kind of ripe-hanging fruit on a bough, on the brink of dehiscence. When he reentered the living room, he burst into song, harmonizing with what, in that golden moment, became the Fab Five—Bert's head sharing a mic scrunched between John and Paul, singing "Hard Day's Night."

While the tangy sauce simmered, he turned the gas burner on for the pasta to boil. The flames leaped up and licked the bottom of the potful of water. It was all too much. His senses began to uncork. He turned and automatically drifted down the narrow hallway toward the light in the bathroom. She looked up in anticipation and smiled at him in the mirror. Bert stepped in behind her and slipped his hands around her waist (artfully avoiding another train wreck of slippers). She put her hands on his arms and squeezed them while he guided her gently backward in a slow dance leading to the accession—and their becoming devoted subjects—of Bert's brand new California king.

The ravishing computational molecular biologist began to tear off the shirt and then the pants of the ravished Social Studies teacher, breaking him down, one layer at a time, to his bare constituents—an interdisciplinary approach he positively savored. As they expressed their desires through their every pore, he knew that this, not some lofty idea, was what put a fire under the legends, giants, and heroes he celebrated in his class. In that instant, before he moved on to more pressing matters, he realized what was so laughably plain: Schliemann was never out to collect a bunch of old museum pots or clumsy statues, not even the priceless gold artifacts he unearthed. Old Heinrich was never ultimately searching for Troy. All he really wanted was Helen, the same way Bert wanted Anna.

As their fevered skins combined—she on her back, he astride her—they were each newly made. No longer merely a presenter of social studies, he was now the subject: an explorer of new worlds, amalgamated with a distinct scientific bent, straddling the bowsprit of the vessel that would take him to his destiny. His hands dove in first and swam to her small yet buoyant breasts as if survival of their species depended on it. When she opened the rest of her waters to him, the fully seaworthy rudder of his being, long up on dry dock, was poised to take the plunge. For the first time in ages he felt like he truly belonged, he was part of all that life offered, and it was exquisite.

33

WHEN THE AROMA OF PASTA PRIMAVERA sauce wafted back to the bedroom, Anna and Bert realized they were both famished.

"I'm going to take a quick shower," Anna said with a dreamy smile. "Then I'll be out to help."

Bert jumped out of bed, throwing his pants, shirt and slippers back on. When he walked into the kitchen, it was a rainforest—an entirely unsustainable one. The pot of water had all but boiled off, and the air was humid with a gallon or more of steam. He turned off the flame, refilled the pot with fresh water, and started the fire again. The flames licked and tongued the bottom of the pot with a renewed hunger that got him to thinking about what had just happened and how he couldn't wait to make it happen again, especially that double-twisty thing the two of them were doing on their sides. He, on his right, draped his left leg over her right with his toes jabbing into the mattress, his other foot pointed skyward while she, for her part, was a perfect mirror of him. The conjunction surely called to mind Franklin's breakthrough proposal to the Continental Congress on July 21, 1775—a draft "Articles of Confederation and Perpetual Union"—the sublime vision of a shared future together tendered by the Gentleman from Philadelphia.

The Beatles sang an encore of "She Loves You" and encouraged Bert's revision of events, both current and venerable. His daydreams continued until there was a knock on the front door. At first he thought Ringo's snare and his own ears had teamed up to play tricks on him. No, he heard a loud rap again. He looked at his watch. It was not yet seven o'clock.

He opened the door to find a vaguely familiar man in a dark suit holding a black leather computer bag in his left hand.

"Hello, Mr. Gropes."

"Hello?" Bert questioned.

"Special Agent Dennis Clamp. FBI, Sacramento." He held out a badge from his wallet at eye level in front of Bert's face. "We met before. Remember?"

"Right." Bert was now recalling the meeting with his mother and the two agents.

"Nice place you've got." The agent's searching blue eyes peered side to side, nodding approvingly. A large and joyless 4-wheel-drive vehicle—a Ford Wasteland, dull white—was parked so as to block the egress of Bert's pickup truck. Bert's blood skidded to a stop, threw itself into reverse, and began hurtling sickeningly backwards, faster and faster. He sucked in a defensive breath.

"I'm following up on details concerning the disappearance of your uncle, Grover Gropes."

"Of course." Bert was slightly relieved that was all, though the agent's timing could not have been worse.

"Mind if I come in?"

"No. No," Bert said but failed to add: *This can't be happening.* After the initial meeting with him and his mother, the FBI could find no evidence of foul play or a motive, kicking it back to local law enforcement. The sheriffs of Yolo, Sacramento, and Placer counties passed the balloon investigation around like a hot-air potato, saying it was not their jurisdiction. The balloon either launched, traveled over, or was found in someone else's county. As a result, there'd been little progress, much to the dismay of his mother.

Special Agent Clamp stepped into the house, and Bert closed the door.

"Have a seat," Bert said.

The agent discreetly scanned the room before his eyes trained on Bert's feet. His was a mind no doubt trained in classifying all manner of information, but he appeared to be struggling with the lion slippers. For Bert's part, his alarm at the sudden presence of the FBI overshadowed any embarrassment or need to explain that he might otherwise feel. He turned the Beatles way down until they were but a sorry muffling of munchkins trapped inside a small box.

"What else can I tell you?" he asked in a hurried voice before they were seated. There would be no offer of iced tea or nibbles. A survival lobe in his brain wanted to believe that somehow this would be over and forgotten before Anna appeared.

Agent Clamp selected the seat in front of the coffee table so as to afford a view of the front hall, access to the kitchen, dining area, and hallway back to the bedroom. It wasn't supposed to be this way, Bert thought, when he realized that a G-man was first in line to sully his virginally new love seat.

Clamp scratched his head at the French windows all fogged up from water that boiled for an hour out of control, turning the living room into a bog at the edge of a rainforest kitchen. Then he coughed and waved a finger at the candle in front of him. "Potent," he gasped. "What is it?"

"A combination," Bert told him. "Cinnamon, with accents of burnt musk and Italian leather." He was given the same look as with the slippers: no classification. "The store lady..." Calming down, he gave up on his compulsive need to explain. "Never mind. Why don't I—?" He licked the tips of his thumb and index finger and pinched the wick, snuffing it out. A cloud of aphrodisiacal smoke billowed up to Agent Clamp's face, causing him to cough six times and lean back while he covered his mouth.

"Sorry about that," Bert said. He wasn't.

Clamp pulled a pad of paper and pen from his computer bag to take notes and left the bag on the table.

"Mr. Gropes," he began, still clearing his throat from the assault on his sinuses. "Do you have any information you haven't shared with us concerning the disappearance or possible whereabouts of your uncle?"

"No," Bert answered. "None." If he just wanted an update on what Bert knew about his uncle's whereabouts, this would be quick, and Clamp would be gone before Anna reentered the room.

"Do you know of anyone who might have had a reason to bring harm to him?"

"No."

"I understand that you've become the trustee of your uncle's trust."

"Yes."

Clamp leaned back. "Like I say, Mr. Gropes, this is a nice house with nice things." He looked around again while, with repeated raking motions of both hands, he kept copping feels of the fabric on Bert's new love seat. "What with the prices of real estate in California, can I ask how someone your age, on a teacher's salary, is able to pull it off?"

"To make it work for the trust, the company that licensed the technology paid me a fee for my time," Bert said, pleased with the way it came out. "I'm a technical adviser."

"Really?" He leaned forward, taking the pen and scribbling notes.

"I still haven't closed," Bert explained. "The owner let me move in. We're waiting for the bank to approve the loan."

"Think it would be possible for me to get a copy of your license?"

"I don't have that here at this place," Bert said. "I haven't moved those papers yet. What is it you need to know?" He wondered: What did this have to do with Uncle Gro's disappearance?

"Now, I know your lawyer is required to file reports with the court to show that you have been a conscientious trustee. I looked at the papers your lawyer has just filed saying you licensed to a company called Mother DNAture Bioinformatics. Is that right?"

Bert nodded.

There was a clatter of something being dropped in the back bathroom that rattled around in the sink.

"It sounds like your lawyer thinks you've been a diligent trustee. You're on top of everything going on. Do you think so?"

"Yes." He drifted momentarily into a recollection that—following the double-twisty thing and, before that, faithfully serving as Professor Anna Brighton's understudy—he'd definitely ended up on top. But that wasn't where the agent was going with his question. This was getting ridiculous. He glanced over his shoulder. Still no Anna.

"If you saw something on their web page you didn't approve, am I right that you would tell them?"

"Of course."

Clamp put his pen down and rubbed his forehead lightly with his right hand. "Mr. Gropes, can you explain how this so-called shock technology actually works on subjects?"

"I'm not a scientist myself, but I understand the basics of it. The software gets downloaded and modulated electric shock is delivered to the user's system. That reboots their libidos and… solves their problems."

"And you get paid a technical adviser fee for 'solving their problems?'"

"Well, nothing is guaranteed," Bert backed off. "The first ones will all be guinea pigs."

"And that's fine with you?" With an involuntary droop of his left lower lip, Clamp's disdain shone through. This had moved beyond an investigation into the whereabouts of his uncle into new territory. Had Bert done something wrong? What? Did they think he should be charged under some cruelty-to-chickens statute? Selling club drugs to roosters?

"Hello?" Anna was perplexed to find the stranger in the room. She looked great wearing a blue "UC Davis Aggies" T-shirt, stretch nylon warm-ups, and Bert's Jungle Heat on her feet. He would have jumped her bones again right then and there but for the not inconsequential problem that he was in the middle of being interrogated by a persistent, love-seat-clawing FBI agent.

"Special Agent Dennis Clamp," he said with a nod after he stood, his teeth showing, his detector jaw aimed at her.

Anna appeared troubled, if not horrified.

"He's investigating Uncle Gro's disappearance," Bert said. That seemed to calm her a little. He turned to Clamp. "This is Anna Brighton."

"Anna Brighton? You are next on my contact list. You're Professor Gropes's assistant, right?"

"That's right," she said.

The three of them sat down—Anna and Bert together on the couch and Clamp all over the love seat again. The agent looked the two of them over before fixing now on the fluffy, yet compact row on the floor: two lions and two monkeys. Finally he looked up and darted his eyes back and forth at each of them. "You're together. You two are—?"

"Good friends," Bert said. He'd written "my girlfriend" in the draft letter to his Dad, but he couldn't bring himself to say it right now. That his first chance to introduce Anna came up with Special Agent Dennis Clamp was totally preposterous.

"I see," Clamp said, the squint of his eyes intimating that

conspiracy charges were next, once the chicken cruelty indictments were handed down. Chicken torture camps.

"I'd like to log onto the Web and ask you just a few more questions, and then I'll let you go," he said. He pulled the notebook computer out of his bag and turned it on. "While that's booting up, do you mind if I use your bathroom?"

"No," Bert said, pointing at a door off the entryway. Clamp disappeared into the guest bathroom.

"Did he have an appointment to meet you?" Anna was not pleased.

"No, he just showed up," Bert said with open palms.

"Well, do they have any leads?"

"It doesn't sound like it. So far he's asked me lots of questions about the trust that seem pointless."

Anna shook her head tersely. The silver lining, Bert considered, was that she really was looking forward to spending the rest of the evening with him, and not anyone else.

When Clamp returned, his computer was already online. He minimized the web browser and pulled up a JPEG image of a frightening looking woman who looked vaguely familiar.

"Do you recognize this woman?" Clamp asked Bert.

Suddenly it hit him who she was. "Yes, that's Tatiana Lurenski. She's my contact at Mother DNAture." It was a surprisingly bad photo for a vice president of public relations. In a black and white shot, she stared straight ahead with blank eyes encircled with smeared mascara, entirely devoid of any of the charm Bert thought he'd experienced when he was with her in person, back when he was on a mission to rescue Anna's paycheck. At this moment Bert didn't glance over at Anna; he didn't need to. He knew the on-screen woman was not going to score him any bonus points tonight.

"What kind of contact have you had with her?" Clamp said.

"We had one meeting at the airport," Bert said. "There's been some written correspondence since. That's all."

"Yeah, well, let me know the next time she comes into federal jurisdiction to see you," Clamp said in a tone of condemnation. "The United States wants her for mail fraud, extortion, racketeering, trafficking of obscene materials, and conspiracy to commit those crimes."

Bert heard Anna gasp. As for himself, he could barely breathe.

"Mr. Gropes, before you had the source code delivered to Ms. Lurenski, did you know that she and Mother DNAture were owned or controlled by Primal Urge Entertainment and its founder, Dick Slayde?"

"I didn't before I signed with them."

"My question is *before* the instrumentality, the source code, was delivered."

"Yeah, I did know before, now that you mention it," Bert answered sheepishly. "But only because the checks I cashed, that they paid with—" He abandoned that explanation, instead adding for Anna's benefit, "I was just trying to keep the trust going."

He glanced over at her. She glowered at him and scooched further away from him to the end of the couch.

"Let's take a look now at your moneymaker website that you licensed, shall we?" Clamp said, relishing his ruination of Bert.

When the page loaded, he turned the notebook so that it faced Bert. Bert couldn't believe his eyes. In big red letters at the top of the page it said: WELCOME TO HOT MONKEY LOVE. Bert had to make sure the address was correct, but he'd seen Clamp type in *www.whatmother.com* and watch it roll into Hot Monkey Love. The photograph that now served as a backdrop was a far cry from the Hallmark image of the heartland chicken ranch that he'd previously seen on the WHAT/Mother home page. The new background photo, which depicted two men and three women—naked and linked together by a chain of unnatural, twisted, gym-nasty contortions—was straight from the Primal Urge site he'd visited two weeks earlier when the FedEx truck delivered the checks. Although two of them were doing a version of that double-twisty thing, it was by no means a copy of him and Anna a short while ago. This shot looked like it had been snapped by Hieronymous Bosch himself. The image could have been a hologram; from the intended viewing angle, it was Primal Urge epitomized and celebrated in pixels, but from where Bert was sitting right now, it was pure human wretchedness.

Anna stood up. "Please excuse me." She walked briskly down the hall. Bert couldn't call after her, not with the agent parked on his love seat.

"My question, Mr. Gropes—"

"No more questions." Bert cut him short. "You'll have to leave now."

"We're almost done."

"Go, please."

He clapped the computer shut, tossed it in the bag, zipped it, and stood up.

"Thank you for your time, Mr. Gropes." He walked to the front door.

Bert said nothing but was tempted to ask if he was some kind of suspect. He knew enough from his own reading and watching TV crime shows that once he became an actual criminal suspect, they'd have to give him his Miranda warnings. There was little comfort in that.

"Perhaps we can finish another time," Clamp said as he opened the door and headed out toward his car.

Bert hurried down the hall, running into Anna coming out of the bedroom. With her bag strapped over her shoulder, she was rushed, her expression tense. The slippers, flung from her feet, lay on the bedroom floor.

"Anna, wait… I think I can explain."

"I don't think so." She made a bee-line past him down the hall. When she reached the front door, she did an about face. "Who are you, Bert Gropes? What kind of…? How could you fall in with that kind of scum? And with your uncle's legacy? I thought I knew you. I was wrong."

She pulled the door behind her, slamming it shut. Bert stared out the window as she sped off in her car as if in a hurry to catch up with Agent Clamp. The only traces of Anna that remained were the dust storm she kicked up and its fallout.

34

WITH A HEAVE, LES HARRY SLID SHUT THE roller door to the coops, quieting the incessant racket of a thousand chickens. As he headed toward the house, he mopped his brow with both hands and wiped the sweat on his pants. Not yet noon, it had been hot for hours. The TV weather lady said last night it would stay hot tomorrow, but by Tuesday all of East Tennessee would see some cooling thunder showers.

Les Harry had been a chicken farmer his entire life. His father raised chickens. His father's father raised chickens here on this farm on the outskirts of Dayton. When he was young, Les promised himself he was going to do something different with his life. Nothing happened until age fifty-five, when he'd suffered a major heart attack, and his wife Noreen urged him to try something new for his own good. Six months later, and nearly bankrupt, Les heard about raising naked chickens. It came at that stage in his life when Les decided he hated anything with beaks or feathers. He figured if he raised *naked* chickens, half of his problems would be solved. The idea was simple: Artificially inseminated bio-engineered birds, born without layers of insulating feathers, would be able to survive in the hot spots around the world. You raise 'em, crate 'em up, and ship 'em. You didn't need to pluck 'em.

More to Les's liking was the government money to be had. The Department of Agriculture, as part of a Peace Corps program, guaranteed qualifying farmers top dollar for every live naked bird shipped off to various hell-hole third world countries, where volunteers helped locals set up chicken farms.

For the first year it had worked like a dream: Les raised birds, shipped them off, and got a nice check from the government. All was easy street until the government got word back from its various projects scattered around the equator: These birds didn't, or couldn't, do what nature intended. Worse for Les, the government spigot was about to be cut off unless suppliers solved the problem. His contact from the Ag Department told him about a scientist from California who'd come up with a cure, some kind of electronic gene therapy that could be downloaded from a website.

Les was skeptical, to say the least, but he was desperate to keep those Ag checks coming in. He went onto the web to where he'd been directed and downloaded the software on a demo basis. The next day, FedEx delivered the little chicken headset he needed to hook up to his notebook computer and that actually administered the therapy. He outfitted a naked hen, followed in short order by a naked rooster. When he introduced them to each other on the coop floor to let them get acquainted, the next thing he knew, well, virtual feathers were flying. Nature was back in business.

Later that afternoon Les was in bed at the Rodeway Motel with Maura LaMême, ten years his junior—his own little bird, right tasty to be sure, and served to him strictly on the side. A transplant from New Orleans, Maura owned the beauty parlor next to the 7-Eleven called The Big Easy. Les told Maura it was the first time he'd "ever seen the deplumed ones do the dirty"—pronouncing it "de-PLOOM-ed"—and that it even made him "a little hot to watch." She laughed and encouraged more such banter for the two hours they were together.

The software demo came loaded with twelve free "therapy sessions," enough to see whether the next generation of birds was able to regenerate under its own steam. Les figured he'd go ahead and order the whole program. Time was not on his side. Besides, the software also came with a money-back guarantee if the next generation turned out to be turned off.

He was about to enter the house when his wife, Noreen, stood up from her rose garden and stretched her back. He regarded her backside, which seemed to have evolved into a double-wide load over the last thirty-five years. He remembered way back when her rig was only big enough to draw maybe a sleek little sailboat astride nothing larger than a two-wheel trailer for highway travelers to admire.

When his foot inadvertently kicked a pebble, she turned around. "Oh, there you are, honey. I've got three big bags of soil up in the shed. They need to be brought down."

"I've got a little business to take care of," he said, slowing his gait but not stopping. "On the computer. I'll get them on my way back out."

"That's fine. Thanks. And, honey, don't try to do too much…"

"Don't worry, hon," he said, reaching the back door. "That's why you and I have a third wheel." He winked even though she couldn't see it.

AFTER WASHING HIS HANDS IN THE KITCHEN, LES went straight into the study and sat down in front of his notebook computer. When he clicked onto the page where he'd downloaded the demo software two days earlier, he couldn't believe what he saw. Gone were the chickens and their domestication. Instead, he was exposed to the words "HOT

MONKEY LOVE" in shocking red. The background displayed a porno picture of three girls and two lucky young guys. The sheer athleticism of these five individuals looked like a programming joint venture of ESPN and the Discovery Channel: *The X Games and The Four-H Club Gone Bad*. Les wondered: Had the chicken people been hijacked by a porn site? He'd heard about that kind of thing happening on the Internet.

Could it be the same people? From a list on the left side of the page—Home Page, About Hot Monkey Love, About Mother DNAture, More Animals, Contact—he clicked on More Animals. Up popped the country farm scene and the exact same page he'd visited before and where he could now go ahead and purchase the product. It would have taken less than two minutes to complete the purchase and be on his way. But now he was more curious than ever to poke around. At the bottom of the page a link lured him back to the new home page: If you like the way our genetic code from jungle fowl lights up your naked chicks, wait'll you see what our monkeys can do for you! CLICK HERE NOW!

He clicked.

Back at the home page, he admired the image again briefly. Fortified, he clicked on About Hot Monkey Love and scanned it:

Libidoan monkeys, the most sex-crazed primates on the planet, are now downloadable into your genotype. The best parts anyway.

He was getting curiouser and curiouser with each click. When he read in "About Mother DNAture" that Dick Slayde, founder and publisher of *Slayve Quarterly*, not only was a giant in biotech but had pioneered something called Shock Technology that was the basis of this gene therapy, Les had the irresistible urge to give this thing a go. And he knew just where to call—The Big Easy beauty parlor—in case that urge needed to be followed through to its natural conclusion.

He gave his credit card info and downloaded the software.

He skipped reading the User Agreement, scrolled down and clicked "I agree." The directions recommended wearing a headset as preferable to earbuds. Les briefly examined the headset specially designed for the chickens and that he'd used on them, but it just wasn't going to work. Try as he may, he couldn't adjust them to fit his own head, or any head wider than a ping pong ball. So he opted for a pair of earbuds he found dangling from Noreen's iPod that she used to listen to classical music.

On screen a bright red button with the words TURN ON MONKEY GENES awaited his command. Ready at his end, he hit ENTER again. A horizontal bar showed that the software was activated and supplied a graphic for how long he should keep the earbuds on. He heard a strange, high, and rhythmic pulse, a sound somewhere between a futuristic computer on the blink and a banshee. Instantly he experienced a pleasant tingle in his head that started to radiate out to his extremities. Graphics of monkeys jumping up and down coaxed the process along. A minute later, he pulled the earbuds off. His flesh felt like it was glowing, and it was getting stronger.

Regardless of the outcome, he decided he needed to share this experience with someone now, not later. He dialed Maura.

"Big Easy," the voice drawled at the other end.

Before speaking into the phone, Les held it away from his head for a second to make sure he didn't miss someone entering the house who might hear him.

"Hi, baby," he said in a soft voice. "What's doin'?"

"Kinda quiet, hon." She did a half yawn. "Just finished my eleven o'clock wax. Now I'm doin' my books, and I'm bored."

"Guess what I'm doing? You never will, so I'll tell you. Remember that software, that genetic juju that I was telling you about last week?"

"You're a strange bird, Les Harry. You're doin' gene therapy for roosters—?"

"No, better than that. I'm doin' their newest one. It's for

people! And get this. They call it"—he dropped into imitation basso profundo—"Hot Monkey Love."

"So that's it?" she said, unmoved. "You want a little phone sex? Am I right? You don't take me nowhere like you used to."

"I'm warmin' up here real good, baby. Yeah, your big rooster daddy's gonna want his honey-baked hen again." She giggled. That was all the opening he needed. "I thought maybe we could meet up at the Rodeway in about twenty minutes." He'd have to come up with a fib for Noreen to put off hauling her dirt. The motel was fifteen minutes away on Rhea County Highway on the outskirts of Dayton. "After, we'll cool down at the Dairy Queen." Definitely feeling hotter, Les undid another button of his Ben Davis work shirt—one of two that Noreen just got him at WalMart on a twofer.

"What makes you think I can leave my business right now?" she said, this time with a full yawn. She was going to meet him, Les knew, but she just wanted to see if she could hold out for, say, a notch up from Dairy Queen. Like maybe a real sit-down place. Les figured the Rodeway was going to run him almost sixty bucks, counting the five-dollar bottle of malt liquor he'd grab at the Piggly Wiggly on his way.

"How's about we stop off at Baker's Square for ice cream on top of some pie?"

"Mmm," she said, perking up. "That does sound good."

"How quick can you be there? This is something, baby. I'm gettin' hot. Real hot." His blood was now racing head to toe and back up in what felt like a wink.

"Ooh, you poor boy, you must be foudroyant."

"Keep talkin' that dirty French." Les was breathing hard now and he felt like his body was balancing on a high wire two hundred feet above the ground, filled with lust and delirium and animal power…and something else that wasn't quite right.

"Now who said it was dirty?" She was still holding out. "Mama used to say we were foudroyant whenever we came down with a fever real fast."

Suddenly he went tight and there was a sharp pain. "Oh!" he cried out loud.

"You're not gonna wait for me?" she pouted. "Pooh!"

He wanted to tell her to call 911, but he couldn't open his mouth. Leaning forward, he slapped his chest with the phone-free hand, the wire still attached. The horizontal bar showed TURN ON MONKEY GENES was "99% Complete." He knew this was curtain time for sure. They'd find, along with some duct tape dangling from his fallen hand, that he was connected by a wire to a computer and by a telephone to a woman named Maura LaMême. He never quite got around to asking himself what was important in life and what wasn't, but now it was too late to start in with those questions. There'd be an inquest of him instead. They'd tape off the space around his study. They'd learn he tried to turn himself into a monkey on the Internet. They'd come and go and whisper jokes outside of Noreen's earshot—all of it funny, excruciatingly funny, there'd be no denying it. Finally, a coroner's report would be knocked out, and a file clerk in a government building in downtown Dayton would chuckle one more time while sliding the metal drawer shut with an unceremonious knee kick.

The screen came alive when "100% Complete" was reached; it lit up with large, pulsating letters in flashing colors:

Go Ape!!!

It was the last thing he saw before everything went black.

"Les Harry, you big goon. What're you doing? Talk to me… Are you there? You promised me pie."

35

BERT BEGAN HOLDING VIGIL OUTSIDE ANNA'S
campus office on Monday morning at 8:30 A.M. It was close to
eleven now. Yesterday, Sunday, he'd tried to call her beginning
around nine, but there was no answer, only her outgoing message: *"Hi. This is Anna. I'm not here right now..."* The cheer
in her voice gave him hope that all of what they had between
them could be quickly restored to the time when those words
were recorded.

*"Anna, please pick up if you're there...I thought they were
legitimate...I mean, what would I know about biotech? I teach
Social Studies to ninth graders. Besides, you'll have to believe
me when I say that Tatiana—the woman in the FBI photo—was
very persuasive in person. I promise you I didn't know about
any business with racketeering and mail fraud. It never came
up. Call me. This would be so much easier to explain in person."*

He left ten such messages on her machine yesterday over
the course of the same number of hours. Only the last one was

remotely clear or thought out but, in all likelihood, after the first one or two she was punching ERASE every time his voice came on.

Just then, like waiting for the world's slowest toaster, the elevator door rang and out popped Anna. It only made him feel worse that she, in fact, looked a little burned—tired and puffy around the eyes. She headed in his direction, sorting through her keys. When she looked up and saw him standing in front of her office, she scowled.

"Anna, please let me tell you how it happened."

"Bert. I *know* what happened." She seemed to draw certainty from her disdain. "You found these bottom-feeders. You made a deal with them. You got *paid* by a bunch of porn peddlars." She stopped in front of her door. "A legitimate biotech company?" She shook her head as she put the key in. "Right." She pushed the door open and retrieved a few pieces of mail dropped on the floor.

"I was trying to help *you.*"

"Helping me by making me the laughingstock of the biotech industry? I trusted you. I turned over the source code—the source code, Bert!—so they could come up with this perversion of your uncle's work. I still feel sick from Saturday night." She picked up two files on her desk and turned to leave the office. "I went home and took a closer look at that disgusting website you and your confederates dreamed up."

"Dreamed up? I didn't—"

"Don't tell me you didn't." She closed the door to her office. "It's clear you would have done anything to get your ranch. And I guess you stand to make a small fortune as a 'technical adviser.'"

"Anna, I never imagined they'd turn the website into—"

"Oh, please." She punched the down button for the elevator, increasingly eager to get away from him. "Any drooling idiot with the dimmest bulb of an imagination would take one look at Cell Shock and wonder if it could be adapted to do the same thing for humans. Even Senator Ray Hoffenworth, who fits the latter category, asked Dr. Gro about that. Remember?"

"I remember. I thought he was asking if it could be used somehow to create chimera. Like half-chickens, half-humans. That's as much as I thought about that."

"If that's true, then you're the biggest drooling idiot of them all. But I don't believe a word you say. What you did speaks for itself."

"That's because you haven't heard—"

"Really? Do explain then."

He was stunned that his request was granted. "Well, they contacted me, saying they were a startup biotech company. We met at the airport. Everything seemed on the up-and-up. She nicknamed me JB." He didn't know why he added that. "They wanted to include me, get me involved, but they needed to cut a deal that day because the books were closing." He stopped talking. All day yesterday, and two and a half hours this morning to think about how best to persuade her of his good intentions, and that was all he could say.

"Right," Anna said, "the books and accounts for Primal Urge from whom you received your take. You knew back then who was behind this, but you said nothing, to get me to go along."

She was seething, indignant. It was over. He'd lost this battle. "Let me just say this, Bert, then I'm out of here. I left Boston because of unscrupulous people in the biotech industry I met there, who would do or say anything for a buck, or an edge. That's why I sought out your uncle because he understood there was more to biology than the molecules, that progress in science wasn't progress unless you followed the enduring genetics of nature itself. That you're not moving forward unless you bring with you the best of what went before you. It's too bad you never learned anything from him."

"He said that?"

The elevator door opened. She stepped in and turned around.

"I do not want to see you, Bert. Don't call or show up. Don't test me. I'll call the police if I have to."

The doors closed. She was gone.

It was over just like that, his vigil a bust. Rather than seeing that he too was a victim, she was now convinced that he'd long yearned to worm his way into the seamy sex trade, that he'd betrayed her and his uncle for money, and that he'd generally ruined her life. She had actually made drooling idiot sound like an attractive alternative to what she really thought of him. Worse, he hadn't said any of the things he wanted to tell her. Staring like a zombie at the closed elevator door, he felt like he was about to explode with frustration. He couldn't bear the rest of today, not after yesterday. Nor could he endure the rest of his life, not under these conditions. Even if it meant making an embarrassing public display, he had to chase her down and tell her what he felt inside. If she heard him out, if she'd only listen to the whole story of how he managed to get into business—into bed, he supposed—with Primal Urge! He had to speak to her or it would kill him.

Bert hit the elevator button. When it didn't instantly spring open and suck him into a wind tunnel that would carry him to her, he took off in a sprint toward an EXIT sign, opened the door and began hurling himself down the stairs.

Clackclackclackclackclackclackclackclackclackclackclack-clack... His cowboy boots clomped down the four floors of the hollow stairwell and broke into a gallop through the door into the lobby, racing out into the parking lot after the girl of his dreams. Her car was stopped, about to drive out of the lot. When she saw him, she hurriedly pulled into traffic. Luckily Bert's pickup was parked right next to the building. He jumped in and took off after her. He could see her six cars ahead as they moved through stop signs on Anderson heading west towards Highway 113.

Anna squirted through the last light, pulled onto the on-ramp and gunned it, as if to blow him back with the exhaust as much as to maximize her forward thrust. He knew he could easily catch her after the light turned green, but he wasn't sure what he would do next. Follow her all the way to Vacaville, about twenty minutes? Roll up beside her and pantomime for her to pull over?

He decided to pull over without her, but it wasn't exactly his decision. A flashing red filled his rear view mirror. He glanced at his speedometer: eight-six miles an hour. There was no mistaking whom the highway patrolman wanted. Gradually he pulled over to the shoulder, slowed and stopped. The lights of the patrol car behind him throbbed and pulsed, animated as a yipping bloodhound. Bert opened his door. Maybe if he could meet and greet the officer, he could charm his way out of this one.

"PLEASE REMAIN IN YOUR VEHICLE," a male voice of authority blared from the loudspeaker of the patrol car. So much for the charm approach.

A Black officer in his early forties, well built, emerged from the vehicle. He approached Bert's car on the passenger side and rapped on the window. Bert lowered the glass with the button on his door.

"Sir, I'll need your license and vehicle registration, please."

Bert handed him his driver's license and the temporary registration. The officer examined the items briefly, glancing up at Bert to compare the photo.

"In a hurry today, Mr. Gropes?"

"Not any more. If you're going to write me up, you might as well go ahead."

"Where did you buy this vehicle?" he asked, ignoring Bert's invitation.

"At the Ford dealer in Roseville two weeks ago." Bert had removed the two license plate frames with the mini-billboards in them that advertised the dealer. He hadn't received his permanent registration or plates yet.

"Sir, I'll need to run a check. Please remain in your vehicle."

Bert could hear the tinny voice of a female dispatcher providing choppy bursts of mumbo jumbo as the officer returned to and seated himself in his patrol car. After five minutes went by, Bert imagined that Anna was almost to Vacaville by now, but he no longer had any intention of trying to catch her. When he turned on the radio, and it started in with a sad song, he couldn't stand it for another second. He looked down and jabbed around until he found just the impenetrable wall of metal rock he was searching for—driving, relentless, and entirely unapologetic in its mindlessness. That's what he craved right now. He remained lost in the sound for a few minutes, and when he looked up again, there were two more highway patrol cars, one behind him and one in front, appearing out of nowhere. The officer jumped out and the car in front of his and, using the open door as a barricade, pointed his drawn gun at Bert's head.

"PUT YOUR HANDS UP WHERE WE CAN SEE THEM. NOW! GET OUT OF THE VEHICLE SLOWLY! KEEP YOUR HANDS UP!" the first officer, still behind him, commanded.

Bert vaulted out of his truck. Trucks, cars, and buses whooshed by, their velocity blasting him with the mid-morning heat of the Sacramento Valley. What was happening to him seemed to unfold to a strange, staccato rhythm, lunging forward and rolling back like a nameless surge in his gut.

"DROP TO THE GROUND. ON ALL FOURS. NOW!"

Bert fell to the ground, cutting his left hand on a broken piece of roadside glass. He glanced over just as a brown station wagon drove by. A boy in the back seat stared through the glass in amazement at the man he saw on the ground who seemed like a dog about to be leashed,his body under the control of others. With the little that was reserved to him, Bert used all of it not to relieve himself.

"HIT THE GROUND AND SPREAD 'EM. NOW!"

Instantly Bert merged with all that was under him, scraping his face on the roadway. As he heard a thunder of feet rushing toward him, he turned his head to the left. Between his grasping hand and the earth, he saw that he was vaguely welded to a clump of dirt and a dried-up banana peel, now freakishly, whimsically intermingled with his blood. Three officers hovered over him. One pulled Bert's hands behind his back and slapped cuffs on him.

"You're under arrest," the first officer shouted above the traffic noise.

"What?" Bert screamed. "There's a mistake!"

"No mistake. A warrant issued this morning out of Dayton, Tennessee. You, John Bertram Gropes, are wanted as an accessory in connection with the murder of one Les Harry—"

"Who? Never heard of him! I've never been east of the Grand—"

"You have the right to remain silent…"

36

SENATOR RAY HOFFENWORTH FINISHED HIS third plate of scrambled eggs, bacon, sausage, and cinnamon toast. He'd barely made a dent in the quantities still waiting in large flame-warmed-over chafing dishes all in a row, each with a white-clad server at the ready in the otherwise empty Radisson Hotel banquet room in Manchester. The primary was seven months away, and only three New Hampshirites had dropped in this morning to meet the candidate for breakfast. That third helping gave him the temporary feeling he craved, filling a much larger void in which his campaign found itself set adrift.

Skip Ferndon, national chairman of the Hoffenworth For President 2020 campaign, approached the Senator with cell phone in hand. Avoiding eye contact, Skip's posture this morning said it all; as if pounded with four days of heavy rains, his shoulders had collapsed and seemed to have fallen into his chest. The road to the White House was a mess and appeared to be closed, at least for now.

"I've got Wayne Tanner," Skip said, head down. "He says he needs to talk to you personally." He quickly turned and disappeared as the senator took the phone from him.

"Is this the finest district attorney in the great state of Tennessee?" Ray Hoffenworth could always put a game face on.

"If I'm good, it's because I learned at the foot of the master himself. I bet you got a million New Englanders wantin' you to shake their hand and kiss their little ones. So, tell me, how is the campaign going for the next President of the United States this fine day?"

"Unbelievable, Wayne. Really unbelievable. How 'bout you? You still pokin' a stick at that seat in Congress? Got your name on it."

"Between you and me, Senator, definitely. In fact, I've hired a high-priced political strategist to steer me."

"Let me guess. If Skip Ferndon is sittin' here with me, then you got Tennessee's other finest. Andy Goodfellow. Am I right?"

"No. I mean *really* high-priced. More like New York's finest. I'm sure you're familiar with the work of Sol Krasputin."

"Krasputin?" the senator spat. "He's a Demo."

"He's looking to expand his sphere of influence, and he's helping me."

"I don't know if I like the sound of this. He's brought down a lot of good men, friends of mine in both houses. That's not even his real name. What'd it used to be anyway?"

"Beats me," Tanner said. "All's I know is it's Krasputin now. And he's come up with something that just might supercharge your campaign, and my prospects along with it. It's a hell of an idea, Senator."

"Really now?" Ray Hoffenworth leaned back in his chair and scooched his butt forward. "Tell me about it."

"Remember that professor from California you had at one of your SICC hearings a few months back? The one on the Naked Chicken Genome Project that cost the government a bundle?

Professor Grover Gropes who came up with a gene therapy so's the birds could make whoopie?"

"Oh, yeah, I remember. Celestial Chickens, or somethin'." Hoffenworth rolled his eyes for his own benefit.

"Well, we just issued an indictment against his nephew for using that therapy on humans, except instead of using bioinformatics from chickens, he's gettin' it from monkeys and zappin' humans with this thing."

"What kind of sick, twisted—?"

"And not just any monkeys, he's using monkey genes from the Isle Libido—"

"Those are the monkeys with the—"

"Right."

A pause ensued, allowing the men to load the mental picture. Wayne Tanner forged on. "They're calling it Hot Monkey Love."

"What do you expect? That's why I put the words 'beastly degradation' in the Act." The senator was salivating again. Instinctively, he grabbed his napkin and mopped up around his mouth. "As I remember, this thing could change germ lines in chickens—genes are changed in the next generation. No doubt it's the same for humans. You got to scotch the snake when it wiggles. You lookin' to make this the first prosecution of the Act?"

"Yep. But hold on, this thing gets better. A fellow here in Dayton died—was out and out murdered, Ray—using this animal therapy. Had a heart attack. I've got an FBI statement that shows this nephew of the professor, name of John Bertram Gropes, was well aware deaths were going to happen. But he was completely indifferent about the risk."

"Animals."

"And there's lots more. Wait'll you hear who this fella Gropes is partnered with on this monkey business: Dick Slayde, as in Primal Urge."

"Don't say! A one-man pestilence of putridity!"

"Right. So here's Krasputin's crazy idea, Senator. How'd you like to have your old job back for one case?"

Hoffenworth looked up at the row of servers standing quietly behind the chafing dishes, their hands idly clasped. "Keep talkin', Wayne. My ears are burnin'."

"Think about it, Senator. A monkey trial in Dayton, almost one hundred years later, but this time it won't be a circus. Of course it'll be daily national headlines because of you, and I ride on your draft just enough to launch my bid. For you, it'll bring into focus the heart of your campaign: morality, common sense, tax cuts, preservation of the species, and the fact that the world is divided into two kinds—good people and bad people."

"I should get you to run my campaign, Wayne." He glanced over and saw Skip Ferndon sitting at an empty table, doodling with a white linen napkin, trying to make bunny ears. "But do you really think we got a lay-down here? I'm completely sold on the upside, but if I don't get a conviction, I'm finished."

"Are you kidding?" Tanner snorted. "These facts? *Your* jury in Dayton? Like old times, Senator. For you, it'll be shootin' fish in a barrel."

"I'll rearrange my schedule and fly down tomorrow to go over the evidence with you."

"It'll be kind of funny to have me deputizing you to try this case, Senator, but you'll have the complete support of my staff, whatever you need."

"Thanks, Wayne. You're doin' me proud."

"It's my honor, sir. And let me just say, especially with all the hubbub that will come with this case, I don't want to lose sight of one thing. Les Harry is dead, murdered. He was a good man. I'd met him, knew who he was. Family goes way back in these parts." Wayne Tanner aspirated, breathing out both anger and grief. "He was one of us, Ray."

37

"GONZALES! GRAND THEFT AUTO. ATTORNEY Weissberg, " the deputy yelled into the holding cell where a dozen other prisoners awaited their cases to be called. Gonzales, outfitted in a polyester jump suit—CalTrans orange—and handcuffs, stood up slowly and then had to step over feet and legs stretched out from slouching bodies scattered around the space. He was led away to a courtroom by another deputy sheriff.

Bert sat quietly, albeit stiffly, in the corner of the fifteen-by-twenty-foot room that featured cinder block walls painted light green and lined with bolted-down metal benches; another six-foot length of seating anchored the middle of the bleak space. The drill this morning was simple: Prisoners were called by their last names only but, to ensure that two prisoners named Gonzales didn't respond, the keepers identified them by their charges and the name of their attorney.

Following Bert's arrest yesterday, he'd simply been called

"Gropes" both here inside the courthouse and his new home at the Yolo County Detention Facility out on Gibson Road near the Fairgrounds—where it was all about livestock. He'd attended the County Fair every year and was certainly familiar with the tradition of putting animals on display. This insistence on last names only seemed to have the effect of reducing him and his cellmates to the likes of Fido, or Bonzo, or Trigger. The bad cats in this holding cell seemed quite comfortable with that protocol and looked upon him, the rigid stranger in the corner with legs too long sticking out of his orange jumpsuit, as if his name were Chirpie or Pecker and who was probably up on charges of shoplifting birdseed from a mall pet store. His cowboy boots might have been of some help, but unfortunately they had been checked in, along with his wallet and personal effects. He now wore a pair of shower shoes given all detainees.

He didn't sleep at all last night, and today he was groggy and slightly nauseous. As a result, traffic was sluggish, if not at a standstill, throughout the major synaptic hubs in his brain. The harder he tried, the murkier it got. As he tossed in his jailhouse bed, he came to recognize the problem was an overturned, impassable, eighteen-wheeler of a question: *Why is this happening to me?*

He was aware that, statistically, his fellow cellmates came from broken families, and more often than not, the absence of a guiding father figure contributed to their trouble. Was it simply fore-ordained that he would end up in prison even if, unlike some of the hardened recidivists who surrounded him right now, he'd done nothing wrong? The single name was demeaning, if not dehumanizing, stirring up old feelings from school days, when other kids started calling him "X Periment"—"X" for short when they learned he was manufactured in vitro in a lab. To think, only a few weeks ago he was JB Gropes, Rancher, Tech Adviser, Babe Magnet. Now he was—

"Gropes!" the deputy shouted, bringing Bert temporarily out of his fog. "Murder, second degree, and..." He squinted to make sure he read it correctly. "Conspiracy to commit beastly degradation of humanity." His eyes bulged in disbelief. "Attorney Tweed."

When Bert rose from his seat, everyone in the cell instantly straightened up. Feet were neatly paired and tucked snugly under their respective benches. Heads lowered as he made his way across the cell, but one—a Black ringleader under age twenty-five, a grizzled veteran of holding cells who looked to be an aggravated assault type—lifted his head and muttered: "Hey, good luck, man." He held his cuffed hands up near his mouth in a deferential, boxer-like pose whose origin, it struck Bert, was a meld of hip hop, life on the inside, MTV, and the cradle of civilization.

It was June 26. As a deputy sheriff escorted him down a back hallway to his courtroom, Bert recalled that it was only a month ago that he'd been here in the same courtroom where he'd been admitted to the world of fiduciaries, those who, by reason of their education, standing, and overall trustworthiness, are deemed suitable to act on behalf of others: bank officers, attorneys, financial managers, executors, conservators, receivers and, following that hearing, John Bertram Gropes. He'd remembered feeling good about himself, proud even, when he read the Order of Appointment, granting him the full powers and responsibilities of trustee.

He'd seen highs before, and his share of lows, but nothing like this. Somehow, somewhere along the way, his life had turned, twisted, and spiraled out of control.

WHEN ELLIS PEEK PICKED UP ON HIS INTERNET bulletin board that the first indictment had issued out of Tennessee under the Abatement of Human Chimera and Beastly Degradation of Humanity Act, he knew the dreaded time had arrived: It was no longer a cold war with the warlords of Planet Lusus Naturae. At the time he got word, he was in

Scottsdale investigating the World Cryogenic Institute, where he had reason to believe hundreds of Lusians were kept frozen in pods that resembled giant ice trays and who, almost too easily, could be thawed out with a few splashes of warm water, the trays cracked with giant robotic tray crackers and the frozen warriors dumped into gargantuan ice buckets capable of mechanically sprouting all-terrain wheels to be deployed as conventional Lusian armored tanks, rolling out of Scottsdale and into the urban centers of America on a moment's notice. In fact, Ellis himself was on the verge of cracking—the investigation, that is—wide open when he learned of the indictment and decided to drive straight to Woodland.

He arrived at the hearing early because he expected there to be throngs for such an historic occasion. To his surprise, there were fewer than a dozen people in the courtroom. That alone was suspicious. A middle-aged man with big ears was talking to a younger woman and suddenly turned to Ellis, who was standing quietly nearby. Big Ears introduced himself as a reporter for the *Yolo County Times*. Then he introduced the woman he knew from before and who'd been recruited to freelance for *The Herald-News*, the local paper in Dayton, Tennessee.

"How about you?" Mr. Let's-All-Be-Pals asked Ellis. "What brings you here today?"

"I'm also a freelancer. I expect to be covering the trial for CNN," Ellis told him. It was a fib, or a partial truth, depending on how you looked at it. If you peeled the letters C-N-N all the way back, you'd find C-I-A unveiled, a secret so jealously guarded by Ellis and his contacts there, the Agency would likely deny any affiliation with him. Meanwhile, best to lay low and act like just another one of them.

"Really?" Mr. Pals said. The woman tried to smile but, due to some unspecified nervous disorder, she was leaning so far back and away from Ellis to the point that she was about to fall over.

"And maybe the BBC too," Ellis added. "They're both bidding

for my services. They may end up doing a joint broadcast. Today I'm doing advance research." He walked away and sat down in a remote corner of the courtroom.

ONCE BERT ENTERED THE COURTROOM AND TOOK a seat next to Ollie Tweed, the clerk read aloud: "People versus John Bertram Gropes...," and she stated the case number before handing the file to the judge. "Appearances, please."

"Timothy Plant for the AG's office, California," a young blue suit said. "I'm here with Wayne Tanner from the Rhea County District Attorney's office representing the people of the State of Tennessee."

A willowy dark-haired figure in a beige suit rose and greeted the court in a Southern accent: "Good morning, sir."

Bert's lawyer stood up, tentatively. His neatly cropped hair that offset his glowing baldness on top was longer than the last time they'd been together in court; hanging flatly from three corners of his head, it resembled ceremonial white bunting. He buttoned his old sport coat and smiled at the other attorneys and the judge. "Good morning, your honor. Oliver Tweed for the Defendant who is present in court."

The judge was as fastidiously groomed as Bert remembered him. "I understand that one more will be joining us by speakerphone." He looked down at his clerk who was speaking in a low voice to someone, likely a phone operator. "However, all parties are represented, and we need to get started." He glanced at his watch and then at the file. "This is an extradition proceeding. Under Penal Code Section Fifteen-fifty-one, a fugitive complaint has been filed against the Defendant on charges pending in Tennessee: one count of felony murder in the second degree and one count of manslaughter, both as an accessory to the murder of Les Harry, a resident of Rhea County in the demanding state. And one count for conspiracy to violate the so-called Beastly Degradation of Humanity

Act. Mr. Tweed, does your client waive his right to an extra-dition hearing?"

"Your honor," Ollie said, struggling to his feet, "if it doesn't displease the court, my client, John Bertram Gropes, wishes to exercise his right to a habeas corpus hearing."

"Fine, then," the judge said. "We'll set a date forthwith."

Wayne Tanner stood and caught the judge's attention before a date was announced. "Sir, we're duty bound to bring to the court's attention a dossier that we were given by the FBI only this morning. I'm not sure exactly what relevance, if any, it has to this proceeding, but it involves this case and the subject of genetic tampering. Let me read the summary paragraph that accompanies this lengthy report." He held up a two-inch-thick bound report. The judge nodded.

"'The Baltimore field office received an anonymous tip,'" the prosecutor began reading, "'regarding subject of investigation Defendant John Bertram Gropes that certain medical files, long held in storage in a warehouse, should be reviewed. A search warrant was issued and the files were located. They revealed that twenty-seven years ago, in 1992, during an in-vitro insem-ination procedure, a very small quantity of genetic material—one gene to be exact—was taken from an anthropoidal ape, namely, a Libidoan monkey, and it was inserted into Defen-dant's zygote, with the result that the Defendant's genome car-ries one gene from said nonhuman animal. The source of the anonymous tip was identified and, upon further investigation, it was discovered that the anonymous informant and the indi-vidual responsible for the genetic tampering was one and the same person: Richard Sleigh aka Dick Slayde, principal of Pri-mal Urge and principal of another subject of this investiga-tion, Mother DNAture Bioinformatics. Mr. Slayde, for reasons unknown—possibly an old academic rivalry taken too far—had attempted to alter documents and lead investigators to con-clude that the tampering was the work of Professor Grover Sey-mour Gropes, the adoptive uncle of subject Gropes.'"

There were a dozen people in the courtroom, some of whom had gasped or uttered "What?" during the reading. Bert rubbed his exhausted eyes in disbelief. A few seconds passed and his heart started to pound more loudly as if trying to deliver a message to his brain, all other means of communication having broken down. But there was no place in his overburdened mind to classify this information. Ollie Tweed stood motionless, stunned.

"That's quite remarkable," the judge observed. "Already in my two weeks on the criminal calendar, I've seen some odd background profiles in probation reports, but this one beats all. Does the FBI think any of that actually happened?"

"Yes, sir," Tanner said. "It's all been verified, including DNA sampling. No surprise, sequences totaling less than one hundredth of one percent of the Defendant's genetic makeup are purely Libidoan monkey, not found in humans."

"Mr. Tweed," the judge said with a calm, even voice, "do you wish to take the position that this information has some exculpatory significance that would dictate against this court's power to extradite the Defendant?"

"I...I...don't know," Ollie stammered, standing but leaning on the counsel table with the extended fingers of both hands. "This is so extraordinary... I am in shock at this announcement and that it comes in this fashion. I am privileged to represent this fine young man, a school teacher and friend of children." He nodded kindly to Bert seated beside him in his orange jumpsuit and manacles. "I guess what I want to say is that I cannot believe that something of this nature would simply be blurted out in open court for my client to hear for the first time. Admittedly, I don't spend much time in criminal courts, but is there no sensitivity, no sense of compassion?"

"He said the report was just handed to him. What more can he do?" The judge hunched his shoulders and displayed open palms. "Sorry, but the fact is you're right. This is a criminal matter. Now, I take it from your comments that you don't believe any of this militates against the petition to extradite."

"I am still weighing the significance of these astounding revelations, your honor—"

"Excuse me, and if I may." A vaguely familiar woman stood up from the gallery. "I'm Clarene Eliza Dare, and I've come here today to petition for the right to appear as amicus in these proceedings." She waved court papers in her hand, presumably a petition.

"I didn't recognize you, Ms. Dare," the judge said. "I must say, I'm aware of your widely-reported verdicts on behalf of celebrity defendants throughout the country, something we don't have here in Yolo County. I'm also aware of your work on behalf of animal rights. But I doubt you're here today on behalf of farm animals, something we do have in this county. What is it, Ms. Dare?"

The famous defense lawyer advanced through the gate into the thick of where the lawyers were clustered. When she brought herself squarely before the judge and began to speak, the other attorneys backed away so as to give her all of the phantom spotlight.

"Our amicus brief, on behalf of the Animal Civil Liberties Federation—the ACLF—will set forth the reasons why the Tennessee law is unconstitutionally vague and discriminates against other living creatures deserving of dignity rights. I have been waiting for the first case to be filed. I received electronic notification this morning at my office in Sacramento. When I saw that a hearing was taking place twenty-five minutes from my office, I decided to come to Woodland myself and file the petition. But this new twist, just read into the record, truly makes this case extraordinary with its animal rights implications. If in fact the Defendant is a mix of human and nonhuman genetic material, I believe that under the narrow definition of what is properly a person as contemplated by the laws of the state of Tennessee, we are faced here with this question: What is a human?"

The judge stroked his chin thoughtfully. "An interesting way of looking at this, indeed, Ms. Dare, but what does this have to do with the extradition?"

"Everything." There was no trace of doubt in her voice. "A fundamental issue is raised. The only statute under which this court has authority reads: 'Upon a proper showing of probable cause, the court may extradite any person to a foreign state.' But I think it's the laws of Tennessee that govern here. Those laws refer to the criminal liability of 'any person.' If the Defendant is not a *person...*" She turned and regarded Bert with the kind of compassion typically reserved for a stray at the pound on day six and counting. "That is, if Mr. Gropes is not a human being—as was the intent of the Tennessee laws under which he is charged—then there is no probable cause for the indictments, and this court cannot extradite the Defendant."

Bert heard a familiar gasp behind him. It was his mother. She was the one who warned him about digging too deep into the biological Bert when he should be devoting himself to investigating his human potential. He was in too much shock to muster his own gasp.

The judge squinted in disbelief. "What are you saying? Are you saying that the Defendant sitting there is not a human being?"

"Not under Tennessee law."

"Then what is he?" the judge pressed her.

"He's a chimera—part animal, part human. The laws as written hold persons criminally responsible, not chimeras."

"If true, this raises a few profound legal questions. How does this court classify for purposes of judicial process?" the judge thought out loud, only feet from his alphabetized wall of forms. "Sometimes the law must do more than cite to precedent. It must consider teachings in science, ethics, philosophy, and look to the deep thinkers of our time for an answer. Is a chimera a nonhuman, as you suggest? Or a human, only watered down some? Or what? Come now, he's a living creature. He has to belong to someone who in turn belongs to a known species."

"That's generally true, sir," Tanner interjected. "I should add something of further interest from this report. The last paragraph of the FBI's summary reads: 'The medical files further reveal that, prior to the described genetic tampering, human artificial insemination was administered at a Baltimore fertility clinic by the same Dick Slayde who non-consensually inserted the sperm of the same Grover Seymour Gropes, the adoptive uncle of the subject Gropes, into the mother's egg, resulting in the latter Gropes becoming the natural son of the former Gropes.'" The prosecutor lowered the file and removed his glasses. "My point is simply this: The Defendant does very much come from someone else, another human being, and therefore he is a person like anyone else, capable of being prosecuted for his wrongdoing."

Ollie collapsed into his seat. Instinctively Bert turned around to look at his mother. He couldn't catch her eye before she jumped up from her aisle seat, covered her mouth, and rushed from the courtroom.

"Right," the judge said, seeming pleased that order was restored. "All creatures by their nature belong to something, don't they? A person is part of a family and a community and, as such, is accorded certain legal privileges. Nonhumans must be part of something else. We speak of a flock of birds, a gaggle of geese, even a confusion of guinea fowl. Monkeys move in troops. So do humans, come to think of it. Then there's—"

"A shrewdness of apes," Dare ventured. "How perfect since they are creatures of the highest intelligence, but they are accorded no dignity, rights, or liberty rights under our laws. The only benefit they enjoy is that they cannot be prosecuted for crimes. Now it seems the prosecution here wants to strip nonhumans of that lowliest benefit of non-personhood."

"A worthy point, I'm sure," the judge nodded, distracted. "Then there's—"

"*A pace of jack asses!*" The speakerphone came alive with a familiar voice. "*That's the one I remember best as a boy growing up in east Tennessee.*"

"Senator Hoffenworth," the judge said. "I'm glad you're finally able to join us. I've been informed that you are going to prosecute this case."

Bert was too beat up to react.

"*On behalf of the people of Tennessee and right-minded Americans everywhere, I am pleased to announce that I will be bringing the Defendant in this case to justice.*"

Dare turned to Ollie Tweed on her right and whispered tersely, "Is that true? Senator Ray Hoffenworth is trying this case?"

While Ollie nodded, Dare continued to stare back at him with an intellectual curiosity that, in a span of seconds, transformed into something that more resembled hunger for fresh meat.

As if the senator's words were being broadcast, and not merely relayed over a speakerphone, people began streaming into the courtroom, some with suitcases.

"I don't know how much of our colloquy you heard," the judge said leaning over the bench and directing his voice at the speakerphone, "but I've decided to set a trial to answer one question: Is the Defendant John Bertram Gropes a person? If yes, he may be extradited to Tennessee for a trial on the charges. If no, then he will remain free here in California. Clarene Eliza Dare is of the view and will file a brief to say, among other things, that Tennessee law should be applied and that under its narrow definition, he does not qualify." The judge was smiling, amused at the possibilities. "What do you say?"

"*I agree that the jackals who've called themselves governors, who haven't been doin' much in the way of governin' in this state for the last ten years, and who, by the way, are the political allies of Ms. Dare, lend a degree of credence to the notion that there's a more liberal definition in California. Now I don't believe that's*

*what Californians stand for. Call me plainspoken, but I have
no doubt that, if asked to do so, we will easily satisfy any reasonable definition of human and prove that the Defendant is
a human bein' amply qualified—legally, genetically, taxonomically and, above all, morally—to be prosecuted for his heinous
crimes before a jury of his peers in Dayton, Tennessee."*

"I'm setting this for a three-day trial on the sole issue beginning Monday, July nine, a week and a half from now," the judge
said. "Are the People ready?"

"*Ready*," the speakerphone said, parroted in turn by the
beige suit and the blue.

"Your honor, despite all the speechifying, nothing has
been proven yet," Dare said, "speaking, of course, strictly in
my capacity for the amicus." She glanced with perfunctory
politeness in the direction of Ollie Tweed. "I believe that the
Defendant should be set free, released on his own recogni-
zance, at least until such time as the prosecution establishes
the threshold fact that the Defendant is legally eligible to face
any charges."

"*Judge, he's proven himself a danger—*"

"Not necessary, Senator," the judge cut him off. "The
Defendant will be released OR."

Ollie, whose mind was anywhere other than the courtroom for the last ten minutes—the defense having been thus
far punted to the ACLF—had been sitting and staring in a
dreamlike state since the paternity announcement. When
he registered that Bert was free, his eyes lit up like the sun
finally breaking through clouds of swirling gases above Jupiter.
"Thank you, your honor," he said, almost breathlessly.

"However, I will order that the Defendant confine himself
to here, Yolo County, neighboring Sacramento County, and
Placer County where he resides. Also, Mr. Gropes, I will have
to ask that you surrender your passport. Do you have one?"

Bert shook his head, too dumbfounded to mouth the word
"no." Or tell the judge he'd never been east of the Grand Canyon.

"Let the record reflect that the Defendant has nonverbally communicated that he does not possess a passport. Now, how about you, Mr. Tweed? Is the defense ready?"

"Your honor, I sense you are struck, as I am, with a dawning awareness of history in the making." Ollie was now standing erect, full of vigor. "And I want to thank you also for offering the defense a trial to be had. But rather than plunge heedlessly in that direction, I think we would be remiss in not pausing to contemplate the extraordinary announcements made in open court today. I am elated. He is the son of my dear friend Grover Gropes. God bless you, Gro, wherever you are! And you, your honor, have seen fit to set him free. You mention that all creatures move in their respective groups; I myself am moved to imagine a murmuration of starlings, a host of sparrows, a soaring bouquet of pheasant, and—glory be!—an exaltation of larks!" For the starlings Ollie threw his left hand skyward, then dropped it only to thrust his right hand up for the sparrows, followed by the left again for the pheasant. The exaltation sent both open hands heavenward together with his gleeful upward gaze.

"Does that mean the defense is ready?"

"Your honor, I'll tell you what we're ready for: A dismissal. Right now. Especially when you consider, it was the People who introduced the stunning evidence today, calling to mind that we all derive from a great harmonious oneness. This extraordinary moment calls for an extraordinary act. As your honor knows, the word *conspiracy,* with which my client has been charged, comes from the Latin, and means *a breathing together.* This fine young man, a school teacher, we learn is a miracle one-creature group, combined as he is with the exalted Grover Seymour Gropes and those who were here first: the great apes, who roamed the earth before you, me, the People, or any of our kind. If there's to be any breathing together, it should be in song, a celebration of life's miracle, but—no!— not a trial. That's what their evidence cries out for. Should I not lead us all in a rousing chorus of, say, *We Are the World*? That would be a fitting response. In fact, let us all join hands right now, the People and the accused, in a display of solidarity, and let us form a life-affirming circle."

Ollie grabbed Bert by his arm, lifted it and took his cuffed hands, then reached out to Clarene Eliza Dare and the prosecutors. Each recoiled. Before the judge could cut Ollie off, a man burst through the gates from the gallery and shouted: "Don't do it! They're Lusians! Believe me!" Dare lightfooted out of the way as the wild-eyed stranger interposed himself between Ollie and the two prosecutors, stretching his arms out in both directions to prevent a joining of hands. "Don't you see? They want you to form a Saturnalian Circle that will make human desires mingle with theirs and spin out of control. Don't be fooled. They want more of them!" He pointed at Bert. "Lusus Scientae. Freaks of Science!"

The judge banged his gavel. "Out of order! Who are you, sir?"

"CNN, the BBC, and principals whose identity I cannot reveal. We want to televise this trial so that all the world can see." He turned and waved a finger at Dare. "Even they admit now that they and their kind are nonhumans. We want the world to see and know!"

"Bailiff, arrest him," the judge said. "Trial next Monday, nine A.M. This court is adjourned." He gaveled, rose, and paused at his bench to watch the bailiff and a newly arrived sheriff attempt to subdue the man.

Bert needed to return to the detention center out on Gibson Road where he could shed the jumpsuit and have his belongings restored, including the keys to his truck.

"Mr. Tweed, may I speak with you for a moment?"

It was the voice of Clarene Eliza Dare, but he could barely hear her due to ambient noise from the lunatic shouting, as the sheriff led him away: "Sex! Don't you see what they want? It's all about sex!"

38

JULY 1, 2019

"MARKETPLACE" SECTION OF *THE WALL STREET JOURNAL*

No one would have picked Dick Slayde to win the race
to bring biotech to mass-market consumers the way he's
done it. Traditional life science companies spend years in
research and development, followed by more frustrating
years seeking FDA approval, only to encounter a jungle
of red tape distributing the product through doctors
and pharmacies. Nevertheless, Mr. Slayde laid down an
obstacle course that could only be of his making. His latest
business venture is also tainted with controversy, involving
pending murder charges against his U.S. technology
partner (see story, A1 "Deadly Surf").

A mogul in the sex entertainment industry, Mr. Slayde
founded Primal Urge Entertainment twenty-five years ago
on the Caribbean island of Libido, first as the publisher of
the monthly, anachronistically named Slayve Quarterly.
Several successful businesses soon followed: The Urge
Casino Hotel, a network of websites that titillate with
his brand of flesh'n'flash cum razzle-dazzle, and the

manufacturing of bedroom accessories, including market leader Great Ape condoms. Epitomizing Mr. Slayde's style of doing business, his condoms come in packages large enough to suggest they will easily sheathe a decades-old vintage cell phone. Ringers all right, they only come in one standard size.

But it is Mother DNAture, a subsidiary of Primal Urge, upon which Mr. Slayde has set his latest site in his quest to retool how the biotech industry does business. Trained as a molecular biologist both at the University of California at San Francisco and Johns Hopkins, his newest venture allows users to download software from the Internet and self-administer an electrotherapeutic shock treatment that, within minutes of application, switches on monkey genes residing dormantly in human chromosomes. The result: dramatic and instantaneous genetic changes that trigger in humans the sex drive of Libidoan monkeys, all without having to endure gene splicing, years of expensive medications or injections, or other time-consuming and expensive therapies—indeed, without even having to hire a gene lab or consult a doctor.

Eschewing the tortured splicing of words and letters of mainstream biotech—with names like Affymetrix, PharmLife, Vaxgen, or his own Mother DNAture—Mr. Slayde dubbed his latest venture Hot Monkey Love. The first generation of HML features a simple user interface (see diagram, B12) employing audio headsets or earbuds. However, Mr. Slayde says he expects within a year to have a next-generation HML app that uses convenient Monkey-izer attachments for smartphones and mobile devices,, allowing users to read e-mail, check stocks, weather and movie listings, or send their earthbound libidos soaring into empyreal overdrive.

The rapid rise—of Dick Slayde, that is—can be attributed
in part to the fact that neither the FDA nor any U.S. law
enforcement agency has any jurisdiction over Libido. He
not only dodges regulation, he avoids criminal prosecution unlike his licensor (see story, A1 "Deadly Surf"). As a
citizen of Libido, he enjoys complete sovereign immunity.
Mr. Slayde has also fully availed himself of U.S. patent
protection, controlling as he does the technology through
an exclusive license arrangement.

Mr. Slayde insists that Gropes has done nothing wrong
and professes to support him in his trial. He says that Hot
Monkey Love indeed turns people into chimeric human
apes, as advertised and just as the prosecution contends
violates the Tennessee statute, but that people should be
able to do as they please without government interference.
Legal scholars are in accord that Mr. Slayde's moral support will not help Gropes should he face trial in Tennessee.

Born Richard Sleigh, records from the now defunct
Modern Means Company in Baltimore reveal that his
father sold electric bed sheets targeted for children suffering from chronic nocturnal incontinence. Mr. Slayde
refused to talk about his father or whether he, when a
child himself, had been forced to sleep on the alarming
behavior-modification device.

39

WHEN BERT REACHED THE END OF HIS LONG
dirt driveway, he found a dozen cars, along with a few television feeder vans and at least twenty-five reporters and photog-
raphers. It was the first time he'd left his refuge since arriving
home after court two days ago.

To think that he used to get practically misty-eyed when
lecturing in his Social Studies classes about the American
justice system and how the courtroom, whatever the subject
of vetting, was "the great liberator of truth." Very little truth
was coming out of his trial, already begun in the media. Just
last night on the news he'd seen a computer graphics display
depicting the silhouette of a blue man and a blue woman hovering over a sperm and egg that combined and formed a blue
zygote. To the side of the couple, a single gene flies out of a
red monkey and is inserted into the embryo. The reporter's
voice-over fairly described the latter process as an "infinitesi-
mally small amount of genetic material now part of the human

chromosome in every cell," but the graphics told a different story. Somehow the nano-speck of monkey turned the whole zygote into a furry brownish color.

Bert navigated his pickup truck through the media throng and headed down the street. Two cars followed him as he drove westbound onto Highway 80 all the way into downtown Sacramento. When he turned into the parking garage of the high rise on Capitol Mall, his two pursuers peeled off.

"I have a meeting with Clarene Eliza Dare," Bert told the young female receptionist on the twelfth floor.

Her eyes widened when she looked up and, for a second, he could tell she was searching for signs of that one rogue gene. "You're Mr. Gropes, aren't you?" She could only see him from the chest up. No doubt she was dying to stand up and look over her counter to see if his knuckles scraped the floor when he walked.

She told him to enter the conference room off the lobby and wait for Dare, who was coming from her small office in Old Sacramento. She had borrowed the conference room from a colleague because of the added security the building afforded. While Bert remained standing, office workers walked by and recognized him through the solid glass wall. Some stopped and pointed, their soundless speech incomprehensible. Although no one tried to feed him, the looks once again reactivated feelings in grade school when the others found out he was a test-tube baby. If they'd known he was part monkey, instead of X they might have called him…what? Gro-zilla? Ape Lincoln?

Clarene Eliza Dare finally strode in, wearing black slacks and a leopard-print blouse. Her hair was pulled back, emphasizing her strong facial features.

"Mr. Gropes," she said. "Eliza Dare. Pleased to meet you." Even in a simple greeting, her shoulders and feet were squared, her voice pleasant but firm as bedrock.

"Call me Bert."

"Please, have a seat, Bert. Let's get acquainted, shall we?"

Before she could continue and steer the conversation, Bert spoke up. "Let me save you some time. My lawyer, Ollie Tweed, told me that you've offered to represent me for no charge. I appreciate that—I really do—but I must decline. I'm not the least comfortable in defending these charges by saying that I'm an animal, not a person. It's simply unthinkable, whatever the consequences."

"I quite understand how you feel," she said with great empathy. "But you're in a criminal courtroom now. It's my job to search for laws they haven't considered and ways of looking at those laws they haven't thought about. That's using the tools we have, namely, the law, to make new tools. Sometimes the new ones are quite sophisticated; sometimes they are mere blunt instruments. You must adapt, and you must do it to survive. The alternative—a life in prison, of course—is that you become extinct, forever eliminated from existence."

Bert felt a chill. With another hot day in the Sacramento Valley, it might have been the air conditioner kicking on down near his ankles, but he knew better.

"I hear what you're saying," he said. "But I'm just not comfortable with the idea."

A secretary walked in. "Excuse me, Ms. Dare. This just arrived." She placed a large three-ring binder on the conference table.

"At Mr. Tweed's office yesterday I reviewed the evidence that's been turned over by the prosecution. I asked him to make me a copy and have it delivered." She pushed the binder toward him. Bert opened it and fanned through it quickly. Among other items, it contained the license agreement he'd signed with Mother DNAture, images from his bank of checks received from Primal Urge, Anna's paychecks that he'd signed, printouts from Anna's computer, reams of material on the Hot Monkey Love technology and its web interface, the affidavit of agent Dennis Clamp, pictures of a tablet computer(presumably belonging to the dead man in Tennessee), medical and coroner reports on the victim, and a dozen glossy photographs of Bert's designer slippers, seized from his home under the search warrant, whose relevance was beyond him.

"None of this proves anything. Right?" He slapped the binder shut and slid it out to the middle of the table.

"It looks like a grab bag and not much of a case, doesn't it?" she said agreeably. "At first, anyway. Let me make sure you understand the law under which you've been charged. If a death occurs during the course of certain high-risk felonies, you can be charged with murder. Say you participate in a bank robbery by driving the getaway car, and your accomplice pulls the trigger and kills a guard. You, the driver, can be prosecuted for the homicide under the state's felony murder rule. Tennessee has categorized the beastly degradation law as one of those high-risk felonies."

Bert swallowed. "So if we had to go to Tennessee, how would you defend it?"

"I think there's a good case to show that you intended to do the right thing and help others. It's in there." She tapped a pencil on the binder. "But that could be irrelevant. The only questions may be: one, whether the online experience triggers a mutation in the gene that creates a human chimera, however thinly; and two, whether, by licensing it for use on humans, a jury can convict you just for being an accomplice in the victim's death. You will be tried in Dayton, Tennessee by Senator Ray Hoffenworth who is revered there and who, with his megalomania to be the next president, wouldn't have taken this case unless he was sure he could win. Add to that you're from California."

"But I'm from Yolo County," Bert said. "Farm country. It's conservative here."

"Nobody understands that out there. To them Yolo sounds like another beach town right next door to Hollywood with pricey restaurants that sprinkle feta cheese on pizzas the size of drain stops. Look, I'm sure that we can find a professor from some northern university, with the same problem you have, who will come in and say that the therapy doesn't create chimera. Will the jury believe him?" She shook her head soberly. "Don't count on it. And it doesn't help that your partner in crime—the one who went into the bank and did the dirty deed, or so the jury will see it—is boasting in ads now that his shock therapy will turn people into human monkeys. None other than the reviled Dick Slayde."

"Partner in crime? But I've never met the man, barely knew he existed until a few weeks ago. And now I find out that from a laboratory somewhere on a remote island he's had more influence over my life than any parent."

"Remember, Dick Slayde and the prosecution share something in common. They're both using, or misusing, biotech to suit their own agendas. To win you'll have to fight fire with fire. You'll have to turn it against them and tamper with nature a little yourself and make *that* your strength. What it must have been like to find out about Slayde's vile behavior... I can't imagine the anger you must feel," she said slowly, inviting him to vent if he cared to.

"I *am* angry," Bert said in a voice that belied his words, "and naturally anxious and naturally fearful about this trial. By all logic I suppose I should go into a ballistic rage, but all I can feel is numb. I can't explain, but it's the same total numbness I felt last night when they interviewed an animal rights law professor on the news who said if I use the nonhuman defense and win, there's nothing at that point to prevent me from being treated like other creatures who face less institutionalized captivity: a petting zoo, a circus, or sold to a billionaire who collects exotic animals. He said if I'm set free, it may be on a hunting ranch—"

"Howard Betts," she interrupted. "I saw that, too."

Still contemplating Slayde, Bert went silent as if popped with a stun gun.

"I know Professor Betts," she said. "He's a jackass, pure

and simple. Trust me, he couldn't get a job as game warden on a hunting ranch if he tried—" She caught herself, taking a breath. "Sorry, but it could never happen. Never mind what the laws might say, people would never allow it. In Tennessee, California, or anywhere. That's why you're in a unique position to not only beat these charges, but draw attention to worthy issues that, until now, have never before come up on the public's radar."

Bert remained perfectly motionless, still numb-*stuck*.

Dare reached across the table, pulled the binder toward her and opened it again. "One other name besides Dick Slayde comes up over and over. Let's talk about Anna Brighton."

His trance broke.

"After I reviewed what's here and with Mr. Tweed's OK, I gave Anna a call."

"You called her?" He turned and looked at her intently.

"She was aware of all the legal goings-on and the news stories. As a matter of fact, a few reporters have tried to contact her."

Bert felt a pain that made his problems more real than the arrest, the jail time, the court hearings, the media attention, even the pending trial.

"She told me what I had inferred from the evidence. That there were the makings of a romantic involvement, but that was no longer true."

Bert felt a pain that was *worse* than the arrest, the jail time, the court hearings, the media attention, and the pending trial. Far worse, in fact, than being dumped on that hunting ranch, stalked, and riddled with gunshot.

"To be accurate, she said that you two 'were not seeing each other right now.'"

Bert was sitting up straight in his chair. Did she say "right now?" His spirit soared, gliding over a landscape of possibilities. His futuristic binoculars zeroed in, to the exclusion of all else, on a heart capable of softening.

"When I talked to her about the case, she confirmed that you didn't understand the technology—that is, what you were licensing—and that, as far as she was concerned, you didn't intend to kill anyone. I asked her what she thought about the nonhuman defense."

"What did she say?"

"Speaking professionally, she could well envision that the one gene could be taxonomically significant. As a computational molecular biologist, she thought the one gene made you an intriguing subject, and that the nonhuman defense could likely be fleshed out with, in her words, 'an interdisciplinary approach utilizing an array of algorithmic and combinatorial equations.'"

Bert felt another chill, this time deep beneath the skin line. "What does that mean?"

"She thinks it's smart."

"She thinks I'm an animal."

"That's simply not true. I think she sees it as I do: Of course you're human, but you have to stretch in other directions to survive in court, throw your adversaries off, and all the while advance a good cause if you can. She even gave me the names of some possible expert witnesses at Davis. She particularly likes the idea that the defense might give Hoffenworth the run of his life."

"That's it?" he pressed. "Did she say anything else?"

"She didn't return the reporters' calls, but she returned mine right away. I'm grateful for that. You should be, too. She said she believes in the work I'm doing on behalf of animals and professed her unwavering support for it. Her work with naked chickens, as you know, improves their lot, and she's looking to do more work with other animals. It was a nice talk."

He'd been tempted to call Anna when he arrived home from jail but resisted. With the murder charges stemming from the seamy website that so infuriated her, he didn't feel that the Total Bert Package was sufficiently attractive right now that he'd be able to charm her, like in the old days, into a lost hour of small talk. But slowly, surely, he was beginning to see the merit of Dare's offer: He'd have a world-class mouthpiece who could make that call on his behalf, and with excellent results.

"What exactly do you propose?"

She leaned back with a smile. "Let me put on the nonhuman defense. If it doesn't work, I'll stay with you and put on the best defense we can in Tennessee. You have my word."

She'd already put on a heck of a case: how to not only beat the charges but maybe win Anna's approval. He felt good enough about it that he was already grappling in his mind with some of his lesser problems, like how successful proof of non-personhood might affect the bank's handling of his still-pending home-loan application.

"You've got a deal," he said.

She leaned forward, extending her hand. "Deal."

40

JULY 6, 2019

FROM USA TODAY

Called Hot Monkey Love, it sounds more like a blue
movie from Disney than serious medicine. What were the
chances of this strange mercurial tonic succeeding against
competitors like Viagra, Levitra, and other mainstays
of the sexual enhancement market. It's not from any
icon of the pharmaceutical industry. In fact, it's from
a rogue nation in the Caribbean having only the most
tenuous trade relations with the U.S. It's not distributed
in pills, tablets, capsules, powders, or syringes. Instead
it's distributed over the Internet with a user interface that
requires that the patient, in effect, electrocute himself with
his home computer. So shocking is the charge that at least
one man is dead. If that's not enough, stern warnings have
been issued from both the United States Surgeon General
and the Food and Drug Administration.

Could there be any future for such a product in the sexual
enhancement industry? The future is here. Overnight,
Hot Monkey Love has proved to be more popular than

anything health officials, or phenomenologists for that
matter, can recall.

Stealth-launched, it first appeared only deep within a
site featuring a similar home-page remedy, a website for
and visited by breeders of naked chickens. Breeders were
encouraged to give it a try on themselves. "We're Letting
Everything Out Of The Barn Now!" the pop-up ads
promised. Hot Monkey Love was neither announced in
advance nor advertised. Jim Bolondolfo of HitManager, an
online media tracking firm, estimates that in its first week,
HML went from one hundred to a thousand hits a day. But
when news spread that the electronic tonic was powerful
enough to kill a man, visits skyrocketed. Now HML boasts
five million unique visitors per day, and rising. Officials
say the public health issues are profound. Among early
developments:

- Employers nationwide report that employees are calling in
  sick by the tens of thousands with what health officials are
  calling Hot Monkey Fever.

- Despite harsh warnings, there is ample evidence that
  employees are logging onto Hot Monkey Love while on
  the job.

- If the trend rises, according the Congressional Budget
  Office, the GNP could take a nosedive. Pfizer, makers of
  Viagra, closed yesterday, off 30%.

Former senator and Presidential candidate Ray Hoffenworth issued a press release, saying that it's more than
an attack on our economy and public health. "Hot Monkey
Love is an attack on the moral fiber by a foreign nation. It's
an attack on who we are as Americans. If elected President,
and if necessary, I would invoke the War Powers Act and
commence bombing Isle Libido." Attempts were made yesterday to contact the Hoffenworth campaign headquarters

for further comment on this story, but calls were not returned due to unforeseen staff shortages.

41

"IF YOU WANT TO BACK OUT OF THIS WHOLE thing, Senator, you can." Wayne Tanner was standing in the main conference room in the Rhea County District Attorney's Office, speaking to Ray Hoffenworth and his new national campaign chair, former advertising executive, Sol Krasputin. The candidate and the storied New York powerhouse political consultant were an unlikely pair, and not just because they were from opposite parties. The senator was unapologetic in firing Skip Ferndon in order to re-kickstart his campaign.

Sol Krasputin, sometimes affectionately called Mr. K—at least when the poll numbers were on the way up—was a slight man with an oversized head of black hair slicked back with what staffers were sure was lard or bacon grease. Quiet but intense, he always wore a dark suit with a dark shirt. Rumor had it, to maintain his juju, he bathed but once a year, reputedly on the day after the first Tuesday of November or All Souls Day, whichever came later. It was always a Wednesday.

"I suppose Mr. K would just announce that the growing demands of your campaign prevent you from trying the case," Tanner said.

"Drop out of the case?" Krasputin, gargling venom, spat at the district attorney. "Are you kidding? Of course the majors don't come out until next week, but my poll numbers tell me we're probably up fifteen percent in just a few days, and climbing, all because of the instant national coverage. CNN, MSNBC, networks, and international press are all in. Vice President Boswell has a gravity problem, an incurable one. We're going straight up. Usually only with a war or a catastrophe do we see such a dramatic rise, and that's for an incumbent. I'm counting on you two to work the legal hocus-pocus so I can do my end."

"Easier said than done," Tanner said. "We got a bit of an old-fashioned conundrum. Clarene Eliza Dare has entered the picture to personally deliver an albatross only she could come up with. Sure, we have a strong shot to bring in a conviction on the first Beastly Degradation case, but to get there we have to decide whether a human chimera is a person or a nonhuman." He looked directly at the senator. "Have you had a chance to think a little more about that?"

"Oh, I've been doin' some thinkin' all right," Hoffenworth said.

"By the way, Senator, let me say: If you want to skip the extradition phase, I'm OK with that," Tanner said. "You can step in and try the case if...*when* we bring it back here to Dayton."

"If you're gonna take her on, you gotta keep it nice an' easy," the senator said. "Let her do the convolutin', turnin' things all upside down and sidewise. I'm about keepin' things straight and simple. Somethin's either good or bad, right or wrong. You're either a human bein' or a human chimera. They're different beasts entirely." He nodded confidently, then quickly added: "Different *things*, that is."

"Agreed," Tanner said, picking up a file. "In fact, I've already interviewed a couple of primatologists and anthropologists to get their opinions. If you want to hear what they have to say before you make a decision, I could—"

"Nah! I know what's what."

"OK," Tanner said, not sure what to expect next. "So, what's your conclusion? Is Gropes a person or not?"

"An animal," Hoffenworth said.

Tanner winced in pain. Not even a trial. There went his conviction. And his chance to leverage a run at Congress. Just like that.

"Without a doubt," the senator said. "Clarene Eliza Dare's his lawyer. His biological father—wouldn't you know it?— invented this thing, all with taxpayer money. Add to that lust, murder, and fraternizin' with porn peddlars. Makes a little ol' monkey gene nothin' but the cherry on top."

Krasputin retrieved a hand recorder and blurted into it: "Note to file. Judge rules Gropes is an animal. Both Defendant and prosecution agree. Run TV ads with grainy photographs of Boswell and Gropes together with series of newspaper headlines re same and reference to Hot Monkey Love threat to health, safety, and morality. Voice-over questions policy of current administration that supports use of federal funds for porn peddlars and human degradation."

"Are you going to tell the judge what you just said?" Tanner asked the senator.

"That from a moral standpoint, Gropes is an animal? Yessir, with no hesitation. But from an extradition standpoint, he's human enough. We need us a conviction, no compromisin' on that."

"Excellent!" Krasputin announced. "Our courtroom strategy lines up perfectly with our core campaign themes. At trial in Tennessee, we'll get the message out that you're tough on crime, strong on moral clarity, and willing to go to the front lines yourself to battle degradation of the species, *Homo sapiens Americanis*—"

"*Anthro* sapiens," the senator corrected him. "That's what real Americans call themselves. Genome may be the same, but—"

"Right," Krasputin agreed. "That's what the country wants. And the position you're taking in the extradition trial is the velvet hammer: What he did was beastly, but he's a person all right. That will highlight key talking points I'm actively developing: that, in spite of your uncompromising law and divine order stance, you truly believe in compassionate inclusiveness, opportunities for all and, regarding those who were born genetically a little different and who stand accused of a terrible crime, you support their right—"

"To be tried and imprisoned," Tanner chimed in.

"Precisely," Krasputin said. "All my secret polls show overwhelming support for that."

"Chimera," Hoffenworth observed grimly. "How else we gonna stop 'em from propagatin'?"

42

"GUEST WATCH, CHECKING IN." DANNY TRATTS spoke listlessly into his radio from his perch above the two guest cottages on the Island.

"Roger," the familiar voice responded. "Anything for the log?"

"Nada. Not tonight. Over."

"Thanks, Danny. Over and out."

No surprise. After all, it was 4:00 AM. The next two-hour check-in was at 6:00 when his relief arrived. Nothing ever went on during graveyard until a week ago, his second day on the shift. That's when each night a few minutes after 11:00, right after he took over the watch, the woman—the looker on Operation Lock-Down—had turned the porch lights on, thrown down an area rug from her room and, to Danny's delight, done forty-five minutes of yoga.

Unfortunately, there had been no show on this night to start his shift. He'd have to confine himself to his thermos of coffee, listening to music on his headset, which was against the rules, and occasionally stepping out of the cart to stretch or take a leak.

It was much cooler later in the evening, but 11:00? It was hard not to believe that she'd been putting on a show for *him*, Danny Tratts. Before, when he was on day shifts, she'd seen him up close when Mr. Slayde had that run-in with the old man. She had to have noticed the work he'd done on himself—pecs, lats, glutes, the whole package. He was pretty buffed, no getting around it.

Just then the porch lights went on. Could it be? Sure enough, the front door opened and the girl trotted out, placing her rug on the ground in front of the stairs. He could see she was wearing a low-neckline raspberry spandex top and her black compression shorts. She had a sexy face and miles of leg action.

When she started her routine, he lifted his binoculars to watch. He knew what kind of girl she was because he'd seen her dance. She was hot; so hot, in fact, that it must be keeping her awake. More than ever, it was obvious she was putting a show on for him. It certainly wasn't to entertain the old man who couldn't see past his eyelids.

With her face down and both hands and feet planted, she stuck her ass high in the air. He savored the moment she held that pose. Then she inverted, stretching the other way, dropping her firm butt down low to the ground and thrusting her breasts right into the sight-line of his binocs. Tropical fruit, tender and sweet, ripe for the picking.

"Ouch!" she yelled, collapsing onto the rug. She rolled over on her back and moaned. She tried to lift herself up to her elbows but fell back in pain. Two more tries at rising ended in failure. She lay on her back motionless and helpless.

Automatically, as if an emergency system were activated, Danny dropped the binoculars and took off in the cart, descending toward her guest cottage.

"You OK? Need some help?" he said as he rolled up to within ten feet of her.

"I did something to my lower back," she said in obvious pain. "A disk. It's happened before."

"I saw you stretch out in both directions, then fall." He couldn't think of anything else to say as he calculated how to get next to her.

"The pose is called down dog, up dog, preceded by cat cow." She gushed a short breathy laugh, then gritted her teeth. "Maybe some things were never meant to be combined."

The names of yoga poses didn't interest him in the least, except maybe the doggie one. The important thing was she seemed eager enough to talk to him. Up close she looked better than ever. Did he read too much from that laugh or did she just flirt with him? In case he misread her, he might have to muffle her with his shirt, but only as a last resort. He didn't want to hear a lot of noise or wake up the old man.

"I might be able to help that," he said. "You need some pressure applied there."

"That might be nice. And then just a little help standing up and walking to my bed… I'm sure I'll be fine."

He could do better than that. He'd carry her in there if that's what it took. He stepped out of the cart, removed his belt with the gun and radio on it, and walked over to her. When she rolled over on her stomach, he pulled his T-Shirt off and dropped it within reach. He leaned over her and touched the middle of her back with one finger. "Is this the spot?"

"Down," she said. "There!"

He held his finger on the target, swung one leg over her back and lowered himself until he was straddling her with both of his knees on the rug.

"Oh yes," she said. "That feels really good."

As he continued to apply pressure with his right hand, he began to explore the rest of the prize with his left hand, moving into the shoulders and neck region.

"Mmmm…" she purred, as he settled his weight fully on her butt. Both of his hands dropped down and held her around the waist. There weren't going to be any problems. He could tell she wanted him as much as he did her.

Suddenly she lifted her head. "Do it! Do it, doll! Now!" she shouted.

Priming this hottie was as quick and easy as the company's new gene tech, like flipping on a switch. And she called him doll! His pecs, lats, and glutes were buff all right, but—just like that, less than one minute into his probing massage action that could turn a woman into putty—she was coming on to him like a she-bitch in heat. No problem moving the timetable up a notch. Truth be told, he only had one notch to go anyway.

At the same moment he heard a rustling from above. He looked up just in time to see a monkey perched in a banyan tree, launching himself from a branch so as to plunge the full twenty feet to the ground. It didn't make any sense. Here he's got a babe who wants him so bad she crawls out of bed at 4:00 AM to snare him and drag him off to her love nest, when out of nowhere a monkey decides to jump out of a tree. But then it got stranger. As the monkey emerged from the dark canopy overhead, he was able to make out that the animal was now clutching in both hands an iron from one of the guest cottages somewhere on the Estate. That made even less sense. Could there be an ironing board up there too? Now why would a monkey be ironing up in a banyan tree? Unless, possibly, someone *gave* the iron to the monkey and...*oh shit!*

As a prophylactic measure, Tina tied up her would-be masseur with complimentary Great Ape condoms from the bathroom of her cottage. Dr. Gro, who emerged from his cabin as soon as Scooter did the deed, instructed her to double-twist two of them together, adapting them into the sturdiest of handcuffs and ankle restraints.

"Is it going to be cool enough today?" Tina asked. That was key to their escape plan.

Dr. Gro took a deep breath. "I think we'll be OK."

Each morning, along with hotel service of continental

breakfast, they were given day-old editions of the *Wall Street Journal* and *USA Today* from which she read to him the regional weather reports. The news stories about Hot Monkey Love, the arrest of Dr. Gro's until-now estranged son, and the pending trial—not to mention Tina's own restlessness—all compelled them to make their move.

Soon her captive was conscious again but still groggy and disoriented. Tina gagged him with the shirt he'd removed moments before. Until then he kept repeating the only two observations he was able to muster: "Bitch!" and "Fuckin' monkey!" Tina and Dr. Gro knew that he would be found shortly after his relief arrived at 6:00 A.M., after which there would be an intense hunt throughout the small island. They needed to make themselves scarce before then.

Tina dragged the Silk UnderAir double mattress off the bed and out of her cottage where, with the help of Dr. Gro, she loaded it onto the roof of the cart. Securing it as best she could with ropes fashioned from strips of bedsheets, she picked up the belt that Bozobreath had dropped, complete with gun, radio, and utility knife, and fastened it around her waist. It was 4:22 when they finally launched their escape.

With Tina at the wheel and Dr. Gro riding shotgun, Scooter appeared to be acting as lookout on the roof, but in fact he provided ballast to hold the mattress down. They headed north on a dirt road into the jungle, in the opposite direction of the security gate on the southeastern edge of the Estate, the only road that led to the city of Libido or the port.

In case someone on the Estate might be able to see them, they traveled for three quarters of a mile under the light of a nearly full moon. When they were far enough away, Tina handed the onboard flashlight to Scooter, who shined it on the road ahead for her.

After half an hour bouncing along a dirt road surrounded by dense jungle, they began to hear a low roar that became louder and louder for the next quarter mile. Within a few minutes they came to the spot where Tina had predicted the road would end: Libidinal Falls, emanating from a height of over one hundred feet and formed by two magnificent spouts of white kinetic energy converging midair and crashing into an egg-shaped pool where the waters—jumping, dancing and ceaselessly grinding at rock, long after it was molten lava—surged forth as the Libido River. From there the driving waters flowed swiftly but silently downstream away from the roar to urban Libido two miles away.

They stood on the bank of the river with the falls to their left at ten o'clock splashing into the pool about fifty feet away. Tina untied the mattress and dragged it off the cart's roof and into a nearby pool of shallow, almost still water.

"Wait," Dr. Gro said, pausing, standing perfectly still, listening to the liquid percussion of the falls. Tina closed her eyes and tried to imagine what the blindman's mind was bird-dogging: frenetic thunder and driving rhythms punctuated by random, intermittent drumbeats tinged with evanescent clarion sprays. That probably wasn't what he heard. He always had some interesting scientific take on things. She opened her eyes and stared into the water. The way the moon played on the rippling waters radiating away from the falls, it looked like there were flickers of hot flames burning beneath the surface. He wouldn't be able to see the fires she saw but, it occurred to her, maybe he could hear them.

"Of course," he said slowly. He'd discovered something. "I can prove there's no such thing as a chimera. Mathematically. They don't exist. They're just a figment of Hoffenworth's imagination. His whole case would vanish. With a computer and a few weeks to run millions of calculations, I can construct the equation later. It would be great right now to jot down a few mnemonics until then."

"Quick! Give it to me." She always had something to write with, just in case she wanted to jot down an observation of something unusual or striking in her daily routine. Today, in the course of escaping a life of imprisonment, having run smack into the fountainhead of the Libido River, accompanied by a blind molecular cosmologist and a monkey, was no exception.

"Ready," she said, pen and paper in hand.

Dr. Gro took a breath. "One."

"That's it?" She'd waited to see if more numbers followed.

"It's not as obvious as you might think," he said, a little defensively. "If it were, the world would not be overrun by fools."

"Got it." She put the pen and paper back in her belt.

"There's more."

"Sorry."

"Nine-two-eight."

"Got it."

Before they all climbed aboard, Dr. Gro christened their improvised craft the H.M.S. Evolution and declared the seat assignments: Scooter in back, himself in the middle, and Tina at the helm.

"Can I recite a poem? Do we have time?" Tina asked. "It's good luck."

"Not exactly scientific, but luck sounds good right now."

"It's the only mattress poem I know," she said modestly. That seemed appropriate since they were entirely at the mercy of her Silk UnderAir to ride a rough and tumble river. The poem was by Samuel Johnson, as best she could remember it—one that he, in turn, had translated from an earlier French writer: "'In bed we laugh, in bed we cry; and born in bed, in bed we die; the near approach a bed may show of human bliss to human woe.'"

For some reason the rhymes unglued Scooter. He burst into uninhibited laughter.

"He's laughing because he understands it's not a poem about mattresses," Dr. Gro humbly observed. "Great balls! Took me a lifetime to figure it out."

After her two companions were settled, Tina smashed an

imaginary champagne bottle over the hull, pushed away from the bank, and jumped aboard. She stroked furiously with her oar fashioned from an upside down broom stick jammed into a tubular dustpan handle. As she started paddling, she couldn't resist tickling Scooter a little more: "Scooter *doll*…used to be *small*…but now he's *tall*…as far as monkeys *go*…in Libby-*doh*." He was bleary-eyed from the hilarity. Maybe it was stress reduction for monkeys. It was for her.

Their moment of mirth over, Scooter edged forward and put his arms around Dr. Gro so that he, too, could better hang on for the ride. Once immersed into the full thrust of the river's current, they undulated at times gently, swiftly, and wildly ahead.

AS DAWN BEGAN TO LIGHT UP THE SURROUNDING jungle, about a mile and a half down river, Tina stroked hard for the right bank, splattering her crew with water in the process. She reached an eddy and stuck her paddle in the volcanic silt beneath the surface as an anchor. They all scrambled onto dry land, and then she pulled the mattress to the shore and left it. They were just north of the dock for the waterbuses that would be arriving later this morning for tours of the Great Ape condom factory, museum, and gift shop.

Tina led the way with Scooter guiding Dr. Gro one step at a time. When they reached the pathway leading from the dock up to the museum, Tina tied a sweatshirt over the utility belt she was wearing, and they made their way to the front of the complex. There, on the spacious decking to the factory and the entry to the museum, was what was billed as "the World's Largest Condom." It maintained its shape with hot air blasted from below the deck. Except right now, during non-business hours, there was no need to keep up appearances. Instead of a buoyant work of art, piles of nylon material were heaped on the deck—shriveled and lifeless.

Out of curiosity, Tina had taken the museum tour after she first arrived on the island. She recalled people standing in front of the giant flesh-colored condom, marveling and awestruck, as if regarding Michelangelo's *David* or Rodin's *Thinker*. The docent delivered the script with the same tone she would have used at a prestigious art gallery: "Primal Urge founder, Dick Slayde, commissioned the world-renowned performance artist, Anarcho, to design the Great Ape Living Sculpture. Its inspired shape is maintained with hot air, not a fixed object, so as to allow it to move, breathe, expand, contract, and respond to its environment. While reaching for the future, note how the object emerges from the earth, intimating a great unfurling towards a shared past. Hence, the words so carefully chosen," she said, referring to the company tagline. She swept her hand up to lead all eyes to what was nothing more than naked commercialism:

GREAT APE®

SLAYTEX® ALL-NATURAL CONDOMS
Because You Can Go Back®
A product of Primal Urge

Above the words "Because You *Can* Go Back" was the face in silhouette of a Libidoan monkey. With her own head crooked back in awe, the docent summed up: "The upward thrust of the artist's work, so deftly implied, suggests that the sky alone is the limit. Mr. Slayde brings the same philosophy to his varied enterprises."

Tina peeked through the window of an exit door at one end of the deck. No one was in that location, but she noticed a large display photograph that she'd only glanced at a year ago. he photo was of a male Libidoan, mugging for the camera, surrounded by ten younger ones. The caption read: "Primo (1986-2014), the beloved Libidoan who was a fixture on the Estate, acted as the model for the silhouette used on all packages of Great Ape condoms. From 1992, when Primal Urge was founded, until his death, Primo was Honorary Chairman of the Board of the company. Photographed here in 2004, he is shown with 10 of his reputed 97 children. Squatting on bench, left to right: Bruno, Sophie, Jojo, Androo, and Jackee. Front: Pluto, Sami, Scooter, Primo, and Rose."

As eager as she was to leave, part of Tina wanted to stay and meet Scooter's brothers and sisters—all ninety-seven. Then she flashed on the stunning revelation made by Dick Slayde at the tail end of their last encounter with him. Ninety-eight, she recalculated.

Tina removed the gun from her belt and released the safety. Folding her arms so as to conceal the weapon, she walked across the deck toward the piles of nylon as if to get a closer look. She'd assumed there would be someone in the building near the front door in the middle of the deck. Sure enough, a security guard in his forties, with a chubby face and glasses, jumped out of his seat inside the museum and hastened out the door.

"The museum is closed," he scolded in a squeaky, nasal voice. "You'll have to leave."

Tina arranged a surprised and stupid look, then turned to him. "Huh?"

"How did you get past the gate?" he pressed, more annoyed. "There are no waterbuses until—"

Tina unfolded her arms, revealing the gun, and aimed it at him.

"Drop your belt very slowly," she said.

He was dumbfounded. As if he didn't believe what he was seeing or hearing, he searched her eyes, but she remained steely-eyed and firm in her resolve, even assuming a wide stance she'd seen Wonder Woman use to great effect. He dropped his belt.

"Sit there and put your hands behind." She directed him to a bench in front of the museum entry. He did as requested.

"Come here, doll," she shouted over to Scooter. After he hurried over on all fours, she pulled out more rope she'd fashioned from sheets to tie the guard's wrists to the bench. She handed the gun to Scooter. "Don't shoot him unless he moves," she instructed. The monkey couldn't possibly have understood a word, but he took the gun and held it with both hands, even widening his stance just as she'd done.

"Are you crazy? You gave the monkey your gun!" the man whined.

"Right. Now don't move!" She grabbed his wrists and wrapped them three times.

"You can't do that!" He spoke without moving his lips.

"Sure I can."

Scooter bared his teeth in a wide grin, shrieked, then started jumping up and down while waving the pistol.

The gun went off, firing a bullet into the deck in front of the security guard, who let out a high-pitched scream. Scooter squawked and tossed the gun. It went off again, firing a bullet into the side of the building. Luckily Tina was finished tying up the guard—her nose for trouble told her that he'd had an accident. Holding her breath, she took the last strip of bed sheet and gagged him with it.

Tina returned to Dr. Gro and led him to the scene on the deck. He touched the deflated nylon on the deck. "Do you see where there's access?" he asked Tina.

"Yep," Tina said. "On both sides." She lifted the eight-foot long trap door on one side revealing a steep ten-foot-deep staircase. "We're in luck! You were right. There's a gondola down there."

Based on her description of the floating condom, the professor had predicted that the artist wouldn't recalculate the specs for placement of the burners, burner platform, and lines for securing the gas-inflated sack to a fixed object. A simple hot-air balloon with gondola, ready-made with the necessary features, was all that was needed. In creating the Great Ape Living Sculpture, Anarcho produced his illusion by merely modifying the standard shape of an aircraft, making sure to hide his artist's trick under the museum's deck.

With help from Tina, Dr. Gro descended the stairs, climbed aboard, and began familiarizing his hands with the features of the aircraft. "See if you can find something we can use for life preservers. We may need them. What's our time?"

"Five-fifty-four."

Dr. Gro took a deep breath. "OK. Let's move. Make sure the radio is on."

Tina climbed back up the stairs and, joined by Scooter, entered the front door that had been left open by the security guard. It was cooler than usual, in the low fifties this morning, yet the guard's gagged face was awash in perspiration. Inside on a bench she found a few foam seat cushions that held some promise of buoyancy. She grabbed two of them.

"*Guest watch. This is Skip. Danny's not here. Over,*" the radio blared.

"*He checked in at four, Skip. Look around the guest cottages and get back. Over and out.*"

Tina hurried back to where Dr. Gro was, handing him one tool at a time. He ran his fingers over each one to identify it and stow it away.

"I heard that," Dr. Gro shouted. "We have fewer than ten minutes. I'm going to fire one of the burners. Go up and keep fluffing the material until it's inflated."

Tina did as instructed. She heard the burner activate and slowly the nylon began to billow. She raced around and untangled the folds, allowing it to fill and take full shape.

"*Skip at guest watch. We found Danny. They hog-tied him. He says they took the cart and an air mattress toward the river. Over.*"

"*Copy. Follow the road out to the Falls and keep an eye out. We'll send security to the port and make sure no watercraft leaves without a search. The only other stop would be the museum. We'll send a unit up there pronto. Over and out.*"

Tina scrambled below and, when Dr. Gro had climbed out, cut one of the anchor lines with Danny's knife. The gondola lifted a few feet and canted to one side. She calculated she needed twelve feet to clear the deck level. With extra rope stored nearby, she measured two Tinas, head to toe, and added a foot and a half for knots. With the gondola raised and pitched to one side, she was able to tie the rope to a spot at the center of the aluminum gondola, a location that would be unreachable by her once she was inside the aircraft. When she secured the other end to the bottom of the stairs, she cut the two remaining moorings. Freed, the gondola clanked off the sides but lifted to a foot and a half above the deck, held now solely by her rope.

She could hear a car engine at the bottom of the drive, accelerating up the hill. Dr. Gro was already in the gondola, firing up the second burner. As the island temperature warmed up, more heat was needed to keep it hotter inside the balloon than the exterior. A gentle breeze was blowing to the west, as Dr. Gro predicted, meaning they had to rise quickly, six hundred feet in the direction of the Estate. Once they cleared the mountain, they would drift with those westerly currents, continually adjusting their altitude for the optimal ride.

"Ready!" Dr. Gro shouted to her.

Tina leaned down and gave a hug to Scooter. "I'm going to miss you. Be good."

She climbed up the stairs and into the gondola hovering a foot over the deck. Two men were running up the stairs to the deck as she tossed the knife down to Scooter. She had trained Scooter to jump off tables onto a pillow-headed security guard and club his head with an iron. She'd also taught him to "cut it" using twined grass as a stand-in for rope and a stick as the knife.

"Cut it, doll!" she yelled down to him. The monkey picked up the knife and didn't hesitate to go straight for the taut rope with the blade. Instantly they were airborne just as the men, breathing hard, arrived onto the deck. Forty feet above, climbing fast and drifting west over the museum, they were clear. She leaned over the side and witnessed the men pointing and shouting into their radio. She didn't see Scooter anywhere. Just then the balloon pitched one way and Scooter, holding onto the bottom of the rope with one hand, swung into view. He was still holding the knife in the other.

"Scooter's still holding the rope!" she shouted at Dr. Gro.

"We're rising too fast, aren't we?" Dr. Gro said. "Reading!"

"Two hundred feet," she said. She looked down and then stood and took in the 360-degree view: the river winding off to the right where they had just come and the mountain, covered with a canopy of trees and dense growth, rising in front of them. On the east side she could now easily see the port, the casino hotel and the Libido cityscape, and the ocean beyond.

Dr. Gro turned the valve on the second burner but it wouldn't reduce the flame. The valve was broken or stuck. He reduced the flame on the first burner to a pilot light. They continued to rise but less dramatically. Within a few minutes they reached the crest of the steep hill.

"We'll have to jettison the defective burner," Dr. Gro said. "We won't need it once we clear the mountain."

Tina peered over and saw Scooter again, quite relaxed, hanging on with one hand at the bottom of the rope, studiously examining the knife.

"Hang on, doll!"

"Once we're over and far enough down the other side," Dr. Gro said, "we'll see if we can lower to where Scooter can jump onto a tree or into a clearing."

A moment later they cleared a last ridge, and they were floating over the Estate at about one-hundred feet and rising. At least two-hundred acres had been clear-cut and replaced with lawns, farming, and scattered buildings.

"We're clear," Tina said. "I see the Mansion ahead and the ocean, all downhill, to the far west."

"Let's find a place to dump this burner, so we can switch to the other." He was already more relaxed. "Preferably an open area away from the indigenous flora and fauna. A lawn would be excellent."

Tina unwound a wing-nut securing the expendable tank.

"Push it a little closer to the edge of the platform so you can shove it off when I say go," the professor said. "What's that noise?"

"We're approaching a large, flat-roofed building surrounded by barbed wire that houses all the computers for the Primal Urge online businesses. You hear roof fans."

Dr. Gro scowled. "Dick Slayde's server farm. That's an ecological disaster of global, not just insular, impact."

Tina pushed the burner closer to the edge. "That ought to—" she gave it one more shove—"do it."

Suddenly Scooter, who must have climbed up to the rail of the gondola, leaped to the platform and pushed the burner free.

"Scooter!"

Dr. Gro needed no description of what happened. Tina watched Scooter's projectile descend, end over end as if in slow motion, and strike the roof below, but not on one of the fans or any of the open rooftop spaces. Instead, it met up with another, larger tank. But the relationship was doomed and short-lived, instantly sending a flame and smoke over a hundred feet into the air, behind and above the path of their balloon. The entire roof was consumed in flames.

"Butane," the old man said. "A refrigerant." He could tell, evidently from the smell.

Before their aircraft dropped more than fifty feet, he fired up the remaining burner.

"Did I say 'do it?'" Tina said, trying to reconstruct how a monkey, acting on cosmic cue, outsmarted everyone, especially Dick Slayde. Just then there was a second explosion, collapsing the roof and pouring the fire into the center of the building.

"We're approaching the mansion," Tina said. "About seventy-five feet. We'll just barely clear antennas. Dick Slayde is on the veranda, talking on the radio."

Tina turned the radio on again. It was Slayde: "*Get every fire unit up here! Immediately!*"

"This is Tina Hallickson, a Slayve who's now been set free. I give you the great Dr. Grover Gropes of the Libidoan Underground. Over."

"*Are you there, Gropes? You've destroyed a billion-dollar business. The future of science. The future of biotech. Bioporn!*" Wearing a vermillion robe that seemed to hang on his haggard frame, Slayde paced on the veranda and gesticulated as he shouted into the radio. "*But not for long. I will be back. And if it's not me, it'll be someone else. You will pay for this!*" He shook his fist at them as the balloon passed overhead.

"How can that be, Dick?" Dr. Gro said. "There are no laws in Libido."

Just then, Scooter finished inspecting the knife and, satisfied that it was no longer of use to him, threw it overboard. It shattered the plates and cups on a breakfast table a few feet from where Slayde stood, startling him.

"No laws except the laws of the jungle," Dr. Gro shouted. "I tried to have the tank meet your lawn, but I'm no matchmaker. I was preempted, and you were eliminated by—as a biologist, you'll love this, Dick—*natural selection.*" He reached up and patted the foot of Scooter, who shrieked once, loud enough to be heard on the radio. "Marvelous, isn't it? Over and out."

Dick Slayde threw the radio down, slumped into a chair, and buried his face in his hands.

The balloon drifted across and down to the far edge of the Estate to the outlying cottages where the two of them had spent the last six weeks together. Nothing further was spoken about trying to drop off Scooter. His passage was booked.

Tina faced the back of Dr. Gro who, taking a deep breath, spread his arms out wide as if to greet the approaching ocean. It reassured her to see him in a moment of complete calm. For her part, she didn't look back, letting her eyes sweep over the magnificent blue canvas straight ahead.

43

JULY 9, 2019

STUDIO ANCHOR: Good morning, everyone. I'm
Janet Jones in New York, and this is LNTV, the Litigation
Network. It was July, nineteen-twenty-five when the
historic Monkey Trial began in Dayton, Tennessee.
Schoolteacher John Scopes, represented by Clarence
Darrow, was convicted for teaching evolution to his
students, a crime in Tennessee. The prosecutor was none
other than the populist and three-time Presidential
candidate William Jennings Bryan. Fast forward to today
when LNTV brings you live coverage of the already historic Hot Monkey Love Trial from Woodland, California.
Defendant, Social Studies teacher John Bertram Gropes,
stands accused of murder for his role in the dissemination
from Isle Libido of the online electronic aphrodisiac Hot
Monkey Love. Gropes was born with a single gene taken
from a Libidoan monkey and inserted into his zygote,
duplicated billions of times in every cell in his body. The
defense says that kind of tampering with Nature calls into
question whether Gropes is a person, in a legal sense, who
can be prosecuted for crimes. The defense says "nonhuman." The prosecution says "nonsense." The lineup. For
the prosecution: former prosecutor and now senator from

Tennessee, and Republican candidate for President of the United States, the Honorable Ray Hoffenworth. And for the defense: the victor in numerous high-profile criminal trials, and advocate for animal rights, famed defense lawyer, Clarene Eliza Dare. Let's go to our legal commentator, veteran trial attorney Ben Griswold, who's standing outside Judge McGrath's courtroom in Woodland. Ben, tell us a little more about this proceeding. We know the murder trial is supposed to happen in Dayton, Tennessee and that we're at the extradition phase.

LEGAL COMMENTATOR: Let me break it down, Janet. Murder trial in Tennessee. Extradition trial in California. This mini-trial here today in Woodland. Typically our viewers would tune in only to the murder trial, but everything is riding on this trial within a trial. Today's trial is a first. A jury will be asked to answer only the one threshold question: Is the Defendant, John Bertram Gropes, a person as that term is meant by the laws under which he is charged?

STUDIO ANCHOR: So is this a preliminary hearing, a habeas corpus, or what?

LEGAL COMMENTATOR: Neither. As I said, this trial is unprecedented, but with the advent of biotechnology, surely we will see more in the future. Since the sole question is whether he's a person, legal scholars I've spoken with are uniformly calling this a personal trial.

STUDIO ANCHOR: Indeed, it's a historic battle of legal titans with groundbreaking questions to be decided. Still, it's preliminary. Why should we care about what happens at this early stage?

LEGAL COMMENTATOR: This mini-trial is likely to tell us the whole story. What will happen at the murder phase of the trial could probably be constructed—cloned, so to speak—from the minute details unfolding here at the personal trial. Ultimately, they'll have to decide what a human being is; namely, whether the activation of dormant monkey genes in users of the Hot Monkey Love technology turns them into part monkeys, part humans.

STUDIO ANCHOR: Speaking of the molecular, won't we be looking at certain sequences of Gropes's DNA?

LEGAL COMMENTATOR: Yes, Janet. Scientists here have already isolated a sequence in Mr. Gropes's DNA composed of about a hundred thousand nucleotides—a staggering, two-inch thick tome, Exhibit A to this trial, with nothing but the letters a, c, t and g printed single space inside—that all parties agree is a Libidoan monkey gene. In other words, among the three billion nucleotides in the human genome it's an aberration, but the same sequence is uniformly found in the monkey, Pan troglodytes Libidoanis. But here's the catch: They don't know what function the gene performs.

STUDIO ANCHOR: Any chance they'll find out during this trial?

LEGAL COMMENTATOR: Unlikely, Janet. They only know what a fraction of genes do, and they take years. In this case—

STUDIO ANCHOR: Excuse me, Ben, we just received this news report. A fiery explosion occurred early this morning on Isle Libido, a few miles west of the city of Libido, south of the Libido River, apparently destroying the server farm that supports all of Primal Urge's online business. The cause—whether arson, accident, or act of nature—is unknown and no announcement has been made by representatives of Primal Urge. But this much we do know. As of about six o'clock this morning Eastern time, the service is down. Hot Monkey Love has been interrupted, perhaps indefinitely.

LEGAL COMMENTATOR: Which may explain why the court is blessed with a full pool of prospective jurors this morning. With chronic absenteeism reported everywhere, court officials were frankly concerned about whether citizens of Yolo County would be reporting for jury duty. Janet, the clerk has entered the courtroom, signaling that session will begin within a few minutes.

STUDIO ANCHOR: Just enough time to go to reporter Pam Schroeder, who's standing in front of the Yolo County Courthouse.

REPORTER: Janet, the ease with which genes can be manipulated by Hot Monkey Love, the revelations about the Defendant's genetic history, and now the trial have all caused people we've encountered to pause and think about the implications of genetic engineering—what it all means, where it might be going. I have some people here on the street willing to offer us their opinions. What do you think the future holds?

YOUNG WOMAN ON STREET: I think it's scary what scientists can do with the genes of people and animals and fruit and dirt clods. I just want it to be, like, over. So the family of the victim can get closure on this. You know what I mean? I don't want to have to think about it anymore.

REPORTER: Thank you. And here's a gentleman I know is anxious to talk to us. You're wearing nothing but a big diaper that says "DNA" on it. What's that all about?

MAN ON STREET: Open your eyes. Everything. Watch how easily I change my diapers. I pull them off—

REPORTER: I see. Underneath, your Fruit of the Looms say "AND."

MAN ON STREET: Exactly! Move a few letters around. Diapers become underpants, Scopes becomes Gropes, and DNA becomes AND. The conjunctive! Combinations without limit. And and and and and without end. Anything can be combined with anything, or nothing at all—

REPORTER: Sir! Keep your underpants on! Never mind. Let's keep that camera waist up.

MAN ON STREET: Elements and physical characteristics that for eons defined and distinguished human beings, animals, and plants are tossed back into a primordial alphabet soup. Imagine Sense and Sensibility folded willy-nilly into War and Peace. Sense becomes nonsense. Who will stop the Lusian technology overlords? They—

REPORTER: The who?

MAN ON STREET: The overlords of planet Lusus Naturae, of course. It's supposed to mean freak of nature, but now we're seeing a new generation of Lusians: freaks of science, neither human nor animal. On the taxonomical chart, they are way, way out there. Look at me. This is Homo sapiens—

REPORTER: Sorry, sir, our time is up, but thank you. Your comments were most revealing. Back to you, Janet.

STUDIO ANCHOR: Thanks, Pam. This much is clear: We will go straight to the courtroom where this personal trial is about to begin.

44

BERT GROPES SAT AT THE DEFENSE TABLE
next to his attorney, Clarene Eliza Dare. Around him the
packed Woodland courtroom buzzed with eager onlookers
and reporters. Senator Ray Hoffenworth had entered the room
a few minutes earlier and, when their eyes met for the first
time in a passing glance, Bert detected a grimace somewhere
between condescension and distaste. No mistaking, the prosecutor regarded him as a something less than human. Bert took
some comfort seeing his lawyer behaving calmly, leaning back
in her chair, her hands folded. At the prosecution table, Ray
Hoffenworth, Wayne Tanner, and a young woman from the
California AG's office huddled, talking in hushed voices.

Bert's mind wandered, searching for company—some good
company, not the misery-loves-company kind. In no time he
found himself thinking about Anna. It pained him that she
wasn't there, but that didn't stop him from fantasizing about
her sitting in the gallery, holding a keepsake of him. But they

hadn't really had enough of a relationship for her to have a keepsake, except maybe the Waldorf salad recipe he'd given her. That's what it was. *Clutching the recipe in her small hand, she sits on the edge of her seat. Seconds later the judge thunders at the prosecution: "The Defendant has been falsely accused! Case dismissed!" A well-worn script, but one he loved all the more. Anna drops the recipe, rushes forward and wraps her arms around his neck. He lifts her up and swings her around as the slow motion camera, synced to a joyful tune, captures the billowing wave of a print dress he had no reason to believe she owned, one that hadn't been made in more than forty years.*

He leaned over and spoke to his attorney. "What kind of witnesses are they going to call?" She had briefly described to him some experts she'd retained, but they hadn't talked much about the prosecution's line-up.

Dare turned around and coolly scanned the courtroom. "None that are here now," she finally said, coming back around and facing Bert. "They'll show up after the jury is picked, and the great Ray Hoffenworth has to finally put on his case." She didn't conceal her disdain. "His team has top experts—primatologists, geneticists, zoologists. But it won't do him any good. That's because the prosecution and the kind of experts whom they tend to hire are all so species-centric and biased against those who are genetically different. They haven't given any thought to how most creatures have a right to look at things. The trial may be over after I cross-examine their witnesses."

Just then the judge entered the courtroom.

"All rise," the bailiff announced. "The Honorable David Winton McGrath presiding."

When the judge took the bench and the room was seated, the clerk called out the case of *People versus John Bertram Gropes.*

"Good morning, everyone," the judge spoke. "Before we get started, let me make some acknowledgments so that we can put things in context and keep things in order. We have a large number of visitors to our courtroom today and, as I'm sure you're all aware, the court has granted permission to have television cameras present because of the great public interest. That won't change anything. As always, we will proceed in an orderly fashion, and it is my intent to have the issue before this court decided swiftly but fairly. Is that clear and agreed?"

Both Dare and Hoffenworth nodded. Hoffenworth was relentless in the competition to appear more agreeable. He nodded three times to the judge, then three more times to Wayne Tanner seated to his left. Still nodding when he turned back to the judge, it bordered on unctuous bobble-headedness.

"Now there is one hitch, but I do not expect it to derail our plans. I've just been informed by the building engineers that we have—how shall we say?—an air-conditioning problem." There were moans. "Apparently a microbe capable of making people sick either has escaped or may have escaped from an exhibit in another courtroom in a case involving a University lab. I am assured that it has not circulated and that it will not. But to be cautious, the building has now turned off the air conditioner and—"

Groans punctuated sustained moans.

"—they are going to install special safety filters throughout the building before turning the system back on. This may take a day or two, but I don't want it to interfere with what we've set out to do. One advantage of an old courthouse is we can open the windows. It's supposed to reach ninety-one today, and it'll be hotter tomorrow. I suggest light-fabric attire. I may have to allow removing jackets, but we will get through this."

The judge paused, only to take a breath. "Now, we should bring in prospective jurors. Are the parties ready to proceed?"

"We can do better 'an that, Judge." Hoffenworth rose from his chair and addressed the court. "We'd like to make an *in limine* motion."

"Very well," the judge said. "Now is the time to decide any preliminary issues."

"It's this simple, Judge. If it walks like a duck, quacks like a duck, and acts like one o' them ol' ducks, by golly, it's a duck." A few approving chuckles rippled across the gallery. "Some things are so self-evident that the court can beg off hearin' evidence about it by simply takin' judicial notice." He turned and addressed the gallery directly. "The sky is blue. There is no man on the moon, and if there was such a man, he wouldn't be plowin' cream cheese on his back forty. Judicial notice, as this court knows, is a fancy legal word for horse sense—just about anything that is common knowledge, beyond reasonable dispute." He faced the judge again. "Now I ask you to look at the Defendant, and tell me, sure as the creek will rise, that's not a person sittin' there."

All eyes were on Bert, sitting next to Clarene Eliza Dare. Instinctively he straightened up in his chair and adjusted his tie by shifting the knot a smidgen to both sides before re-centering it. Then it struck him that a monkey wouldn't straighten his tie and try to look prim and proper. But what about a man mixed up with monkey? He wanted to follow the course his attorney had charted, but it was all so counterintuitive, if not downright unnatural. When he realized too late that he'd just helped Senator Hoffenworth make a case against him, Bert automatically began rubbing his eyes deeply with the thumb and middle finger of his right hand, only to discover he'd assumed a pose of tortured cogitation.

"Allow me to explain. Mr. Gropes here has defined himself, by more than his physiology or genes—by his choices. The kind of choices monkeys don't make. Why should we have to put in evidence? The court knows full well that there's no monkey anywhere that's negotiated and signed an agreement. If it was for buyin' or sellin' a bunch o' bananas, that'd be one thing. But this agreement licenses over some sophisticated technology to a purveyor of pornography, the kind of filth and degradation that only a depraved human could dream up." He held up a copy of the license agreement. "Maybe a million monkeys with a million typewriters could eventually knock out a masterpiece like *The Book of Virtues*. But what are the odds a monkey could do what the Defendant did here? No, those are moral choices. If he weren't in a Tennessee prison next year, I'd be willin' to bet he'd be votin' for a tax increase spawnin' another kinda monster, combinin' Democratic fiscal policy with the Internal Revenue Service, creatin' a mutant creature so large, threatenin' to come in an' crush under its foot poor innocent taxpayin' citizens."

He paused as if not sure how he got to where he was.

"This is the way we see it, your honor," he began again. "A real monkey's evolved himself up from the slime and ooze to become a monkey. I have no doubt the critter is sincerely desirous of raisin' himself up even higher by his furry little bootstraps so's he can walk in the company of men. Not gonna happen, but what creature wouldn't want that? What the Defendant and his attorney have cooked up is just the opposite. It's evolution upside down, turned around and goin' the wrong way on the evolutionary highway. It's growin' a fur coat and divin' into a Swimmin' Pool Primeval, back with the bugs an' slugs, locusts an' pornographers. It's no evolution at all. It's *devolution*. You rightly hear a familiar name tucked inside the word devolution, concoctin' a scheme of turnin' things back in a way that only the devil himself"—he said, rotating his head in the direction of Dare without looking at her—"or *her*self could have hatched. It's a man sayin' he's not a man. He's sayin': 'I renounce my humanity, my precious rights as an American citizen, and I declare myself a monkey who answers only to the law o' the jungle.' Sad truth is, only a human bein'—one who's lost his way and who don't know who or what he is anymore, all with help from the clever and like-minded—could conceive o' somethin' so twisted."

Bert, leaning back and away from the defense table, gazed down at his gray slacks covering his thighs and held his head there. The prosecutor was trying to convict him for crimes he did not commit, but he found himself strangely agreeing with at least half of the terrible things said about him.

"But it's nothin' more than their words and their choices," Hoffenworth continued. "Nothing more than familiar sophisms from criminals and their lawyers who will say anything to avoid responsibility. We're askin' the court to go ahead and exercise its power to recognize the immutable truth: declare what's as plain as the days are long and this great land is wide." He bounced on his heels and placed his hands on the fore of his girth. Then he turned and pointed a finger at Bert. "That there is a person, however misguided and morally led astray. A person who under law must be held legally accountable for his crimes against his country and humanity.

"That's my message today," he said to the gallery. "Now let's move this campaign…" He caught himself mid-sentence and turned to the judge: "…this *trial* to Tennessee where it belongs. Thank you. Thank you." An approving murmur of voices sounded through the room.

The judge looked at him wide-eyed, as if trying to digest all that had been said. "Ms. Dare," he said. "A motion has been made that the court take judicial notice that the Defendant is a person. Your response?"

With great resolve and composure, Clarene Eliza Dare placed the pen in her hand on the table and stood erect. "Your honor, the only thing the defense asks is that the law be applied as it always has—no exceptions. I know I have come before courts on prior occasions and argued for the rights of non-humans, that they be afforded basic rights like bodily integrity, liberty and dignity. Quite often, well meaning jurists have hunched their shoulders at me and said there is nothing they can do. The law is as it always has been. It's refreshing to see Senator Hoffenworth wear the progressive mantle, but the logical extension of his argument today is a little too much. The biotech era has only commenced and, with no case precedent or even so much as a law passed on the subject, he is asking the court to immediately accept a human chimera with a monkey gene—and perhaps a chimeric monkey with a single human gene, and everything in between—as legal persons entitled to full benefits under the law. It's beyond refreshing. It's breath-taking. Our laws are rooted in the past and engraved in stone, whether the Senator likes it or not. *Hominum causa omne jus constitum.* That's what the Roman judge Hermogenianus wrote seventeen-hundred years ago. 'All laws were estab-lished for men's sake.' All laws, without exception, were and are grounded in an anthropocentric teleology that teaches that the purpose—if not the divine *reason* for existence—of nonhumans and things is for use and exploitation by humans. Nothing has changed throughout the millennia. Nonhumans are not persons. Going back several thousand years B.C., cune-iform tablets make clear that Mesopotomian humans could own nonhumans, namely, sheep, donkeys, asses, oxen, pigs, goats, bees, and dogs."

Bert was sitting up straight and detached from the back of his chair. She'd lost him with the Latin phrase. He tried to pay attention to her with a respectful, studious gaze.

"Taking judicial notice in this case is simply fancy legal phrase for 'taking it on faith', a throwback to a bygone era. Stripped away, the prosecution argues that you should take it on faith that the Defendant is a person. Never mind science or the evidence. Let's just take it on faith that Mr. Gropes is a person—a human being—as defined by our laws, and ask no further questions. What is the case precedent for Senator Hoffenworth's motion? I have to reach way back to a dark and bygone time to find anything that approaches the leap of faith and logic requested. It calls to mind the Great Rat Litigation of fifteen-twenty-two."

There was a scattering of chuckles in the courtroom. Bert was more lost now than with the Latin.

"Because the poor folks in the French village of Autun were having a terrible time with barley-eating rodents, they filed a petition against the rats before the ecclesiastic court. That's right; they sued thousands of rats for destroying their crops. Why, you ask, did they treat rats as if they were entitled to the same due process as humans? The peasants of medieval France believed that the pestilence of rodents was visited upon them because of their sins. Their faith informed them that the only way to lift the just punishment was to petition God's agent on earth, the Church. The judges obliged and appointed a lawyer to represent the rats. You can imagine how ludicrous it was mixing divine law with their very earthly rodent-abatement problems. The lawyer for the rats complained that his clients were reluctant to appear in court because the cats of the suing villagers were menacing and interfering with their access to the courthouse. The judges considered this and ordered that the villagers restrain the cats. The rats were given every chance to respond to the petition but, as should be no surprise, they never did. Their defaults were finally taken, and the suing villagers were given a judgment upon which to execute—in every sense of the word."

Ripples of delight spread across the room as Eliza Dare poured herself a glass of water and drank a third of it before continuing.

"What does this absurdly generous view of the rights of the lowest nonhumans have to do with this trial? Plenty. Today, ninety-four years after the first Monkey Trial, when the prosecution insisted it was unlawful to teach anything but Biblical creationism, the prosecution appears to be advancing the argument that science should again be disregarded in favor of a belief, unencumbered by evidence, that Mr. Gropes is a person, a human being. This, in an age of reason and unprecedented scientific knowledge and capabilities—" She went over and picked up the two-inch thick Exhibit A and held it before her with both hands. "The undisputed fact is that the Defendant was engineered not by God but by another human, a scientist—a maliciously mischievous one to be sure—and the scientific fact is that the Defendant is part monkey, part man. This gene is all monkey." She let the heavy exhibit drop to the table with a loud thud heard in every corner of the courtroom.

Just when he felt like he was starting to acclimatize to the shocking revelation, the words "part monkey, part man" hit Bert over the head like a blunt instrument. It made him feel numbingly, even epochally stupid.

"If anyone should be asking the court to take judicial notice, it would be the defense. A human chimera has never been held to be a person. The short response to your honor's question is that the court ordered a jury trial last week. That's the law of the case. The defense is ready to pick a jury and get on with it. Let the prosecution then put on its case, if any it has." She sat down.

Before the judge could speak, Hoffenworth rose quickly. "Judge, if anything's been generous here, it's the helpin' of bull feathers we just heard. They're tryin' to confuse everyone into thinkin' that's a big ol' gene that'll make a tail sprout outta the back o' that man any day now. A lot of codswallop, that's what we're hearin'. The same science counts no more than twenty-five thousand o' them genes in the human genome. It also says the human genome and the monkey's genome are more than ninety-eight percent carbon copies. Meanin' that of the twenty-five thousand, around twenty-four thousand gotta be the same in both. The sayin' in this court and throughout this country is: 'The law abhors trifles.' What's one little piddly ol' gene other than a trifle, purely inconsequential, and we should not waste any more o' the court's time contemplatin' somethin' so trivial."

The judge opened his mouth to speak, but Eliza Dare was up again. "Your honor, with all due respect, I concede Senator Hoffenworth is an expert on what is a trifle, piddling, and inconsequential, having spent so many years in Washington—"

Laughter ensued, while the senator silently fumed.

"But his characterization of genetic phenomenology is misleading and wrong," she continued. "The truth is—"

"Thank you, Ms. Dare," the judge cut her off. "I've heard enough. I've decided I am not going to take judicial notice as requested by the prosecution." She flashed a confident smile at Bert who, in turn, could see Hoffenworth growling something at Wayne Tanner, seated next to him.

"However," the judge said, "there is no question in my mind that some adjustments need to be made. We are going to move this trial along. Ordinarily, the prosecution goes first," he said, looking beyond the attorneys, explaining to the gallery and indirectly to the viewing audience. "They must prove their case and, if they don't, their case doesn't survive." He leaned over and spoke directly to Bert's lawyer. "Because, however, I do agree with the prosecution that it is your defense that raises the issue and not the prosecution's case, Ms. Dare, you will go first and prove non-personhood, if you can."

Hoffenworth leaned back and beamed.

"But, your honor," Dare protested, "it should be their burden—"

The judge put his hand up, stopping her. "And if it's true that you don't know what function the Exhibit A gene performs, we will be done quickly. Your burden. That's my order. We will recess for twenty minutes and then begin jury selection."

He gaveled, rose and walked out.

Bert knew it was bad. She'd expected to score most of her points cross-examining the prosecution's experts. Now she stared down at her papers as if to avoid meeting the eyes of her gloating adversaries.

"Are we going to be OK?" Bert asked.

She looked at him and forced a smile. "We'll make some adjustments. It'll work out."

Bert was no lawyer, but his animal instincts told him he was in danger.

45

CESSNA PILOT: This is T3789, Skyvoyer out of St. Bart's. Do you copy? Over.

AIR TRAFFIC CONTROLLER: We copy, Skyvoyer. This is ATC, St. John. Over.

CESSNA PILOT: I'm just south of Virgin Gorda, about fifteen miles due east of St. John, and I'm in view of…um, an aircraft you should know about. I was able to make brief radio contact with the crew, then lost 'em. They're losing altitude, headed your way. Over.

AIR TRAFFIC CONTROLLER: We don't show anything except you in that area. Describe the aircraft.

CESSNA PILOT: It's a giant condom, sir.

AIR TRAFFIC CONTROLLER: Did you say condom? Charlie-Oprah-Nathan-Daniel-Oprah-Michael?

CESSNA PILOT: Ten-four. And it says Great Ape Condom on the side. Over.

AIR TRAFFIC CONTROLLER: Oh, for crying out loud. Sounds like something that could only originate out of that infernal tourist trap, Libido. Over.

CESSNA PILOT: You are correct, sir. It's a hot air. And by the way, crouched up on the tank platform, they got a real Libidoan on board. Over.

AIR TRAFFIC CONTROLLER: One of those native monkeys with the large—?

CESSNA PILOT: Right.

AIR TRAFFIC CONTROLLER: What's its destination?

CESSNA PILOT: Which?

AIR TRAFFIC CONTROLLER: The hot air.

CESSNA PILOT: This much I got. The pilot is totally blind but hellbent on his ultimate destination: that Hot Monkey Love Trial in Woodland, California.

AIR TRAFFIC CONTROLLER: Crazy tourists.

CESSNA PILOT: First though, says he'll need to land, and soon, what with the rising ambient temperature. But it'll have to be a crash landing. He means it when he says he can't see a thing. Over.

AIR TRAFFIC CONTROLLER: Damn. Should have taken that early retire. Listen, see if you can make contact again and suggest they pass over us. Unless they can guarantee touchdown at or near our runway, we're not set up for the rescue op this might call for. Now, Skyvoyer, can you give us more visual on this? We'll want to alert low-flying aircraft. Over.

CESSNA PILOT: It's big and red and definitely taller than wide. Its head is listing westerly, dropping and hurtling toward your lovely little island. Unbelievable. Wait'll you get a load of this thing. Over.

AIR TRAFFIC CONTROLLER: They should continue west and give San Juan a try. Tell the hot air: Sorry, we can't accommodate. And not just here. I speak for controllers throughout the Virgin Islands. Over.

CESSNA PILOT: How do you guys feel about a name change?

46

BERT SAT ALONE ON THE NEW COUCH IN THE
living room of his ranch house, facing an empty fireplace, the
toes of his cowboy boots huddled against one another. On
an impulse he'd selected Anna's abandoned recording of the
Beluga whales to fill the room with sound. Oddly, it seemed
right. He'd tried playing one of his favorite groups but the
sound, composed of notes sequenced in comfortable, predictable order—unlike his life—made a mockery of him. The random cries of whales transformed the room into an aquarium,
shutting out everything beyond the walls.

Not that the whales chased all the troubles out of his mind.
Hardly. The constant stream of bubbles rising up to the surface
were his thoughts about what was going to happen to him and
what he should do. If Eliza Dare managed to pull another animal out of her hat, he might still walk. She told him this morning that she could make adjustments, and they could succeed
with their defense. Although they knocked off early afternoon

because of the heat, Dare seemed confident picking the jury, adeptly screening jurors to determine any bias against Bert or his defense:

"Mr. Li, do you own any pets or have any nonhumans in your home?"

"No. Cats I hate and, country I come from, dogs we eat."

"You see Mr. Gropes here. You don't hate him, do you?"

"No."

"Mr. Li, do you think you can put aside your own experience of declining to form friendships with nonhumans and promise me that you will give Mr. Gropes a fair trial?"

"I think so."

Bert really wanted to believe her when she told him that he could emerge a hero after all of this. What self-respecting Social Studies teacher wouldn't yearn for that? She'd even told him in earnest that he could become "the George Washington or Simón Bolívar of the Animal Kingdom," conjuring up images of bronze statues of Bert on display...where? At museums of natural history? No, more like in lobbies of vet clinics. It all seemed preposterous now, and not just because it had gone badly in court this morning.

Just then the phone rang. He was screening his calls, and he let the machine kick on.

"*Bert...*"

A hauntingly familiar voice, but he couldn't instantly place it.

"*This is your, well—*"

Bert fumbled and snatched up the phone. "Hello?"

"You're there."

"Uncle! Where are you? Are you all right?"

"I'm all right. It's a long story. I was abducted by Slayde and taken to Libido where I was held captive. I escaped to the Virgin Islands. That's where I am now."

"What a relief." Bert exhaled. "Does Mother know you're alive, and all right?"

"I just got off the phone."

"*You* escaped?"

"I'm with two others. My fellow travelers."

"Who?"

"A marvelous young woman. A friend." He sounded different. "And my other companion is…" His voice was definitely different. "Bert, you know, of course, I'm not your uncle."

"I know."

The old man paused. "It came as a shock to me."

Bert was stung. His real father, forced into fatherhood, wanted out. Bert felt like he'd been adrift for decades in a deep genetic pool except finally, now, instead of reuniting with his father, he'd washed up on shore only to encounter Cyclops, blind, and not happy about it.

"The DNA doesn't lie. In this case it's ninety-nine point nine percent accurate, with a margin of error of point zero zero one percent." He spoke with a smile in his voice. Maybe he wasn't so distant after all. "Now, where was I?"

"You were about to tell me about the other one who escaped with you."

"Oh right," he said. "My fellow fugitive is the son of Primo."

"Who?"

Another pause.

"You know the gene you have?"

Now it was Bert's turn. "You mean the one…"

"Yes. It's from Primo. A beloved and respected—" his father paused. "An alpha male, to be sure. I'm told he passed away about four years ago."

Bert thought for a second. "That makes your traveling companion my—"

"Technically your brother. But not full or half. Times have changed. They come in all sizes now, but it's no reason for anyone to become disoriented. I know that to most people it sounds outlandish to describe him as your one twenty-five thousandth brother. But if you've ever studied the math of the galaxies as I have, or how many atoms can dance on the head—"

"What's my brother's name?"

"Scooter."

"I hadn't really thought about all the new relatives I have."

Bert tried to form a picture of a family tree, but then he couldn't help but notice some of his relatives swinging from the branches.

"Scooter will be coming out with me tomorrow," his father said. "You'll like him. Tina, my other friend, is also joining me. She's not just a friend. She's a teacher."

"What does she teach?"

"Not professionally like you and me, but she has a gift. She's taught me about the world as it is, as I wasn't seeing it. She's shaken up my hierarchy of the cosmos. She wants to help me help you. She's even postponing plans to reunite with her family. Bert, I think you'll find that I've changed. I'm looking forward to our reunion. It's a funny combination of curiosity, survival reflex, and genuine paternal…you know. Imagine me… saying that. I'm sure you recall, I'm the one who used to say visiting relatives were like bananas: They come in bunches—"

"And just grow rotten," Bert finished for him.

"Bert, I think I can help with your trial. I'm already in the middle of fleshing out a mathematical calculation whose proof, when completed, I believe will force the judge in Tennessee to dismiss all charges."

Bert felt a tremendous lightening of his load. Most amazing, the lift was not so much from the prospect of proof that would be his ticket to freedom. It was the sheer offer of help from the man who was his father. Bert thanked him, said goodbye and put the phone down. He'd never felt so connected in his whole life. He leaned back and draped himself over the couch. For a moment he forgot about the trial and all the problems he had, and he let himself enjoy an exquisite comfort that tingled out to his fingers and toes and filled him up with a new and powerful sense of well being. He'd just talked to his father. He—could he call him Dad now?—was eager to get together with

Bert, and he was going to bring his considerable knowledge to bear on his son's thorny problems.

A series of fresh images gradually developed in the dark room of his mind. He could see the two of them—father and son—sitting right here on a warm summer evening, in the living room of Bert's ranch house, some time in the not too distant future...

His fantasy ended abruptly and with a rude wake-up. That same quiet, dreaming face tucked away somewhere inside him got slapped out of it by the harsh open hand of the inevitable: Tomorrow morning, nine o'clock sharp, the trying of his case would resume like a threshing machine set with an automatic timer. If his lawyer successfully presented the non-person defense, he would be seen, at least for his kind, as the crown of evolution. But if the Dare defense proved to be another bone-headed move, well, then...

Never mind how the judge, or scientists for that matter, described the issue on trial. As far as Bert was concerned, the taxonomical riddle was whether he was *Stupid Man* or *Highly Realized Monkey*. Obviously, neither classification was going to win him favor with females of the human variety, but that was beside the point. Right now he was feeling every bit of the 98.9% the two creatures shared in common, and nothing else.

47

STUDIO ANCHOR: Good morning, everyone. I'm Janet Jones in New York, and this is LNTV, the Litigation Network. Welcome to day two of the Hot Monkey Love Trial: Phase One, the Personal Trial. Yesterday, in a dramatic turn, Judge McGrath announced that the defense would have to go first, requiring that Clarene Eliza Dare proceed to present the proof that John Bertram Gropes, the Defendant, is not a person. Right now we're going straight to Pam Schroeder in front of the Woodland courthouse. Our viewer response to the man on the street in his underwear yesterday was so unprecedented and overwhelming that we plan to feature this unique social commentator, Mr. Ellis Peek, each day throughout the trial. Pam?

REPORTER: Thanks, Janet. I have here beside me Mr. Ellis Peek. Welcome, sir.

MAN ON STREET: Wello.

REPORTER: Hello?

MAN ON STREET: No, wello. It's a combination of welcome and hello. Anything and everything can be combined. Hellbye.

REPORTER: Hello and goodbye? Why would you combine those two words?

MAN ON STREET: Precisely. Allow me to explain. With Lusian technology the DNA sequences of natural law descend into a swirling bowl of genetic gibberish. Where we could count on the true and predictable order of a-b-c and one-two-three, instead we'll have one-hydrogen-c-ham-sandwich-b-three, and so on. Lusians not only combine molecules never intended to be joined, don't forget that they're creating real living, breathing creatures. But unlike ham sandwiches and hydrogen molecules, living creatures engage in sequences of acts that produce their own consequences. Especially with human chimera, there's no telling what kind of acts we'll see triggering sequences of events—comic strips on the obituary page, news and interview shows chockablock with nonsense, consequences so bizarre they'll overtake our planet. Combine the ordinary with the unnaturally improbable: guess which is dominant and which is recessive?

REPORTER: I think I know, but why don't you explain?

MAN ON STREET: See this outfit?

REPORTER: I thought we'd get to that. On top you're wearing a bright red monkey costume, and on the bottom you're wearing a quite ordinary pair of gray slacks. I see your point. The improbable is clearly dominant.

MAN ON STREET: That's why the Lusians will dominate the planet unless we act to stop them.

REPORTER: All right, so let's talk about the trial. Are you saying that John Bertram Gropes is a Lusian and therefore a nonhuman, or do you believe he's a real person who should be held accountable? Which is he?

MAN ON STREET: Yesterday Senator Hoffenworth spoke of devolution, evolution in reverse. Which defines a species more in this case: his genes or his actions? Get a flipbook picture in your mind of the Descent of Man. Now flip through a couple of million years as an ape on all fours moves toward Homo erectus and walks into Homo sapiens. Keep flipping. As Lusian technology combines with Homo sapiens, you think you see forward progress, but—no!— it's only an illusion. Suddenly your eyes can make out that the creature is sliding in the opposite direction. Just like this, in real time, he's moonwalking straight back into a future of—Monkey sapiens!

REPORTER: There he goes. Gone. Our Man on the Street, Ellis Peek. Back to you, Janet.

STUDIO ANCHOR: Thanks, Pam. That was Pam Schroeder with our Man on the Street, Ellis Peek: LNTV guerrilla theatricalist and special trial commentator who managed to nimbly dance around the big question. So let's go right now to the courtroom where day two is about to begin.

IT SEEMED LIKE THE TRIAL HAD BEEN GOING ON forever. Court employees, onlookers, legal support and news people, everyone seemed to arrive in Judge McGrath's court-room, find their place with a sense of purpose, and carry on as if part of a decades-old routine—everyone except Bert, that is. He felt as if he'd pulled a rock back to find that there were armies of creatures working day and night to ensure that what happened to him happened. He wondered for how long this had been going on. Was it because he was simply too ignorant to notice before, or did it have anything to do with the lone gene that made him different?

"You promised me, win or lose, I'd come out looking better for putting forward our defense," Bert told Eliza Dare as they sat at the table waiting for the judge to enter. "But yesterday you used rats to argue on my behalf. Believe me, I'll do just about anything not to face charges in Tennessee, but I'm not exactly feeling ennobled by what we're doing."

"The rats? That was about the prosecution taking things on faith, not you," she told him. "Hang in there. You may not see it that way now, but you'll be the one sitting on top when this is all over."

She slid a yellow legal notepad and pen over to him. "Take notes." She tipped her head toward the prosecution table. "I'm going to expand Hoffenworth's definition of the Animal Kingdom, and he's not going to like it."

The jury filed into the courtroom and found their seats: seven women and seven men. Two of the men were alternates. Judge McGrath immediately acknowledged that the air conditioning had not been reactivated; installing the new filters was a bigger job than the building engineers thought. He told them it was going to be much hotter today: 9:15 and already eighty-seven degrees. When the judge shared the day's forecast—by noon in the midnineties both inside and outside, over a hundred degrees later—there were groans anew, followed by dozens of hands using whatever they could find to fan faces.

"We must use our time wisely. If we're lucky, we can remain in session until twelve-thirty, maybe one, and then we must adjourn."

The judge relaxed the dress code for everyone, including attorneys. Several jurors and members of the gallery jumped up, removing layers of clothing. Seeing that his attorney made no move to take off her jacket, Bert didn't either. He was already feeling the heat. Wayne Tanner kept his cool, or at least the appearance of it, but the corpulent senator already had a good sweat on his forehead. Bert wondered if the removal of jackets by one side would represent to the jury a meltdown of its case.

"However, I am not going to remove the robe," the judge announced. "As you can imagine, it's already plenty warm, but a certain place, that can't be too far from here, will freeze over before I abandon the trappings of the office. No, I'm not being heroic. There's another reason besides protocol. Think of me more as the canary in the coal mine. If it gets too hot for me inside this robe, I'll know that our time is up for the day."

The judge turned to face the lawyers. "Now, with a short day, this court will also exercise its inherent power to control the pace of this trial. We hardly need a warm-up act; hence, we will dispense with opening statements. The jury was told yesterday during selection what the issue is in this trial. Let's get on with it. The defense may call its first witness."

Clarene Eliza Dare rose and stood beside Bert: "The Defendant calls Professor Anton Marlowe."

Amidst shuffling and turning of heads, a man stood up from the back row with a binder in his hand and advanced toward the box. Professor Marlowe was in his early sixties, had big ears and proportionately large and high cheekbones that grew larger when he flashed a smile at Bert and his attorney. His head seemed to sprout out of his brown sport coat and white starched shirt with a beard that covered his face right up to the base of his cheekbone, complemented by thick eyebrows and a rush of long grayish yellow hair that bent back like a field of wind-whipped wheat.

The witness was sworn in.

"Professor Marlowe, please tell the jury what your area of scholarly expertise is."

"I'm a professor of zoology at the University of California at Davis. My specialty is in the area of genetic taxonomy." He turned and faced the jury. "Using genetic data as a guide in classifying new species of plants and animals."

"Judge," Hoffenworth said, standing and pointing his gut directly at the professor. "I'd like to voir dire this witness if I may. However, an honest offer of proof from the defense would go a lot further in speedin' things along here." He pulled a handkerchief out of his jacket and mopped his brow slowly, dabbing his forehead once in the middle, then twice on both sides. "With all due respect to the learned professor, unless the relevance can be verified, his testimony may be nothin' more than a long courtroom filibuster we can ill afford."

"I hate to do this," the judge said after a few seconds of thought, "but I think ultimately it will save time. Before we commit to an hour or more of testimony from this witness, I agree we need to find out if it's going anywhere. My apologies to the jury, but I'm going to excuse you for five minutes or so."

After the jury filed out, Dare protested: "Your honor, this witness is impeccably credentialed and his testimony squarely addresses the pivotal issue in this case."

"Let's cut to the chase." The judge faced the witness. "Professor, briefly summarize your ultimate conclusion."

The witness looked like he'd been slapped. That, in turn, was followed by a sulking expression, as if he'd been ordered to give away the plot to his new movie about to be test-screened to the jury: a story that folds Professor Doolittle of *My Fair Lady* into *Planet of the Apes*.

"But for my work to be credible, *optimally* that is," he began to explain, "you have to see the charts and models I—"

"Please, just your conclusion on the effect of the Monkey Gene."

"But you see," the professor said, looking around the courtroom as if to rally support, "the gene was from an anthropoid, not a monkey. Although they are called Libidoan monkeys, they are anthropoidal apes like chimps, orangutans and gorillas. When we speak of real monkeys, we refer to our long-tailed cousins, the macaques, baboons—"

"I'm sure you're technically correct, Professor," the judge said, "but the record already refers to Exhibit A, the Libidoan restriction map, as the 'Monkey Gene.' We can't go back and change that now."

Resigned, Professor Marlowe took a deep breath and began: "The Defendant's genetic makeup shows a near match to the human genome, but not a match, because of genetic material uniquely found in the anthropoid, *Pan troglodytes Libidoanis*. Given how genetically proximate anthropoidal apes are to humans, it would be taxonomically incongruous to not also separately classify the subject, however close to human he may be. Accordingly, I have classified him as…*Homo troglodytes Gropius*."

A buzz of animated whispers rose up. Bert felt another wave of heat hit him. He didn't know what to think about that testimony, but he did know he was dying to rip off his coat.

"My other experts will confirm the same," Dare chimed in. "If he's not per se a *Homo sapiens*, it follows that he's not a person under law."

Smiling confidently, Hoffenworth shook his head. "Even if the jury were to believe that foolishness, it surely does not prove a thing, Judge. Where's the proof that a *Homo-Troglio-Gropio*, or whatever names the professor wants to hurl at him, is not a person under the law? Bear in mind what we've cited in our brief. In courtrooms across this beautiful land, including the United States Supreme Court, they say, sure as the day is long, that a corporation is a person under law. Are you goin' to tell me that one o' those biotech companies with mishmash names, like Xyloid Proteomics Incorporated, is a full-fledged person but ol' Mr. Gropes here is not?"

The judge mopped his brow with one stroke of his bare hands from his forehead over the top of his head and that ended with him holding the back of his neck for a reflective moment. As he let go, he spoke: "I agree that the ultimate conclusion of the witness, even if found true, falls short of proving that the Defendant is not a person."

Dare flailed. "But your honor, you can't do this. I've got other experts whose testimony builds on this witness. It's essential to the defense."

Hoffenworth smiled broadly, positioning himself for a nice profile shot for the LNTV cameras.

The judge frowned. "The issue here is whether the Defendant is a person as contemplated by the California extradition law. The prosecution is correct that under the law a corporation is a person and so are various other 'legally engineered' bodies, like trusts and partnerships. The Defendant possesses a unique but seemingly trivial genetic variation that has no known effects." The judge stretched himself over the bench and addressed the witness. "Is it true, Professor Marlowe, that you don't even know what the gene does?"

"I don't know?" the witness repeated with an incredulous tone, frustrated that his film's distribution contract was canceled. "Of course, I know what it *does*. The gene causes there to be need for a new classification and a new name for a new species."

"But you don't know the actual biochemical function of the gene," the judge said. "You don't know if it causes actual gene expression or, if so, what proteins are expressed or what they do. Isn't that right?"

"No, that would be outside my area of expertise," the witness conceded.

"Ms. Dare, do any of your experts know what the gene does?" the judge asked.

"No, but some functions have been ruled out."

"I'm afraid among countless possibilities, that won't do," the judge said. "Professor Marlowe, you are excused."

The professor picked up his notebooks and stepped out of the witness box. The gallery watched him walk hang-dog to the back of the courtroom and slump into his seat.

"The record shows that the gene we're talkin' about is an extra gene," Hoffenworth weighed in. "He's got all of his human genes plus the bonus one. He just wants to take advantage of the legal system by tellin' this court he was flimflammed out of somethin' not even missin.'"

The judge turned to Bert's attorney. "Do any of your experts have an opinion about what the lone Monkey Gene does and, specifically, how that contributes to nonhuman or uniquely animal characteristics?"

"Here's what we have," Dare answered. "Together, our other scientific experts will present data showing that, at least statistically, where a unique gene from closely related species A is introduced into species B, it is likely to suppress otherwise natural gene expression in species B. In other words, it's more likely than not that some uniquely human gene has been rendered non-functional in the Defendant where it is fully functional in normal humans. So, no, we haven't identified a specific human gene where this has happened, but—"

The judge raised his hand, cutting her off. "Ms. Dare, with only one thin gene—and from a species that already shares ninety-eight point nine percent of our genome—and you don't even know what this gene does, I don't see how you give me any choice but to make a ruling at this point."

Bert wrote on his note pad: "Human gene believed MIA," and stared at it. Not knowing what to conclude from it, he began doodling pictures—monkeys wearing dark glasses for possible footwear applications. He would soon be manacled and dragged to Dayton, no doubt about it, but he felt a strange calm come over him.

Hoffenworth strutted back to the defense table and whispered something that evoked a smile from Wayne Tanner. He then looked back up at the judge with his mouth partially open, fixing on something over the judge's head that could have been a giant overhead television screen in a noisy hotel ballroom displaying scrolling footer text:

5% Precincts Reporting—Exit Polls: Hoffenworth President-Elect

Dare's eyes flashed at Bert. In that instant he could see that she was cornered and frightened but in a ferocious way. She was not about to go down without the fight of her life.

"One moment, your honor…" She stared down at the floor, then looked stoically up at the ceiling before continuing. "The court has wisely suggested that it would be instructive to look at evidence of what the California Legislature intended by the word *person* when it wrote the extradition law—the committee reports, the transcripts from the hearings on the proposed law, and such."

The judge nodded and stroked his sweaty jowl. "Since this is a case of first impression, that legislative history could be quite relevant, but I doubt it would be here. The extradition law was passed decades ago, making it extremely unlikely you'd find what you're looking for—statements suggesting that California legislators discussed human chimera and meant to exclude them as persons when passing the law. But let me ask you: Did you bring any of the legislative history?"

"No," she said. "None." She looked down again in regret.

"Judge, we'd welcome any evidence like that," Hoffenworth said. "We have nothing to hide. But now's the time to bring it on. Because if it's goin' to mean any kind of delay—"

"There will be no delays," the judge said emphatically.

"What I have is better," Dare added in a serenely sly voice.

"Better?" the judge repeated.

"That's right," she said. "It was counsel for the prosecution who suggested in an earlier hearing that California's definition of a person may prove to be broader than Tennessee's. So let's cut out the middleman—or middle*person*, if you will—and cut to the chase instead, as your honor has urged."

"We can do that, Ms. Dare," the judge said with an incredulous tone. "You're referring, of course, to the Tennessee criminal statute." He leafed through some papers and read: 'It shall be a crime for any *person* to create or cause to be created any human chimera,' etcetera, etcetera. If we decide that, and skip the California extradition law, I agree that would knock more than a few seconds off the judicial stopwatch. Do you mean to tell me you didn't bring the California legislative history but you happen to have it from Tennessee?"

"No. I don't have those papers either."

Hoffenworth guffawed. "No delays, Judge."

"I won't take up the court's time or bore the jury with a bunch of stale and musty old transcripts," Dare said. "For the meaning of the Beastly Degradation Act, I'd like to call the author of the bill himself." She turned and faced the prosecution table. "The Defendant will call Senator Ray Hoffenworth as its next witness."

The courtroom erupted in disbelief. The judge sounded the gavel.

Wayne Tannner was on his feet. "We vehemently object, Judge. The court has a strong policy of not permitting attorneys to be called as witnesses, especially in a criminal trial. It is only allowed in exceptional cases where the attorney is a percipient witness. The law speaks for itself."

"The prosecution will confer. If you object," the judge said, speaking to both Hoffenworth and Tanner, "we may need to have a hearing and perhaps briefing on this."

"I'm at a loss, your honor," Dare said, wide-eyed. "The Senator just said: 'Bring it on.' I was so sure there was nothing to hide."

Hoffenworth grimaced. The jury was still absent, but the cameras continued their silent stare. America was watching. He sat down while Wayne Tanner hovered over him, speaking rapidly but inaudibly. Hoffenworth nodded his head to the advice being imparted. Tanner finished, smiled, patted Hoffenworth on the back, and nodded toward the judge.

"Very well," Judge McGrath said. "Senator, do you object to being sworn as a witness?"

Hoffenworth stood, straightened his tie and hitched up pants. "If the defense wants a good old-fashioned Sunday schoolin', I'm happy to oblige, Judge. I'm from the Volunteer State, and I'm a Vol, dyed in the wool. I got nothin' to hide."

Assuming a fresh man-of-the-people look, he peeled off his stuffy prosecutor coat, picked up his ready-made cheater notes—a three-ring binder whose spine bore the title *PLATFORM: Hoffenworth for President 2020*—and ambled toward the witness stand with a smile on his face. Wayne Tanner, now seated, quietly buried his head in his hands. Bert turned around and for the first time noticed Sol Krasputin, the senator's new campaign manager, standing in the back of the courtroom, glaring in the direction of his new client.

Nothing to hide. Those were the same words Bert used when Special Agent Dennis Clamp came knocking. That was before he had any idea what lurked below the surface. Improbably— perhaps perversely—Bert found himself feeling empathy for his tormentor.

48

STUDIO ANCHOR: Let's go to our veteran trial attorney and commentator, Ben Griswold, standing outside the courtroom. Ben, isn't it extremely unusual for a prosecuting attorney to testify as a witness?

LEGAL COMMENTATOR: Rare indeed, Janet. Judges will look at legislative history when there's a question about the meaning of certain legislation. But testimony from a legislator? Rare. And letting the jury hear it? The meaning of the law should be for the judge alone to decide.

STUDIO ANCHOR: Why didn't the prosecution object?

LEGAL COMMENTATOR: There's no secret that Senator Hoffenworth's ambitions extend beyond obtaining a conviction in this trial. He may need a unanimous jury inside the courtroom, but a mere plurality will do on the outside. On the front burner we've got the Hot Monkey Love Trial, but don't forget that on the back burner a Presidential election is heating up.

STUDIO ANCHOR: We're seeing history in the making, aren't we?

LEGAL COMMENTATOR: Or remaking, Janet. What's so remarkable is that we are seeing a legal drama repeating itself—a little warped, perhaps, by time—but nevertheless repeated. Recall that in the original Monkey Trial in nineteen-twenty-five, prosecutor and three-time Presidential candidate William Jennings Bryan, a beloved figure and devout Christian, invoked the Bible—Genesis, of course—as the ultimate authority on the origins of humankind, categorically repudiating the teachings of Darwin. It was an excruciatingly hot summer day in Dayton, Tennessee when the judge refused to allow Clarence Darrow to call scientific experts to explain the basis for evolutionary theory. That's when Darrow called Bryan as an expert witness to explain passages from the Bible that, at least from the defense view, defied a literal reading. So yes, it's the same storyline.

STUDIO ANCHOR: But is it the same gene line, Ben? Does it mean the Defendant will be found guilty just as John Scopes was so many decades ago? That the outcome is genetically encoded?

LEGAL COMMENTATOR: Well, first of all, I would observe that the facts of this case aren't exactly identical to the Scopes trial. This trial is a different organism. Mutation is in evidence, definitely. Is it the result of natural selection and adaptation, or human tampering? I don't know. What I do know is that none of this has escaped the watchful eyes of defense maestro, Clarene Eliza Dare. I expect she will stop at nothing to introduce radical new material intended, at least this time around, to produce a happy ending for the Defendant—

STUDIO ANCHOR: Or, from the prosecution standpoint, a miscarriage of justice. Thanks, Ben. Let's go back to the trial where they are about to start again.

AS THE JURY MARCHED IN, THEY FIXED THEIR EYES straight ahead to where Senator Ray Hoffenworth, coatless, was seated, prepared to testify as a witness. It was at least ten degrees hotter in the courtroom than it was before the break, as if the open back door had blasted heat in from a convection oven.

"Ladies and gentlemen," the judge explained, "the defense has called Senator Ray Hoffenworth, the prosecuting attorney, as a witness. The relevance of the testimony will be clear to you. However, if in the course of it I see something immaterial, I will make that known to you, and I may ask you to disregard it."

Bert played that back in his head, the part about seeing something immaterial, and wondered if the heat was getting to the judge already. Judge McGrath sipped some of his water; his cheeks were a bright pink, as if from a fresh slapping. He turned to the clerk. "Swear in the witness."

The senator rose from his seat.

"Raise your right hand," the female clerk asked him. "Do you swear to tell the truth, the whole truth, and nothing but the truth?"

"So help me God, if my hand were on the Book itself."

"Please be seated, Senator," the judge said.

Clarene Eliza Dare addressed him from the lectern: "You are an expert on the meaning of Tennessee's Beastly Degradation Act. Isn't that true, Senator?"

"It's the *Abatement* of Chimera and Beastly Degradation of Humanity Act," he corrected her. "It's the only law in this great land that looks to put a stop to the willy-nilly foolin' and fiddlin' with the American genome. I wrote the law and I am proud of it."

"When you wrote it, Senator, you didn't have in mind that someone of Mr. Gropes's unique genetic makeup, with its non-human elements, should be included in the class of creatures referred to as *any person* in the law. True?"

"Not true." he said, brandishing his platform. "My position has always been—"

"That was a yes or no question, sir. This is not a candidates' debate."

"Can't I explain my answer?" He looked up to the judge with false humility.

"I'm going to let him air, his full answer that is," the judge said.

"My position has never changed," the senator continued. "There are three childishly simple things you need to know, Ms. Dare. It's so simple that right-thinkin' people don't need to wrangle over it. Number one…," he held up a pedantic finger, "a person is someone who can be held accountable under the law because only a person—not a horse, a cow, or a monkey—can tell the difference between right and wrong. Number two: Only human bein's fit into that definition of a person. And number three: your client, Mr. John Bertram Gropes, knows the difference between right and wrong, and he's a person who can be and will be prosecuted under the law." He leaned back comfortably in the witness chair. "Now you tell me if there's somethin' you don't understand."

"There is."

The witness guffawed. "You want me to explain right and wrong?"

"Sorry," she said with a cunning smile. "Just a few questions about that. Forgive me, your answer was excellent, but I'm a little unclear on the application."

Hoffenworth shook his head, slowly and superciliously, from side to side. "Now, why doesn't that surprise me, Ms. Dare?"

"Not everyone is blessed with your moral clarity, Senator. You can tell the difference between right and wrong, can't you?"

He chuckled. "I most certainly can. And take responsibility."

"There's a company called Mutexis, based in the Bahamas, that does nothing but develop organisms that are GE, genetically engineered. They're currently developing a chimera that's a cross between a goat and a gopher that they're calling a Goatpher to be marketed as a commercial lawnmower. My question sir: Is that good or bad?"

"It's immoral."

"All right, I'll accept that," she said. "Mutexis also holds U.S. and international patents on GE crops that they license to third world countries. If the farmers are caught taking the seeds from the corn or rice they've grown and replanting them without paying new fees and royalties, the company has the right to destroy or repossess the unauthorized crop. What do you think, sir? Is that moral or immoral?"

"Reprehensible."

"Now let's talk about PharmLife, the giant agricultural and pharmaceutical company. It's true, isn't it, Senator, that PharmLife is a longtime financial and political partner of yours?"

"Objection!" Tanner was on his feet. "Irrelevant. What does this have to do with the senator's work as author of a bill while in the Tennessee Senate?"

The judge took three shallow breaths and spoke: "The witness opened the door by agreeing to testify. Now it's a barn door he pushed wide open with his right-and-wrong answer. Overruled. You can answer."

"I am proud to have worked with the thousands of hard-workin' men and women of PharmLife. It's a fine taxpayin', God-fearin' American corporation."

"Now what I neglected to tell you earlier is that a careful reading of its recent SEC filing reveals that PharmLife is the majority shareholder in Mutexis."

Hoffenworth winced. Tanner tossed his pen down and rubbed his eyes.

"Do you wish to change your earlier answer?"

"No, certainly not, but I'd say—I should have said—it all depends. I mean, first off, we're talkin' vegetables, not people.

And they got a corn that grows on rocks and resists plagues, typhoons, and herds of stampedin' water buffalo. Some of these countries would have no food at all if it weren't for companies innovatin' with crops the way they do."

"So only human beings create and disperse dangerous GMOs. Monkeys don't. It's true, isn't it?"

"That's an absurd way of looking at it. How humans exercise their knowledge is one thing, but only they know the difference between right and wrong."

Eliza Dare reached into her trial briefcase and produced her own copy of *PLATFORM: Hoffenworth for President 2008*. She thumbed through it, making sure to let the jury see what she was examining.

"It's true, isn't it, Senator, that you have advanced a proposal for a national MPS—a so-called moral positioning system?"

The white-shirted senator, whose figure was starting to melt into the corners of the witness box like a big scoop of vanilla ice cream, suddenly perked up.

"Could I trouble you to explain to the jury this technology that's a centerpiece of your presidential platform?"

"I'd be most happy to oblige, Ms. Dare." He looked directly at the jury and the camera that hovered over them. "Because of the difficult moral issues facin' scientists and research centers, they need guidelines, especially where government money is used. The MPS software is chock full of the best thinkin' on bioethics and faith-based logic found anywhere in this great land of ours. It's about time we put those national treasures to work for us."

"Please tell us how it works."

"Before undertakin' use of government grant money or property, a scientist would ask the MPS to evaluate the morality of the project, research, or experimentation. The MPS will set to work evaluatin' it with the wisdom and moral fiber that's been distilled from our best doctors, scientists, and moral thinkers. It then generates detailed guidelines for the project. If it's not correct in its moral positioning, well then, you can't do it, not with government money or property. Everywhere I go in this blessed land people tell me they are sick of seein' their money spent on immoral, amoral, and *un*moral programs."

"Is it only for scientists?"

"The initial roll-out, yes. But if I can persuade members of Congress to put some giddyup in their appropriations, soon enough the MPS will be there to help everyone, includin' businesses and average Americans usin' any kind of government property: interstate freeways, frequency spectrums, online government databases, national parks, what have you. You see, except for a few plainspoken and necessary laws like the Abatement of Human Chimera and Beastly Degradation of Humanity Act, people don't want Congress spendin' a lot of time passin' more laws, fillin' up more books with more regulations every time some bumpkin comes up with a foolish new idea that'll monkey up the works, if you'll forgive the expression. There needs to be somethin' in place that takes care of that, somethin' quick and plain and just common sense."

A smattering of applause and cheers erupted in the gallery. Senator Hoffenworth smiled and nodded his appreciation. The judge gaveled once.

"Now, let's see," Dare said, flipping through some financial papers. "The estimated cost to develop and deploy the System is between eight and twelve billion dollars. Twenty billion if satellites are used. Money that could be spent on school lunch programs for unfed or underfed children. Is that your idea of right?"

"Nobody's takin' money away from budgeted programs. We're comin' up with long-held but under-reported capital reserves to fortify—or in some places build from the bottom up—our nation's moral infrastructure. It's a steal at that price. In my view, satellites are the way to go."

Dare tossed the financial report on the table. "So if a government-funded scientist is on a camping trip, in a canyon out in the middle of nowhere, and he looks up at the stars and starts thinking about an assay back in the laboratory involving molecules from roundworms and human toe nails—why, he can point his wireless device at the heavens and find out what the last word on it is from Senator Ray Hoffenworth's satellite-deployed MPS."

"You can't pay enough for guidance like that. And yep, that easy to access."

"But it's true, isn't it, Senator, that in the world order you've now described, a computer has a higher, better and clearer—distilled, as you put it—sense of morality than a human being?"

He gazed at her with his jaw open. "That can't be right, but I see where you're goin'. Nobody said you weren't clever, Ms. Dare. Better and clearer, perhaps. Let me think here."

He reached for his handkerchief, but it was in the breast pocket of his coat hanging on the back of a chair thirty feet away. He started to lift his left arm to squeegee the top of his head but, wearing a spanking clean white shirt, he must have thought better of having a stain on it. Instead he tore the back page out of his platform, crumpled it into a makeshift hanky, and he wiped his face with it. When done, he hoisted it toward the jury and smiled, his eyes sagging at the corners with heat. The jurors smiled back. Dare stood her ground, not for a moment considering retrieving his handkerchief for him.

"But now that I've done some ponderin' on it," he continued, licking his dry lips. "MPS is only possible because of the good minds and intelligence of the people behind it. Only humans could program it. Apes can't program computers." He assumed a preachy expression. "The moral faculty requires a high level of intelligence that only humans and humans alone possess."

"So it's higher intelligence that separates humans from non-humans?"

"Includin' moral intelligence, yes."

"And that's what you meant by a *person* in the law you wrote?"

"Yes. You see because only a guilty and misguided person would use their intelligence to license a sleazy business turnin' people into sex-crazed guinea pigs, buyin' a ranch with ill-gotten gains, and twistin' logic around so's he can say he's not accountable for what he done."

"So that any normal human would easily outperform a non-human in an intelligence test?"

He sat up, as if he suspected a setup. "That's right, but Mr. Gropes *is* a person. I'm sure there are subjects he has more knowledge about than I do, like surf-ridin' on porn sites or makin' easy money."

"Your honor," she said, turning to the judge, "I am not through with this witness, and I request that he remain where he is while another witness is called."

"One witness at a time, Ms. Dare," the judge. "If you want this witness to be temporarily excused—"

"No, that won't be necessary. It's possible and time-saving to combine testimony with this witness."

"What witness?"

She glanced over her shoulder at the back doors and then announced to the court: "At this time the defense calls Mr. Scooter Primoson."

The double doors were flung open by a tall, beautiful young woman wearing a white skirt and a stylish watermelon red and aqua blue top with the message I ♥ Virgin Islands written in sparkled script. Holding her hand and fully two feet shorter, a Libidoan monkey waddled into the courtroom. The ape stopped and, despite his crooked legs, stood as still as a tripod. He took in all the faces staring back at him by pointing and touching an index finger to his crown. When Clarene Eliza Dare extended her hand toward the ape from the lectern, the ape began his knobby-kneed procession toward the front of the courtroom.

"Objection!" Tanner was on his feet. "This is highly inflammatory. Besides, this so-called witness is—incompetent!"

Dare faced the judge and calmly nodded her head. "That's exactly right. Indeed we want to establish—"

"That you've called an incompetent witness?" The judge's eyes bulged with disbelief.

"That's right, your honor," Dare replied. "This goes to the heart of what a person is or isn't. I only have a short series of questions, and I believe we'll be done for the day."

"Let's take a ten minute recess," the judge said. "I'd like to speak to the attorneys at sidebar." It was difficult to read whether the judge, trying to appear in control and quietly stoic, was reassured or resigned—whether the reaction, written on his overly ripened face, stemmed from the words *done for the day* or simply *done for.*

That's when Bert had to admit to himself he had no idea what the judge was thinking. That concession, induced by heat, exhaustion and stress, caused him to realize that he was merely using the judge's face as a mirror for his own. He'd had that kind of insight before but, for some inexplicable reason, this time he was filled with a sudden dread and foreboding. He glanced at his attorney in search of where else he'd been projecting his own reflection. He even stared briefly at Senator Hoffenworth, still seated in the witness stand, while the two attorneys, Dare and Tanner, moved toward the judge.

Just then Bert felt something bump his chair from behind. He turned his head around to find the face of a Libidoan monkey grinning straight back at him.

49

"WE NEVER TALKED ABOUT THIS!" BERT'S WHIS-
per was shrill, but outside earshot of the prosecution. Dare had
just finished the conference with the judge.

"Don't worry. I told you I spoke to your father last night. He
said he'd do whatever he could for you. When he told me he
was traveling with the ape, I told him you'd need that witness
on standby."

"And you're just now mentioning you've arranged this little
sideshow?" Bert was flustered and angry.

She put a patronizing hand on his shoulder. "Look, we're
not talking about rats anymore. This is as close as you can get,
and you know it. The judge won't allow our experts. We have
to do what we can."

"What?"

The clerk announced that session was about to begin again
after the judge briefly left the courtroom.

"I've got some ideas. You'll see. I gave you my word we'll end up on top. To be honest, we're going to have to be a little more aggressive to make that happen. But I *will* make it happen. I promise you *Hoggen*worth is going down if I have to chase him down there myself with a meat ax."

She'd led him this far, but he wasn't sure how he got here. No longer were they talking about heroic causes. For Bert to survive, Hoffenworth had to go down.

When the trial resumed, the ape stood quietly at Dare's left, between the lectern and the jury, as the two of them faced the witness.

"You agree, don't you, Senator, that Mr. Primoson here"—she gestured to her side—"is not a person recognized under law?"

"If you can assure me he's not a card-carryin' member of the Trial Lawyers' Association, why yes, I'll have to agree with you."

A hearty laugh spread through the courtroom. Dare deflected the barb by lifting just enough of a good-sport smile around the corners of her mouth.

"Good," she said. "Since we agree Mr. Primoson is incompetent to testify, he will have to be marked as an exhibit. I will, however, attest to the veracity of any remarks he may provide." She smiled, reminding the jury that she, too, had a sense of humor.

Wayne Tanner sat mutely at the counsel table, the dry heat slowly evaporating him.

The clerk wrote on an exhibit tag and handed it to Dare with an extra long loop of string running through it. Dare draped it over the exhibit's head to be worn as a pendant. Scooter lifted the tag in his hand and thoughtfully examined it.

"Exhibit B," she continued, "as in *beastly* intelligence, will be easy to remember. Now, Senator, can you remind the jury what the *sapiens* means in *Homo sapiens*?"

"I prefer *Anthro sapiens*."

"Very well. What is *sapiens*?"

"In Latin it means *knowin*'." He was smug.

"Thank you." She turned and signaled toward the back door.

A female employee of the courthouse cafeteria walked in carrying a plastic tray bearing three brown bags. The girl whispered to the attorney while pointing to the tray. Dare thanked her, gave her two twenty-dollar bills for the special order. While standing at counsel table, the attorney leaned over and peeled away three Post-it notes. She wrote a number on each—"1," "2" and "3"—and stuck one to each bag. But no one, except Bert, was watching what she was doing. All eyes were on the newest witness designated an expert on beastly intelligence. Positioned next to Clarene Eliza Dare, he was crouched under the table admiring her shoes.

When done, she lifted the tray, walked over and laid it on the ledge of the witness stand. The ape followed her. "Senator, on this tray, as you can see, there are three bags. Childishly simple," she said, echoing his earlier condescending words. "One of them contains two bananas while the others hold raspberries. Now, using all of your faculties for knowing—the English word for *sapiens*—and without touching the bags, tell me which one has the bananas. Number one, number two, or number three?"

The contempt in her voice was palpable. Hoffenworth's eyes narrowed, and he scowled. It was no secret that testifying was supposed to be a ripe opportunity for him to gain utmost exposure and to spread his message. Instead, it had overheated, ripened too fast, and was about to go rotten.

"You may think you can make a mockery of these proceedings, Ms. Dare, but I will have none of it."

They glared at each other, but it was the interrogator, Clarene Eliza Dare, who brandished an invisible chair, poking and jabbing the growling face of Senator Ray Hoffenworth.

She looked to the judge. "I request that the court instruct the witness to answer the question."

"You must answer the question," the judge said, then turning back to Dare. "That doesn't mean I won't cut you off if I think you're too far afield."

Miffed, Hoffenworth squinted at the three bags, then aspirated in anger and frustration. "I don't know. I'd be guessin.'"

"Guesswork is a form of knowledge, albeit a low one. But go ahead, give it your best college try."

"One." That's all he said, glowering at her.

"The *Homo sapiens*' knowledge informs him that it's number one. Let the record reflect that I am now offering it to Exhibit B, the ape." She lowered the tray to him with one hand. Instantly he reached for number 3 but, before he could lift it, her quicker right hand shot out, cat-like, and snatched it away from him.

"The record will reflect the ape selected bag number three. Let's see who is more knowledgeable." She walked back to the defense table. "Let's look in number one, the *Homo sapiens*' selection." She opened the top of bag number one, turned it upside down, and dumped it on a yellow pad. "Raspberry," she said with mock disappointment, all but blowing through her lips the rude noise of the same name. Along with raspberries there were several pieces of crumpled paper used as filler to make the bags appear uniformly full.

"Now let's check number three." She opened it and, with a smile, out plopped two bananas. "Let the record reflect the ape knew where it was. Round One goes to Exhibit B."

"That's not intelligence," the senator retorted. The red heat in his cheeks was now self-generated. "No more 'an a huntin' dog or a truffle-rootin' pig, sure, he's got himself an A-one snout. But 'cept for a banana tastin' good, he doesn't know the first thing about biology, botany, or the order of the animal or plant kingdom." He turned and gave an aside to the jury. "But of course it takes common sense to understand that."

"An interesting point," she said. "You're saying that, independent of *intellectual* knowledge, each of the species has some innate physical advantage, like a snout or fast legs or long neck. In that light, do you agree that humans are blessed with incredibly dexterous hands and fingers?"

"I do, but that's not what makes us more intelligent."

She picked up one of the bananas, marched over and handed it to the witness. "Show us anyway. Let's have a demonstration. Peel the banana from the top down as fast as you can."

He shook his head again to show his simmering annoyance. While continuing to glare at her, he held the banana up, wrapped his fingers slowly around the stem and, with a sudden motion, cracked its neck. His hands remained perfectly still for a second, enough time to allow a quietly vicious smile to settle in around the corners of his mouth. He then stripped the entire banana in two swift peels.

"Impressive," she remarked when he was done. "Indeed, the human's manual dexterity is not to be trifled with. Now I'm handing the other banana to Exhibit B, the stand-in for non-human intelligence, and I'm asking him to peel it from the top down as quickly as he can."

The ape, with no shame about the fact that you are what you eat, took the second banana from her and sat down on the middle of the floor as if it were as good a place as any to have a picnic. The way he briefly looked at the long fruit in his hand, he could have been inspecting the label on a wine bottle. Then he popped the end opposite the stem, peeled it in three strips, and took a bite. Evidently pleased with its pith, texture, and fruitiness, it was clear that he was not sending it back.

"Not as dexterous, I'll admit," Dare said. "But the instructions were from the 'top down.' True, anthropoids are in the habit of always peeling bananas that way, but surely it's because they are knowledgeable enough to know the stem is the bottom of the fruit."

There were some laughs and a few guffaws.

"Round Two. The ape," she announced.

"Who says the stem is the bottom?" Senator Hoffenworth glowered at her, sweating profusely. In his right hand he continued to hold a peeled, uneaten banana.

"Its growth is closest to the root, isn't it?" she retorted. "But I want this to be fair, Senator. We'll handicap it and call Round

Two a draw to keep you in the hunt. Are you ready to admit now that genetic differences, especially artificially engineered differences, separate human beings from nonhumans?"

"Hardly, Ms. Dare."

"Are you aware that the Monkey Gene was inserted into Mr. Gropes's zygote using a primitive version of electrolytic shock technology?"

"No," the witness answered dismissively.

"Shock is what's needed for it to take," she said as she started to advance toward him. "Let me take that banana off your hand before you spill any seeds."

He glanced down at it. She saw him hold it up for a brief closer look.

"I'm sorry," she said, "I was kidding. Of course there are no seeds. Are you aware that bananas reproduce asexually—that, unlike humans and monkeys, they are not sexual organisms?"

"Those are your words and your beliefs, Ms. Dare. Except for a few lost souls that would deny their humanity, like Mr. Gropes there, who want to have us believe that they are monkeys, or who'd turn others into monkeys, no one believes humans are nothin' more than a plague of sexual organisms, as you'd call us, overrunnin' this earth."

The ape had moved to the side of the witness box and, facing Dare and the gallery, was imitating the senator. Both were facing and poking a finger in the air at Eliza Dare.

"But how an animal reproduces, including *Homo sapiens*—or *Anthro sapiens*, as you say—is a major factor in classifying the species. Isn't that true, Senator?"

"Call yourself what you want. We got a brain that no animal, includin' a monkey, comes close to. It's the meetin' hall of higher thought and intellect that only we got. The hands, two arms, and head of those monkeys"—he gestured toward the Libidoan monkey—"may resemble a human, but it's plain as day they took a different evolutionary off-ramp. The proof's in the puddin'. Their brains are much smaller. Instead they put their stock in beastly sized you-know-whats, all the better for runnin' through the jungle to pleasure themselves."

"Let's explore that thought, Senator, shall we?"

"Ms. Dare," the judge intervened, "you promised us you were almost done. Do we really have to explore that line of inquiry?"

"Your honor, this wasn't my idea. I also really hoped it wouldn't come to this." She was standing in the well less than ten feet from the witness, rubbing her hands, ruby-colored and so warm they seemed to glow. "But the witness has opened another door, offering his most compelling macroscopic distinction between the species. I promise we're just going to peek in with a few questions, and then I'll be done."

The jury leaned forward while the judge sighed and sat back. "Please be brief. The heat is nearly unbearable, and it's not yet noon."

Wayne Tanner was not about to weigh in. He looked like a Smoky Mountain trout, non-native to these parts, his gills desperately sucking the furnace blasts.

"Senator Hoffenworth, let me make sure I understand what you've just said. The Libidoan monkey's priority is sex and, accordingly, it has evolved a magnificent... a decidedly large sex organ, whereas the human being has a much larger brain, indicating its higher priority of knowledge and understanding. Is that a fair summary?"

"I suppose. I think what I said was clear. You can say it however you want." With the presidential platform resting flat on his lap, he was fanning himself with its binder cover.

"Size matters?"

"Brains, yes."

"We heard earlier about the MPS that you propose—the Moral Positioning System, didn't we?"

"We did, Ms. Dare. All a part of elevatin' the discourse of these proceedin's above that monkey's head." He looked down at the monkey, now seated under the witness stand, his head about three feet below the senator's, "but you keep bringin' in bananas and jungle cavortin'."

"But the heart of the Moral Positioning System, what defines it, is the mainframe back on Earth, not the satellites in space. Am I right?"

"I suppose you're right. Yes, that's true."

"It's true, isn't it, that the human brain, exclusive of its satellites, weighs in at a full three pounds?"

Hoffenworth nodded.

Just then a hundred heads gawked at the open-legged ape, sitting below the senator stroking his chin. At the same moment there were a hundred calculations being made. Bert computed just under three pounds.

"You're aware it's been proven that a male human being thinks of sex every fifteen seconds."

"Oh, please, Ms. Dare. I've heard that."

"And you knew that when you wrote the law?"

"I wasn't thinkin' about it when I wrote it."

"Are you telling the jury that you wrote the Beastly Degradation Act in less than fifteen seconds?"

"No, it's not—no. I wasn't thinkin' about the clockwork business—"

"I understood that. You were thinking about sex."

"Right. I mean, no—"

"Are you aware of how the sex organ of the human male, with counterparts to the female, takes its direction from the brain?"

He shook his head in disgust. "I got better things to bide my time, Ms. Dare, like readin' from the Good Book. I can't believe you're headin' down this sleazy and slippery path—"

"Ms. Dare," the judge jumped in, apparently to the rescue of a numb Wayne Tanner. "I realize the witness pushed the—door wide open." This time his mouth swerved to avoid the word *barn*. "But now you're badgering the witness. I don't care if it's ninety-eight point six degrees in this room. The code of conduct is the same. I'm going to terminate this line of questioning that's impertinent to the point of appalling. *Shocking.*"

"Believe me, your honor, therein is my higher purpose. Please bear with me. The shock, if any, is merely the probative method I must use to serve that higher purpose of stripping away the prejudices, misconceptions, and group-think mindset that has brought us to this trial and to such a fundamental, yet unanswered question. I promise, if you'll just allow me a few more minutes—"

"Go." The judge waved a hand and leaned back. "But make it brief. We need to adjourn." His head must have been swimming in an Olympic-sized hot tub.

She went to the table, unplugged her notebook computer and brought it back to the lectern, taking a moment to pull up a file. "Now I want you to stop me if your intellect can supply any knowledge or understanding—your words—about any of the following major sexual functions of the brain I'm going to identify. If you can't, that's fine. I'll understand that the large brain performs these sex acts and nothing more."

Senator Hoffenworth's mouth hung open in quiet protest. No matter which way he went, her whipsaw was going to get him.

"Let's begin, starting with regions of the hypothalamus, including the medial preoptic area which aggregates, organizes and redirects sexual data and stimuli from throughout the brain; or the paraventrical nucleus which also crunches data and releases oxytocin, a pro-erectile neurotransmitter centered in the hypothalamus. If you want to stop me, or I'm going too fast, just raise your hand."

Hoffenworth's eyes drooped as if she'd started working a whammy on him—a wicked sex hex.

"And we've already touched on the vigilance of the cerebral cortex. Imagery and fantasy techniques make it possible to associate sexual arousal and orgasm with uniquely individual or commonly shared predilections. The possibilities for the higher brain functions to leverage the simplest acts into far-ranging and, for all practical purposes, irreversible, obsessive, paraphilic disorders are well documented: sadism, masochism, exhibitionism—breather-ism, scopophilia, necrophilia, or what in the seamy underbelly of the sex trade is called mondo-bondo zoophilia—"

"Huh? What?" He looked like he'd been clubbed over the head. "Bondo...*philia*?"

"Bondophilia? Really, Senator? I'm guessing that would be an obsessive, unnatural, sexual attraction to fixed income securities or, perhaps more impossible to resist, a seductive array of high-yield instruments that have fallen below investment grade, slumming it tonight, as it were, maybe looking for a little company. Tell us about it." She waved her hand at all the people gathered in the courtroom. "Speak freely, as if among friends."

"No, I don't—can't...."

"Fine. If you shed the inhibitions holding you back, or if you have knowledge or understanding of any of the following, stop me. The next category is purely a product of so-called higher intelligence: fetishism, mental fixation resulting in sexual arousal that occurs only with a particular object or body part. Scientists know it's purely begotten of higher brain function that's, well, gone clinically bananas. So where are we? Bizarre foot fetishism—"

"Please stop, Ms. Dare!"

The ape shrieked spontaneously.

"You know about foot fetishes?"

"Please... Enough. I want to go sit down now."

"You are sitting down, Senator, and you can go back to your air-conditioned hotel. But first, admit it: The human brain is the biggest sex organ of them all."

"You could look at it that way, but—yeah, you could, but it's all so subjective."

"And yes, Senator, you could look at it that way, but—" She hurried over to the clerk's table and picked up Exhibit A. "This gene, painstakingly spelled out, letter by letter, nucleotide by nucleotide," she waved it around like a flag that demanded saluting, "is *not* subjective. There's no such thing as genetic relativism. Isn't that right?"

"It's objective. Yes."

"You have to agree that what separates us from nonhumans is the genomic blueprint that defines our physical makeup?"

"Yes."

"However small those verifiable differences may be?"

His head nodded pliantly.

"Is that a yes, Senator?"

"Yes."

She paused. "There is a revelation I am duty-bound to make at this time. Mr. Scooter Primoson here is the son, you might have guessed, of one Libidoan monkey by the name of Primo. Now what I haven't told you is that Primo is the same source of the Monkey Gene inserted into Mr. Gropes's embryo."

There were gasps.

"That's right," she continued. "The Defendant, John Bertram Gropes, and the Libidoan monkey sitting before you are brothers—brothers by blood."

Voices of astonishment filled the room.

The judge sounded the gavel. "Order! Continue with your questions, Ms. Dare."

"There are only two creatures in this entire courtroom—include, if you want, the millions watching this trial on TV—two creatures who share this gene. Right, Senator?"

He leaned over and gazed directly at the Libidoan monkey seated below him. The ape looked up and treated the bedraggled witness to a wildly toothsome grin, bouncing his eyebrows just enough to say *Welcome to the realm.*

Hoffenworth looked back at the attorney, his mouth agape. "It's true."

"And you agree, don't you Senator, that Mr. Primoson is not a person?"

"No—I mean, yes, I agree."

"Admit it: When you wrote the Beastly Degradation Act, you never intended to include as a person someone with genetic makeup unique to Mr. Primoson's species?"

"It's true. I can't argue with you," was all he said.

Both Clarene Eliza Dare and Ray Hoffenworth were breathing hard, their faces awash in sweat. Mascara was running down Dare's cheeks and her hair, worn up, had two wild clumps that had come loose on either side at the back of her head and bounced as she walked away from the witness.

"I have nothing further," she finally said, sitting down and slumping back in her chair, sated.

The courtroom itself, more than the people in it, seemed to yearn for the air conditioning to kick on, but it remained quiet and subdued throughout, the sharp smell of body odor in the air. With puffy, redolent jowls, and his mouth slightly open, Hoffenworth stared blankly ahead, absolutely motionless. He was a courtroom sketch that the artist fleshed out to a full oil on canvas, finished with a coat of pungent shellac, entitled "Still Life of Fallen Senator."

"The witness may step down," the judge said. "We will adjourn until nine A.M. tomorrow. The jury is reminded of its duty not to discuss these proceedings with anyone," he added, making it sound like the reason was discretion and avoidance of shame, not due process. He banged the gavel.

Slowly Senator Hoffenworth stood up and made his way back to his chair. He climbed back into his suit jacket, but it wasn't the gladiator outfit with which he began the day. He resembled more a man—straddling somewhere between the morning after a fitful night's sleep and the moments that follow a ten-round knockout—who crawls into his robe to stumble off to the showers.

50

EAGER TO DEPART THE SWELTERING COURT-house, Bert and his attorney agreed to meet at his mother's home nearby for lunch and to go over the case. Before leaving the court, Bert was disappointed to learn from Dare that his father was a no-show at the trial because he had work at the University urgently requiring his attention.

When Clarene Eliza Dare arrived, Bert was already sitting on a couch enjoying the refreshing coolness of the air-conditioned living room. She used the bathroom to freshen up her smudged makeup that had her resembling the fearless and indestructible action figure who, after the bomb explosion, the building collapse, and the train wreck, looked more determined than ever to corner the faceless perpetrator. She finished up a cell phone call before entering the living room and sitting down opposite Bert and his mother. Dare's dark suit was in stark contrast to his Eugenia Gropes's bright green cotton pants and floral top.

"It's all my fault," Eugenia blurted out.

"What?" Dare looked at her quizzically.

"I told Bertie that if he wanted to know himself, he should go out and find love. I didn't think it would come to all this." She fluttered her fingers once, presumably to indicate international pornography rings, interstate murder charges, and a televised trial.

"That doesn't seem right, Mrs. Gropes," Dare said. "Aren't you being hard on yourself?"

"Oh, my…" Eugenia's eyes grew big. "It's like you see right through me. I took a course once—a rather expensive one, as I recall—where for a week you wear nothing but this flammable burlap-like material that feels like a thousand toothpicks piercing your flesh. To 'rise above'—that's the goal of the course— you have to walk across coals in your bare feet. On the last day, in a one-on-one with my group leader, he told me that I have a tendency to be hard on myself. Those were his exact words. And you got it right away."

"I never blamed you, Mother," Bert said, embarrassed that he was having this conversation in front of his attorney. "It was my decision to go to the speed dating."

"That's supposed to make me feel better?" she said to Bert with gentle scorn. She turned to confide with the lawyer: "I've told Bert"—her voice became sing-songy pedantic—"'you can't be truly happy unless you know yourself.' Then I told him there's no better way than love to find out."

Bert glanced into Dare's eyes; he could practically hear inside his lawyer's head the burning question for this witness: *So you want Bert to find the kind of love you did in a sperm bank?* Instead she took a sip of lemonade and said: "Just like there's no better way to know the truth than to have a trial. It's certainly true that one's true character is revealed when put through the grueling conditions of a trial. Your son has conducted himself admirably. It's been a pleasure representing him."

"I'm happy to hear that." She smiled at Bert. "It's not been easy to watch on TV."

His mother hadn't come to the courthouse since that first hearing when, after the paternity bombshell, she'd rushed out covering her mouth as if about to hurl. Bert was fine with her watching from home where she could perhaps remain calm and rational. He feared that if his mother were present in court, she might make a bigger scene. What if, all choked up with emotion and while the cameras rolled, she began reading to him from her dog-eared copy of *Chicken Soup for the Human Genome*?

"I know it went well for us today," his mother said. "Something gave at the end there. That was the feeling I got, but I'm not sure how to explain it."

"Hoffenworth admitted that only humans can be prosecuted," Dare said, "and that the smallest genetic differences separate humans from nonhumans. When he conceded that only Bert and the monkey share the gene, I think the jury connected the dots."

"That's good news… if it's going to set my Bertie free." She patted his knee. "I support whatever decision he makes to come to terms with his shadow, to reset his personal atomic clock, to slay his Issue Dragons." She stopped and put her index finger on her chin. "I must say, I'll be glad when this is over. It may be a winning strategy but, as a mother, I worry about how it might play on his self-image. I know, like me, Bertie can be hard on himself. Or am I projecting? You know, they say you point your finger, and you've got three of your own pointing back." She pointed at Bert and then, in a show-and-tell for Dare, pointed with a finger from her second hand at the three little tattlers crouched under the first.

Bert stared out the window behind Dare, willing his eyes rubbed without so much as touching them.

"So…lunch is ready. Why don't I let you two talk while I bring it in?" His mother disappeared into the kitchen.

Dare leaned forward. "Tomorrow I'm going to move to dismiss the extradition proceedings. I think the jury will find for us, but I think our position is stronger than that. The judge can take the decision away from the jury and grant our motion."

"Really?" Bert said, hopeful.

"I didn't think you'd disapprove."

"So where's this going to leave me?"

"Try free. Or at least as free as you could hope for. You would not be free to travel to Tennessee, where you can still be prosecuted. Not that you would want to after this. In fact, my advice would be that you not leave California. If you were to travel to, say, Nevada, it's possible that Tennessee would initiate extradition in that state. Nevada would not be bound by any decision in California."

"I'd never see the Grand Canyon again," Bert said quietly to himself, as if referring to an old friend.

"Consider the alternative. I've told you: If you skip this phase and go straight to Tennessee, you'll be eaten alive."

"I'm still confined, only in a bigger prison. How long's my sentence?"

"There's no statute of limitations for murder. But, hey, you live in California! It's a huge state. What more could you want? Cities and towns of all sizes, mountains, deserts, rivers and oceans. It's not like you're stuck in Rhode Island."

"But what's going to happen to my life? People already look at me strange. Not because of what I've been charged with, not because of the Monkey Gene, but because of what I've said I am."

"People understand. To beat this thing, you have to do what you have to do and be resourceful, work with what you're given."

"What if you had me testify?"

She shook her head emphatically. "Nothing to be gained. Much to lose."

"But if we've proven it's purely a matter of gene makeup, what harm is there? I can explain how I never intended to hurt any-one and that I was trying to help out a friend."

"Get into your motivations?" she asked, intimating that was a sure way to lose everything. "It's irrelevant. Besides, they'll get into that if you face charges in Dayton. They'll focus on the money you were paid. Then they'll really go after you. Painting you as a leech if they can get away with it. They'll bring in the Chianti, the pasta primavera, the aromatic candle, and over-sized animal slippers you used in furthering of your designs to seduce a nice girl."

"That's a lie."

"I'm not saying it's true. You just need to know what they'll say."

It was true. But it was just as true that he wanted to help Anna. Bert was asking his lawyer what he should do, and he was getting the best legal counsel there was: duck, dig in, dodge, and delay.

"Your father has some ideas, based on science, which could beat the charges in Tennessee. Perhaps you don't have to feel like you're under house arrest in California. After we get the extradition dismissed, we could go into Tennessee with your father's challenge and have the law stricken from the books. We'll look at that. One thing at a time."

His mother came in and put a platter on the table stacked with sandwiches cut into halves: deviled egg and olive, tuna with pickle, ham and cheese, and Bert's favorite, sliced knock-wurst with marinated bell peppers. Bert waited politely for their guest to make her first selection. She plucked two halves of knockwurst onto her own plate, even going to the trouble of moving tuna and ham around like a Chinese puzzle to get at the second spicy sausage.

"You eat meat?" Bert didn't conceal his surprise.

"Sure. Just because I'm an animal-rights activist doesn't mean—I respect their lives, their right to reasonable liberty and autonomy, especially those of the highest intelligence, and

I will do whatever I can for them to avoid suffering or needless pain." She took a giant bite of knockwurst, her mouth half full. "But once they're dead, they're dead."

Bert was silent while she continued chewing away. "Animal clients," she said with a chuckle. "Not people, for crying out loud."

Her cell phone rang. She quickly retrieved it. "Hello?" Her face transformed into courtroom grave. "And what is it I can do for you, Sol?" She stood up, signaled her apology for taking the call, but it was clearly important and related to the case. She retreated to the hallway for privacy.

"Bert, eat something." His mother still hovered over the platter she'd served. "There's more knockwurst underneath—your favorite."

"No thanks, Mom. Maybe later." He'd lost his appetite for cold cuts.

A minute later Dare came back into the room, her face still solemn. "That was Sol Krasputin."

"Who?" Eugenia asked.

"Hoffenworth's new campaign manager," Dare explained to her. "Bert, it has to do with Anna."

"What?" he said.

"There's something she told me in my conversation with her more than a week ago. I probably should have mentioned it to you. She's moving back to Boston. She may have left by now."

An alarm went off. With his focus on the trial the last few days, he hadn't been actively thinking about Anna. He didn't need to. Somewhere in the back of his mind, he held a foolish belief that she might come around, that somehow she might see him as a man of greater stature than he'd previously revealed. That wasn't happening. He was on his way to beating the charges, but the hero side of the equation was the product of a gross miscalculation. Now she was moving three thousand miles away to a place he'd be forbidden to travel.

Clarene Eliza Dare was grave but determined. "It's no

surprise, but Hoffenworth will stop at nothing. He needs a conviction. Sol Krasputin just told me that if I get you off, they'll simply re-file charges against Anna. She's implicated with you. She prepared and supplied the software. And, of course, she can be extradited from anywhere."

Just when he thought he'd pulled back all the muddy, filthy rocks in his disastrous quest to find the true Bert Gropes, something underneath this one stung him to the very core of his being.

51

BERT DROVE STRAIGHT FROM HIS MOTHER'S to the lookout above his home in the foothills. The sun had shrunk to a burnishing gold coin across the valley in the western sky. As he gazed out, he tried to hold on, at least to that bright and promising image, but it slipped away and into a bottomless dark below it rimmed with pink-orange ooze. Meanwhile it was seven o'clock, and the long summer day's heat had only loosened its vice-like grip down to 98 from a high of 104.

He drove down the hill to the foot of his driveway and jumped out to grab his mail. Letting the motor run, he quickly opened and read each of four pieces that sat on top of a larger stack of junk mail.

The first was from the bank: "In view of our inability to obtain income verification from your principals in Libido, we regret that we must therefore decline the loan."

The second was from the owner of the ranch, who had let

him move in while he applied for the loan. The owner noted that the sixty days he'd been given to obtain the loan was about to expire, that Bert would need to move out, forfeiting his down payment of $48,000.

The third came in a yellowish envelope with colorful stamps postmarked from Libido. He opened it to find a letterhead marked "Mother DNAture, a subsidiary of Primal Urge Entertainment" with a subject line "Notice of Termination," and signed by one "Simon Debree, Chief Operating Officer." Debree wrote: "WHAT licensed Mother DNAture to develop its Hot Monkey Love technology, and then Dr. Grover Gropes of WHAT conducted a bombing mission over the same operations his trust had licensed. Accordingly, our agreement is canceled. No further royalty or consulting checks will be sent to you."

The letter he opened last was the one whose content was already known to him: "This will notify you that your teaching contract with Mansfield Academy, set to expire at the end of July 2007, will not be renewed." It was signed "cordially" by Margaret Tillman.

It was a perfect storm: four catastrophic letters, all colliding inside his mailbox on the same day. Bert pictured one of those storms in L.A. as if there'd been a confluence of four gushing aquaducts of rainwater, creating one wild and turbid roar that sweeps everything up. Rescue choppers look down at a ranch house being tossed like a toy, disintegrating second by second, and a pickup truck being hurled with… *Wait! There's someone inside! He's flailing his large hands up at us, desperate! Who is it? What is it? Could it…is that the Abominable Gropesman? Now what kind of trouble has he found, and what are we supposed to do? Is this a standard life extraction and rescue op for us, or should we call for help from the Marine Mammal Center?*

True, no one had yet asked for his truck. The Credit Kings at the Roseville Ford dealership qualified him on the bare assertion of his endless cash flow from Libido. Of course, with no income now, the repo man would take his wheels soon enough. Not that he had anywhere to go. If all went well, he'd be confined to the state of California. With no vehicle and no job, that meant living with Mom indefinitely, if not forever. California was way too big for him. A few blocks around his mother's house would do.

He opened the front door and trudged inside his...his... The notion that it was *his* home was a castle in the air to begin with. Holding onto the four letters, he tossed the rest of the mail onto the front table—a table he'd have to pay some storage rental to hold for him, along with the rest of his new furniture. Or maybe it would be cheaper in the long run to simply give it away.

He paused before the entry hall mirror whose future, if not a U-Stor locker in Citrus Heights, was steeped in uncertainty. Bert's ears looked bigger and stuck out more, perhaps because his face looked rounder than he remembered it. His eyes were definitely browner than a week ago.

"Don't just stand there feeling sorry for yourself," a voice from the living room said quietly. "Come in."

Even though the voice sounded familiar, it startled him. Then he made out the gray-headed figure, a wingspan silhouette above his ears, sitting motionlessly in the upholstered chair. Bert wandered into the living room, at first to get a closer look to make sure it was who he thought it was. When he saw the face, he didn't say a word. He sat down in the sofa opposite the old man.

"How'd you get here?" Odd that was the first thing he said to the man he'd only recently discovered was his father. Not exactly the gushing reunion he'd pictured, but that was the first thing on his mind.

"A student on his way to Tahoe gave me a lift. I had him crawl through the window in the back and let myself in."

"Where are your two companions?"

"Davis," he said, referring to his home near the campus. "It's nice and quiet here. I've been sitting for three hours. The silence is immense. Funny how that works. Like unheard planets hurtling through space."

Bert had looked forward to seeing his newfound father. Now that the two of them were together, he couldn't help but feel disappointed. He was a skinny, funny-looking old man, just as he remembered him, the same one who ignored him all these years. Now he was carrying on just like before with gobbledygook science only he understood—a prolonged conversation with himself.

"I guess you know I became... friends with your... with Anna. That's why I became your trustee. She asked me to help and—"

"You fell for her."

"I did." Suddenly realizing he was still holding the four letters, Bert let them fall onto the floor. "Talk about doomed from inception. Anna's moving back to Boston, and my attorney tells me that if I get off, Hoffenworth's people said they'll simply re-file charges against Anna."

The last thing he wanted was Anna dragged into this mess, although it did occur to him that sharing a defense table with her lawyers might be the only way they could start seeing each other again. Realistically, there were a variety of legal and personal reasons that she would demand a separate trial.

"Doomed," Bert repeated somberly.

"I don't know if you want any advice from me," the old man said, taking a pipe and a pouch of tobacco out of his pocket. "I understand the mathematical relationship between celestial phenomena and phenotypes, between crop circles in Zanzibar and migratory patterns of North American birds. Those—"

"That's it!" Bert exploded. "I don't want to hear it! I've got enough problems. You've ignored me my entire life. Now you're doing the same thing."

"What?"

"Nothing has changed. Now you're talking to me like I'm a lecture hall. Anyone could be sitting here."

There was silence. The room was beginning to darken.

"I was going to say: Those mathematical relationships I can explain." He lit his pipe with a match and shook the flame out. "But the kind you have, I know virtually nothing about. I'm sorry, Bert. I want to help, but I'm grossly out of my element."

His words were earnest and utterly disarming.

"I always felt invisible around you," Bert protested, less forcefully.

"All I've ever known is science," his father said. "That has come at a cost. I honestly didn't even know I had a son."

"Forget it. The truth is everything's different now. I'm in the middle of a trial that's up close and way too personal. The world is watching me. I'm hardly invisible anymore."

"Are you serious?" the old man said with calm conviction. "The trial is about the lawyers—or lawyers and politicians. I've not seen anything about you. The Man with the Monkey Gene? That's not who you are. They invented that."

"It's killing me," Bert backtracked. "I sort of fell into the monkey defense."

"Elementary physics," his father said. "An empty space will be occupied."

Bert sighed, once, this time with more tolerance. "Then the legal strategy sort of took on a life of its own. It seemed right at the time. It's definitely me showing up at the trial every day."

His father didn't react.

"If that's not me, then who is it?"

Still no reaction.

"All right, tell me what you think I should do even if you have to put it in cold, scientific terms."

"Don't ask me. I'm a blind old goat, but you cause me to think of a black hole."

"That can't be good."

"Black holes are black holes. They're neither good nor bad.

You said you 'fell into' the monkey defense. The gravitational pull of black holes is so strong that once a body enters the horizon of one, it becomes an object without dimension and of infinite density." He paused to consider his own words. "Not flattering, I realize, especially the part about being dense." Then he bounced his pipe out in front of his beard, describing unseen circles, as if to soften the impact. "The thing is black holes can be full of light, but one small problem: Light can't escape. That's why they're black and invisible in the skies."

"So how can light escape? Better yet, just tell me what I'm supposed to do."

"I don't know. I'm just a simple country molecular cosmologist. Seems that light would have to be inside something other than a black hole. Capiche? Or the black hole would have to alter its nature."

Bert pondered all the science and concluded: "The black hole is my life. By all measures here on Earth I was stupid. Falling for Anna, playing the cat's paw in the license deal, and then going in for the monkey defense."

"Who said it's too late to change?"

"I'm telling you it's got a life of its own. I made a decision early on that I'd rather be classified as a Highly Realized Monkey than the Stupid Man I was."

When Bert was done hanging his head, he looked up to see the old man had removed his dark glasses and was rubbing his eyes. "Since we're on the subject of stupid, I've got something you should know that's been weighing on my mind, that needed to be said in person."

He could see that his father, even in the darkening room, was uncomfortable, suddenly agitated.

"What's that?"

"It's about your...genesis. *I'm* the black hole, not you. You're but a chip off the old dying-star block."

"Huh?"

His father took a deep breath and bowed his head. "Back

when Slayde and I were at UCSF, I was teaching and he was a brilliant and promising graduate student. Frankly, I was jealous of the success and the work he was doing on what became shock technology. I saw great things that could some day be done with it, and I knew he would do terrible and foolish things. Slayde shared with me the astonishing breakthroughs he'd made, and I knew he was at an early point where he wouldn't be able to recreate the mathematical calculations he'd stumbled upon if they were taken from him."

"You—?"

"Stole his notebook and later denied I knew anything about it." He shook his head in shame. "Pretty stupid, isn't it?"

"So I don't get it. Why is this something I need to know?"

"I am so sorry. Please forgive me." He tilted forward, his dark glasses still in his lap, and showed Bert his dark, pained eyes that dimly reflected back. "Don't you see? Slayde wouldn't have tampered with…with you—the in-vitro—if I hadn't done what he knew I'd done."

"I get it," Bert said. "You're saying it's all your fault. That I wouldn't have the Monkey Gene but for what you did. I wouldn't be going through this trial if you hadn't done what you did. You wouldn't have been kidnapped. I wouldn't be trustee. None of this could have happened."

"It's true, and it can be shown with mathematical certainty. I feel terrible, but grateful not to be in the dark anymore."

"Seems to me, once you start parsing it that way, you wouldn't have been my father, either. I wouldn't *be*. Period."

His father's voice was heavy. "I know it doesn't make sense, but I fear you would've been happier without me, being someone else."

Bert fell back in his chair. "Did people have conversations like this before biotech? For a while there, I imagined I was someone else's son. I think that father needed to make sure I didn't want money before he agreed to see me." He leaned way forward, as close as he could to the old man. "And here you are.

You know what kinds of problems I have. The serious financial ones are just the beginning. Yet you've been in that chair for hours."

"It's what matters," the old man said.

Bert played that back, savoring it.

"How do you feel about me calling you *Dad*?"

"For every action there's a reaction. I'd like that, *Son*."

They sat and talked for two more hours, letting questions bubble to the surface, both fundamental and far-flung. The last hour and a half they searched for answers together in total darkness since Bert didn't see any reason to get up and turn on a light. When he did, it was to prepare something for his father, who hadn't eaten since breakfast. A tuna sandwich with two end pieces of rye bread scraped out of the refrigerator was the best he could do.

That night, as he lay in bed wide awake—after wrestling with the trial and going over in his mind the long talk with his father—Bert stared at the ceiling and visualized, of all things, a favorite stretch of freeway between his home in the Sierra foothills and the Woodland Courthouse out on the valley floor. Tomorrow morning, near the end of the drive, accompanied by his father, he'd be heading west again on Interstate 80 on a stretch hatched by highway engineers to bypass downtown Sacramento. From less than a mile away, it lifts high up over the Sacramento River, creating an illusion that the road ends where it crests. But the smoothness of the ride and the supernal lines rising before him always instilled a blind faith that he wouldn't sail off a high ramp at the top into the waters, ooze, and muck below. Instead, at its zenith, and transcendent of the past so unforgivingly cast in concrete, he would rise up even higher and somehow merge seamlessly with the pure ether of the western horizon.

With sleep, it became his dream. Improbable, yes, but what a way to go.

52

STUDIO ANCHOR: Good morning, everyone. I'm Janet Jones in New York, and this is LNTV, the Litigation Network. Welcome to day three of the Hot Monkey Love Trial: Phase One, the Personal Trial. Yesterday, in a steam-cooker cross-examination of the prosecutor Ray Hoffenworth, Clarene Eliza Dare forced Senator Hoffenworth to admit that Mr. Gropes and Exhibit B, the Libidoan monkey, were the only two creatures in the courtroom who shared the Monkey Gene, all but conceding that Gropes wasn't human. Veteran trial lawyer and commentator Ben Griswold will show us how the defense attorney used an eclectic mix in her recipe for success—Hoffenworth's campaign platform, bananas, and spicy bits from human sexuality—to cook the senator's goose. But first we go to reporter Pam Schroeder who has a special guest with her in front of the courthouse. Pam?

REPORTER: I'm standing here with Professor Grover Seymour Gropes, who just escaped from Isle Libido where he was held captive by self-styled biopornologist, Dick Slayde. There's something you want to say, Professor. What is it?

DR. GROPES: I'm holding here a notebook that was prepared by Dick Slayde thirty years ago while in a state of intellectual satori, which later proved to be a nervous breakdown. The notebook, nicknamed The Shocking Details, reveals state-of-the-art catalytic shock technology, capable of producing wildly chimeric creatures, beyond anything we've ever seen. The technology was, of course, used to launch Hot Monkey Love, and, before that, Cell-STL Force that I developed to help naked chickens, and before that the Undercurrent shock tech used to create the Fowl Man gene so that COUTHH could apply for a patent it didn't want. The first use ever was twenty-seven years ago when a crude facsimile of the technology was reconstructed by Dick Slayde when he used it to splice the Monkey Gene into my son during the in-vitro procedure. I say reconstructed because at that time he no longer possessed this notebook. That's because I stole it from him. When I was held captive, Slayde demanded that I return the notebook to him immediately.

REPORTER: What did you tell him?

GROPES: I lied. I denied that I had it. This notebook, The Shocking Details, ingeniously brings us about as close as we may have ever come to the mysteries of how life began. The technologies I just mentioned only scratch the surface of what this notebook reveals, of what the future holds. It is indeed Dick Slayde's legacy, his lifework, his soul, if you will. I've decided to do the right thing and return it to him as he requested. I'm putting it in this FedEx package and sending it to him today.

REPORTER: But he kidnapped and imprisoned you, among other things. Why would you do that for him?

GROPES: He gets the notebook back, but I should also mention that it's all going up on the Web later this morning, for the world to see at www.theshockingdetails.net.

REPORTER: Doesn't that make it worthless to Mr. Slayde?

GROPES: Mere worthlessness would be PharmLife's patent application for its Undercurrent technology, since the disclosure will prove PharmLife didn't invent shock tech. But as to the notebook itself, recall that I likened it to Dick Slayde's soul: a yellowed and rotting pile of trash bound together by a lone and twisted piece of wire.

REPORTER: I get it. You're no fan of his. But how will revealing The Shocking Details affect the outcome of the trial and trying to help your son?

GROPES: You'll have to excuse me now. I must go. I'm wanted inside. My son is holding a seat for me up close.

REPORTER: That's Professor Grover Gropes, the molecular cosmologist who recently discovered he's a father. Back to you, Janet.

"ALL RISE," THE BAILIFF ANNOUNCED. "THE Honorable David Winton McGrath presiding."

The jury hadn't been brought in yet as Bert stood with his attorney. Evidently prepared for more heat, Dare wore a very short cream-colored skirt and a matching light-weight silk blouse, already open an extra button.

"Early this morning," the judge began, "a motion was delivered to my chambers from the defense seeking to have the petition for extradition dismissed. Has the prosecution received a copy?"

"We did, Judge," Hoffenworth said, still standing. After yesterday, he must have decided to take 'wearing it on one's sleeve' to a new sartorial level. He had on an ill-fitting tan suit with a bright aqua-blue shirt—oceans of gently curving fabric—atop which a tie floated, belly-up silver. Whereas Clarene Eliza Dare dressed today like she was ready to turn a few more legal tricks, Hoffenworth might have been her steady John back for more.

"With your permission," the senator continued, "I got a bone to pick with it. Yesterday's heat in this room was downright insufferable, and I'm not sure what all slipped into the record. But I do know there's no basis whatsoever for bringin' this motion."

"The heat yesterday indeed was excessive," the judge responded. "I'm told they've solved the problem and that the air will be switched on no later than ten o'clock this morning. I will hold the engineers to that, or in contempt if I have to. Now, I'm not going to grant the motion, but"—he turned to Bert's attorney—"I may yet take the decision away from the jury and rule in your favor, but not before the prosecution puts on its case."

"While we are on the subject of procedure, your honor," Hoffenworth began, "the prosecution's been doin' some research on the order of proof. As much as we hate to admit a mistake, we think we must."

Dare's ears seemed to move around like a feral cat's, taking aim at the voice of the senator.

"What are you asking of the court, Senator?" The judge seemed genuinely puzzled.

"The first day we argued that it was not our burden and, on account of the defense they raised—thin as a mangy dog—you agreed with us. I'm always mindful when draftin' up a bill in the Senate, last thing I want is for it to bounce back on a veto, or worse, a court sayin' it's unconstitutional. Same here. We think if we don't shift the burden, the conviction we get will flip-flop on appeal."

The judge pinched the bridge of his nose and closed his eyes. "Are you saying now that it's your responsibility to prove that Mr. Gropes is a person?"

Hoffenworth bowed his head. "I'm afraid so."

Judge McGrath put down the motion papers he'd been holding. "Senator Hoffenworth, I don't want you to have the wrong impression. Just because I am not granting the dismissal motion doesn't mean you don't have an uphill battle. By shifting the burden, you may be over your head."

Hoffenworth held his tie out in a humble gesture, then let it plop back from where it came. "We accept the consequences, Judge."

"Ms. Dare," the judge turned to her, "what do you say? At this stage I won't change the order of proof unless both sides agree."

Dare leaned over and conferred with Bert. "This proves I was right. It's what we wanted from the beginning."

"OK with me," Bert said.

She stood up and, practically bobbing with exuberance, addressed the court: "Fine with us, your honor."

"Very well." The judge lifted his eyebrows as if there'd been a request that the defense hold the prosecution's sword so that Senator Hoffenworth could charge at it to carry out his new shish-kabob strategy. "To be clear, do the parties stipulate that the prosecution now has the burden of proving that Mr. Gropes is a person?"

"Yes," both attorneys agreed.

After the jury was brought in, the judge told them about the change in procedure, but they were far more interested to hear that the air conditioning would be coming on soon.

"We will treat the evidence we heard already as testimony taken out of order from the defense," the judge explained. "We will now let the prosecution put on its case as if it were first. After that, the defense may put on additional evidence following the prosecution's case in chief. The prosecution may call its first witness."

Hoffenworth rose. "The People call the Defendant, John Bertram Gropes."

Instantly Bert felt himself being lifted up by a powerful and uncontrolled force. Could this be the mythical freeway ascent, or was it the same one that seemed to have delivered him this morning, rising up above the Sacramento, but letting him down on the other side, locking onto the awaiting tracks and railroading him straight into the Woodland courthouse?

Expressions of shock erupted throughout the courtroom. Clarene Eliza Dare shot to her feet. "Objection! There's been no waiver of the Fifth." She lowered her voice in disgust. "This, from an experienced prosecutor."

The judge squinted at Hoffenworth. "It's true, Senator. Please explain yourself."

"Your honor," Hoffenworth drawled with newfound confidence. "The Fifth Amendment applies only to persons. The prosecution must prove he is one. Until then, he's not."

The judge stroked his chin. "I think he's right, Ms. Dare. You just agreed to the presumption of non-personhood."

Dare was stunned, fuming that she'd been the object of Senator Hoffenworth's sting operation. Her nemesis stood nearby, gloating.

"Mr. Gropes, please take the witness stand,"the judge said to him.

Bert couldn't believe it. All eyes were on him. He turned around and looked at his father seated right behind him. His father, a grizzled survivor of the senator's interrogation, must have sensed the eye contact because he gave Bert a quiet but firm nod.

The bailiff hadn't moved when other witnesses were called. But he jumped to his feet and hurried over to escort Bert to the stand. This wasn't a good sign. For a second he felt like he was in a scene from *Dead Man Walking: The Sequel*, except Bert was worse off. The guy in the movie, while being escorted to the electric chair, was presumed to be—or at least portrayed by the filmmakers as—human.

Bert sat down and looked out at the gallery and the LNTV cameras.

"Raise your right hand," the clerk said, matching her own with Bert when he obliged. "Do you swear to tell the truth—"

"Objection!" Bert's attorney was on her feet. "He's not a person. That's the presumption we just agreed on. That means he should be treated the same as was Exhibit B yesterday, Mr. Scooter Primoson. Therefore, I move to have Mr. Gropes marked and tagged as Exhibit C to these proceedings." She spoke forcefully, evenly, as if the packaging, repackaging and commoditizing of clients for legal gain was all in a day's work.

"Granted," the judge ruled.

The clerk began preparing the exhibit tag, same as yesterday with a loop of string, as Bert remembered ejecting himself from his truck at the command of a CHP officer, lying face down on the hot freeway shoulder, his eyeballs within inches of tiny insects who, in spite of him, went about their business as usual and, unlike him, refused to act like they'd been squashed. This was lower.

"May I approach the witness?" Dare asked the Court.

"You may." The judge's demeanor hovered between amusement and pity.

When Dare reached the witness box, she leaned over and whispered: "They've actually played into our hands. The jury will only remember seeing this. Just keep your answers short, and we'll be fine." She draped the Exhibit C tag over his head, then straightened it on his chest below the knot of his tie.

As he watched his attorney walk confidently back to her seat, Bert felt the day's first flush of heat rise up from the floor, causing his head and neck to swelter.

"Now, Mr. Gropes, you've been sayin' in this trial that you're not a person, right?"

"Yes, that would be a fair summary." Rather than grunt yes like a trained hyena, Bert couldn't resist wanting to sound smarter than that. Dare flashed him a stern look.

Hoffenworth stood squarely at the lectern. "I'm a plain-spoken man, Mr. Gropes. Let's you and me cut out all the head-fakes and parsin' of words. You tell me straight in the eye: Are you a human bein' or not?"

The senator's confidence was back. It was clear he had a sharp angle in mind whether Bert answered yes or no.

Bert cleared his throat and began. "I want to answer you, Senator, but being me can be very confusing." He paused. "The truth is, lately, I've felt like a combination."

"Ohhh…," went half the courtroom, from loud to soft. Others just shook their heads in disappointment. Dare unfolded her hands and leaned back, pleased with his answer.

"That don't answer the question, Mr. Gropes." Hoffenworth addressed the court: "Kindly instruct the witness."

Bert looked up at the judge, who clearly was less than enthralled.

"May I explain?" Bert asked.

"You may," the judge said, "but if I determine that you are being disingenuous, I will hold a—" It seemed the judge was going to say "contempt hearing," but wasn't sure if Bert qualified. "—a hearing on how best to punish that conduct." He nodded for Bert to proceed.

"First of all, I'm not a geneticist or any kind of scientist. So I can't answer it that way. I'm just a ninth-grade Social Studies teacher."

"Well, then, Mr. Gropes, maybe you can tell us. Is the social in Social Studies about humans or nonhumans?" Hoffenworth pressed him.

"In my class, we focus on very *special* human beings. Giants like—"

"I must make a continuing objection to this whole line of questions, allowing a presumed incompetent witness to give narrative answers," Dare interjected.

"So noted," the judge confirmed, then nodded at Bert.

"First off, I'll tell you who we don't study, who, by default, are the nonhumans in the universe of social studies. In studying American history I tell my class that Tories is an easy word to remember. Sounds a lot like snores and bores. They were the ones who remained loyal to the Crown during the Revolution. Like politicians today who never stray from party lines. They're all like dogs—not humans—never leaving their litter, living at home with their mothers."

Bert's distaste for social-studies nonhumans was audible in his voice.

"We call them *ohs*, or zeroes in social studies."

Hoffenworth searched his face for signs of impertinence, but Bert gave him none. Dad smiled wryly at the backhanded dig at the prosecutor.

"And humans…" Bert began again, then noticed for the first time that his class was sitting in front of him, taking up two rows right in the middle of the courtroom. The faces of Robert, Megan, and Linda stood out. Even Trevor had sacrificed time from his summer vacation to be there. They were escorted by Ollie Tweed who looked intensely, compassionately, back at Bert seated in the witness chair. Bert had forgotten the judge had scheduled this visit at the end of the trustee hearing. No surprise. He hadn't looked at a calendar in two weeks.

"My class is here today." Bert smiled at them. They liked the attention and smiled back. Trevor even smiled, as if he finally identified with Bert, being in more trouble than his young mind had ever dreamed of.

"Good," the senator smiled. "Then you can tell them what a social-studies human is, and whether you're one o' them or one of your own zeroes."

Just then Bert saw Margaret Tillman walk into the room and take a seat in the back next to a fellow faculty member.

"I can, because I'm a good Social Studies teacher."

Tillman glared at him, then appeared to notice that Bert's class was there with Ollie Tweed. She stared at them, and seemed fidgety and unnerved, probably because she believed it didn't reflect well on the school that her students could be seen on national TV listening with rapt attention to their teacher on trial for murder and Beastly Degradation charges.

"But, frankly, I lost my focus the last week of class," Bert continued, "due to…matters pressing on my mind, and I really need to make it up. I feel bad about it. You see, we studied in class about what we call adventurers of the human spirit, or *a-h-s*. The *ahs*, the likes of Benjamin Franklin and Heinrich Schliemann—"

"Who?"

"The German expatriate, transient Californian who found Troy in Turkey."

"Never seen him on a stamp," the senator bellowed, "and I assure you Congress never declared no Hein-lick Schliemann National Holiday."

"He's a hero."

"You got a lot of big ideas for someone who's been callin' himself a monkey, Mr. Gropes. Now you want to answer the question?"

He was buying time, all right, but he just needed a little more encouragement. "We have a way of conjuring up our adventurers of the human spirit. It's invigorating and breaks the monotony of class. Since they're here and they're so good at it, I'm going to ask my class to give us an air bath, our updated but sedentary version of Ben Franklin's 'morning constitutional.'"

Hoffenworth's mouth was open, about to cut him short, but Bert preempted him. "On the count of three. One…two…three…!"

"Ahhhh…!" went his entire class in unison.

Bert was completely gratified and beamed at his class. Just then he heard a loud *clunk*, succeeded by a rapid *clickclickclick*, and then an emphatic *HAWOOOSH*. The air conditioning kicked on and blew the first wave of cool air into the room.

"AHHHH…!" sighed the entire courtroom. That was followed by laughter and the low hum of voices.

"Let the record reflect that the air conditioning resumed at nine fifty A.M.," the judge said, smiling.

Margaret Tillman seized the distraction as an opportunity to jump up, beeline down the aisle, and whisper furiously to Ollie Tweed. Seconds later the entire class stood up and was ushered out of the room by her. Her message to a national TV audience was clear: Bert Gropes was ostracized.

"Seems your little bit of voodoo worked, Mr. Gropes." With the air conditioning working its magic, Hoffenworth was more poised and confident than ever. "Conjures up the human spirit, you say? We'll see about that. Right now some truth would be a breath of fresh air. Can we just get an answer, Mr. Gropes?" The Senator sounded impatient. He knew the longer and more complex the answer, and the more he drew out the conversant Social Studies teacher, the more preposterous became the defense constructed by Dare.

Bert took a deep breath and pushed ahead.

"The truth is I fell in love. Everybody knows that. With a really great girl. A computational molecular biologist butwith a big heart. And I'm a Social Studies teacher but kind of a loner. Odd combinations combined with odder combination and recombinations. The truth? I got carried away... really carried away. I would have done anything for her."

Bert could feel the heat building inside him. "Was it *normal* behavior, or was it me, a creature with a Monkey Gene? What I do know: I was half mad with desire. But not mad, like crazy."

With more cool air arriving, Hoffenworth started to twitch, as if unseen ions—pesky ones to be sure—were swirling and dancing around his head.

"Was I like everyone in this room... or not? Human or non-human? Free will or *Free Willy*?"

That triggered another reaction from Hoffenworth, his mouth now quivering. He and Bert were hurtling closer to their inevitable flashpoint.

"When I was approached by Dick Slayde's people, and they

told me about the money I'd make, and they offered me a license deal that would turn people into hot monkeys with thrilling, but probably dangerous results, and that I too would have all the gratification of a Libidoan monkey, well, I just couldn't say no. To get what I wanted, it was important to keep all of this secret from everyone else, especially the woman I mentioned who happened to be the software developer. I realize this is all shocking to say, but at times I felt like a normal person and at times I felt like some kind of monkey-gened animal. It's hard to put in words, but…"

Bert paused as if to think, then opened his mouth again, this time to douse the floor with verbal gasoline.

"Have you ever imagined yourself in a group scene letting yourself go? Acting like a monkey—eight or nine Libidoans roiling, grinding their hips at one another, shrieking with abandon—and you're there, you're a part of the scene, having the time of your life?"

Bert remained matter-of-fact, determined, as courtroom observers gasped.

"Have you ever lost yourself completely, Senator?"

Incensed, Hoffenworth looked ready to lose it, all right, if not explode. Bert pressed on before his own questioner or the judge cut him off.

"Losing it doesn't have to be good or bad, Senator. When it's good, it's great. When it's bad, you feel like you don't exist. You're not part of anything. For a long time I was nobody, but then falling in love the way I did changed everything. Is there such a thing as too much animal desire? It made me a different being, the who and what of which seemed like moving targets. So, to answer your question, I could give you a different answer depending on at what point in time in the last few months you asked, but—"

"A human bein', Mr. Gropes!" Hoffenworth struck with all the force he could muster, standing in the well, thrusting his girth forward, ready to pounce. "Are you now or have you ever been—?"

Bert looked his interrogator straight in the eye. "Yes," he said in a low but sure voice. Then he sat up, broadened his shoulders, leaned forward and spoke in an even firmer voice, never losing his lock on the senator's eyes. "I'm Bert Gropes, and I've made my share of mistakes. I suppose that alone makes me what I am. I'm one-hundred percent human... and proud of it."

What happened inside the next second seemed like all of evolutionary time, compressed.

The shot of virtual electricity he felt coursing through his body was frightening, but he was buoyed by the sight of his father over the senator's right shoulder. He'd resolved to be a lightning rod for Anna; he'd take the charges, all manner of them. Like one of those tens of thousands of genes she analyzed, it was what he was supposed to do—his singular instruction—the only thing he knew for sure.

Last night his father had explained the science to him. Lightning occurs naturally when a looming thundercloud becomes polarized, and its negatively-charged bottom gets into a face-off with a positively-charged object on Earth, creating an electrical potential that reaches a flashpoint of some 10,000 volts per centimeter. A long ionized swath tears the sky in half, all the way down to the ground, bursting its path into celestial fireworks.

Of course, he and his father weren't talking about real lightning. Bert had in mind something else—bigger, brighter, and vastly more dramatic. He was not only covering Anna; he was paying homage by copying something of the man who, in the world of Social Studies teachers, was simply the Dean, the go-to guy in all of Americana: Ben Franklin. As a revolutionary, by definition Franklin had known very well that sometimes doing the right thing meant breaking all the rules. For Bert, even if—as an uncredited, unnoticed extra in the epic film, *Grand Scheme of Things*—he merely played the part of the instrument Franklin invented, it would be a noble destiny realized. The smallest part, it was heroics taken down to the molecular level, but it was the part that was all his.

Such was the heft behind that first second after Bert answered the question—the discharge of his dream—all because he came clean.

And then there was thunder, exploding inside the courtroom, frightening everyone, nearly shattering the windows that looked out on downtown Woodland, until then a sleepy farm town.

"Objection!" Bert's attorney yelled, jumping to her feet. "The witness is incompetent! I move to strike!"

"Animal!" Hoffenworth mouthed the word right at Bert, but it didn't go into the record.

"He's a Lusian of Grandeur!" a familiar voice shouted at the back of the room. "That's Las Vegas on his planet! Don't you see? It's all an act!"

There were loud gasps and yelps and howls scattered about. Underneath those sounds there were even a few hushed sighs of relief that bubbled up to the surface. The man shouting in the back, wearing an Elvis outfit, was tackled by a sheriff, wearing a sheriff outfit, and a scuffle ensued.

"Order!" the judge demanded, pounding the gavel three times.

The world's skinniest Elvis was hauled off, flailing a pantomime version of "Jailhouse Rock."

"Objection overruled!" the judge announced, looking at Dare. "Motion to strike denied!"

"Judge," Hoffenworth bellowed, "the People move at this time for judgment against defendant John Bertram Gropes on the grounds of his confession of humanity."

"Your honor, that would be reversible error." Dare was shuffling for a new file, no doubt for a fallback stratagem to stay in the game. "If you'll give me—"

"That won't be necessary," Bert cut her off, turning to the judge. "My attorney is mistaken." He took hold of the Exhibit

C tag hanging on his chest and pulled it over his head. "It's over. I accept the judgment." He tossed the tag onto the floor.

"I'm afraid he's right, Ms. Dare," Judge McGrath said. "There's nothing left to decide here."

Clarene Eliza Dare dropped to her seat, resigned. Senator Ray Hoffenworth stood nearby, quite full of himself.

The judge enunciated carefully so that the court reporter would get every word right and in its proper sequence: "Based on the Defendant's unequivocal testimony, the court finds that as a matter of law the People's burden has been met—namely, beyond a reasonable doubt—that John Bertram Gropes is a human being and therefore a person, as defined by the laws and statutes relevant to these proceedings."

"With due respect, Judge," Hoffenworth politely interjected, "shouldn't the judgment state that the burden was met to 'a moral certainty'? Given the waywardness Mr. Gropes just told us about, I think the People would feel more comfortable knowin' the word 'moral' had a place in your decision."

"In California, we haven't used that language in decades, Senator," the judge explained. "Be assured, however, the burden I recited is the sole standard, but the certainty is the same we've always had. The petition for extradition is therefore granted and judgment is entered accordingly. The Defendant is remanded into custody, pending further proceedings, Friday, July thirteenth, at nine A.M. to deliver him over to law enforcement in Tennessee where he will stand trial for the murder of one Les Harry. This court is adjourned." The judge gaveled, stood, and exited the courtroom.

In the last sequel to *Dead Man Walking*, another sheriff— older, more portly—approached Bert in the witness box and cuffed him. But this time was different. With the slow-moving, would-be jailer struggling to keep up, it was John Bertram Gropes who led the way, striding purposefully towards the back door and the cell awaiting him, his manhood a certainty.

53

IT WAS ANOTHER PERFECTLY QUIET AND PRIS-
tine morning up in the foothills, far from it all. Bert putzed
around the house, savoring it, trying not to think about the
hearing tomorrow or being handed over to law enforcement to
be whisked off by jet to an arraignment in Dayton, Tennessee.
He was grateful for these last two days at home. If his father
hadn't put up bail yesterday after the judgment—only after
Ollie Tweed had come in to convince the judge he should be
afforded the chance to post it—Bert would still be in the Yolo
County Sheriff's Detention Facility.

He sat on his couch wearing his cowboy boots that never
got the chance to get down and dirty on the working ranch he
envisioned. As well he should be, he was anxious about what
was in store for him, but the feeling was surprisingly mild, controlled. He thought about how he'd feel right now if he hadn't
done what he'd done. That actually had a calming effect. It was
strange to discover that the strongest of balms was composed

of his thoughts about how it could be worse, that he'd successfully dodged a deadlier bullet. The Monkey Gene was nothing
but a distraction, a sideshow.

He called his mother a little while ago to assure her once
more that he was all right. Because she's a mom with the mom
gene that's coded for worry production, Bert had to act calmly
as an inhibitor of gene expression. She also told him how proud
she was. "You had to make a you-turn, Bertie, and you did it
in the face of speeding and honking and swerving oncoming
traffic. Bravo! It's a mover, you know, but in the good sense of
the word, and it brings with it a steep fine. Now, you know why
they call it a fine? Because it is. Isn't that marvelous?"

She must have had the headset on because he could hear the
clasping of hands. He simply listened and let her talk until her
worry subsided, at least for the time.

Just now, the phone rang. He picked it up.

"Hello."

"Bert?"

Suddenly his heart was pushing up against his throat.

"Anna? Where are you?"

"I'm in Boston."

"Are you OK?"

"Everything's OK." She hesitated. "I saw the end of the trial."

"I'm sorry. I got carried away, I know, answering a simple question. I'm sorry for taking advantage of you the way I
described—"

"None of it's true, and you know it."

"What's not true?"

"I just got off the phone with your attorney. She told me
about the call she got from Sol Krasputin. They threatened to
indict me if they couldn't get you."

"I promise you, Anna, I was just looking for an opening.
Whether or not Krasputin ever called, I had to end up where I
did. Besides, Hoffenworth's a politician, not really a prosecutor.
They promise lots of thing. I don't take much stock—"

"Shush, Bert."

He held his tongue.

"What you did was the most wonderful thing any human being has ever done for me. I wish you luck. I really do. I'm praying you beat the charges in Tennessee."

"Thanks, Anna. That means a lot to me."

"I have to go now. I just had to call and say that."

In the warm quiet that followed—all of two full seconds— he almost said: "Have a great life, Anna." But he didn't. He said his goodbye and leaned back into the couch where the two of them had sat not that long ago. His calm was deeper.

He heard activity outside, the sound of new arrivals. He stood up, walked to the front door and opened it. His father's hybrid brown bomber had arrived. Tina, his traveling companion, was his chauffeur. Bert had yet to meet her, having only seen her in the back of the courtroom the other day. She was out of the car, leaning over, her back to Bert, helping Dad out of the passenger side. Suddenly Bert was feeling all of his oats again. He could marry that in a Woodland minute. Definitely. She was a dream package to be sure: a writer, like Benjamin Franklin, and a stripper—or at least she had been for a while on Libido—in the great tradition of Heinrich Schliemann. Well, technically Schliemann hadn't been a stripper, but he'd completely denuded the Turkish countryside—in a good way—to reveal the lost city of Troy, as the world, mesmerized, stood by.

Bert's imagination started to drift. He could see himself now... *a small but private room at the men's penal colony, away from all the noise and riffraff, Tina arrives for her first conjugal visitation. No candles allowed, but she wears a favorite eau de cologne that sets the mood and makes it special...*

Bert stopped. He was getting way ahead of reality again. He laughed at himself.

"Hello!" he shouted to the new arrivals.

The third passenger jumped out and took the old man's hand.

The two of them—one waddling, the other moving slowly—approached, with Tina following behind. Although his father had posted bail for him, this was the first they'd actually seen each other since court yesterday. Then the old man let go of Scooter and put both arms around Bert. Their embrace must have lasted a full nine seconds, and it wasn't complete until his father patted him firmly on his upper back five times for good measure.

Stepping back, the old man waved his hand up at the house. "How's it look?"

Tina drank it in with her eyes. "It's perfectly lovely. I see you living out here."

"Good," the old man said. "The contingency is removed. I'll tell the owner we have a deal."

"Dad, that's great news! But, hey, what's wrong with the description I gave you of the house?"

"Great balls, Son! You'll never see the way she sees, and you'll never look the way she looks."

Bert curled his mouth humbly at Tina as though to say: *Who can argue?*

"Bert, that's Tina," his father said.

"I'm so glad to finally meet you." He shook her hand as his father and Scooter made their way into the house.

"I've heard so much about you," she said to him. "Good things."

"You should hear my father talk about you."

Big ice-breaker smiles were exchanged.

"Can I just say?" she began again, in a can't-hold-back kind of way. "I know all about what you did yesterday." She breathed in. "That you would do that for a woman, for anyone—it's positively inspirational. Incredible."

Her eyes seemed to plunge headfirst into his—a swan dive. Somehow she already knew his waters would refresh her, were deep enough and safe. He hadn't expected this. He remembered when he met Anna at speed dating for the first time, and she'd regarded him in a similar way, right after he'd revealed who his uncle was. Tina's blue eyes looked more directly into Bert.

"Yeah, well, I heard what happened to you, trying to help my father. Come inside."

His father was seated in the same chair Bert had found him in the other night. Tina sat down on the couch, leaving a space for one more. Bert was about to offer everyone coffee, when his father leaned forward and preempted him. "Bert, with your permission, Ollie and I are going into federal court tomorrow to challenge the constitutionality of the Beastly Degradation Act. We think we stand a good chance of turning this thing upside down—or right-side up, as we see it—one more time and stopping the judge from handing you off to authorities tomorrow. What do you say?"

"You know I'm fine with leaving tomorrow. I'm ready. On the other hand, it's true I'd be even finer staying right here." He and Tina exchanged tepid smiles.

"Good," his father said, pleased with the answer. "To adapt the words of a noted Social Studies teacher, who quoted someone else: 'We have not yet begun to fight.'"

Just then Scooter arrived from the back of the house.

"Scooter doll!" Tina exclaimed. "Look at you."

Sure enough, the Libidoan had gravitated straight for Bert's closet. He was upside down, walking on his hands, wearing two pairs of slippers. His feet, sticking straight in the air, were covered with Jungle Heat—twin monkey heads, hanging loosely, staring down at the floor—while his hands shuffled forward in Comfort Kings.

"Hmm, slippers comfortable enough to wear on both your hands and feet," Bert observed out loud so that his father knew what was going on. He gestured to Scooter for the benefit of Tina. "My new partner tells me the potential market is twice the size I'd projected. It's not too late to get this business venture—"

"Back on its feet," Tina joked.

"Definitely." Bert laughed. "But I still need a name for it."

Scooter right-sided himself, and hurled the hand slippers playfully in the direction of Tina. When they landed squarely at her feet, Tina and Bert laughed together.

"I was thinking of Gropes Brothers—Genuinely Furry Footwear," Bert said. "What do you think?"

"Good," his father said. "Building on the Gropes name." He turned in the direction of Tina to seek her opinion.

Tina picked the Junglers up off the floor, slipped her hands into them the way Scooter had just done, and waved them mirthfully at Bert.

"I like it." She flashed him as full smile. "Anything with Gropes in it is smart."

Aftershock

JUDGE MCGRATH WAS ABOUT TO HAND BERT OVER to Tennessee law enforcement officers, when Ollie Tweed suddenly made a grand entrance into the Woodland Courthouse to deliver a stay of proceedings. Even Clarene Eliza Dare stood by dumbfounded. Ollie had managed to convince a federal judge in Sacramento to issue the stay in order to give that court a chance to fully review the Tennessee law. After looking over Professor Gropes's thesis, composed of "mathematical and molecular arrays and microarrays," the federal judge issued a final ruling a month later that the Abatement of Chimera and Beastly Degradation of Humanity Act violated the Equal Protection clause of the Constitution because chimeric humans were potentially exposed to different treatment than others and, more controversially, the law infringed the ability of citizens to retool themselves—possibly with life-saving improvements—into chimeric humans, contrary to the First Amendment, the right to freedom of expression, and possibly a freedom of *self*-assembly that may be implied in the U.S. Constitution.

Bert Gropes remained free on bail while the State of

Tennessee appealed. It was a good move on the part of Ollie to go to federal court when he did, rather than wait to do it in Tennessee. The Ninth Circuit Court of Appeals, covering several Western states but based in San Francisco, was known to be liberal and likely would be sympathetic to Bert. Legal scholars who closely watched the Hot Monkey Love Trial were generally in agreement that Hoffenworth's and Dare's political and ideological motivations were transparent. Some argued such biases paled compared to those of judges on federal appellate courts like the Ninth Circuit.

Meanwhile, in the fall of 2019, after moving into his new home in the foothills with Bert, Professor Grover Seymour Gropes founded the Center for Molecular Humanism, based at UC Davis, the first of its kind in the world. Dr. Gro was fond of saying that, informally at least, the motto of the Center was "It's Not What You Think." Initial funding for the Center came from a commitment from PharmLife where, as part of obtaining a license of Cell-STL Force from Dr. Gro (and abandoning its eco-disastrous VigoRoost launch), the agri-biotech pharmaceutical and chemical giant agreed to provide five years of seed money. Tina Halliksen, after spending a few months with her family back in Iowa, moved to Davis upon accepting the position as editor-in-chief of the Center's quarterly journal, *Life Force.*

Bert didn't even try to look for work as a teacher, not with the appeal pending and his shocking, self-incriminating testimony so notoriously familiar to school officials everywhere. Instead, and with qualified help from Scooter, he worked hard on completing his line of slippers in order to scout a license deal. He also worked part-time for the Center in both administration and research.

On April 1, 2020 the Ninth Circuit upheld the Federal District Court's decision. Bert continued to remain free on bail while Tennessee appealed once again. On July 14, 2020, one year after the stay of the state court judgment, the United

States Supreme Court agreed to hear the case of *People v. Gropes*. Bert's fate was now in the hands of the highest court.

Following the nationally televised trial in Woodland, Hoffenworth's Presidential campaign took off. He was seen as a man of action, willing to fight in the trenches himself, in order to "root out" the scum of society, like John Bertram Gropes, who would jeopardize the "future of America as a species of people." The unmasking, in the course of the trial, of evil-doers and perverts, also brought into high relief the need for Senator Hoffenworth's Moral Positioning System. In November 2020 Ray Hoffenworth was elected the 44th President of the United States by a comfortable margin.

After his server farm was bombed in July of 2019 and his online business destroyed, Dick Slayde suffered a disabling stroke. For the next year and a half he was completely out of circulation and made no effort to re-launch Hot Monkey Love. Nevertheless, as one of his first acts in office, President Hoffenworth invoked the War Powers Act and imposed a naval blockade on Libido to prevent the delivery of the hardware necessary to re-plant the Primal Urge server farm.

Shortly after Hoffenworth took office, the truth began to percolate to the surface about what actually happened at the trial, but not from Bert Gropes, who remained quietly out of public view. It started with a few newspaper articles suggesting that Bert Gropes had set himself up as the fall guy for Anna Brighton. The story went big when Sol Krasputin switched camps again, taking the helm of a Democratic candidate for President for the year 2024. (It was later revealed Krasputin was hired months earlier on the same day as Hoffenworth's Inauguration.) Krasputin told reporters that, upon Hoffenworth's orders, he'd called and told Dare that they'd go after Brighton if the Gropes charges didn't stick and, following that, Gropes chose to fall on his sword for her. Assured by new advisers of plausible deniability, the President's position was that he was unaware of any such details.

Following those developments closely, and convinced of an intergalactic conspiracy to destroy the Presidency, was none other than Ellis Peek. After the trial, he landed an offer he couldn't refuse as an anchor on Fox News. He was anxious to get back to his first love—hard news—but not before he satisfied himself there was nothing alien or chimeric about his would-be employer, what with a fox somehow mixed into news for humans. As part of the deal he negotiated, he was free to do broadcasts wearing monkey outfits, chicken feathers, thong underwear or nothing at all if he chose, provided that his fashion editorials were always from the waist down, that is, well below his talking head.

On March 21, 2021 the United States Supreme Court affirmed the federal appellate decision, ending Bert's ordeal and decreeing his freedom, but only because the vote was 4-4, split along ideological lines. The computer logs clearly showed that the ninth Justice, one of the more elderly and conservative members of the Court, had been a user of Hot Monkey Love even before the demise of Les Harry, requiring that he recuse himself from the case.

Unfortunately, Bert's slipper biz never got traction. To put it more bluntly, it was a complete bust. That didn't stop Scooter. He derived endless hours of entertainment climbing up on the roof, laughing and clomping around in them. Bert, however, still believed in his destiny and, despite everything he'd been through, yearned to reach a higher branch.

Soon after the Supreme Court decision, and with the legal cloud gone, Anna Brighton gave an interview on *60 Minutes*, confirmed Krasputin's version and added: "Bert Gropes is a hero in my book." With the positive press that followed and his revision in the public eye, Bert started smelling opportunity again—big opportunity. He put a few feelers out and, sure enough, a chance came. He was invited by a middle school in Sacramento to address the student body, giving part of a series of lectures he'd prepared, entitled *Life, Liberty, and the Pursuit of Social Studies.* A local TV station covered it, and the story was picked up nationally.

It was a thundering success, simply huge. Soon Bert had invitations to give talks to more middle schools. With corporate sponsors signed on and a hot website, *www.MisterSocialStudies.com,* not only was he traveling in style, he was making a fortune compared to what he earned at Mansfield Academy. It was a milestone day when, setting out for a lecture tour along the Eastern seaboard, he looked out the window and realized he was sailing over the Grand Canyon.

In April of 2021 Tina published her first novel, *Not Far From the Madding Shrewdness,* a bodice-ripping-stripping Victorian biotech novel with comic overtones. It received strong critical acclaim, which brought even more well-deserved attention to the Center for Molecular Humanism and her journal, *Life Force.*

As to whether anything ever came of Bert and Tina, that's really none of our business; they're both happy and enjoy their privacy. But, not to speak out of school or anything, let's just say molten-hot monkeys got nothin' on them, and leave it at that.

Schedule of Exhibits
People v. Gropes, Case No. 19-300241
Yolo County Superior Court
Superior Court for the State of California
Unlimited Jurisdiction

EXHIBIT	DESCRIPTION
A	Restriction map Gene present in both *Pan troglodytes Libidoanis* and, per stipulation, Defendant John Bertram Gropes but not in Homo sapiens ("the Monkey Gene")
B	Scooter Primoson Species: *Pan troglodytes Libidoanis*
C	Defendant John Bertram Gropes Species: TBD

Special thanks to:

Lynn Duryee, my dear friend, who is a brilliant writer and a gifted editor. Liz Trupin-Pulli, who achieves trifecta as my agent, editor, and friend. Lynn Vannucci of Water Street Press, whose talent and dedication to quality in publishing, reinvented, should make us all proud. Laura Witter and Peter Logan, writers extraordinaire and friends, for their sharp eyes on everything written I put before him.

I am deeply grateful to each of you.

The Scopes Monkey Trial

The True, Unmutated, Unrecombined Story

The 1925 case of *The State of Tennessee vs. John Thomas Scopes* pitted true believers in "old-time religion" and its fundamentalism against proponents of evolutionary theory and its scientific rationalism. The trial, the most famous in U.S. history, was the first ever to be broadcast nationally on what today we might call "reality radio," an amalgam of the real, surreal and unreal masquerading as all real. Journalists from all over the world descended on Dayton, Tennessee, including the famed H.L. Mencken, covering it for the *Baltimore Sun,* who coined the name "Monkey Trial."

Responding to the threat that children would be taught that humans were descendants of monkeys, in January 1925 the Tennessee state legislature passed the Butler Act, making it a crime to teach "any theory that denies the story of the Divine Creation of man as taught in the Bible, and to teach instead that man has descended from a lower order of animals." John Thomas Scopes, a substitute biology teacher, was approached by activists seeking to challenge the law. Scopes urged three students to testify against him before the grand jury, assuring that he would be charged with the crime.

A noted Baptist pastor persuaded William Jennings Bryan—three-time Democratic Presidential nominee, former Secretary of State, and devout Presbyterian who traveled the country preaching against "the menace of Darwinism"—to step in as the prosecuting attorney. Thereupon Clarence Darrow, the country's most famous criminal defense lawyer and a vocal agnostic, volunteered to defend Scopes.

Amidst sweltering summer heat that only increased in the days that followed, the trial commenced on July 10, 1925. Judge John T. Raulston, hardly reserving judgment, started each day of trial with a prayer or a reading from the Bible. He prohibited any challenge to the law itself, excluding any evidence or expert scientific testimony offered by the defense that would challenge the Butler Act on the grounds it violated the Establishment Clause of the U.S. Constitution (separation of church and state). Bryan rejected the scientific view that humans were but one of thousands of mammals, and he lamented the evolutionary notion that humans were descended "not even from American monkeys but old world monkeys."

On the seventh day, when the defense had no one else to call—and the trial had moved outdoors due to the insufferable heat—Darrow called Bryan, the prosecuting attorney, as a witness to testify as a "Bible expert." Darrow put Bryan in the hot seat, grilling him on such scientific factual questions as where Cain's wife came from, whether Jonah was actually swallowed by a big fish and spewed out three days later, and whether the seven days in which God created the world were of the "twenty-four hour" variety or something slightly more epochal. Judge Raulston swiftly "expunged" the testimony from the record, and allowed no further witnesses on the subject. With no defense evidence allowed and Scopes having admitted to teaching evolution, on July 21, 1925 the jury took only nine minutes to render a guilty verdict. The judge imposed a fine of $100 (almost $1500 today, adjusted for inflation).

The Tennessee Supreme Court rejected all the challenges to the law, but set aside the conviction on a purely technical ground. Although the Butler Act specified a minimum fine of $100, governing Tennessee law did not allow judges to impose fines of more than $50. The Supreme Court also made its views known about the prospect of *Monkey Trial: The Sequel*, declaring that it saw "nothing to be gained by prolonging the life of this bizarre case." Tennessee's attorney general promptly announced the State would not seek a retrial of Scopes.

If John Scopes, only one of the millions either part of or following the story that took on a life of its own, could be likened to one gene of an entire multi-million-fold genomic sequence, he was a gene never activated, never allowed during the trial to testify on his own behalf. But after the verdict was rendered and his guilt was established, he did briefly achieve gene "expression," declaring before the fine imposed and to the world that it was his intent "to oppose this law in any way I can. Any other action would be in violation of my ideal of academic freedom—that is, to teach the truth as guaranteed in our Constitution, of personal and religious freedom."

ABOUT THE AUTHOR

LARRY TOWNSEND is a fourth-generation intellectual property attorney who lives and works in the Bay Area. But beneath that calm exterior lurks a mind gone bananas! His first novel, *Secrets of the Wholly Grill*, was praised by *Kirkus Reviews* as being "the perfect gift for everyone who has ever cursed Windows—a not insignificant market." It will be reissued by Water Street Press in 2017. Townsend clearly has his finger on the pulse of technology...gone berserk.

Virgins & Martyrs
A novel by Hugh Mahoney

New Yorkers open their Sunday morning paper to find a photo of Virgil Quinn, teacher of history at St. Lucy's School for Boys, splashed all over the front page. How did he get there? Scandal, of course. Virgil has made enemies—the Cardinal of New York not the least among them. The Cardinal's research reveals that Virgil has lived many lives, all of them scandalous. Was he really a ranking nun in the Sisters of Mercy of Baton Rouge? Did he really walk the ramps of Seventh Avenue as the city's highest paid supermodel? Just how did he come to know all those men whose names appear in his notorious (and deadly convenient) Black Books? *Virgins & Martyrs* is shrewd and malicious fun, a wicked commentary on love, life, gender and the history of our nation, a work in which the peripatetic and intrepid—yet all-too-human—Virgil Quinn lets no one off the hook.

F*ck Art (Let's Dance)
A memoir by Sally Eckhoff

What would you give to shoot the moon in the greatest city in the world?

F*ck Art (Let's Dance) is a chronicle of ten slam-bang years in a very slam-bang part of New York City, and of one young painter's crusade to make that place her own.

This memoir, by a former Village Voice writer and critic, starts in 1977 with the Summer of Sam and ends with the Tompkins Square Park riots—two notorious incidents that defined an age. After a last, desperate summer in the beach towns of Long Island, the naive young wannabe artist borrows her dad's El Camino, finances a trip to Manhattan with the change on his cufflink stand, and rents an apartment on East Tenth Street with a floor so crooked that everything that falls off the kitchen counter rolls under the bathtub. And then she begins to paint, eat, dance, and feel her way around New York.

F*ck Art might remind you of what it feels like to be a beginner in a land of crooks and geniuses.

Water
street
press